THIS CLEAVING
and
THIS BURNING

**Canada Council   Conseil des Arts
for the Arts   du Canada**

**ONTARIO ARTS COUNCIL
CONSEIL DES ARTS DE L'ONTARIO**

an Ontario government agency
un organisme du gouvernement de l'Ontario

Canadä

Guernica Editions Inc. acknowledges the support of the Canada Council for the Arts and the Ontario Arts Council. The Ontario Arts Council is an agency of the Government of Ontario.

We acknowledge the financial support of the Government of Canada.

THIS CLEAVING
and
THIS BURNING

J.A. Wainwright

**GUERNICA
EDITIONS**
TORONTO · CHICAGO · BUFFALO · LANCASTER (U.K.)
2020

Michael Mirolla, editor
David Moratto, interior and cover design
Guernica Editions Inc.
287 Templemead Drive, Hamilton, (ON), Canada L8W 2W4
2250 Military Road, Tonawanda, N.Y. 14150-6000 U.S.A.
www.guernicaeditions.com

Distributors:
Independent Publishers Group (IPG)
600 North Pulaski Road, Chicago IL 60624
University of Toronto Press Distribution (UTP)
5201 Dufferin Street, Toronto (ON), Canada M3H 5T8
Gazelle Book Services, White Cross Mills
High Town, Lancaster LA1 4XS U.K.

First edition.
Printed in Canada.

Legal Deposit—Third Quarter
Library of Congress Catalog Card Number: 2020933143
Library and Archives Canada Cataloguing in Publication
Title: This cleaving and this burning / J.A. Wainwright.
Names: Wainwright, J. A., 1946- author.
Description: Series statement: Guernica prize ; 2
Identifiers: Canadiana (print) 20200189549 | Canadiana (ebook) 20200189557 |
ISBN 9781771835664 (softcover) |
ISBN 9781771835671 (EPUB) | ISBN 9781771835688 (Kindle)
Classification: LCC PS8595.A54 T55 2020 | DDC C813/.54—dc23

for Marjorie

So sleep, dear brother, in my fame, my shame undone.
—HART CRANE

All stories, if continued far enough, end in death ...
—ERNEST HEMINGWAY

Prologue

Miller retreated to the island after the debacle in Havana, telling Manuel on the crossing only that his friend had to leave. He shouldn't have used his fist and mouth so cruelly, but his altercation with Hal had threatened him in ways he didn't understand. All night he sat at his desk and tried to write about it by hand, but the words didn't make sense. Just before dawn he gathered up the letters Hal had sent him through the years, placing them in a small metal box. On the path to the limestone cliffs he could smell the sweetness of the jasmine and tang of the pines. From the edge of the precipice he threw the box into the sea, wondering idly if Hornsby's arm was still as strong as ever. Back at the house he sat at his desk and poured himself a whiskey. They were lost to each other and he'd never see the bear again.

Under Fire

1.

He giggled nervously as they crept along the edge of the meadow just inside the tree-line, Miller's lever-action 30.30 clutched tightly in his hands, the sun warm on his cheeks, and the sound of the shallow creek blending with the birdsong.

"Shut up!" Miller whispered fiercely. "You'll scare him."

The bear was about two hundred yards away chewing on the spring grass. Occasionally, it raised its head and sniffed the air, casually it seemed, as if it had nothing to fear. But they were up-wind and froze when it broke off from its meal to look around, so the only betrayal from Miller's point of view would be Hal's stifled laughter.

Where the trees began to thin out Miller, who was in front, raised his hand to signal this was the place. "Rest the barrel on a branch," he said. "And remember, don't jerk the trigger."

Hal had never planned to be the shooter when his friend spotted the bear in the flat land beyond the junction of three streams where they emptied into the river. All he'd killed were pigeons in the Sark barn with a .22 and the occasional squirrel with Miller in the woods. But this morning Miller insisted they had to bag some "big game," and he had to admit more than a mild curiosity as to what that would be like.

"Have you ever shot one?"

"Sure. In the spring they hang around the cottage looking for garbage. They'll get right up on the porch if you don't deal with them. How do you think I learned to use the gun?"

Hal didn't know whether to believe this but told himself that Miller would never have passed up the chance to bring down this animal if he hadn't killed such a creature before. He knelt beside a tamarack, feeling his knees press into the soft earth, and found a bole protruding far enough for a rest. The bear was less than a hundred yards away now, its flank exposed and glistening in the sun. He sighted down the barrel and was amazed at the bulk in front of him. He could see the flank moving in and out with every breath. When he squeezed the trigger and heard the report a split second later, the bear grunted and lurched sideways.

"Hit him again!" Miller yelled, as he levered out the shell and slammed a new cartridge into the chamber. But the bear was lumbering off now across the meadow towards a distant hill. Hal felt sick as he watched it drag its hind leg where the slug had ripped into muscle and tendons. He hadn't even been able to hit it properly, and he didn't want to hurt it anymore.

"Give me the gun," Miller cried, grabbing at the stock. By the time Hal released it and his friend raised the rifle to his shoulder the animal had dropped into a gully on the meadow's edge. Miller waited calmly for it to emerge and put a bullet in its spine as it climbed the last few yards to safety. "I hate tracking when you've blown a shot," he said. Hal knew the comment wasn't personal, but also that Miller never missed.

When they came up to the carcass, Miller cut out a claw from one large paw, tossed it to Hal, and pressed his fingers into the shining pelt. "It'll make a great rug," he said, then added nonchalantly: "You lifted your arm. That's why you hit him where you did."

Hal crushed the claw inside his fist. Just then he hated his friend. Hated and loved him.

2.

As far as the pecking order in high school was concerned, sandy-haired Miller was at the top of the heap. Part of him obviously liked his prominent position, based largely on his physical prowess and winning smile, but mostly he spurned efforts to bring him into various social circles, preferring the company of a few loyal hunter-fishermen his age and the giving of his spare time to the rivers and woods. Hal, raised to believe any stretch of trees and grass beyond his back yard was wilderness, was later impressed that the fearless frontiersman always put books in his pack along with ammunition, flies, and various camping items. Miller bragged not only about the size of the trout he caught but also about having ploughed through a Tolstoy or Stephen Crane story on a weekend trip.

They met when Hal moved with his mother back to Oak Park where she had been born and attended school. After the separation and divorce from her spendthrift husband she focused all her attentions on her only child and demanded his unwavering fealty, often forcing him to choose between time spent with friends or with her. Miller's mother had died when he was six, but he worshipped his father who taught him everything there was to know about guns and rods. In their first casual conversation, as they leaned against their side-by-side lockers outside the classroom where spinster teachers and the occasional young man attempted to impart the wisdom of words or numbers, they learned they had been born on the same day in 1899. Not only that, but their mothers were both named Ruth and their fathers Henry.

"I guess that makes us brothers," Miller said excitedly. "We'll just have to make it official."

"What do you mean?" Hal asked, nervously sweeping back a dark lock from his forehead. He had some idea of his new acquaintance's reading capabilities from his performance in class but was a little leery of any commitment to what seemed a rough-hewn if kindly character. He liked Miller's broad chest and big hands, but he'd already gained more information about local fishing holes than he needed to know.

"A blood pact! Here, give me your hand." Miller drew a pearl-handled pocketknife from his jacket and pricked his own thumb until a red droplet appeared. Hal instinctively pulled away, but Miller grabbed his fingers and forced them back. "Come on, it won't hurt."

It did hurt, of course, but Miller's bleeding thumb was up against his in an instant and Hal felt a powerful rush of affection for his new kin. He'd always wanted a sister but this big, aggressive boy was what he had been given. He wanted to talk with him about books and writers and hoped that wouldn't involve any treks outside of town.

"Done that with lots of guys," Miller announced, "but you're the first birthday brother I've ever had."

Hal looked out the window of his tower bedroom in his mother's house and thought things over. It must mean something to have been born on the same day in the same year as someone you just happened to meet. And it must mean even more that your parents had the same names. It was like God had made them twins, not identical, of course, but joined in time and lineage. He peered up at the darkening sky looking for the constellation of Gemini. Miller probably knew exactly where it was because he was always talking about how you could never get lost in the woods at night or even on the ocean if you paid attention to the stars. He remembered that Castor and Pollux were the patrons of sailors, but how much did their protection extend to wilderness trails?

The ocean seemed safer for now so he lay on the bed, grasping the sides of his coverlet as if it were a raft tossed on a wild sea. Squeezing his eyes almost shut he imagined the ceiling light was Polaris and he was moving north into unexplored waters. It was a very dangerous voyage and he might not survive. But just as he was about to give up hope and surrender to the cold waters, he saw an island ahead and Miller waving to him from the beach. He was eager to land and begin a new, adventuresome life, but his mother's voice broke into his reverie, calling him to dinner.

They ate in the wood-panelled dining room with the stiff-backed chairs. Her one concession to comfort was that they each had thin cushions to sit on. The room was crowded with heavy furniture and knick-knacks, and when the thick drapes were closed on winter evenings he often felt overwhelmed by the weight of ancestral taste and his mother's conversation. Tonight, though, a little distracted by the raft and promise of happy exile he failed to hear her patter until she chided him for his lack of attention and manners.

"Harold, you're dreaming, and your poor old mother is left talking to herself."

Hal didn't like it when she addressed him formally, pronouncing his given name in a pinched, pretentious fashion and always with some critical intention. When she was relaxed and affectionate, he was her 'Prince Hal,' but her moods shifted rapidly, and instead of remaining the wild, eloquent hero of *Henry IV* he could, without warning, be banished to his tower room like one of those doomed young royals in *Richard III*.

"Was I in your dream?" she now asked, smiling.

"Yes, mother," he said, lying. "We were on an island together having a wonderful time."

"An island, indeed! Well, where did we live? I hope we were comfortable."

He wanted to tell her they had to sleep in the sand and eat raw fish but said instead: "I built you a house of palm leaves and we ate figs and drank coconut milk." He took a chance. "You were very happy there."

"Perhaps, for a short time," she replied. "But I'd want to be rescued before too long."

Yes, it would be nice for her to be rescued and for him to stay on the island with Miller. Maybe he'd write letters home once in a while. After all, he couldn't abandon her completely. "That's another dream," he told her, but she was already standing to clear away the dishes.

Miller told him that when he was a very small boy his mother had dressed him in his older sister's blouses and dresses and called him Millie, at least until his father put a stop to it. Both his sister and mother had died of heart conditions a few years apart, and his father explained that sometimes women became emotional in ways they couldn't control.

"It's lucky she didn't try it when I was any bigger!"

"What would you have done?" Hal's own mother hadn't dressed him up like that, but he couldn't tell Miller of his attraction to her clothes and how he loved to press their folds to his face as they hung in her closet or bury his nose in their scents as he lifted them from her chest of drawers. Once he'd even slipped a dress over his head and felt it encase him like silken armour until he caught sight of himself in the closet mirror and felt slightly nauseated at what he had done.

"I'd have popped her one right on the snout," Miller declared. But he kept his head down as he said it, and Hal wondered how long his friend's bluster would last if another Ruth were ruling his house. If Mr. Sark was right about women and their loss of control, what about him and his desire for his mother's garments? No, he wouldn't ever tell Miller, but he might try to write about it one day.

They both wrote, but very differently. Miller kept a journal in which he recorded the numbers and kinds of fish he caught and birds he shot. He also recorded sketches of local characters like the Indian guide who lived near the Sark cottage and the town druggist who had one eyeball significantly larger than the other. Miller wrote simply and directly about such people without any fancy words and Hal thought these portraits, like those he provided of birds on the wing or tiny mammals scurrying though the forest, were completely honest and real. His own work was, well, not so straightforward. For starters, he seemed able to write only poetry, or he wanted to write only poetry, which was pretty much the same thing. Where Miller saw the world for what it was and attempted to capture its visible dimensions in description and dialogue, he tended to cloak the world in images that brought to mind what it could be like on the other side of some imagined watershed. He didn't think deeply yet about symbols or metaphors, but he knew what he was trying to do with words was meant to alter everything.

One day Miller read him a short story he'd written about Roosevelt's charge up San Juan Hill. Hal almost cried when the horses fell, and he applauded when the Colonel and his brave men attained their goal.

"That must have been just how it was," he said.

Miller beamed with pleasure. "The old guys were good," he replied. "Melville, Hawthorne, Crane, but I can't write like them yet. Have you read 'Maggie, a Girl of the Streets'? Hal shook his head. "Crane doesn't fool around, just goes straight for the throat like he does in *Red Badge*. That's what writing has to do today." He smacked his palm with his fist. "Of course, I'm nobody right now, but one day ..."

Almost right away Hal felt he wasn't born to write just short poems about his feelings or what he saw immediately around him. Later on, he realized it was because there was so much history out there, and while prose could talk *about* this only poetry on a grand scale could *embrace* it and bring out its consequence. Look at the *Odyssey,* part of which they'd studied in school. Look at Whitman whom he'd read on his own and who saw his personal development mirrored in his nation's progress. It didn't take Hal long to discover he didn't want to write a song of himself but sing in new ways of a larger past that spilled into the yearnings of two blood brothers and shaped their lives.

When he tried to express his feelings publicly no one but Miller seemed to understand. They'd both joined the staff of the school newspaper, which mainly featured stories about the football team and social events. Miller was on the team in a starting fullback position and wouldn't hear anything bad said about the school's sporting life, but he did agree with Hal that stories and poems should be published as well. So he submitted one of his fishing tales about an old couple who trudged through the woods to their favourite river spot only to have the rain come down so heavily they couldn't catch a thing. Most of the story centered on their seemingly inconsequential dialogue, but as Hal read through their exchanges for a second then a third time he realized it wasn't only what they were saying that mattered but how they were saying it. They talked in monosyllables about the beauty of the woods in the rain and how the tug of the trout on the line made them feel attached to the water. Hal couldn't figure out how people who spoke so simply could convey such depths of perception, but he also knew his friend wasn't cheating with words by using them to replace experience. It was that language and the senses were one and the same in what Miller wrote and there was no need to distort this union through flowery diction. The student readers of this story liked it because everything looked and sounded and smelled familiar, from the way the river flowed in the dull light to the patter of raindrops on the birch leaves to the aroma of the wet, dark earth. They didn't take it for anything more than it was, even though Hal grasped an undertone of loss and perhaps despair in the old folks' condition. Who were they before they began their trek and who would they be after? When he asked Miller about this, his friend happily clapped him on the shoulder. "You're on to something there, my boy," he said. "The tip of the iceberg hides a whole lot, doesn't it?"

But when one of Hal's poems was published the reaction wasn't the same. He'd seen some kids playing on the beach with their dog near the Sark cottage but wasn't satisfied just to present their commonplace noise and energy. Instead he saw rapture in their bodily expression at odds with the timeless lapping of water on sand, and was fascinated by their brilliant unconcern for anything but the moment that would trap and kill them in the end. He didn't employ end-rhyme or bother with a constant metre, and no one but Miller caught the rhythms and alliterations he worked so hard on in each line. The other kids told him it didn't make sense and he must have copied it from a book somewhere, but he was happy to see his work on the page and determined to pursue this muse who didn't care so much about clarity as evocation.

Mainly the difference between them was that Hal's quest was more private. Content to let things come in a rush and take joy in editing draft after draft, he kept his sheaves to himself most of the time and did not submit another poem to the paper for many months. Miller, on the other hand, loved to share his work-in-progress, handing single paragraphs and even individual lines to Hal for approval before he gathered them into a finished tale he wanted the whole world to read. Hal had to admit to himself that almost everything Miller put down on paper was worth reading, but sometimes he wished the woodsman-writer would play his catch a little longer before pulling it from the stream.

3.

The Sark summer home was a cottage on the shores of a large lake about two hours away from the city by train or auto. Hal was often invited up for a week at a time, though his mother didn't like him to be away for longer.

"I get lonely without you here," she told him each time he made plans to leave. She'd attended school with Ruth Sark and had liked her down-to-earth, honest character, but she was gone and Henry Sark lacked proper manners and stability, always gallivanting off into the woods with a son who, while not openly disrespectful of more staid existence, always had a glint in his eye and a little too much vigour to suit her. Still, the father provided hearth and home for Miller and managed to be a reasonably dignified character when she occasionally saw him in town, so she couldn't refuse Hal's holiday requests. Besides, she had to admit he always came back to her with colour in his face and looking stronger. Without Miller, he would spend too much time alone in his tower room. Wanting to be a poet was just fine for a sensitive boy, but you had to get out in the world and get some practical training for manhood. Swimming and fishing skills would take Hal only so far, of course, but the self-confidence he gained from his time with the Sarks was undeniable and could be turned toward accomplishment in business that would lead to his unquestioned success. That he didn't talk to her about the details of his poetry was somewhat troubling, but she was willing to let him have that private space for now, and truth be told she was happy he wouldn't be writing any verse when he was out and about with Miller.

He and Miller had taken many day hikes in the country around the cottage. Through the woods they'd follow the river that fed into the lake on the edge of the Sark property and emerge by another, smaller lake filled with bass that took the lure and leapt like circus acrobats. Sometimes the fish would shake the hook from their open mouths but more often they surrendered to the hand-net that swept them from the water and onto a gill-rope beside their dead companions. Or the two boys would climb the hill behind the small barn and move down the far slope to a spring-fed stream where trout hovered in the current beneath the skating water-bugs and fallen floating leaves. Miller would bring his .22 and they'd pot squirrels and the occasional rabbit, which Miller would skin and his father would later make into a vegetable-laced stew they would all devour. As they walked, Miller would point out the various species in the deciduous and coniferous mix, indicating to Hal how to distinguish between tree leaves and barks and counting the rings on fallen trunks of oak and pine. He was always drawing maps in his notebook that showed the heights of land and directions of stream flow, reverently marking the spot where they killed a small animal on these maps as if, Hal thought at first, the pencil dot contained some part of the creature that could never die. But as he discovered later, Miller was only matter-of-factly recording an inevitability, and the mark represented his role in a task fulfilled. For his part Hal was happy to take things in without instantly capturing or representing them, but back in his tower room he would recall the wind on his face or the rush of wings as the birds flew off in an attempt to protect their nests, and search for ways to convey the carving force of the air or how his own eyelashes fluttered in time with feathered anxiety.

Then one night as they lay in their bunks in the back bedroom of the cottage, Miller announced the next morning they would begin a longer hike, one that would take four or five days into the country beyond the far side of the lake to a series of streams his father told him converged into a river holding the biggest trout imaginable. The land there was covered in pine forest cleanly-spaced for walking, the ground carpeted with needles, and the sky so clear in summer and fall you wanted to throw a line into its blue depths.

Hal listened to Miller's description with a mix of excitement and apprehension. He'd always wanted to camp out with his friend and get past the usual borders no matter how distant these already were from home. There was something out there he wanted to explore or run up against to test himself, but he also knew he could never do so without Miller. What if they got separated? Miller had the compass, and even if he could survive for a while by catching fish and eating berries, he wouldn't know how to get himself out of the wilderness. Well, he'd just have to stick close to his guide. There was another issue as well. His mother would forbid such a trip, and he knew he would never be able to tell her that he'd betrayed her assumptions about his safety with the Sarks. When he announced this, Miller laughed.

"She's really got you by the short hairs, hasn't she?"

Hal didn't like the image but wondered how he could fit it into a poem.

They walked uphill towards the pines, the tumplines from their packs tight against their foreheads and their boots leaving soft impressions in the thin soil that covered the rocky slope. Miller was ahead, the big Winchester 30.30 his father had recently bought him slung over his shoulder.

"We might run into a deer or moose up there," he'd said when Hal had raised his eyebrows at the size of the rifle. "You can't bring one of them down with a .22. Of course, we'd have to dress the meat and carry it out."

He was also carrying the tent as well as most of the cans of food and cooking and eating utensils. Hal had a groundsheet, two wool blankets, and most of their clothes, which consisted of changes of underwear and several pairs of socks each. Mr. Sark had ferried them to the other side of the lake in the skiff powered by a three-horsepower Evinrude. Miller thought Ole Evinrude who lived near Lake Oconomowoc in Wisconsin was the tops.

"He came over from Norway and realized our lakes were just too big for paddling all the time, so he invented the motor. Isn't she a beauty?"

Hal inhaled the fumes from the gas-oil mixture and coughed. The bilge water at Mr. Sark's feet was tinted in reds and greens, and the steel and brass casing of the motor shook as if it was about to disintegrate, but he had to admit to the benefits of cutting out an hour's paddle from the beginning of their trip.

"Sure," he said, nodding enthusiastically to bolster the monosyllable.

Mr. Sark cut the engine to idle and they clambered out, wading ashore through a patch of reeds and turning to wave as the boat circled away to the south. In five days they'd stand here and fire a couple of shots to signal their return. Miller had figured one night on the trail and a morning's march to the sweet spot of streams and river. That would give them two full days of fishing before heading back. They had to count on the weather, of course, but it was mid-August and any storms would pass through the area quickly.

The first afternoon took them through stands of oak and maple, Miller pointing out the biggest trees and speculating on their age. In clearings the grass and wildflowers grew to waist height, and Hal watched the bees and other insects flit from stem to stem and the pollen rise into the air like mist. Each hour or so, they'd stop and sip from their canteens, and he would feel every inch of his body stretching and pushing out of its usual complacent form, not aching yet, though he knew that would come. When he wiggled his toes in his boots something stirred in his brain. Not an image exactly, but an impression words were in the offing waiting to shape this day. When he looked over at Miller his friend was scribbling in his notebook, already composing the landscape.

They stopped before dark and set up camp in a grove of hardwoods. Hal gathered some fallen branches and a few small rocks for a fire circle. Once Miller roused the flames he pulled out a frying pan from his pack, cracked four eggs sunny-side up, and when they were almost done threw in a can of stew, the mixture bubbling within a matter of moments. They ate right from the pan. It was one thing to bring spoons along, but another to lug plates. Hal could hear his mother's expostulations about table manners as he slurped the delicious mess. Then Miller reached into his pack again and brought out a flask.

"Stole this from Pop's supply," he announced proudly. Then he winked. "He knows. I don't even have to add water to the bottle."

Hal had been allowed to sip a little wine at the family table at Thanksgiving and Christmas, but he'd never had anything stronger, and now the whiskey burned his throat even as he listened to Miller's admonition to take it slowly. Burned yet cleansed as well, clearing out passages that led all the way to his heart. The fire shimmered and the shadows danced beyond the fingers of light. Sparse clouds drifted across a crescent moon above the treetops. They were alone together where no one could ever find them. He'd read about the biblical prophets out in the desert searching for God and for the first time understood such isolation as akin to a state of grace. Once under his blanket he drifted off into what Miller later called "whiskey-dreams," full of possibility and desire.

The next morning everything was damp and steam rose from the tent and their clothing as the sun came through the leaves. They chewed on some hardtack while Miller boiled coffee in a small pot then poured it into their tin mugs.

"We'll have fish for lunch," he said as Hal complained about the texture of their breakfast. "And dinner. It's all trout all the time from now on."

They packed up and headed north again. The land rose before them and Hal could see the range of small hills that marked the watershed above the confluence of streams. After two or three hours they climbed above the old forest and walked into the pines, the odour of resin filling their nostrils and the damp blanket of brown needles absorbing their footsteps as if they had never touched the ground.

Stopping to lean back against a smooth trunk and take the pack's weight from his shoulders, Miller said: "Just down below us now. Listen."

Hal thought he could hear the sound of running water, but he couldn't be sure. There was a slight breeze mixed with birdsong in the green grove, and the pounding of his heart from the climb seemed louder than anything else. He was excited by the prospect of arrival after they'd come so far, but there was more to it than that. He and Miller, born on the same day, were exactly here seventeen years later when so easily they might never have met or, once acquainted, never have hit it off to the extent of learning about their twinned emergence into the world. For the first time, he wondered which of them was older.

"What time were you born?" he asked.

"You mean what time of day?" Miller stepped away from the trunk and hitched the pack up to a comfortable position.

"Yes, a.m. or p.m.?" Hal knew, because his mother had told him, of his early morning delivery after her night of prolonged anguish.

Miller thought for a moment. "Around noon, I think. Why?"

Hal felt a sudden rush of affection for his younger sibling. Miller might know all there was to know about the woods and would certainly protect him from any physical danger, but that was because he was bigger and stronger. Hal was older and therefore wiser by a few hours, and it was up to him to put that extra time to good use. He would begin now.

"Poetry's been around longer than any other kind of writing," he said.

Miller wasn't stupid. "What time were you born?"

"Way before noon."

"I'll bet it was raining."

"What's that got to do with anything?"

"Sound gets distorted in the rain. You hear things that aren't there."

They started down the slope together, Miller still slightly ahead.

"Why did I lift my arm?"

They were talking about the bear. Miller had skinned it with his hunting knife that afternoon, removing the fat and flesh from the hide as well as cutting out the toe pads and the toe bones behind the claws. It hadn't been pleasant to watch, but the worst part had been when he'd scooped out the brain and tissue through a hole in the back of the skull, flushing out the remaining bits with water. Since the kill had occurred about a mile from camp, Miller left the carcass to rot rather than bury it.

"The coyotes and turkey buzzards will have it down to bones in a few days anyway," he'd pronounced as they walked away with the smelly pelt. "We'll have to salt the hide until it's tanned. I figure the live bear weighed close to 300 pounds. That means about twenty pounds of salt." He chuckled. "Got any with you?"

Hal stared at the head and the dull, dead eyes looking back at him. Miller had split the lips and eyelids and turned the ears inside out to prevent spoilage. A few hours ago the animal had been alive, feeling the ground beneath his feet, smelling the wild grass and clean northern air, and paying little attention to possible danger. Then these two small creatures, hardly worth his attention, had crept along the edge of the meadow and exploded his world into pain and desperation. Of course, such disturbance hadn't lasted long, less than a minute until Miller had shattered his spine with a single massive blow.

"Why did you lift your arm? Because you were thinking about yourself, not the bear."

"I was thinking about him! I didn't want to hurt him, that's all."

"Then why did you have the gun in your hands? Why did you pull the trigger?"

Hal looked away. "Because I was with you," he wanted to say, but didn't. "I don't know," he finally replied.

"You did it because you're no different than any other man who's come up against big game. It's in your blood, just like it's in mine."

Then, as if taking pity or, at the very least aware that veins weren't always the same shape or size, Miller told him: "Don't worry, you'll write about it and find some relief."

It bothered Hal that this was true, at least the writing part. He'd already composed some lines in his head. Florid, imprecise ones while Miller made exact skinning strokes that elevated the troubling event into a frontier confrontation between man and beast. He couldn't use words the way Miller would, focusing on the report of the initial shot, how the bear ran with one leg torn and dangling towards the hill, and finally cleansing any dark moment of guilt or doubt for his hero with his own lethal marksmanship. For that's what Miller did, he realized— turned himself into the hero of any story he wrote and so got rid of real-life complications. Hal knew his poetry was meant to cleanse as well, but it never relieved him of daily responsibilities or misgivings. You could make the bear represent whatever you liked, but that never really changed the fact you'd pulled a trigger and that something in you had wanted to do this. What he'd meant by 'Because I was with you' was that he wanted Miller's approval, but he'd only partly attained it be-cause his friend still saw him as a junior woodsman and, yes, a junior writer whose work was a salve for experience rather than an accurate reflection. For just a dark second, Hal wondered what would happen to them both—to Miller when he could no longer substitute words for guilt or doubt, and to himself should he ever lose his balance on the high tier of his expression.

They fished beneath the boulders where the main stream tumbled into a long pool, standing in the cool water up to their waists and flicking their lines out into the current where the trout rose to their flies, jump-ing until they tired and drifting into the waiting net. Hal was adept at placing his feathered hook below a particular rock or at the edge of the rill where it swirled against the bank while Miller mostly propelled his fly great distances from his rod tip through sheer strength as if he could knock the fish out when it landed. Both methods seemed to work as by the end of the second day they had put roughly the same number of trout in their wicker creels. Miller cooked up two big ones in the skillet, throwing in some flour and a little water as batter and frying a couple of wild fennel bulbs he said had a sweet taste and would help their digestion. After they'd eaten he pulled out the flask and they took turns sipping the whiskey as they leaned back against a log, the fire flickering lazily at their feet, talking over their work plans when they'd finished school the following year.

Miller was adamant about his future. If the country got into the war in Europe, he'd volunteer, not just out of a sense of duty, he said, but because he wanted to test himself in the soldier's life. If they refused him for any reason then he'd join the Red Cross and do hospital work or drive an ambulance. After that he was going to become a reporter with some big-city newspaper. That way you could make money doing the thing you did best. He wanted to write a short story collection first and then novels.

"What about?" Hal asked.

"That's another reason why I'll join up. See the world and all that," he declared exuberantly. Then, lowering his voice: "It's pretty terrible over there, you know. Guys like us getting killed or shot up so bad they'll be cripples all their lives." His voice rose again. "If they won't let me in, I'll write about it like Crane did." He laughed. "After that, I'll just have to convince Mr. Hearst I'm worth a chance."

Like Miller, Hal had read the news reports about the battles in France and Italy. "It's stupid," he said. "Everybody dying over nothing."

"It's not nothing! You can't just let people like the Kaiser take over your country."

"I didn't know you were such a patriot." Hal flung his arm out toward the river. "Meanwhile, I don't see him around here."

"I'm not a patriot, I'm a democrat. But what if the Kaiser did show up? Wouldn't you defend all this?" He lifted his chin toward the river.

Hal thought it over. "Maybe," he replied eventually, "but I can't see him wanting it." Now it was his turn to laugh. "Too far from Berlin."

"Okay, wise guy, what do you want to do when school's over?"

"Well, I could keep going to school, but there's no money for that. So I'm going to go to New York. My mother has some cousins there who'll put me up and maybe even find me some work. I don't care what

I do, just as long as I've got time to write." An excitement came into his voice. "That's where everything's happening—magazines, art galleries, publishing, interesting people who actually read poetry."

"Where'd you learn all this?" Miller asked.

"My mother told me some of it. But if you get past those headlines about the war, you'll find it too."

"Well, I'm pretty sure Paris has everything you're talking about and a lot more besides. Just remember I'll be over there defending your right to read those magazines and write your poetry. I want to be part of those headlines, one way or another."

Hal was confident about one version of the future. "You will be," he said. "You will."

The next morning he carried the gun and tent while Miller hoisted the bearskin across his shoulders. As they set off, he wondered aloud what it weighed.

"Maybe forty or fifty pounds."

"It's a good thing I didn't give you that salt, then."

He wasn't going to tell his mother about the trip, but soon after he got back to town she asked him what he wanted to do beyond his graduation, and he recounted his exchange with Miller beside the campfire. When she called Miller a braggart who would never amount to anything, he fired back that he'd never have survived for five days without his friend's knowledge and leadership skills.

"Five days? What do you mean?"

He began to describe their journey, but she cut him off angrily when she realized Mr. Sark had turned the boat around and left them stranded, yelling that he was never to go out to their cottage again. Surprised at his own composure, he insisted she listen and went on to relate every detail he could recall. She had covered he ears with her hands, pretending she couldn't hear, but screamed when he shot the bear.

"I'll never forgive you, Hal. Never. You could have been killed."

"The bear was terrified, mother. He ran away, not toward us." He felt superior to her, stronger, but he should have known this was an illusion.

"Why did you kill it? You wouldn't have done it if it hadn't been for Miller Sark!"

He remembered his feelings when Miller tossed him the claw. And now he loved and hated her too.

"You're right," he told her. "And I'm glad he made me do it." It was all so ugly because they weren't sitting in the woods, the smell of the fish they'd caught and fried lingering in their nostrils, the fire warming their feet in the night chill, their shared determination to be successful writers covering everything, including the death of the bear, in a positive light. Instead, here in the stifling living room he and his mother stalked one another, alternately hunter and prey, in killing ways that couldn't be redeemed.

But she eventually backed away from the confrontation, apparently confident time was on her side and that boys who would be boys would inevitably go their separate ways. She hoped Miller would join up like he wanted to, she said. She didn't want him to die in the war, of course, but soldiering was probably what he could do best. Then as if aware of her dismissive tone she murmured sweetly: "You mentioned New York, dear."

4.

Through his last year in school Hal worked sporadically on a long poem. He began with *ursus americanus* in a high field overlooking what would soon be named the Hudson River as Dutch sailors met the New World for the first time. The bear had a consciousness that let it sense the coming change for the hills and woodlands. In a series of layered images he contrasted the animal's instinctive wisdom with the mercantile aspirations of those the crew represented, having the animal look down the years through its descendants who would eventually witness certain key moments in American history—the Revolution, the Civil War, the conquest of the west, and the ruthless rise of commerce everywhere. He intended this violent past to lead ultimately to the murder of a single bear in a wilderness field by a boy who, ironically, would reveal himself as the voice and vision of a natural world gone wrong. It would be his way of expiating his personal guilt, but instead he found himself crossing and re-crossing a national fault-line that cut off understanding between man and his fellow creatures. So he created a youthful figure who, meaning well, straddled that fissure but often overrode his good intentions with a desire to control what he encountered and be victorious over it.

At first it was Miller he was writing about, but he soon ambitiously saw far beyond what he believed about his friend, and imagined this figure, like the bear, present at crucial historical sites and events he would then fictionalize so he could tell a story about them. Thus, the Young Man, as he decided to call him, would begin in idealism and possibility as he signed the Declaration of Independence and helped shape the Constitution, only to own a Plantation or lead Union troops in their pillaging of southern countryside, shoot down the buffalo and ride west on iron rails, tell General Custer the 7th Cavalry was almighty and the Sioux had better cooperate—no, here he would have to stop and begin again with the bear's relationship with the Indians before the Dutch arrived and how the tribes took only what they needed from the land, never leaving a carcass to rot and wearing claw necklaces around their necks as protection against their human enemies. Then there would be the growth of factories to contend with and the suffering of people who worked in them during the 19th century—this imagined out of Dickens' *Hard Times*, which he'd found at the Sark cottage—and he'd describe how the Young Man turned his back on entire communities and looked out only for himself. It was all a jumble in his mind. Eventually some sections were roughed out on the page but covered by crossed-out words and lines while others were barely conceived and lacked any definite images. The only part he finished with a little satisfaction was about the bear watching the sailors, which he submitted to the school newspaper just before graduation. Miller wasn't aware of his own behind-the-scenes contribution but had plenty to say just the same.

"The thing about animals is that you can't predict what they're thinking," he pronounced as they walked home after class the day the passage appeared in the paper. He was dragging a stick along the white picket fences of the equally white houses, making loud, gun-like reports that echoed through the neighbourhood. "That's what makes them so interesting and dangerous to hunt."

"Even squirrels?" Hal asked angrily.

But Miller was off on one of his instructive jaunts and didn't notice. "Yeah, remember that bear you shot? Well, I didn't tell you at the time, but he could just as easily charged us as run off into the woods."

"But you would have killed him anyway."

"I would have stood my ground." Then he added in a voice so low Hal almost didn't hear him: "That's all you can do."

Suddenly Hal felt badly that he'd so thoroughly connected Miller to the Young Man in his poem. He'd make some changes so his friend wouldn't recognize himself in any of it. That is, if he ever finished and published the whole thing. It would take years, and he didn't know if his ambition would measure up to the task. Besides, there were other things he wanted to write. He didn't know yet what they were, but he knew they were waiting for him down the road. He thought again about New York and whether he'd ever see Miller there, a war survivor and famous reporter who might or might not give him the time of day.

His mother wasn't altogether happy about him going off to New York without her, but he made it clear he didn't want to stay in a town where employment possibilities were minimal and the kinds of people he wanted to meet simply didn't exist. So she wrote to her cousins to enquire about Hal staying with them until he got his feet on the ground and received a welcoming reply. They had a large house in Brooklyn that would also accommodate her during the frequent visits she planned. Meanwhile, she had a surprise for her son whom she declared to be her favourite boy.

"I'm your *only* offspring, mother."

"Yes, but I mean out of all the boys your age I've known."

He wondered what she meant by that, never having been told much about her life before she met his father. Then he wondered if she was making a direct comparison between him and his father. He'd been too young to remember when Henry Pierce walked out, but he did recall her telling him when he was in elementary school that his father was a profligate. When he looked the word up in a dictionary he found it meant wasteful but also immoral. To be wasteful didn't seem too much of a flaw, but the utterly damning synonym of immorality left him breathless and he never pursued an explanation.

Her surprise was that this improvident husband and father had, strangely, left each of them a trust fund, Hal's that he could begin to access at graduation and hers that she had been drawing on for years so she could support them both in proper style. They were sitting, Hal observed to himself, in a room without any style, but that didn't matter anymore. His heart was thumping with excitement as he considered the prospect of New York funding. He wouldn't have to stay very long with the cousins. He wouldn't have to depend on his mother for money or come home as often as she'd want him to. He was making plans for his independent living when she interrupted his reverie.

"Hal, do you hear me? You'll have forty dollars a month. Isn't that grand? You'll be able to buy your own food and even have a little left over to save for your trips home."

"Forty dollars?" he said, puzzled.

"Yes, your father wanted to make sure you didn't spend it all at once. It's only $500, though I'm sure he could have given you a lot more. But it will last you for at least a year. Isn't that grand?" she said again.

"Do you know where he is, mother?"

"Why on earth do you want to know that?"

"I'd like to write and tell him I'll need more."

"I've absolutely no idea where he is," she said in a shocked voice. But he'd seen the colour drain from her face and knew the lie.

Then, as if to gain the upper hand again, she announced that she had another surprise. "I have enough money left in my fund to allow us to take a little trip together."

"A trip? Where to?"

"Well, I thought as a graduation present we could go to San Francisco. I have an old friend there I haven't seen in years who could put us up for a week or so while we see the city."

At first, he was going to protest vociferously. A week with his mother, first of all in the closed confines of a train and then in the undoubtedly Victorian house of her spinster ally, would suffocate him. Besides, he wanted one more trip with Miller before they went their separate ways. When the U.S. had entered the war that spring his friend had immediately applied for the Marine infantry with the Expeditionary Forces, had been accepted, and would go to training camp in the middle of August. Hal wasn't interested in combat of any kind and held his fire now with his mother. He could put up with her and her friend as long as he had time to explore the city on his own. He should see the west coast if he was to write properly about American advancement to the edge of the continent—the manifest destiny that his history teacher had celebrated but had squeezed his bear into smaller and smaller wilderness pockets and destroyed anything that got in its way. He'd been trying to sort out a long passage about former President Roosevelt who'd established a national park system but also went off on an African safari and killed over five hundred wild animals. If he and his mother left by train right after school ended, he and Miller would later have lots of time to head north and fish.

"All right," he told her. "But I will want some days to myself out there."

She knew he was working on something important to him but guarding it closely. Perhaps, she thought mistakenly, a new, relaxed environment would prompt him to share it with her.

"Of course, dear, I understand. Now let's make our plans."

5.

He hadn't been anywhere, really, unless you counted a thirty-mile northern trek to some untouched country and unnamed streams. They boarded the Chicago and Northwestern line at Terminal Station with its sixteen tracks elevated above street level. Miller had told him to look out for the Mississippi a few hours west of the city, and when the bridge took them across he imagined jumping down into the blue water that would carry him all the way to the Gulf of Mexico. When he wasn't gazing out the window at Illinois and Iowa, he wandered the length of the train through the dining car with its carefully-arranged napkins and a fresh flower on each table all the way to the mail car at the rear where the men let him watch as the big net captured the hanging grey bags filled with letters and small packages at stations where they didn't stop. All the while, the wheels rumbled in a steady rhythm beneath his feet, and he wished Miller was with him to feel the train's power and speed. That first night he and his mother slept in their separate berths across the aisle from one another. There was a tiny reading lamp behind his head, and he wrote some notes about the sights and sounds of the day before he fell asleep as the high-pitched whistle blew them through rural crossings. In the morning they entered Nebraska and came into Omaha around noon, the back walls of houses and fenced-in factory yards lined up in dusty rows that stretched away from the tracks. The land was flat as Miller had said it would be almost all the way to the mountains.

Their next ride was on the Union Pacific that would carry them right past Promontory Point in Utah where the famed line had joined up to the one coming from the west coast in 1869. His bear would watch from a distance as the last spike was driven into the last tie and the celebration of machine over nature began. Now he was part of that mechanical victory he wondered lazily if some things weren't just meant to be, but quickly admonished himself at the memory of countless buffalo shot from trains by tourists who stopped only when they ran out of bullets or their barrels became too hot.

The Wyoming Rockies didn't disappoint. To the north he could see a chain of peaks rising from the plains into the clouds, and through the opposite window was a view south to similar Colorado heights. On the fourth day they rode out of Utah, through Nevada, over the Sierra Nevada range, down to the Pacific. All through the journey his conversation with his mother had been negligible. She'd been immersed in a romance novel, looking out the window only when they were seated in the dining car or Hal shouted excitedly that she just had to see a particular feature of the landscape. Not even the Rockies could tempt her for very long, and he realized she was just moving from home to home, from what she knew to what she knew. After a while he gave up trying to capture her interest, concentrating on what he had seen and adding to his notes. Once, however, he caught himself viewing her opposite him as Miller might have done. "The old woman did not lift her eyes from her book as the train smoked and shook," he wrote. "The country swallowed her like a hungry snake, but she did not notice."

That week in San Francisco everything changed for him. His mother was happy to relax with her friend, a spinster, as he had suspected, who lived off a family inheritance, while Hal explored the city. The rule was simple. He could go out after breakfast and be gone for hours as long as he was back by six for dinner. He loved the cable car ride up Powell Street and the view from Telegraph Hill. More than once he took the ferry across to Sausalito and wondered if they'd ever be able to build a bridge across the bay with its treacherous currents he'd read about in the stories of Jack London, who had died the year before at his ranch up the coast. But most of all he loved the Embarcadero district. It was the place where the trolley looped in front of the ferry terminal and ships from overseas dropped and took on cargo. Teeming morning and afternoon with people of all shapes and colours, it was a roadway along the shoreline facing the mudflats where the young London had been Prince of the Oyster thieves. There were fishermen's stalls, fruit and vegetable stands with produce from San Mateo County, and eateries ranging from proper restaurants to corrugated iron shacks that served crab legs and a beer for fifteen cents. He wandered among it all, brushing up against dark skins with strange bodily markings, Chinamen with topknots, and Scandinavians with blond hair and ruddy cheeks, hearing alien accents he couldn't decipher and seeing gestures he hadn't known to exist. On a postcard with a picture of a ninety-pound sea bass that he sent to Miller, he wrote simply "Catch me if you can!" All the while, he wrote down his impressions in his notebook, thinking this was the storied end of the continent he had yet to describe in his poem. It was almost too much, as if it deserved its own separate work in response, but he was content for now just to record its details and dimensions.

Each evening his mother demanded a strict accounting of where he'd been and what he'd done, not because she mistrusted him, he realized, but because, now she was safely settled, she was genuinely curious about experience she could not or would not access herself. So he described the din of humanity down along the docks, the raucous laughter and sometimes tough exchanges as men came up against one another, sailors usually, on ship's leave for a few hours or even a day or two, testing the city waters and all who swam there. He didn't tell her many were drunk by mid-afternoon and cut the air with their curses sharp as the filleting knives that flashed over fins and scales.

"You should be careful, son. Boys disappear from such places, caught by press-gangs and other rascals."

He'd heard of the press-gangs and, even though they didn't exist anymore, he wondered what it would be like to be clubbed and dragged onto a foreign ship bound for the Orient or around Cape Horn. Miller would put up such a fight they'd back off, but he knew he wouldn't have stood a chance if anyone came after him. Then someone had.

He'd been walking at the edge of the morning's crowd on his third day of adventure, watching the gulls dip and glide above him and thinking how free they were, when suddenly there was a voice behind his ear and a hand on his shoulder. He whirled around to find an attractive young man in sailor's garb with a toothy grin and green-flecked eyes.

"You aren't from around here, are you?"

He hesitated, not sure where the question was leading, but finally stammered: "No, I'm from the mid-west."

"No kidding! So am I! Whereabouts?"

"Oak Park, just outside of Chicago." There was a heat coming out of those eyes that Hal responded to though he didn't understand why. At least that's what he told himself. This past year Miller had been around with a few girls, disreputable ones from across the tracks, and he'd boasted about lying with them in hay mows or orchards on the edge of town. Such talk mildly excited him, but he found himself more involved with Miller's storytelling than with the physical act between male and female. He'd never been out with a girl, though his mother often asked him if he'd met anyone at school he'd like to bring home for dinner. He told her he hadn't but didn't add he wasn't especially attracted to any of the girls he knew in class. As far as relationships with boys were concerned, except for Miller he drifted along, friendly to just about everyone but indifferent to the development of anything that would take up his time. Now, looking into the young sailor's eyes he realized he was anything but indifferent. He wanted to lie down in their green heat and let it cover him like a second skin. The image of his mother's dress sliding over his shoulders came into his mind, and he almost put his hand on the stranger's arm. He was going to ask the name of his hometown, but said instead: "How long are you in port?"

"Tonight's my last night. Are you free?"

He saw the gulls' flight once again as the birds broke away from earthly prisons and spread his wings for the first time. "Yes," he answered. "My name's Hal. What's yours?"

"Nick," the green man said, "but my friends call me Nicky." There was no last name.

They spent the afternoon voyaging from bar to bar along the waterfront. Hal, who had only sipped tentatively from Miller's whiskey flask, got gloriously, loudly drunk for the first time in his life, shouting out to crowds of sailors an embellished version of his life story, including his wilderness trek with Miller, while managing to divulge little information about his family life, especially his mother. When they found out he was a budding writer, and wanted to be a great one, they shouted for recitations. He gave them bits of Whitman, Shelley, and of course the Bard himself, failing to make clear it was not his own work he was quoting until one old salt began to declaim "When in fortune and men's eyes" along with him and he had to admit he was mixing his own with others' verse. In fact, he couldn't bring himself to speak aloud in his bear's tongue, though he longed to, and, drunk as he was, promised himself an eventual poetic response to these layered dens of word and flesh. Pressed up against so many bodies in blue and white he could feel his bones and skin relax and reach out to touch the raw warmth offered without hesitation or shame. Occasionally he would catch Nicky's eye and become aware of a true reckoning in the offing, as if clarity and a way on resided in this focused moment in the nautical blur around him.

Amidst the din and smoke he completely lost track of time, but it was dark when he and Nicky staggered out of the last bar, their arms around one another's shoulders, signing vocal treaties with the night that affirmed their lasting friendship, and laughing uproariously at the slightest slip along the edge of the gutter. In some small buried part of him Hal knew his mother would be frantic. He was always home for dinner, rain or shine. Every day of their life together he had never let her down.

"Rain or shine …" he began to sing, and since the rest of the song was unknown to him he began to improvise. "Rain or shine, 'cause it's a crime if mother pines," but Nicky was pulling him down a dark alley into the shadows of different rhymes.

Swollen with desire, Hal felt his clothing ripped away like sails from masts and rigging on a rudderless ship whose cargo was no longer familiar distinctions between up and down, let alone right and wrong. He fell over against the base of a wall and felt Nicky on top of him, his mouth where only his own fingers had been before urging Hal to let go let go let go and then he did with wondrous relief as if the heeling vessel had suddenly righted itself in the storm. Just before he encircled Nicky with his bear's tongue, he glimpsed his mother's horror and Miller with his eyes closed, then calmer waters enveloped him.

"You must never abandon me like that again!" Ruth Pierce was yelling at him in the bedroom of her friend's home and every syllable was a blow against his already pounding head. Somehow he had found his way back in the early hours of the morning when Nicky had told him they couldn't bunk at the cheap hotel where he spent his shore leave because he was shipping out in a few hours. Hal had woken the two women when he stumbled into some flowerpots on the porch and swore vehemently as he went down into a profusion of petals and shards. Now she was standing over him, apparently unconcerned about his wellbeing and anxious only to berate him for his betrayal.

"I'm sorry, mother," he said, enunciating each word as clearly as he could though his mouth was parched, which surprised him considering the thirst that had been quenched just a short time ago.

His memory of the exchange with Nicky was by turns delicious and terrifying, but most of all he was afraid of her wrath and her reaction if she ever found out where he'd been and what he'd done. He'd known all along if he didn't want to stay in the alley or end up in the cheap hotel for any length of time he needed her to come home to. But he was confused about her role as well because the tranquil seas he'd reached with the sailor seemed preferable to any port she was able to provide.

There were only two days left before they boarded the train back to Chicago. He was tempted by the Embarcadero, but with Nicky gone he knew he'd have to start over, and he didn't know if he had the mettle. His body tingled when he thought of doing so, then troubled feelings overwhelmed him. Had he always been this way? He recalled again the pleasurable sensations as he put on his mother's clothes when he was young. Was it a sickness as she would undoubtedly claim or just a harmless diversion? Diversion from what? He had never kissed a girl or really wanted to, but maybe his hormones hadn't fully developed yet. He had listened politely when his mother had pressed him to bring home one of his female school friends, though now he had to admit there was never any future in such a gesture except the matrimonial one that obviously meant so much to her. On the other hand, had he displayed any attraction to boys? No, he had only one close male friend and, searching his memory, he couldn't find a single trace of sexual desire for Miller. Indeed, the thought made him ill, not because Miller's good looks and physical prowess weren't enough to pull anyone into a forbidden sphere but because they had shared too much other joy with their bodily exertions to twist them into carnal forms. More than that, Miller was entirely normal, and Hal didn't want to associate him in any way with what would only threaten his friend's muscular sense of self.

On the way east he sat opposite his mother half-listening to her chatter about the climate and beauty of the coast. She had not again mentioned his night away from her, and he knew she assumed there would be no repetition of such behaviour. He wasn't sure there would be, at least not for the rest of the summer. After all, Oak Park was a small place where, compared to San Francisco, dark alleys were few and far between. There must be a night life there and in Chicago where

Great Lake sailors frequented bars and clubs, but there'd be a strict curfew for him, and unless he wanted to abandon her altogether, he'd better conform to the house rules. He shook his head to clear away such oppositions. They were what he'd have to deal with once he'd figured out what sex with a man meant to him, if he could ever do that with any confidence. Given his easy surrender to Nicky, was he a kind of predatory sailor himself open to a quick tryst with the first good-looking youth he saw unaccompanied by a female companion? Or was he, as he would prefer to think, a lover-in-waiting looking for a constant partner with whom he might share his visions and poetry? He didn't know, but he would have to wait to find out in New York. On a walk to stretch his legs, he stopped between train cars and scribbled in his notebook, pulling his jacket up over his head against the rush of cinders and smoke:

The pole-star left a mark
Within your green eyes
A fiery fleck
To burn the brine
Without crime or shame
We swam in keener
Currents of the sea

About to scrawl 'For Nicky' above the opening line, he realized that if such personal passion ever became public every word he wrote would be interpreted to correspond with that identity. Sailor or lover, he wasn't sure why he was the way he was—by blessing or by curse—but he couldn't allow his poetry to be dragged by others through moral mud and be reduced to what would be called a faggot's verse. Whatever was implicit in his words was no more or less so than Miller's sexuality when he wrote about fields and streams. He had to shape his poetry in ways that resisted personal categorizations as he was trying to do with the bear's vision of America. He read over the seven lines and scratched the dedication from his mind. Now their ardour was neutral. He would work hard to keep things that way.

6.

Miller showed up the day after Hal returned, full of news and plans.

"I think I got a girl pregnant," he announced, his voice flat to disguise any worry or perhaps self-satisfaction.

"Who is she?" Hal cried, trying to picture his ex-classmates and gauge their charms for his friend.

"Ah, she's an Indian from up the cottage country who sleeps around so maybe it's not mine. She says it is, but I think she just wants some money. Not to get rid of it. They breed like rabbits anyway."

"Have you told your father?" Hal wondered if Henry Sark would angry or proud of his son's potency.

"Naw, the old man's an honorary chief or something, of her tribe, I mean. He'd feel responsible."

"What are you going to do?"

"Pay her, I guess. She made some noises about getting married, but I told her I'm off to the war soon and she'd never get me to settle down. She'll take fifty bucks, I'm sure."

"I've got forty," Hal blurted out, then quickly realized he didn't have anything until the fall except his mother's largesse.

Miller beamed. "That's great!" he said, "but I can raise twenty or thirty right away if I sell some pelts. I'll pay you back the rest."

Hal tried to keep a straight face and didn't back down from his offer, but he didn't know how he was going to get the money. Ruth Pierce would be horrified by any subsidizing of the wayward Miller or a destitute Indian girl she was likely to consider a whore, if that term ever passed the narrow lips of her mind. Miller didn't notice anything amiss because he was now off into talk about their big mid-summer trip.

"The country's right up under the Canadian border. Nobody but Indians and stray old frontiersmen have ever been up there. We'll have to ride a freight halfway then hike in the rest. A week in and out. The fish will be bigger than anything we've seen before."

"A week after the train?"

"Yup. If we get lost nobody will ever find us. But we won't get lost, will we?"

Hal knew this was true. Even without the compass, Miller's inborn sense of direction meant they'd always know where they were. He laughed. Hell, with a 30.30 and a fly rod why should their position matter at all? Then he thought of the Embarcadero at night. How would Miller survive where the pole-star shone on a different kind of traveller? Could he ever tell him about Nicky or his newly-awakened desires that didn't include women? He desperately wanted to. Miller was certainly the only one he could trust, and perhaps the only one strong enough to accept his being different, but he also saw the world clearly and keenly as a territory where rivers of behaviour flowed and forests of feeling stood tall, opposing encroachment and betrayal. Everything else was a side-show filled with scenery and characters that were second-rate and therefore dangerous to what he most valued. Hal recognized that if he revealed his inner self with all its doubts and blatant appetites he might become one of those characters, so he swore himself to silence on the subject. Besides, they could still talk about writing because, as he'd determined, sexual desire wasn't at the heart of what he wanted to say, so Miller would hear the true beat of his blood when they shared a tent together or stood in streams whose force and beauty confirmed the balance of their bodies and minds. That's what he told himself, but the Embarcadero had made him dizzy and he couldn't help but feel some part of his woodland poise was gone forever.

There were no railroad bulls to chase them off when they jumped a freight by a water tank ten miles north-east of the Sark cottage. They had a boxcar all to themselves, save for a few bales of hay in one corner, and sat with their feet dangling over the door sill while the trees flashed by and the sun played on their eager faces. He was excited by the prospect of crossing into another country where he'd heard they spoke French as well as English, but Miller let him know it was nothing special.

"There's no fence or markers. Just a river running east to west. We could swim across if you want, but it'll be only the birds and squirrels that notice."

"How do you know about this place?"

"My father met an Indian guide years ago who told him the smallest trout up there were ten pounds. He always meant to go but kept putting it off. When I said we were heading up he almost decided to come along. That would have been okay, but not much of an adventure for us. We'd be second mates instead of a couple of captains on the loose."

Hal knew there was only one captain on this trip and that he'd signed up as first mate if not an able-bodied seaman under orders. He remembered the *Pequod* whose crew had all died because their captain went crazy over a white whale. Well, Miller wasn't Ahab and he wasn't Starbuck or even Ishmael. For the first time he wondered about the relationship between Melville's narrator and his dark-skinned, south sea companion. Was there anything in the novel to suggest they were more than brothers-in-arms? Lots of sailors were, given their time at sea without women, but it didn't mean anything.

They were six hours on the train before it stopped on a spur line to take on logs that a small band of waiting lumberjacks would load. Hal saw their arms corded with muscle and their stringent faces that spoke of a hard life. They nodded at him and Miller as they passed and headed away from the rail bed.

"Tough as nails," Miller said under his breath. "Some of them never leave here."

"Where do they live?" Hal asked, somewhat in awe of the men's staying power.

"Oh, they've got proper cabins back in the woods. Don't believe all that garbage about them eating only beans and bacon. My old man says they hunt deer and small varmints and keep little gardens of vegetables."

Hal took a chance. "What do they do without women?"

Miller laughed. "They fuck themselves," he replied gleefully.

The first night they camped by a stream too small to fish, but Miller shot a rabbit with the .22 they'd brought along to supplement the 30.30, skinned it, and made up a stew with the meat and some raw carrots he'd toted in his knapsack. They were both tired from the day's exertions and quickly fell asleep on their beds of pine boughs, their blankets protecting them from the chilly passage of the wind soughing through the branches overhead. All the next day they marched, stopping for snacks and a light lunch of bread and cheese. The country was ridged and fairly open, and they saw no game, though flocks of ducks passed in the distance, their wings far back on their bodies, their formation wavering and without the true form of geese as they flew.

"Wish we had a scattergun," Miller said. "There's no chance of bringing one down with a rifle."

When they stopped for the second night, Miller told him they'd get there the next day by noon. "That'll give us almost three whole days before we have to head back in time to catch the return train. If we miss it we'll have to bunk with the lumberjacks for another week. I guess your mother would get a bit worried."

He'd been one night away in the Embarcadero and she'd not forgiven him. But maybe if he didn't return for a week after he was supposed to, she'd think him dead and be overjoyed when he showed up. He'd tell her about the lumberjacks fucking themselves and how he and Miller kept their distance from such an exhibition.

The next morning they hiked along a ridge above a valley whose slopes were lined with conifers and stands of hardwood. The woods were very dry and, except for the occasional bit of birdsong, they heard only their thick-soled moccasins crunching the needles and fallen leaves. Then Miller held up his arm and pointed to his ear. Hal listened to the silence and, after a long time, caught the quiet rush of liquid sound though the river wasn't yet visible through the array of trunks and branches. When they emerged from the trees and dropped down from the ridge towards the steep banks a few minutes later, Miller pointed his chin at the far shore a few hundred feet away. "Canada," he said. "Maybe we'll swim over tomorrow. Right now let's get our lines in the water."

Years later Hal could still recall the amazing numbers of fish they caught and their impressive size. The Indian guide had been exaggerating, of course, but no trout of the half dozen they each brought in that first afternoon was under five pounds, and the biggest that Miller fought, whooping and hollering for over a quarter of an hour, weighed twice that. It was, Hal said, as if living along the border meant they had to grow for two countries. They had a feast that night, fish in batter with wild asparagus they picked from a nearby field. Miller tossed most of what they hadn't eaten back into the river and they glumly watched the remnants of the corpses float downstream. "From now on," he declared, "we'll keep a couple and let the others go."

They sat by the fire, sipping Henry Sark's whiskey once more while some thunderheads gathered in the evening sky. There was a hollow booming in the distance as if the thunder hadn't quite made up its mind. Miller hit the hard ground with his fist. "Hasn't rained up here in weeks," he said. Then, matter-of-factly, his face in shadow: "You didn't have much to say about San Francisco."

Hal tried to look relaxed as he poked a stray log back into the flames with his foot. "I had a good time," he said, "when mother let me off the leash."

Miller laughed. "You and your old lady, Anyone would think you were married."

He could feel his cheeks burning as he yelled: "You take that back!"

Miller appeared genuinely surprised as he put up his hands in self-defence. "Hey, I was just kidding. Don't take it so hard. At least you've got a mother," he added quietly.

That final comment cooled Hal's anger and let him duck any accuracy in the original affront. "Sorry," he said. "I guess I take that for granted." He was about to ask Miller what he remembered of his own mother, but the half-orphan had moved on.

"So what *did* you do when you were off the leash?"

Hal took him down into the docklands in all their glory, vaunting the colourful characters who frequented the district and the energy they gave off just in passing by. He guided Miller along the fish and vegetable stalls, emphasizing the smells and sounds of commerce, and by the parade of ships from all over the world—venerable three-mast whalers and up-to-date steamships as well as naval vessels.

"Must have been a lot of our boys in uniform," Miller said.

"Yeah, there were, plenty of them."

"Were any of them off to Europe?"

Hal hadn't even asked Nicky where he was bound and regretted it now. He'd read in the papers that the Germans had some south sea colonies, and at the beginning of the war there'd been a big battle between them and the British off the coast of Chile. "Maybe," he replied. "But I think they need to guard against a sneak attack in the Pacific."

"Nope, the big one's where I'm going. The Western Front. You should join up. We could win the war together."

Hal laughed nervously, fearing his friend would pressure him, but Miller began to regale him with tales of trench warfare and aerial combat over France. His own prospective army career and the Embarcadero were forgotten for the time being.

That night he dreamed he was fishing with Nicky. They were standing naked in the middle of a cold, fast-flowing stream, the water purling around their knees, the sun hot on their shoulders. Hal knew they weren't going to catch anything, but he'd promised Nicky a good time, so they kept on. Suddenly he had fallen into the current and was drifting away. Nicky didn't seem to notice, and he was carried swiftly downstream to where Miller was on the bank waiting to rescue him. As he came near his friend Hal saw his eyes were closed even as he reached to pull him to safety. Then he awoke, lying warm and dry beneath his blanket but shivering violently as if the stream still enveloped him. He swore to himself he would tell Miller who and what he really was before the trip was done.

The morning air rippled with heat. "Okay, let's swim across," Miller said.

"What, now?"

"Why not? The fish will wait. Besides, don't you want to see Canada?"

"Looks pretty much like the U.S. of A. from over here."

Miller shucked the shorts and shirt he'd slept in, ran the few yards to the bank, and launched himself. "C'mon," he shouted. "It's great!" He turned and began a determined crawl towards the opposite shore.

They'd swum naked together many times before, but Hal was troubled by the dream and especially Miller's seemingly intentional blindness in the face of emotional alarm. But he couldn't very well stay where he was so he stripped down and yelled: "Wait for me!" His subsequent slow motion movement towards the river contrasted with the racing of his brain as if his body and mind were at war along this undefended borderline.

Miller was a powerful swimmer and stayed ahead of him all the way across. The Canadian bank was steep when Hal stood up in the shallows. From above, Miller leaned down and held out his hand. "You look like you could use some help," he said. Hal glanced up. His friend was smiling and looking at him with affection.

"Miller—," he started to say.

"Jesus!" Miller said. "Look at that." He'd stood up suddenly and was pointing back at the American shore.

Hal spun around in the water and saw the smoke on the ridge above their camp.

"I've seen it happen before," Miller cried. "Dry as a tinderbox and a spark just jumps up. The whole place could blow any minute. We've got to get back and over that ridge or we'll be trapped!"

Hal had never swum so fast in his life, powered by the need to escape and the survival instinct that came with it. He wasn't too far behind as Miller leapt from the river and reached their jumble of clothes and equipment. Looking up he saw flames shooting across the treetops on the ridge summit. They dressed quickly then carefully packed up the tent and blankets, broke down their seven-foot rods, slung the guns over their shoulders, and headed out. The wind was blowing from the west, so Miller steered them upwards in that direction towards a point where smoke and flames had not obscured the sky.

"As long as the wind doesn't shift, we'll be okay," he said, turning to Hal. "But if it does, stick close to me. Here, take this." He reached into his pack and extracted a small whistle. "If we get separated, use it. And stay low if you're in the smoke. There'll be more air down by the ground."

"Do you have one too?" But Miller was already moving.

The western edge of the ridge, which they obviously hoped to skirt, was very steep and strewn with boulders so they had to backtrack somewhat. Hal could feel the smoke in his throat and stinging his eyes. If only he had some goggles or a handkerchief over his mouth, then he'd be fine. But all he could do was follow Miller upwards, barely keeping him in sight at times as the grey pall descended around them. They'd travel faster if they dropped some of their gear, but he knew the loss, even if they made it through the fire, would lessen their chances of survival on the subsequent march. They'd need food to reach the rail line, which meant fish or game had to be caught, so the guns and rods were imperative, but did they really need the tent? He tried to call to Miller but began to cough heavily then stumbled over a pile of fallen branches. Trying to catch his breath he peered ahead but couldn't see beyond the next tree. He took the whistle from his pocket and blew loudly two or three times. Maybe there was a distant reply, but he couldn't be sure, and besides it seemed to be below him. His throat tightened as he panicked and began to run downhill with no sense of direction, terrified he'd lost Miller and certain that even if the flames didn't get him he'd never make it the rest of the way by himself. In a short time he found himself down by the shore again, the campsite nowhere to be seen, trembling very much as he had after the dream. He looked across at Canada, knowing he could swim there if he had to. But then what? He still had the .22 and his rod, but Miller always carried the compass. As far as he knew there were hundreds of miles of wilderness on the other side. Maybe he could follow the river downstream. It would spill into a lake eventually. Did the lumberjacks work along the border? Did trains cross it? He cursed his lack of geographical knowledge and his dependence on his friend. Then he heard the faint sound of a whistle and perhaps a cry.

He blew his own whistle sharply and listened for a response. When it came, shaky and thin, he was sure the source was uphill to his right. The west wind had picked up so the line between thick smoke and a thin swirling haze was fairly constant on the slope of the ridge as he climbed. His whistled pleas received muffled answers, but in a short time, despite distortions of vision and sound, he discovered Miller lying beside a small boulder, his lips clenched together and his face and arms blackened by dirt and ash.

Hal couldn't understand. "What are you doing?" he yelled. "Get up and let's go!"

"I can't. I think my ankle's broke."

"What happened?"

"I turned and couldn't see you so I started back. Then I slipped and slid down under the edge of this rock. My leg got caught, that's all. Don't worry, though, I can make it."

Hal saw the beads of sweat on Miller's forehead and could hear the strain in his voice squeezed through clenched teeth. "Here," he said, putting out his hand. "Hold on to me."

For a few moments as they surveyed the situation there was an eerie calm.

"The wind's going to shift," Miller said flatly. He had propped himself standing against the rock, all his weight on his good leg, and was staring up at the ridgeline. His face was very pale and the pain showed with each intake of breath.

"Which way should we go?" Hal was worried, but Miller was still his true guide.

"If it comes around completely we'll be okay. The ground up there will be hot but we can get through to the east. If it's a south wind the only place we'll have left is the river. And I don't know if I can get down there fast enough."

They stood still and waited. "When we move we'll leave the tent and blankets. Just take the guns and rods." Then came the words Hal had never heard before. "You'll have to help me. Uphill or downhill."

Nothing happened right away. Without any wind the smoke settled, and Hal could see the burned remnants of the trees looking like scarecrows with too many arms. Off to the east flames still licked at the sky but without much conviction as if they knew their time was passing. All they had to do was get over the ridge and maintain as steady a pace as they could with Miller's ankle and things would be fine.

Miller nodded at him. "We might be lucky. Let's go."

Hal had the heavier Winchester over his left shoulder while Miller's palm grasped the other, his right hand clenching the barrel of the .22 he used as a cane. They were both wearing their packs with rod tips protruding. Hal hated to leave the tent and blankets but knew they wouldn't fit through the slim portal waiting for them at the top. They staggered upwards, somehow making progress as Hal panted under his companion's wounded weight and Miller grunted and swore. In the lull there was no other sound at all. Wisps of smoke rose in almost straight lines from trunks and branches and bits of ash floated lazily through the air. Hal felt they were in another world from which all life had vanished but for two tattered human forms that remained. They had just reached the summit, its more or less level surface stretching in front of them for thirty yards or so, when Miller slipped and fell hard. His sharp cry was cut off as his head struck a half-exposed rock and he rolled over on his back, unconscious and bleeding from his temple.

Hal bent over him, screaming: "Wake up, Miller. Wake up." Then he felt the wind on his face, though he couldn't tell from which direction. There was a roar in his ears and smoke again in his eyes and lungs. He grasped Miller by the collar and dragged him toward the far side of the ridge, each step a torture as the dead weight caught on every obstacle and the rifle banged sharply into his side. There was no relief and he knew there wouldn't be until they were safely over the far edge, so he focused without respite on his task, his friend's face twisting and rolling but strangely peaceful beneath him. When he finally had to stop to recover for a moment, he could tell there was no one bearing for the wind. It was coming from everywhere. The renewed fire was all around them now, a circle of flames that allowed no exit, rearing up like an enraged animal on its hind legs, a blazing bleeding bear, he thought, come to take its revenge. He slapped Miller's cheek but got no response and thought crazily of hoisting him on his shoulders and running full-tilt at the northern wall, crashing through so they rolled all the way down into the river. But he knew he could never lift him let alone move with any speed. They'd burn into cinders. He sat down abruptly, coughing and gasping, pulling Miller closer to him. That horrible death was going to happen anyway, wasn't it? The circle was closing mercilessly.

"Miller!" he cried. "We were born on the same day! We can't die on the same day! We just can't! Tell me what to do." He moaned and held his friend, curving him into his chest, trying to imagine what *he* would do if he weren't the one injured and Hal's life depended on him. Images of his mother collided in his mind with ones of Nicky. He loved her and he had loved the sailor in a way she would abhor. But now he saw his tower bedroom and the Embarcadero burning together. What was left? He looked down at Miller's face and with so little time remaining tried to admit his greatest love aloud. "Miller," he said softly, rocking back and forth as the roar died away, "listen, I ..." But the words weren't good enough or strong enough to carry all it was he felt. So he bent lower and pressed his lips against the forbidden, sleeping ones, tasting ash within the lingering scent of pine. As he drew back, Miller opened his eyes. "Dig," he said, his voice a rasp against Hal's smooth retreating cheek before he was insensible again.

At first he didn't know what Miller meant. Dig? Why? With what? Then, as he gazed at the encroaching flames blocking any escape back or on, he knew there was only one direction for them to go. Into the ground. He rolled Miller away and began to claw at the baked surface, throwing clumps of sod aside until his fingers would work no more and he drew the hunting knife from his belt to stab and cut his way deeper. A shallow grave gradually emerged from the soil while the fire loomed like a cresting wave about to break, the smoke searing his lungs as he thrust the blade into the heart of the ridge. When the wave was almost over them he dragged Miller into the crater face-down and covered him with earth, careful to leave a tiny cavity beneath his nose and mouth. Then he lay down beside him, scooping the rest of the dirt over himself as best he could, his back and scalp still exposed beneath the edge of the hole.

He cupped his hands in front of his nose and mouth and tried to breathe shallowly, but the feeling of being buried alive was overpowering. The heat above him was intense and he wondered if his hair would catch fire before his shirt. His eyes shut tight, he could see himself and Miller riding the train north and swimming the river into Canada, the giant trout accompanying them, as dolphins had done with mythic Greek heroes, or so he thought, their last glorious adventure gone awry, their futures as great writers lost in a whirlwind of blackened pages. He saw his visionary bear wandering bereft of voice amidst so many histories untold. He saw himself kissing Miller and his desperate, unrequited love. Then he saw nothing at all.

When he came to and pushed himself up out of their tomb the desolation was complete. Although the sky was bright and clear above him, there was no vegetation left on the ridge. He could see down through smouldering trunks to the river flowing undisturbed and across to the far shore with its green blanket of growth intact. His head throbbed, and when he touched the back of his skull he winced and stared blankly at the sight of his bloody fingers through the haze of pain. He heard someone cough beside him. "Miller," he wanted to say, but his throat was parched and made only a croaking sound. The mantle of earth in the grave cracked and shifted as Miller tried to turn over. Hal reached down and helped him roll, seeing his friend's face emerge from the dirt, looking for all the world like an exhausted negro except for his blue eyes. He cleared his throat and spat ineffectively so the phlegm spotted his shirt front.

Miller tried to lift his leg and grimaced in pain. Then he looked around and laughed. "You got us out, Hal. I thought we'd had it. What made you think to dig the hole?"

"You told me to. Don't you remember?"

"Naw, last thing I recall was stumbling uphill. Then I felt warm and comfortable. Now here I am."

"You fell and hit your head. What do you mean 'warm and comfortable'?"

"I don't know. Like everything was okay and I never had to worry anymore."

"About what?"

Miller thought it over. "About being alone, I guess."

If that's what the kiss gave him, Hal thought, then surely it had been a good thing to do. After all, he'd been saying goodbye, hadn't he, not a hello of any kind. They were about to die, so what did it matter if he kissed his friend? Only it did, of course, because they hadn't died.

"We'd better get going," he said. "We need to make that train."

7.

It had taken them just under forty-eight hours to hike from the lumberjack's log pile to the border river. With Miller's injury slowing them down and Hal having to support him much of the way, it was on the fourth morning of their return journey that they came to the spur and the dark scattering of bark where the stack of logs had been. All along Miller tried to keep his pain to himself, though Hal could hear his frequent gasps and feel the tension in his body. His ankle bound with cut-off shirtsleeves, he hobbled on. The bugs were bad, but the dirt and ash on their skin and in their clothes helped keep the horde at bay. They spent the fortunately dry nights huddled under pine boughs by dying fires after cooking some small partridge Hal shot with the .22 and saving a few scraps for the next day. Early one morning they ate one of two small trout he'd caught, wrapping the other carefully in dry leaves to keep for lunch. He was far too busy with survival to think about what had happened as the fire closed in, though sometimes as he walked in step with Miller's limp, he reminded himself happily they hadn't died on the same day. Tired but grateful to be alive, when they heard the train engine in the distance they shook hands as if to formalize their accomplishment.

"I might have had trouble without you," Miller said, a long way from his admission below the ridge-top when the wind had quit.

Hal told himself this was as close as to a declaration of affection he would get. Whatever Miller could or could not acknowledge, he felt as if he had escaped death not only by fire but by excommunication as well. However much he had wanted to speak openly about Nicky, he was almost certain now his confession would have destroyed their friendship. There would always be the touching of their lips, born from the terrible need that had accompanied terror, but he wasn't sure if this affirmed or betrayed his love.

> *The flames passed over*
> *Without descending*

he wrote,

> *Flowers and ash bloomed*
> *From the bodies below*

They didn't see much of one another for the next few weeks. Miller's ankle had been severely sprained but not broken so it would be healed by the time he was ready to head for boot camp, first near St. Louis then in New Jersey. Meanwhile Hal was busy collecting information about New York and writing to his relations there, saying he'd like to arrive at the end of August and stay with them until he could find a job and place of his own. He was excited about the possibilities and eager to taste the freedoms of the famed metropolis wholly away from his mother's prying eye. There would be other sailors, he knew, but he was determined to fix his emotional attention on his writing and especially on bringing modern New York into his bear's line of sight. He didn't think of such inclusion as any kind of ending. The poem was still too formless for final stanzas, but, after all, he had begun with a view of the Hudson, and the imposing city on the river should be given its due.

One weekend, just a few days before Miller's departure, he went up to the Sark cottage where, with all its shared memories, they both agreed it was best to say their goodbyes.

"What do you think it will be like over there?"

They were sitting at the end of the dock, their feet hovering over the limpid water of the lake. It was still summer, but cool at night, and the occasional softwood was already changing colour. Hal watched a silvery school of minnows dart above the sandy bottom, seemingly without direction but always in search of food.

"I don't know. Pretty rough, I'd say. None of us have been in battle yet, but the British and French have been getting pounded."

Miller's tone was different from that of the eager advocate of war on their fishing trip a month ago, more serious and subdued.

"Why are you going?"

"I told you before. You can't just let the Hun ride roughshod over everything. Wouldn't you want some help if they were on our shores?"

"But they're four thousand miles away from New York."

"Thirty-five hundred, actually. Besides, their submarines have sunk ships right off our coast. They'll be *in* New York if we're not careful."

Hal had read the reports of these attacks in the newspaper, but he knew Lake Michigan was safe because even German ingenuity couldn't get around Niagara Falls.

"So you are doing it because you're a patriot."

Miller flushed angrily. "You make it sound dirty."

"Sorry. I guess I'm just not a fighter." He wanted to ask Miller if he was scared but knew there'd be no admission of that. "Aren't you worried?"

"About what?"

"About dying, or even about getting badly wounded."

"Well, I'd rather go up all at once than lose a leg or arm, if that's what you mean. When I come back I sure want to be able to hunt and fish."

"And be a reporter. And write your stories."

"Yeah, that most of all. There'll be lots to write about, won't there? Look what Crane did with the Civil War, and he wasn't even there!"

Hal recalled the tale of Henry Fleming, their age exactly, trying to rid himself of "the red sickness of battle." Henry had survived, but Crane himself hadn't lived long after writing the book, dying of tuberculosis in his late twenties after covering Roosevelt in Cuba as a war correspondent. He wanted Miller to live a lot longer than that. Crane wrote some wonderful short stories and he knew Miller admired them. Wouldn't it be swell if his friend could find that kind of fame! Naturally, he wanted to stick around himself. Whitman *had* been in the Civil war, not as a soldier but as a nurse, and he'd written about the carnage from first-hand experience. After the Embarcadero, the male love he'd alluded to in *Leaves of Grass* became more obvious, and Hal wondered if he would ever have the nerve to be that open in his own work. There were those lines about flowers and ash and his earlier ones about Nicky, but he'd disguised everything, hadn't he? Wasn't that because words mattered to him more than flesh in the end? Nicky was gone, but the constellation of Gemini was not and never would be. Suddenly he was certain Miller would survive the war and return to write stories that would make him famous, while he would get through his own campaign in New York and become ... well, if not equally renowned (he was a poet, after all) then at least respected by critics and a certain level of readers. Of course, while he'd write even if there were no critics or readers, he was fairly sure some part of Miller would constantly be driven by that notoriety.

They swam and fished off the dock, but Hal sensed that even if they'd had the time neither of them would have wanted another wilderness trip for a while. However much they regaled Miller's father with descriptions of the wind and flames, they knew they'd escaped by the skin of their teeth. Even after he'd washed them the smoke still lingered in his clothes until Mr. Sark told him to use a vinegar solution, so when he went home all he had to do was explain the patch of burned scalp to his mother as an accident with some water he'd boiled up for a shower in the woods.

"I was washing my hair," he said, "and got soap in my eyes. All I could think of was pouring water over my head to get it out."

It might have been the only time she *chose* to believe rather than confront him over her doubts about his time with the Sarks. Maybe she had softened a little because she knew Miller was going off to war and because Hal would soon be gone to New York where she couldn't watch over his daily ablutions or anything else for that matter. She had wanted to accompany him and stay for a week or two with the cousins, but he'd managed to convince her he'd be wholly occupied looking for work as well as finding his own place and it would be better if she waited until Thanksgiving when he could entertain her in style.

"We'll be the toast of the town," he told her, "once I'm making some money."

She beamed proudly. "You'll always be my dearest boy," she said.

He wished he had a brother she could say this to. Miller didn't count.

On the morning he left the cottage he gave Miller a small leather notebook he'd bought in town.

"You'll need some new space to jot some things down, I'm sure."

Miller smiled broadly. "Thanks," he said. "But I'll send you some words, as well." Then he walked over to a chest of drawers and took out a sheaf of papers that he handed to Hal. "This is for you. It's all I can say right now."

They shook hands and Miller tousled his hair. He was taking the train to St. Louis that afternoon. "Watch out for yourself in New York," he said. "Don't do anything I wouldn't do!"

Hear the Wind Blow

The younger boy followed the older boy around. It had been that way for a long time. The older one didn't mind. They were brothers and that was what brothers did.

Jim liked to hunt and fish, so that was what Billy liked to do as well. They knew the woods because their father taught them everything he knew about the outdoors, including the animals and birds. Jim always carried a compass, but he could find his way home from a long way off just by reading the stars or the moss on the trunks of trees. On the water they were expert too. Billy wasn't as strong, but he could handle a canoe just as well as Jim, maybe even better. They would paddle for miles across the lake and leave the craft at the mouths of streams where the big trout lay in the shadows dappled by the sunlight through the branches of the pines. It wasn't that they thought about it very much, but if someone had asked them, they would have said they could live this way forever.

One morning they set off to the farthest end of the lake to a river that poured down from the hills in fierce rapids strewn with boulders and twisted trunks of trees. They were both very tired when they got there and set up camp on the shore where the river current slowed into a large pool and the air was sharp with the smell of pine. They built a fire and had bacon and eggs and coffee for lunch, and because the sun was high and there would be no good fishing until the evening hours, Jim went for a swim in the pool while Billy lay down for a nap. He didn't really sleep but drifted lazily like a water-bug as his brother splashed and sang to himself, "Down in the valley/the valley so low/hang your head over/hear the wind blow."

Billy imagined himself out west, riding a pinto pony along a trail and listening to the wind. He was lost in the aroma of sage brush and the clip-clop of his horse's hooves when he suddenly realized he couldn't hear Jim anymore. Sitting up he saw only the empty pool. "Jim!" he cried, "Jim!" Then he got to his feet and ran down to the shore. A sheen of light burned his eyes as he stared over the water. Something terrible had happened and he didn't know what to do. Shucking his boots he dove in fully clothed, his arms windmilling him to the centre of the pool. Jim had to be beneath him, so he held his breath and dove down, eyes open wide to any sight of his brother. The water was cold and clear, and he stayed down a long time fighting the current. He saw the flicker of fins and tiny pieces of plants suspended above the sandy bottom but nothing else. When he surfaced he paused only for a moment before turning his body once more into the depths. Three or four times he did this and then he had no more strength. He made slowly for the shore, his mind racing with possibilities. Had Jim swum over to the base of the rapids and got in trouble there or had he drowned in the pool and been swept out into the lake? He was crying now because he didn't have the answers and because his brother had left him alone. Then as he neared the sandy strand he saw Jim lying there in his swimming trunks with a big grin on his face.

"Though I'd have to come out and rescue you," he said. "What were you doing, anyway?"

Billy emerged from the water and walked up to him. "You bastard," he said, then he bent down awkwardly and slugged him in the face.

Jim yelled and grabbed him and they tumbled across the sand, their breath fast and hard, their thoughts scattered like startled quail or trout at the shadow of a hawk.

"Why, why did you do it?" Billy cried as his brother's heavier weight bore down on him, pinning his arms to the ground with no quick promise of release.

Jim gazed down at him mercilessly and brought his face closer, but behind the hardness Billy could hear the catch in his voice. "To show you what it would be like without me. I

The Sons of Liberty

1.

Miller slipped from his hammock and made his way past the rows of sleeping doughboys to the head. It was the third day of their voyage and the winter seas were rough, so he braced himself as he pissed. He looked down at the steady stream and told himself he was in good shape for what was to come. He wouldn't kid himself though. The casualties among the first Allied Expeditionary Forces troops had been high, and those had been seasoned veterans not untested recruits with just three months of training under their belts. The vets had been fighting alongside the British and French and mostly using their heavy weapons, but now General Pershing wanted Americans to make their own mark. At least they wouldn't be in trenches but taking on the Germans in the open somewhere northeast of Paris. He hoped the 'open' had some cover and all the trees hadn't been blasted into smithereens the way they had in so many newspaper pictures of the front. He hoped there was solid ground to stand on and not just mud.

At first the St. Louis training camp had been a lot of laughs as he watched the collection of country and city boys struggle to get in shape and master their Springfield rifles. They fell on the obstacle courses, heaved like winded horses on the long-distance runs, and missed their range targets wildly. Given his skills and general fitness, he soon made the temporary rank of corporal and was put in charge of a squad of five men he pushed into believing was better than most. Things became more serious when they began to use live ammo, and at first he thought he had a good idea as to which of them had the best chance of making it over in France, not just in his squad but in the rest of his platoon. There were the ones who placidly chewed gum and followed orders without blinking, and there were those who twitched nervously every time he looked at them as if he were an incoming shell about to explode in their midst. But he came to see that being a nervous Nelly could keep you wide awake at crucial moments while a gum-boy in his relaxed state might be a tad slow when quickness of movement was required.

He'd been ahead in the game because he could shoot. The Springfield 30.06 was supposed to be accurate over 700-800 yards, but the sights on it were lousy, the rear one too far away from his eye and the front one unprotected and easily damaged. His father had showed him how to adapt to the quirks of different rifles he kept at the cottage, and the officers soon realized there was nobody better at finding the bull's-eye. Of course, he'd brought down deer and bear, and even a few moose, but shooting at a man would take another kind of talent, and he worried sometimes about having it or not. His enemy would be armed and able to shoot back, which just meant he'd have to pull the trigger first, but he'd be exposed for a split second in a way he'd never been with the animals. He wasn't scared. He just didn't like being vulnerable under any circumstances, as he had been with his bad ankle when the flames surrounded him. He owed his life to Hal, but he wanted to make damn sure nothing like that exposure or dependency ever happened again. A local forest fire was one thing, an inferno of artillery shells and machine-gun bullets entirely different.

He remembered, when he was very young, his father carrying him on his shoulders to the end of the cottage dock, standing there as if admiring the view he had seen a thousand times, then throwing him in the lake without warning. After he struggled and spluttered for a few moments, going under and surfacing more than once, Henry Sark had pulled him out and sat beside him on the wet pine boards.

"Things will sneak up on you like that, Miller. You need to deal with them."

He was trying not to cry and was mad at his father for surprising him so. "Yes, Daddy" was all he said.

Now the lake was wider and deeper than the one in his boyhood, and there were a lot more 'things' to contend with, but at least after that first lesson in self-defence he wasn't likely to drown since his old man had taught him to swim.

In the New Jersey camp the officers had fine-tuned everything, keeping the men in shape with three-mile runs daily, having them strip down their weapons and reassemble them in a race against the clock, and pitting them against one another in battle-like situations. His squad was becoming tough and cynical, but he began to understand reluctantly that chance would play a larger role in a man's survival than his attitude and all his training. If you stood up for a moment because your legs were cramped rather than remained in a half-crouch; if you hesitated because you felt a twinge in your shoulder when you lifted your gun; if you turned one way instead of another when you came to an obstacle; if the wind changed direction as the Germans released their gas—you could be dead or badly wounded instead of able to step intact into the next moment. He wished he could meet up with Hal and share such thoughts, but he couldn't get enough leave time for a trip into New York. When his departure date was firm he sent a postcard that Mrs. Pierce would forward. *In best shape of my life. Could say 'wish you were here,' but we both know that wouldn't work. Leaving USS Madawaska Nov. 17 from New York.*

He'd stood for as long as he could by the rail, looking down at the crowd gathered for the send-off at Pier 35. There were car horns blaring and countless arms waving, but the faces were blurred beneath all the Homburgs and boaters. Hal wouldn't wear either he was sure, but he couldn't make out a bare head in the bunch. It was too bad he hadn't got leave. They could have got drunk together. He was sure Hal was doing more than merely sipping whiskey by now. And maybe they could have talked about killing a man. Hal had said he wasn't a fighter, but he did show his guts back there on the ridgeline. He'd understand, wouldn't he? Soon, with all of them at attention on deck, the ship left the pier to steam with three other vessels into the channel past Ellis and Liberty Islands and the giant French statue welcoming refugees. Now he'd be an immigrant to France, trying to save the freedom the statue represented. He gazed back at the mainland where he'd been young and happy. Ahead was the gathering convoy of merchant vessels his cruiser and others would accompany across the Atlantic to where another Miller was waiting.

In his hammock he tried to curl his body into a comfortable sleeping position. The grunts and farts of his shipmates were amplified in the cavernous space, and occasionally he'd hear a rough curse or plaintive sleeping cry and wonder at the cause of each. Young men swore publicly and to themselves at the slightest provocation, and welcomed any audience, but the emotion of the private call was something else, an unacknowledged admission of the inside getting out that no one else was supposed to hear. He didn't think he did this. Who would he call to? Hal undoubtedly would speak his mother's name. That old bitch certainly had him under her thumb. If he tried hard he could remember a little of his own mother's face, but not the sound of her voice. He knew he was supposed to love her, and he guessed he did, but he didn't like the memory of her dressing him in his sister's clothes, not at all. No, he wouldn't say anything to her. As for his father, Henry Sark didn't listen for such contact so he wouldn't hear any outburst, unless there was some imminent danger in the woods and even then you were expected to keep your self-control. That didn't leave anybody, did it, except for Hal? He remembered telling him as he came to in the blackened landscape that he'd felt okay because he hadn't been alone. Is that who you cried out to, the one who kept you from isolation in a world in which death was all around? Maybe he could keep quiet aboard the ship, despite the U-boat dangers, but in the carnage over there such silence might be the first to die.

He used the notebook Hal had given him to write down observations of his surroundings. Sometimes the words emerged from his pencil tip in an unrelated way that left them on lists for later perusal, but often he could see connections that expanded rather than merely reflected his experience. *The chocks that held the lifeboats in place could be knocked out with a single mallet blow. He'd done this often during drills, but now during the storm, with the ship listing heavily and the sea in his eyes, he swung his arm four times without result.* Many of his entries were drawn from the appearance of his companions. *The farm-boy from Iowa had tiny furrows in his cheeks that looked like the surface of a ploughed field. Now they resembled the endless rows of waves rolling toward him as he struggled to stay afloat.* These lines suggested the beginnings of stories, and he wanted to believe they were unlike anything he had read before. While that wasn't completely true, as Conrad and London reminded him, he knew he was still learning. If he kept on with his work, by the time he got through this war maybe he'd be doing things the old masters hadn't thought of.

One morning that farm-boy, who was really from Ohio, asked him shyly what he was writing.

"Only the simple things," Miller said. Then when he saw the puzzlement, added: "You know, how beautiful the sunsets can be out here. But no big words."

"When I look at the sun going down, I get sad thinking of my folks," the boy said.

"That's it exactly," Miller told him.

The ship docked in Brest where the troops climbed on to passenger trains for the trip east. Civilian workers were everywhere on the dock, cigarettes dangling from their lips as they unloaded equipment and stacked it by the tracks. It was very crowded inside the railway cars, and some of the men had to sit on their duffle-bags in the aisles. Miller dozed like the rest of them, then woke to stare out at the flat winter landscape dotted by hedgerows and copses of trees. The rain left large puddles in the fields, and he imagined trying to march through them and the mud beneath. Once he saw a farmer using his horses to pull a tractor from the mire. The animals were very big with heavy brown manes and fetlocks and white markings on their mostly black heads and bodies. They were having a hard time with the tractor even though it appeared to be smaller than them. This was not his kind of country, and he considered what birds and game they hunted here. Pheasants, perhaps, certainly rabbit and fox. The train would occasionally cross a wooden bridge over a wide, slow-moving river. There'd be bream down there, most likely, and maybe even some fat, lazy pike. He wasn't sorry he'd joined up, but he did miss the freedom of walking into the woods when he felt like it and the little snap of the fly-line before it settled on rushing water. *There were flakes of rust on the housing that covered the tractor's engine and a broken fuel-line beneath. The horses didn't notice the rust as they pulled it from the mud, but they could smell the gas. The farmer knew there was more rain coming, so he pushed them hard.*

Some of the men were playing poker, and he listened to the soft slap of the cards on the tops of packs they propped between their legs as table-tops. The same men had played on the boat and from what he could tell the amounts of money won and lost probably evened out over time, so there were only short-lived hollers of victory or clucks of disgust as individual hands were played out. Others slept with their heads back on the seat, their mouths slightly open and their eyelids fluttering as dreams unfolded, while a few read weeks-old newspapers they'd carried with them from the States and the occasional book. He could see Zane Grey's *Riders of the Purple Sage* clasped in the hands of one sleeper. The men of his squad were scattered through the car, and he did a roll-call in his mind, putting names with faces and chief characteristics.

The Ohio boy was Munson, and the same hesitancy with which he posed his question about Miller's writing was evident in all his actions. But he didn't shirk in his tasks and, despite his slight build, could march all day without complaint. There was a smart-mouthed kid from Newark named Kincaid, who played the tough guy. Although Miller got tired of his patter, Kincaid's self-confidence wouldn't hurt in a tight spot. Scott was from Idaho, an obscure ranching town in the center of the state. He was a good shot and could read the country around him with great accuracy. Miller liked him especially because, unlike Kincaid, he always thought things over before he replied to a question, and his response never wasted any words. Tall, thin Davis from Oregon enthusiastically told Miller about the fast-flowing salmon rivers that came down from the Cascade Range where Mount Rainier's summit broke through the clouds at over 14,000 feet. Finally, there was Phillips, whose North Carolina accent was so thick he often had trouble making himself understood, though he remained good-natured about his difficulty. The other men called him 'Rawley' because the state capital was his home town. Of the five Rawley was the relaxed gum-boy while Kincaid, whose city tongue often flew faster than his thoughts, was the most obvious nervous Nelly, but he didn't think either of them would let him down.

The train stopped at a station in the western outskirts of Paris. Miller was excited to see the city he'd heard so much about. He wanted to climb the stairs of the Eiffel Tower and the older cathedral towers of Notre Dame where Quasimodo had lived and died. But they were billeted with no leave in an abandoned factory lined with cots and only two bathrooms with holes in the floor for shitting and one shower whose hot-water valves were shut off.

"I've seen cleaner heads in the Bowery," Kincaid announced.

"Then you should have stayed there," Scott told him.

Scott's eyes were flat and his voice without emotion. Kincaid was about to reply but thought better of it. Miller figured he could take down any one of them in a tussle. But Scott wouldn't be easy.

After a few days of confinement they boarded another train that took them into a central station. Through the compartment window Miller glimpsed the Eiffel Tower with its curving iron columns rising into the sky and wondered how long it would take to hit the ground if you ever fell from the top. Your last view from up there would be spectacular. He was disappointed with the orders to stay on the train when it stopped, and even more so half an hour later when they started up again and he realized they must be heading straight for the front or somewhere pretty close to it. As he fell asleep he reminded himself to write a letter to his father and a longer one to Hal.

Dear Father

> *Things are fine at our base camp where we arrived yesterday. I can't tell you exactly where it is, but let's say we left Paris in our dust. I like most of the boys who've volunteered for action. There's no question of their bravery, and we're going to make the Germans pay. You taught me a lot that I can use over here, most of all how to shoot straight and stay*

calm when things get rough, and I hope I will acquit myself
well when the time comes.

   You'd like the country we're in now. Lots of forests and
streams. But we're not allowed to use our bullets for hunting
anything but the enemy, and as for fly rods, well, they're not
exactly lying around. I'm trying to stay in shape, but we don't
do any marching except through the camp and along the edge
of a nearby grain field. I trust you are well and looking forward
to summer at the cottage. Catch some big ones for me.

   Miller

Dear Hal

   There wasn't much I could have done to get ready for all
this, except read Crane and Tolstoy. We're camped on a
hillside above some grain fields. Beyond the fields is a forest
of considerable size, thick groves of oak and beech, from what
I can tell. The Germans are on the other side though our
scouting parties have run into a few of them in the forest.
Back of our hill is a small town with all the conveniences. By
that I mean a post office, a wine-shop, and a brothel, all of
which are serving us well. The French girls, unlike their
excellent burgundy, are very sweet and say all the things you
want to hear in the night. We were told they were clean, but
unfortunately one or two of the boys got the clap. They
tracked down the guilty parties and they're gone to Paris or
points west. Every day we drill, then sit around, then drill
again. The routine doesn't stop. When I say 'drill,' I mean
running with fixed bayonets through the one of the fields
along a protected edge of the hill, yelling ungodly things, and
hoping we don't trip and fall on our faces. It's hard not to look
at the sky when you're running, it's so clear and blue, and
when you're out there with the heads of grain exploding from

*your passage, racing to an invisible finish line, the war seems
far away. I know the Germans are just a few miles off,
probably doing the same thing, but until we see some action
they aren't my enemy.*

*I'm in charge of a five-man squad and wear a corporal's
stripe. It doesn't mean much except I get to order them around
occasionally. 'Squad attention!" and stuff like that. When we're
not drilling we sit on our duffs and shoot the shit. You'd like
most of the guys. Munson, he's from a farm in Ohio, kind of
small but never quits on you. I'd really like to take him fishing
with us. Then there's Scott from the wild west—somewhere
near Hailey, Idaho. He's practically a professional tracker and
could take us fishing and hunting as well. Davis is a fisherman
too from the Cascade country up in Oregon. Then there's
Rawley from North Carolina, a sweet kid with a southern
accent you wouldn't believe. The only one I don't like much is
Kincaid, a Jersey city boy with a big mouth. I'm probably going
to have to close it for him one day, but I have to admit he's got
a way with words, not to put down on paper of course—yours
truly is the only one over here who writes anything besides
postcards. I'm filling that notebook you gave me, mostly with
sentences and short paragraphs about people and places.
When all this is over I'll have lots to put into stories.*

*I never got to spend any time in Paris. We had to stay on
the train right through the city, but I could see the river and
the Eiffel Tower in the distance and all the houses and other
buildings that are older than anything back home. Maybe
when the Germans leave you can come over and we'll look
around the town together. I'm picking up some French from
les madamoiselles but I need to learn to say things besides "Je
m'appele Miller, and "Vous êtes belle." I mentioned the wine,
which is cheap and in great supply. The French down it
morning, noon, and night. We smuggle bottles into camp but
can only drink when it's dark and the officers have gone to
bed. It's hard some mornings to wake up with a headache,*

*especially when the camp coffee is so lousy. Now, go into town
and sit at an outdoor café with a croissant and real French
java—that's something!*

*We've got a newspaper that General Pershing started up
called* Stars and Stripes. *You get some news about how
American soldiers are faring, but most of the boys are more
interested in the sports scores and cartoons. There are some
poems in there every issue, but not for you, more like 'I miss
my hound/ and I know he's pining around' kind of stuff. Still,
there are a few enlisted journalists from* The New York Times
*and other places who give us some serious reports of battles
and how things are going generally. Jesus! a fifteen-year-old
kid from Massachusetts was killed the other week in a skirmish
not far from us.*

*They say we're going to advance into that forest any day
now. There'll be cover in there, but it will be hard to see the
Germans coming. We've got some heavy artillery to back us
up and so have they. I'll just have to depend on my trusty
30.06 to get the job done.*

*How's New York? What kind of work did you find? Get
ready on another front because we'll have to submit ourselves
to the pleasures of an American brothel one day. When I talk
French to those dames, they'll swoon! Write me c/o 9th
Infantry, 5th Marines, AEF.*

Miller

Things heated up with Kincaid rather suddenly. Miller was sitting outside
his tent one afternoon, writing in the notebook. The rest of the squad
was standing nearby, chatting idly amongst themselves and trying to
toss some coins into a helmet, when he heard Kincaid call to him.

"Hey, Corporal. What's the deal with all your writing? Trying to
learn your ABC's?" He turned to the others, who, except for Scott, were
already laughing nervously. They knew Miller wasn't to be interrupted
when he had pencil in hand.

Kincaid snickered. "Maybe he's talking dirty to a lady friend," he said in an exaggerated whisper to all of them. The laughter stopped. Miller might have taken it as a joke, but the edge in Kincaid's voice, and the fact that he'd called him 'Corporal' rather than by his first name, as was the custom unless they were with officers in the field, underlined his challenge.

Miller twitched, but didn't respond. He was angry that his line of thought had been interrupted, but he wasn't going to rise to the bait like a trout that didn't know any better. So he kept writing.

After a few moments of silence Kincaid tried again. "How about sharing some of your ... ah, sentiments." He drew the last word out and winked at his companions.

Miller sighed. Trout or no trout, he'd known this was coming. He had little doubt he could outslug Kincaid, but things wouldn't be the same afterwards, even if everyone knew the Jersey jerk deserved it.

He put the notebook in his shirt pocket, stood up, and walked over to the group. "I would share them, Private, but I think 'sentiment' is the biggest word in your vocabulary, so there's not much point."

Kincaid spat and swung at him as Miller ducked and threw an uppercut into his belly. There was a loud grunt of surprise and pain. When he slowly tried to uncurl, Miller put a straight left into his mouth and watched him fall.

Kincaid lay on the ground, blood running from his lips. "I think you chipped a tooth," he complained sullenly.

No one else spoke as Miller opened the notebook and read his last written line aloud. "Words aren't dirty, just the minds that read them."

2.

He'd bragged to Hal about the French girls, but the truth was he lacked confidence in their presence. The first time he went to the brothel he nodded quickly at the one nearest the door who took him upstairs. *"Je m'appele Amélie,"* she said, looking over her shoulder. Tall and slim, with fair complexion and long curls, she was obviously a few years older than him. He worried about all the experience she must have as she led him by the hand to a small room at the end of the hall with its narrow bed, washstand, and dusty mirror smeared with fingerprints. The shade over the window was only half-way down. He'd been in the bushes several times with the Indian girl back home, but in the patches of moonlight he'd glimpsed only parts of her body. Now this French woman was undressing as the glow from the oil lamp revealed every emerging piece of her flesh. When she was naked she spread her arms and shrugged, as if to ask him if he approved of what he saw. His fingers trembled as he unbuttoned his shirt too slowly for her taste, and she stood close to him and opened his belt buckle. He was already erect and wanted her badly, so when she had pulled his pants and drawers to the floor he pushed her back on the bed and tried to force an entrance.

"*Lentement,*" he heard her say softly, then she wet her fingers with her tongue and rubbed the saliva between her legs. "*Maintenant, mon chéri,*" she told him, and he slid inside.

A voice in his head tried to insist that he find words for each sensation, and for a moment he thought he was murmuring them, but suddenly all his individual impressions plunged into a giant pool of pleasure where language could not draw a breath and he had to let it go. Laughing gently, she stroked his shoulders as he swam silently to shore. "*Mon soldat avide ...*" she began, but he put his hand over her mouth, not wanting his inner voice to respond too soon yet strangely afraid it might not come back at all.

When he returned the next week she was gone. Hiding his frustration, he eventually settled on a pretty girl who spoke a little English, finding out from her that Amélie helped to run a brothel somewhere else and came by only occasionally. He was lucky, the girl announced, as she lowered her head, to have had such a *grande dame*.

While he enjoyed the physical contentment his weekly visits provided, and how they released him from camp drudgery and responsibility, each time he entered the pleasure pool he tried, not always successfully, to waterproof a small part of his mind where words could stay safe and dry. He avoided thoughts of Amélie and began to associate sex with this need to protect the writer he was struggling to become.

Dealing with that struggle, he decided to send in a piece to *Stars and Stripes* and sought out the approval of his commanding officer.

"You can't say anything about where we are, Sark, or speculate on our attack plans."

"I know, sir. I just want to write about what it's like to wait."

"Wait? Wait for what?"

He wanted to say 'to die,' although he didn't like to think about that happening to him, but any such honesty would only get him a reprimand. There was probably something in official regulations that said Marines never thought about dying, just winning, so he kept it simple.

"I just mean, sir, that we have to pass the time while we wait to attack. You know, the ball games we play and things like that."

The colonel relaxed a little. "That's fine, Sark. It might boost the morale of the men in your company if they could read about themselves in a positive light. Go ahead, then. Dismissed." Miller saluted then asked politely for the newspaper's address. "Get it from the adjutant," the colonel said.

Before long he did submit a story based on a few innings he watched one day in which a gang of Americans tried to teach some Frenchies how to play. It was a carnival-like atmosphere as boys who had grown up on stick-ball streets and country sand-lots tried to show their allies, who were only adept at kicking a ball, how to swing a bat and run the bases. Whoever had made the decisions about what non-essential gear to bring from the States had been a fan of the game. There was plenty of equipment to go around, though some of the Gallic crew refused the gloves, insisting instead on trying to field grounders and catch flies with their bare hands. There wasn't much order to things as players shifted positions constantly, and there was a lot of leeway to the number of strikes allowed the home team members. Miller wrote of the smack of the leather against their palms, and how they smiled with cigarettes dangling from their mouths as they occasionally managed to hit a single. Meanwhile, the Americans were cracking home runs over the outfielders' heads and jogging noisily around the bases, raising their clenched fists like victorious boxers and bragging about whose ball had gone the farthest. For the first time, Miller created a first-person narrator who participated in the action.

I'd always liked playing ball, but you played the same
teams over and over. This was a new team we were facing,
and we knew we might never see them again. We taught
them the rules, but rules were normally for soldiers and out
there on the dusty field of the camp we were combatants
of a different kind.

"Hey Miller," Davis called out as he ran toward him one morning, waving the *Stars and Stripes*, "Is this you?"

Kincaid snatched the paper from his hands as he went by, and the others gathered round as he snapped the page dramatically then read the headline aloud. "'Take Me Out to the Ball Game! by Miller Sark, 9th Marines.'" Davis grabbed it back and there was a tussle that resulted in a rip across "the dusty field of the camp."

"Okay, okay," Scott yelled. "Let's calm down and read it together."

Miller sat in front of his tent awaiting the verdict. Surprisingly, it was slow-talking Rawley who spoke up first. "Geez, Miller, it's jus' lak we was watchin' the game rat nayow."

Miller smiled. There was no greater compliment, and it stood up to Kincaid's gripe that he hadn't actually been on the field but made it sound as if he had.

The next time he saw her she was sitting at a street-side café table with a distinguished-looking older man in a tailored suit. He was in the cab of a transport truck on its way to pick up supplies and turned his head to watch the breeze push her hair back from her forehead and ruffle the edge of the white tablecloth. Two nights later he asked for her at the brothel, his stomach tight with potential disappointment, and when she came through the curtained doorway that led to the bar and sitting-room he gave a high schoolboy giggle before clearing his throat and chuckling like a man. She was wearing an open-necked blouse beneath an embroidered vest and her skirt rustled silkily against the tops of her buttoned boots as if a wind, he thought, were blowing through meadow grass.

"*Mon soldat avide,*" she said with a smile, taking his hand in greeting.

Embarrassed by his juvenile titter Miller kept his eyes on the floor as he tried in his broken French to say how much he had missed her, but she put her finger under his chin and pulled his gaze level with hers, and he saw a shifting slice of obsidian in her pupil that the blur of the sexual act had hidden from him previously. To his surprise the English words tumbled over one another in his head trying to get out, and he was sure this sliver of blackness would find its way into a love story or at least a story about love.

With a brief apology she mentioned her schedule for the next hour or two, indicating that if he came by later they could share a glass of wine. Glancing over her shoulder between the parted folds of the curtain he saw the same well-cut suit and his stomach clenched again only this time with jealousy rather than possible let-down. As if sensing his anxiety, she stroked his cheek lightly.

"*Sois patient, mon jeune.*"

He sat in a smoky tavern sipping a cognac, trying to calm himself and understand his agitation. She was beautiful alright, and he ached with desire for her attentions. It wasn't just that, though. He had come to believe after their only tryst, followed by lesser couplings with others, that all women could sap the strength he reserved for his writing. And it was true that at every climax he dissolved on speechless shores where there was no promise of future expression. Even back in Michigan with the Indian girl his inner voice had abandoned him as the rolling of their bodies in the bushes became the sole measure of who he was. He'd bought her off, with Hal's help, but it seemed the fifty bucks had put paid to something more than prospective fatherhood because when he'd tried to write about her and the pregnancy it was as if creativity along with the child had been aborted. He never told Hal about this. In fact, he realized, once he'd got the money together he never mentioned the girl again. Now there was Amélie and that glimpse of obsidian releasing the words. He took the notebook from his shirt pocket and scribbled with a pencil stub. *The Ojibway girl moved softly beneath him. In the moonlight the dark pearl of her eye loved him more than he deserved.* He copied the lines on the bottom of the page then ripped that portion from the book and folded it in his wallet. Tomorrow he would send it to Hal.

The bottle of wine was open and waiting beside two glasses. She beckoned him to the table and patted a chair beside her as he approached.

"*Bienvenu à mon château*," she said.

She sat at an angle to the low-burning lamp on the wall above with her face in shadow. He wanted her beneath him, but he was happy to stay here for awhile waiting for the promise of her glance. Everything was so clear. The table's dull grain marked by stains, the fine stitching on the cuff of her blouse above the blue veins of her wrist, his own heart beating in time to the quiet passing of the moments. Then she moved slightly and the line of shadow disappeared. She was staring down at her glass so he reached across and lifted her chin with the tips of his fingers. When she looked at him he wanted to give her everything he would ever write.

Upstairs they undressed and lay beside one another in the dark, her head resting on his shoulder. She spoke quietly to him, and the best translation he could come up with was that he was different from her regular clients. She was mostly with officers, married men who said they would take her back to Paris or Lyon when the war was over where she would be their mistress with a fine apartment and all the comforts she desired. Such things didn't interest her, she declared. Her freedom was more important, and part of that meant making love with whomever she liked. That included him, she said. The French officers would be shocked not that she shared their competing favours but that she lay with a mere corporal and an American to boot! He listened without replying, wondering what he could offer her back home. The only way he could take her there would be as his wife not his lover. Only rich people like Rockefeller and Carnegie had mistresses, and they didn't live in Oak Park or rural Michigan. But it would be hard enough for his father to understand his choice of a foreign woman, let alone ... a whore. He blinked. That was what she was. But he didn't care. He'd make her respectable, and no one would ever know about her past. To hell with anyone who spurned her because she didn't speak English. He'd teach her. And maybe they wouldn't go back to the States anyway. They'd live in Paris where Hal could visit them. He'd like her, that's for sure. He was lost in this flood of thoughts when he heard a murmured "*Assez,*" and she turned and pressed her body against him. His preoccupation must have passed for patience. *"Plus vite,"* she had to tell him more than once.

3.

As the days passed base-camp nerves became frayed. Rumours had filtered down from headquarters of an impending attack. Loaded supply trucks deepened the muddy tracks around the hill and heavy artillery pieces ringed the summit. Officers barked orders as if lives suddenly depended on them, and the men paid more attention to the details of their daily routines, constantly checking the bolt-action of their rifles and keeping the weapons and their boots as dry as possible. They knew they would be sent into the eastern grain field that led to the forest. There was no other place to go.

"There's no cover out there," Scott said, gesturing to the field. "All they have to do is lay down a few lines of shells and we'll be juice."

Miller nodded in reply. He'd heard of the men in the trenches going over the top into murderous machine-gun fire, hundreds of them falling in a matter of minutes over a few yards of mud. If he and his men set off in the dark and crawled on their bellies they might get a bit farther, but it was at least a quarter of a mile to the first trees and then more pummelling for the survivors. He was angry because there weren't any tactics except to advance. The field should be used as a feint with a larger force sent around it to the south to take the Germans by surprise. He hated the thought of those oaks and beeches being destroyed, but why not put a barrage down on those woods that would surely take out every enemy position? They'd been told there was a hill beyond the tops of the trees where the German artillery was dug in. So even if the Americans did the impossible and took the wood, they'd be sitting ducks for the big guns. The forest would burn from the heat of the shells, and he already knew what that kind of fire was like.

The other men shifted audibly as if a single unit of response to the accuracy of Scott's judgement and Miller's immediate assent.

"Shit," Kincaid said, "I'd like to push some of them officers out ahead of us. Maybe a few heads blown off would make them think twice."

"How they gonna think without their heads?" Davis asked, and they all laughed, even Kincaid.

Munson sighed loudly. "That's a beautiful field," he said. "My daddy's got four hundred acres that shines the same way in the sun."

"That's one thing the Frenchies have got going for them besides wine," Davis said. "Those skinny loaves of bread, I mean."

"Any way you look at it, we're fucked," Kincaid replied. Then he turned to Rawley. "What do you think, North Carolina boy?" But Rawley had dozed off, his Springfield cradled in his arms like a child.

"That's worth a court-martial at least," Davis said.

Miller barely listened to their banter as he tried to figure out how to see Amélie one more time. They were confined to camp with no prospect of release not only because the men had to be ready to move at an instant's notice but also because command didn't want any loose lips in the bars and taverns. There was no wire, but guards patrolled the perimeter, some with dogs. Even if he could evade them, the trek to town would take him a couple of hours since he'd have to go around the hill and stay off the road all the way. He'd sent a message to her via a mail-truck driver he'd bribed with a sawbuck and got one in reply telling him she'd be at the brothel for the next while since the roads clogged with trucks and artillery prevented any travel. He wished she'd said she was staying because of him. Something about her emphasis on her freedom had kept him from speaking to her about their future together. That and the real possibility he didn't have any future beyond the grain field.

Dear Hal

I guess we're up against it here. I can't tell you exactly where we are because they'll just black out any specifics. But since we're probably going to attack the Germans in the next week by the time you get this I could be dead. I sure hope not because there's still so much to do. Did you get the two lines I

sent you about the Ojibway girl? They're the beginning of a
good story, I'm sure. I've got lots of beginnings in my notebook,
and when I get home I'm going to deal with the middles and
endings. I also sent you a piece I wrote for the Stars and
Stripes about a ball game we played against the Frenchies. It
was fun writing that, and the boys in my squad really liked it.
If only I could tell the truth about the war, about how hard it
is to get up every morning and know for certain you're going
to have to go out and fight pretty soon and maybe not come
back. You see yourself in the faces of your pals and you know
they're thinking the same thing. We'd all rather be at home
hunting and fishing, but of course we signed up for this so we
can't blame anyone else for our predicament. I've got a girl.
Well, not a girl, a real woman. There's no other way to put it
but to tell you she's a whore in the local brothel. She's older
than me, maybe three or four years, and there's something
about her, some beauty spot inside I can't put my finger on.
Oh, she's gorgeous enough outside, but you'll just have to learn
French to know what I mean. I'd like to marry her when the
war's done, if she'll have me, but that's up for grabs. What
about you? How's civilian life treating you?

Write the usual address.

Miller

P.S. Do you ever dream about the fire? I don't, but I can
remember every inch of the ground we took together. Well,
except for when I was in that trench you dug. I don't want to
have to go through that again.

The mail driver told him about a night-time supply truck run that could
include him for another sawbuck. They'd leave after dark and return
before dawn. He confided his plan to Scott only because he had to leave
someone in charge.

"You get caught, it's desertion."

"I won't get caught. I'll be back before reveille. We're not going anywhere before then."

Scott didn't sound convinced. "I hope she's worth it, Miller."

They shook hands. "That's what I'm trying to find out," he said.

The driver piled a lot of canvas sacks over him that would later hold turnips and potatoes. He lay in the back of the truck as it jolted along the dirt road, breathing in the dust and trying not to think about what would happen if they were stopped and searched. There was no reason for that, the driver assured him, not on the way in at least. And only sometimes did an over-eager camp guard decide to make sure the loaded cargo was only vegetables and do some prodding with his bayonet. There'd been other boys who'd snuck in this way, and none of them had been caught.

The town was in black-out and when he emerged from his lair there was only the starlight to guide him.

"Be back by 4.00 a.m." the driver told him. Miller heard him hawk up some phlegm and its smack against the cobblestones. "If you miss the bus you're on your own."

"I didn't think you'd come," she said. "It's too dangerous now." She closed the door on the darkened street. Only one wall lamp was lit, its tiny flame flickering like a firefly.

"I had to see you. After the attack …" He shrugged.

"Yes, I know," she said.

"Let's go upstairs now." There was so much he wanted to say to her.

"Miller," she said.

He started. She knew his name, of course, but she had never called him by it before. He looked for the obsidian fleck but there wasn't enough light. Then it was her turn to shrug. She took his hand and led the way.

The light scent of her perfume rose from her skin as he traced the outline of her breasts with his fingers. There was a tiny star-shaped mole near one nipple, and he watched it rise and fall with each breath she took. When he moved above her she wrapped her legs around his waist and thrust upward as if she were entering rather than receiving him. So he took her deep inside him and when they came together he did not want her to withdraw. "Amélie," he whispered, over and over again.

They fell asleep, and when he awoke he lit a match to look at his watch. It was 3.00 a.m., no need to rush before a coffee downstairs and the walk to the truck. As she stirred he placed his hand between her legs.

"No," she said. "It would not be as good."

He knew that was true, and if he died in the field or among the trees he would take the best of their love-making with him.

They dressed without speaking then he held her close for a long time. When she put her hands on his chest and pushed him gently back he said, "I want you to marry me."

She smiled. "Yes," she said, but because of a catch in her voice he couldn't tell if she was consenting or merely acknowledging his proposal.

"We'll live wherever you like," he said. "Paris or the States."

"Let's go down," she told him. "I'll make some coffee."

As he followed her he wondered if he should have waited. Who could blame her for not wanting to embrace probable widowhood? But he hadn't mentioned when they should marry, had he? He could have meant after the war not now and all she had to do was agree to that. At the foot of the stairs, as he put his hand on her shoulder and opened his mouth to explain, a familiar older man came through the curtain between the hallway and barroom. Miller saw the tailored suit.

"Miller," she said, "this is Georges, *mon fiancé*."

He couldn't remember finding the truck or getting in the back. Somehow he was lying on a sack of potatoes staring through the wooden slats of the vehicle that rose above the metal sides. The heavy load helped settle the ride, and slowly he was able to gather his thoughts.

They had shaken hands, he and Georges, and then through a haze he listened to her words about his goodness and his youth and how she had known her countryman for many years. She told Miller she had never promised him anything because she knew she was going to wound him one day, and now it was that day and there was nothing to be done about it. Her beauty remained clear to him as did the correct, upright posture of the man old enough to be his father. He wanted to take her back upstairs and he wanted to hit Georges on the point of his strong Gallic chin, but he did neither. All the time she was talking her eyes were wide open and fixed on his, but there was no trace of the obsidian lure. He felt rather than saw this was so, and when she had finished he smiled numbly, gave a slight nod as if he had accepted her explanations, and stumbled outside. Lying now on his vegetable mattress he couldn't believe that two people could be lovers as they had been and let go of such a bond. What did it mean to have murmured her name and heard his own spoken in a naked union that was fleeting rather than timeless? What were his words about marriage worth when she had always been ready to spurn them? He swore he would never put himself in the same position again, not with any woman. Then he cursed her aloud, but his pain was swallowed by the thunder of exploding shells as the truck swerved to a halt inside the camp gate.

Over the woods beyond the field of grain the early morning sky was bruised by bursts of fire and smoke, and Miller could see men with fixed bayonets lining up on the edge of the field as if ready for a charge. He raced to his tent where Scott coolly handed him his Springfield.

"The 5th are supposed to take the wood," he said. "The Frenchies are going to sweep in from the north, but we're going straight for the trees."

Miller looked at his squad. Kincaid's lips were closed in a thin line; Munson pushed down a cowlick before settling his tin helmet over it; Davis, standing awkwardly, gave a mock salute; and Rawley just grinned as if it was all a joke whose punch-line was in the offing. There was no inflection at all in Scott's voice when he told them: "Stick together boys, all the way across."

4.

The din of men and artillery shells was deafening as they approached the field, and Miller knew the Germans would be ready for the coming attack. If he'd been in charge, they would have crept through the grain in the dark with surprise on their side. That way when the bombardment ceased they'd have only yards to cover to the German positions not a quarter of a mile lit up in the dawn. But here they were, at least five hundred Marines totally exposed and ready to do their duty even if that meant throwing their lives away. Squads had joined together to form platoons and platoons to form companies that drew up in tight formation where the grain began. Officers strode up and down before them shouting orders that could barely be heard. It didn't really matter. There was no plan except to advance and take the wood. When they'd done that they'd see about the other side and the hill waiting there. It had a number, 142.

"Does that mean we've already taken a hundred and forty-one?" Kincaid said. "Or there'll be a hundred and forty-one to go?"

"Shut up," Miller told him. He stood there, a one-stripe soldier in loose command of five men who might or might not be able to stay together, whatever Scott's instruction. He just hoped they'd keep their heads down and their rifles pointing toward the enemy. His 30.06 with its fixed bayonet was heavier than the Winchester. It had hurt Hal badly when they had killed the bear while he hadn't given it a second thought. Now here he was, disguised by a uniform, just another great dumb animal trying to make it to a distant hill. Suddenly the barrage stopped and they could see smoke drifting above the trees in the sunrise.

The signal to advance was given by a series of sharp whistles that cut violently through the air anticipating the bullets and shrapnel to come. Miller looked down the line and saw some men begin to jog into the field while others walked determinedly ahead their bayonets glinting in the sun that had cleared the tree-tops and now shone in their eyes. Scott was on his right with Rawley, and Kincaid, Munson, and Davis to his left. When they stepped into the grain he motioned them to bend low. No one spoke except the occasional officer whose resonant "Steady!" seemed to apply to the entire group not just a particular section. He was waiting for the machine-gun chatter to break the silence when he heard a sharp exhalation of breath, like someone blowing out a match, and turned to see Scott topple forward, the bullet from a single German Mauser having exited precisely between his shoulder blades. There was no time to think about the loss of his best man because the

Spandaus opened up shredding the stalks of wheat and bodies hiding behind them. He waved to the others and began to run in a half-stoop, knowing their only chance was to reach the woods and the charred cover there as quickly as possible. Men were screaming as the relentless hail of bullets tore through layers of cotton, skin, and muscle, ripping into organs and severing arteries, crippling what they did not instantly kill and leaving bloody trails through the grain. The lucky ones took head shots that blew their brains onto the jackets of their comrades, at once oblivious to suffering and fear. Miller tripped over one body then another and twisted his bad ankle. He thought he heard Davis's voice shouting nearby, but in the noise and confusion he couldn't be sure. There was no point in stopping. The Germans were back in large clumps of trees untouched by the shelling and he couldn't understand why that was so. Why hadn't the artillery taken out the entire wood before sending in the infantry? His eyes were level with the tops of the remaining stalks, and he could see the first stumps and piles of rocks, so close the striations in stone and bark stood out like sign language warning him of danger and calling him to safety at the same time. He came clumsily out of the grain and lurched sideways toward a fallen tree whose greenery was miraculously still intact. Munson, Kincaid, and Rawley gathered beside him. He knew Scott was dead. "Ah saw Davis go down," Rawley told him.

All morning and through the afternoon the Americans fought and took the ground foot by foot in the face of devastating machine-gun fire and the Minenwerfer mortars with their three hundred-yard range, which were set in pits protected from anything but a direct hit. The sound of the projectiles was lost in the clamour, but the squad could see them tumbling through the air in a high arc and prayed for them to pass over while knowing someone else would pay the price. For a while they had dug in behind the tree, but the cries of other Marines on either side told them the line was pushing ahead, however slowly, and that they'd better be part of the advance. Miller peered through the branches and saw a possible zigzag route through the smouldering underbrush leading to the trees still standing. The Germans were back inside, at least the ones with Mausers and 100-round Bergmanns were, maybe a hundred yards away, laying down a constant fusillade that targeted no one in particular while destroying everything in its path. He knew they'd have to crawl below the metal storm but couldn't tell if that was possible. Signalling to the three others to wait, he slung his Springfield across his back, slipped under the tree trunk, and wriggled forward on his belly like a six-foot garter snake, his chin ploughing a shallow furrow through the twigs and leaves. Tiny worms that had survived the flames squirmed with him and a slug took a free ride on the back of his hand. Rivulets of sweat coursed into his eyes and he had to turn his head into his shoulder to wipe them away on his tunic. This must have been what it was like lying in the trench with Hal as the fire passed over them, only he wasn't awake then, and if he had been he wouldn't have tried to get anywhere except deeper into the earth. A mortar shell passed so close he could hear its rapid plopping noise followed by a blast that left his ears ringing. At great risk he pushed up on his elbows and twisted around. The fallen tree had disappeared in a grey plume of smoke.

"Goddamn it!" he cried. "No!" Then he felt a bump on his boot-heel and lowered his gaze to see Kincaid lying there with Rawley and Munson stretched out in single file behind. I'm just the head of the snake, he thought.

"Lucky we didn't listen to you," Kincaid said, but there was relief in his voice rather than the usual challenge.

The now-longer reptile crept on and Miller's mind went into a slow-motion state so the tumult around him subsided and all he could see was the slug inching forward with each thrust of his hand. He watched its slender antennae bobbing ahead of the thin smear of slime that helped it stay in place. It became very important to him that this fragile creature remain with him all the way to his destination. If the slug dropped off every one of them would die. He knew that for sure. He'd never been superstitious, but he was now. If he and the slug could just get there together he'd stay superstitious the rest of his life. Hell, he'd throw spilled salt over his shoulder at every opportunity and find a lucky charm to rub three times a day or just whenever he felt like a little protection from an unpredictable world. He'd have to write about that, about a man who needs a kind of internal armour to keep going so he builds a whole web of rituals to live by and when the wars come is able to survive. He'd have to be an old man when the story opened in the midst of one last battle. Then he felt the snake's body shudder as if a descending beak had pierced it to the core.

"It's Munson," Kincaid yelled. "He's hit bad."

They broke apart and circled back to Ohio. Where in Ohio? Miller wondered as he crawled. He saw another grain field untouched by violence and a barn gleaming in the afternoon sun. "Munson," he called out. "I'll take you home." But when he got there the farm-boy had rolled over on his back and was staring into a brighter sun as if he wanted to go blind.

"Sorry," he said. Then, just before he died, he reached out and touched the slug. Miller didn't try to hide his tears and he noticed Rawley was crying too. Kincaid pulled off Munson's bandolier. "We've got to keep going," he said.

They reformed with their tail section now gone. The assault of weaponry had returned and Miller knew that while snakes were immune to airborne sounds they picked up vibrations through the ground, hunting their prey this way and with their developed sense of smell. But what happened when they were the prey and it was their blood that had been spilled? What happened when the shock-waves were ceaseless and they couldn't tell one from the other? He crawled on without any answers.

When they finally managed to reach the relative safety of the trees he propped himself against a living trunk and looked back to where they had been. The German shells had obliterated the neat rows of tents, and it seemed strange to him that they hadn't done this before the attack. There was no haven to return to, and even if there had been there was only complete exposure in what was left of the field. Giant sections of ruptured earth were strewn with broken stalks of grain and the still bodies of Marines. Scott and Davis were out there somewhere, and he could only hope a medic had found Davis before it was too late. They were brave, those guys, if they could trek through that slaughter carrying only bandages and stretchers. He wondered how many officers were left and what the orders would be with half the men as casualties and so much of the woods left to take. Had the French got farther in to the north and what about that waiting hill on the far side of the trees? Higher up than the apex of any shell he saw a circling hawk, but he had shed his snake's skin for now and the danger of impalement was over. He glanced at the back of his hand, but the slug was gone.

Word was passed up and down the line to stay put for the night. They were told to remain under cover with no fires allowed. The Germans could send up flares and spot anybody moving or in the open.

"Guess what?" Kincaid said. "If either of you have to take a shit, make sure you move away from me."

Miller smiled in the dark. Scott, Munson, and probably Davis were gone, but he could still smile at Kincaid's refusal to change his ways. He put his hand up to his chin and rubbed his day-old beard. What did regulations say about hygiene in the field? Probably something about the required square footage of latrines and their distance from mobile kitchens. Well, they didn't have to worry about that tonight, did they? Whatever food they had in their packs was what they'd dine on. He shook his canteen and was relieved to find it still half-full. He couldn't remember drinking any water during the day then realized such had been his hurry to join the squad on his return from town that he'd grabbed his equipment without checking it over. Scott had given him his Springfield and he'd slung on his pack without thinking. That was the trouble with war. You depended on other people's plans. There was no way he'd go into the woods without knowing what he was carrying and how long it would last. He reached into his pack and brought out his food supply. There were three cans of bully beef, some dry biscuits, and a chunk of cheese covered with specks of mould. He couldn't find his can opener, but Rawley or Kincaid would have one. At the bottom he discovered a pack of chocolate wrapped in tin foil and after taking a bite put the remainder in his shirt pocket, buttoning the flap securely. He'd read somewhere that the first recordings on phonograph cylinders had been made on tin foil. Back in the cottage he and his father had listened to cowboy songs and even the speeches of Taft and Bryan from the 1908 election on a wax cylinder. In his last year at school his teacher had a wind-up gramophone and discs with negro music and band tunes that everyone danced to. He wished he could wind up one of those songs now. What would the Germans do with "Down Home Rag" or, better still, with John Philip Sousa marching into their ears?

A flare lit up the sky a little to the west, and he could see the ghostly forms of the medics and stretcher bearers as they went about their work. Apparently, the Germans weren't interested in killing the dead or wounded or even those rough angels who closed their comrades' eyes or gave them solace because no mortars rained down or bullets whined through the damp night air. While the flare lasted everything seemed peaceful and acceptable as if the devastation of the morning and afternoon had been an appalling illusion and now ordinary human dignity had reclaimed its rightful place in the world. But as soon as the red magnesium glow died out and they were alone in the shadows again, it was the sense of serenity that had been fantastical. The only rightful place for those who would survive was as small as they could possibly make their fragile bodies that had carried them through the day.

Miller wished he could write down his impression of the flare and its aftermath. He wished he could hold forever on the page Scott's final startled expulsion of breath or Munson's last wriggle as a vital segment of the snake. He wished he could call out to Davis and record a reply from the Cascade peaks with their swiftly-flowing streams. None of this was possible since it was too dark to put anything in the notebook, but he promised himself he would find his pencil stub and write the words if not tomorrow then soon, whatever demands the battle brought. Then he realized such words would be all he would leave behind if he fell, the only testimony to who he was and what he had seen and heard and touched and smelled on this continent of love and death. Amélie was in there and those he had fought with, their features crisp and clear in a landscape that had not yet been destroyed. If you held on to them in this way they could not vanish completely because someone else and then someone else again would pick up the threads of your observations and make their own stories about strangers and comrades and foreign terrain. He patted his shirt pocket and felt the pieces of chocolate and crunch of foil. In the other pocket was the notebook, which he took out and held against his mouth and nose. The aroma of leather was barely discernible above the whiff of his sweat and the soggy odour of the earth on which he lay, but he was sure it would never entirely evaporate. As he inhaled, he realized there was another trace of his passing as well, his letters to Hal. He couldn't write one now about what he'd been through, not on paper at least, but if he was still here because of Hal he owed him more than silence.

Dear Old Pal

I'm lying behind some rocks on a bed of loam and branches. It's dark now so I'm writing this in my head and hope you receive it before a Mauser bullet does anything to my brain. We're at the edge of a wood or I should say the new edge of a wood because artillery fire destroyed the original border of trees. It all looks pretty much like those blackened stumps left over when we got up out of that trench and started our walk back to the train. I've got two men left out of the five who went into the field with me this morning. Scott, the best hunter of us all, went down early without knowing what hit him. Poor Munson was crawling along with the rest of us when a German singled him out and we had to leave him in the dirt. I don't know what happened to Davis, but he's dead or wounded that's for sure. It's crazy how one minute they're all beside you and their faces and voices are so real, and the next they're snatched away as if they were feathers in the wind, and all you can do is keep moving without really saying goodbye and hope you stay anchored to the ground for a while longer. We're trying to take the rest of the wood and then a hill on the other side, but the Germans are dug in pretty good and their mortar and machine-gun fire is hard to avoid. Tomorrow we'll push ahead deeper into the trees and maybe get to see the base of the hill. The Frenchies were supposed to come in from the north side, but we haven't heard anything about them. Probably the officers know, but they're not saying.

*I've still got Kincaid and Rawley with me and I'm more
afraid of losing them than of getting hit myself. I don't want to
be the only one left. Imagine what it would have been like if
you'd stood up alone back there when the fire had passed and
I was dead in the trench. I know how I'd feel if it was me
looking down at you. Rawley's a special boy with a way of
taking in the world I'll never forget. As for Kincaid, he's got
his own approach to things, most of which rub me the wrong
way, but I have to admit he knows how to keep his head above
water, and I figured he'd be one of those to make it this far.*

*Last time I wrote you about a woman I'd met in a
brothel. Her name was Amélie and I was sweet on her, more
than I have been about anyone else. But it turns out she's
fixed to be married to some older guy, a sharp dresser who's
probably got lots of francs. I don't get that either, how you can
be so close to somebody and then they just go away from you
like there was no yesterday and there'll be no tomorrow. She's
no different from Scott or Munson or Davis, just another
kind of death, that's all. Well, you can't do anything about the
battlefield—they didn't have a choice about leaving, did they?
But she did, and I'll never put myself in such harm's way
again. Love 'em and leave 'em, that'll be my motto from now
on. Hah! Ah shit, Hal, remember how it was when we pulled
those big trout in from the Canadian side and the sunlight
came through the pines as if it would shine forever?
Everything was alright then, but I don't think it can ever be so
again. We can write about the world all we want, but really
what we're saying is it's the only thing we can do when we lose
so much every day. Maybe by the time you get this I'll be lost.
Maybe one day you'll write a poem about me.*

Miller

His head jerked to the side as he nodded off and his eyes opened wide. He could feel rather than see Rawley and Kincaid beside him, and he almost put out his hand to touch their sleeping bodies. Hell, he'd never get a chance to take that letter out of his head and send it to Hal. He was already unsure of exactly what he'd said about who had died and was never coming back, but he knew it had all been a rope of words designed to deal with the departed. As long as that rope didn't break, he'd drag each member of the squad and Amélie behind him until he forged it and them into a storied chain so bright and strong on the page that yesterday, today, and tomorrow would be as one.

5.

Over a lacklustre dinner of cold bully beef and complaints about the biscuits, Rawley had talked softly about where he had come from and what he wanted to do when he got home.

"Ah'm goin' back to Ocracoke. Ah kin work for mah uncle there just lak ah did when ah was a kid."

Miller had heard of the island on Carolina's Outer Banks because that was where Blackbeard had been captured and beheaded back in the early 18th century. When he mentioned this, Rawley said some old fishermen had claimed to have seen the pirate's head, full beard and all, floating in Pamlico Sound. "They was joshin', jus' tryin' to put a scare in us kids, an' it worked too!"

His parents sent him down to his uncle's in the summer, and when he left school at fourteen that was where he found full-time employ-ment for awhile, moving goods from larger ships offshore to his uncle's schooner for delivery to small towns at the mouth of mainland rivers.

"They wuz good days. Nothin' but sun and sweat." He chuckled. "An' a few island girls in the pot too."

He told Miller about the sixty miles of dune beach that ran up the Atlantic side of the Banks where the surf ran high almost every day be-cause of the prevailing wind and where, on his one day off a week, he would watch the pounding of the waves on the shifting sands for hours at a time.

"Ah wanted to be one of them birds driftin' high over the ocean, high as the clouds, yuh know. Then ah could see everthin'." He paused. "Ah woulda seen that storm comin, sure."

"What happened, Rawley?" Miller was surprised by the sound of Kincaid's voice and at his apparently genuine interest. He'd thought cynicism or sleep had kept him quiet until now.

"Why it was jus' the biggest damn blow the island ever had. Hell, we wasn't more than a coupla feet above the sea anywheres around. Use'ly we'd have some warnin' and take ever'body over to the mainland. Sometimes we'd come back and find the houses flooded out, but we all chipped in and made repairs and such. Yuh jus' got used to it, that's all."

Miller thought about the forest fire. "But there wasn't any warning this time?"

"No sir, there weren't. Late summer was what it was, and nothin' but sun and sweat, lak ah said. Then the wind come up sudden and we could see a black cloud on the horizon movin' fast at us, flat an' black an' coverin' the whole sky. We wuz in the Sound not on the outside, otherwise ah wouldn't be here tellin' you this. One minute we wuz bobbin' up and down and the next we wuz almost arse over tea-kettle them waves wuz so big an' strong. Uncle Davey he got us turned about an' headed for harbour an' when we finally got in that wind was screamin' lak ah never heard before. Mah uncle told me to git mah aunt and cousins, we'd haftah go out again, that wharf wasn't gonna hold." Ah ran with the wind in mah face the whole way and found them all huddled under the kitchen table, two neighbour's kids as well. They wuz plenty scared but no more'n me. Ah yelled they hadda git to the boat an' pushed them out the door. The wind helped us along, ah figure, 'cause we got there lickety split an' ever'body got on board. Jus' after ah untied the line an' mah uncle gunned the engine, that wharf broke inta splinters. We headed out on the Sound and threw down a sea anchor with the wind pushin' the bow toward the mainland. For two hours we rode it out, them six kids bunched around mah uncle's feet in the wheelhouse and me holdin' onta mah aunt the whole time. It was right strange when that cloud passed and the sun come out. We all laughed and hollered at one another, we wuz so happy to be alive. But when we hauled anchor and headed home we could see there weren't much left of the village. Houses crushed inta one another and no trees left standin'. We pulled forty-six bodies outa that wreckage an' knew ever'one of them. The Coast Guard came by later on an' tol' us there'd bin no warnin' up and down the coast. Jus' God's hand, ah guess."

Miller took it all in, the rush of narrative, the rhythms of Rawley's voice, the resilient characters. They added up to a short story pure and simple, and he wondered how he might make it his own.

"Hell, Rawley," Kincaid said, "this war must seem like a cakewalk so far."

Miller couldn't detect any edge to the remark, just a hint of envy and perhaps admiration that mirrored his own. He was going to tell Rawley about the forest fire, but realized it might sound like a competition, and he didn't want that now, so instead he asked Kincaid why he'd enlisted.

There were a few moments of silence, and Miller had just about given up on a response. Then he heard the slight shift of a body in the dark. "I didn't have much choice," Kincaid murmured.

He told them he'd been a numbers runner back in Trenton, carrying the cash and slips between the local betting parlours and headquarters where the big boys wore Homburgs and fancy suits. One day this Hungarian pulled him aside in a parlour and asked him if he wanted to make some sure money. It made him nervous, Kincaid said, because he knew the guy had grift on his mind and the big boys counted every penny from the runners. But he was curious enough to ask what was up, and the Hungarian told him he had a foolproof method for sliding some cash into their pockets. Some friends of his would pull a stick-up while Kincaid was on his route to headquarters. They'd rough him up a little to make things look good, but here's the thing, he said. Kincaid would make a lot of noise and some other friends would rescue him. He'd be a hero to the big boys since half the money would be safely delivered in the end.

"Who are your friends?" Kincaid asked the Hungarian.

"That's your protection," the man replied. "You don't know any more than I've told you. Just play your part and you'll get paid down the line."

Kincaid thought he was crazy but didn't protest the plan. He kept expecting the phoney robbers to show up, but they never did. Next thing there was a knock on his door and two heavies told him headquarters wanted to see him. He asked if he could take a leak first and they said sure. He went out the bathroom window into the alley and never looked back.

"I figured they knew all about the scam but just wanted me to confirm it. I'd be as guilty as the Hungarian because I hadn't spilled the beans to them. I knew where he lived and ran over to his rooming house a few blocks away. He lay down on his bed and smiled when I told him they were coming for him. He wasn't going to run, he said. There wasn't any point. But I ran right down the street into a recruiting office and signed on the dotted line. For two days I hid down on the docks and then reported to the Marine training camp outside the city. That's it. Here I am."

"Do you think they killed him?" Miller asked him.

"Sure they did. He had it coming, didn't he? But it's a double whammy for me. I'm an accessory to murder and I'm on a hit list myself." He laughed. "I guess it's a cakewalk here for me too."

Miller had a vivid picture of the Hungarian lying on his bed waiting for death. He didn't know whether the man felt he was going to die for something worthwhile, but that was part of the lesson in Kincaid's story. What was missing, however unintentionally, was just as important as what was there. He recognized they'd both given him the tip of the iceberg as far as their lives were concerned, and they knew even less about him. But their choice of words promised hidden depths, and if they were going to fight and likely die together tomorrow that was enough.

Runners brought the orders, boys younger than themselves whose voices hadn't dropped and whose razor blades were as yet untested. Three whistles just before dawn would be the signal to move ahead and take the rest of the wood. They were informed the Germans had apparently left only a token force among the trees and gathered their main strength back on the hill with the unexplained number as its name. Miller checked his Springfield's bolt action well aware he hadn't fired it the day before. Come to think of it, none of them had used their weapons. They'd been too busy trying to survive the German onslaught. Now he heard the snap of Rawley's and Kincaid's bolts and wondered how all three of them would react when the time came to shoot. If yesterday was any indication, it would all happen so fast there wouldn't be time to think. He knew Scott and Munson had died because some kid from Berlin or Frankfurt had lifted his rifle to his shoulder and squeezed the trigger without planning a death. He knew most of what happened on the battlefield was instinctive and completely unlike hunting down and killing an animal. When Hal and he shot the bear, everything was arranged and, of course, the bear didn't have a gun. His guilt over Scott, Munson, and Davis was like a pack of heavy stones on his back, even though he told himself they died by chance and short of throwing his own body in front of them he couldn't have saved their lives. But he was determined to get Rawley and Kincaid through the woods and up that hill. They hadn't said anything about their dead friends. That was what you did. You avoided the dead to keep yourself from joining them. Maybe when it was all over they could talk freely.

As a thin line of light flickered in the sky, Miller looked at the dirty hair and stubbled cheeks of his companions and saw their tiredness and resignation in the slump of their shoulders. He wanted to take a shit, but his bowels were locked tight, and all he could manage was a kneeling piss accompanied by two other streams pattering on the dead leaves. Then the whistles pierced the silence, and he could hear the lifting of equipment all along the line, men coughing and hawking up phlegm, and an officer's occasional sharp command. They began to walk forward in a half-crouch unsure whether the remaining Germans were directly in their way or off to the right or left. A Mauser bullet zinged by Miller's ear and another ripped a chunk of bark that slammed against the bridge of his nose. He dropped to the earth and waited, hearing some far-off machine-gun rattle and an occasional Springfield reply. Kincaid crawled up beside him.

"It's a sniper above us. That first bullet ploughed into the ground behind me."

Miller gestured to Rawley about six feet away on his right side, motioning him to move ahead in a semi-circle then told Kincaid to do the same on his left.

"I'll keep straight and try to draw his fire. You might see his muzzle flash, but it's his shell ejection you need to locate. Space your shots in a line and you're bound to hit him."

Kincaid smiled. "Sounds easy enough. But keep your head down just in case he doesn't cooperate."

Another machine-gun opened up close by, and he could hear the desperate cries of Marines who had been hit and the aggressive yells of those still mobile. Someone lobbed a grenade, but it must have fallen short because the fusillade was unrelenting after the explosion. At least the thick clusters of beech and oak prevented effective mortar use in the wood, and the Germans weren't about to lob down any shells from the hill while their own men were still holding their ground below. Now several rifles joined the fray, and he wasn't sure where their owners were hiding. They could get the man in the tree but miss another half-buried behind a trunk or rock. He wasn't happy about being separated from Kincaid and Rawley, but he couldn't hold their hands. That wasn't the way to keep them alive. No, their best chance and his was to move like they were related parts of the same body and brain. Then he remembered the snake and his image of unity crumpled.

He hadn't realized all this time he'd been crawling, knees and elbows akimbo, in a more or less straight line toward the German's position until a bullet then another smacked into his backpack and he heard Kincaid's Springfield answer with three shots and what must have been Rawley with two more. Fifty feet in front of him a Mauser hit the forest floor followed by a spiked helmet that spun like a top for a few seconds then settled against an exposed root. The body took its time, perhaps caught on a branch or twisted into a last painful position it was loath to leave for death. Whatever the cause, it descended in such slow motion that Miller could hear the leaves rustled by its passing and the soft thump of flesh against each limb. When the man finally came to rest he was leaning upright against the base of the tree, his eyes open but unfocused, the fingers of one hand fluttering as if in time to a familiar tune. A trickle of blood ran from one of his ears. Kincaid and Rawley carefully made their way to his side and the three of them knelt before their enemy, listening to his rasping breath but well aware he could outlive them yet.

"What'll we do with him?" Rawley asked quietly.

"We leave the bastard here to rot," Kincaid said bitterly. "I don't feel sorry for him."

"Ah do."

Miller stared at the young, fair-haired German dying as much from the fall's trauma as the obvious damage from the 30.06s. He hadn't wanted the bear to suffer. That's why he killed him outright rather than let Hal keep shooting. That's what you did for an animal that didn't understand the origins of its pain, only that a two-legged creature was involved. This man would have known at some point where the pain was coming from. Maybe deep inside, even though he probably spoke no English, he could translate what they were talking about.

"We won't treat him worse than the bear," he declared.

"What?" Kincaid said.

"We have to make sure he's dead before we leave him."

"To hell with that."

"What do you say, Rawley?"

He could hear the furious battle sounds around them, but they were cut off from the main struggle now, absorbed in a quandary they couldn't side-step and had so little to do, he realized, with instinctive actions of the moment.

"We could wait here an' jus' let him die on his own."

"There isn't time."

Rawley sighed. "Nope, but ah sure wish there was."

"You're crazy, both of you. Let's get out of here." Kincaid was livid.

"Listen, Rawley, if we wait for him to die, we still killed him, don't you see."

"Ah guess ah do. But that was to protect ourselves. If we kill him now, it's lak, well ... murd'rin him." The conviction in his voice was undeniable.

"Fuck that!" Kincaid shouted, contradicting himself. "He'd be getting what he deserved."

"Even if it got rid of his pain?"

Kincaid grimaced. Miller could see he was darkly torn.

"You two go on," he said. "I won't be long."

When they had crept away, Rawley promising they wouldn't go far without waiting for him, he looked at the German again and saw he was really just a boy like himself, his face smeared with dirt and bits of greenery but still young and unlined. If I were lying there like you, he thought, what would I want you to do? He picked up his Springfield and placed the tip of the barrel against his enemy's forehead. What were the rules concerning a prisoner?

They'd put the bear out of its misery, hadn't they, even though it hadn't been any threat. This man or boy who had attacked them was now helpless. There was a torn seam in his uniform collar and one of his boot-laces was undone. His eyelids fluttered and he seemed to be trying to speak, but only a garbled sound came from his throat. Then he coughed and there was a splash of blood on his chin. It would be a mercy, Miller thought, as his finger tightened on the trigger. But despite his pity, Rawley's image of murder wouldn't dissolve. Which was the moral high ground? Was there any such territory in war? He was crying when he took out the notebook and wrote down the protective words. When he left the German was still alive.

6.

"Ah didn't hear a shot," Rawley said. "Did he ...?"

"Yeah, he's gone."

"What happens if we bring down another sniper?" Kincaid said. "We gonna talk it over again?"

A sergeant crawled by behind them. "Good work, boys," he cried out. Miller knew he was referring to the whole battle and not just their own close-up encounter with the enemy, but he flinched just the same. He heard the sergeant tell them and all the others within hearing that the attack was to go forward. There was only a quarter of a mile or so of wood left to win then they'd be at the bottom of the hill.

"We've got to get them off there," the sergeant said. "Too much fire-power on top to leave behind."

They had no choice but to move more or less straight ahead. That's what everyone else was doing, so your luck just depended on whether there was a machine-gun nest in your way or a stray bullet picked you out. When the whistles blew, he patted Rawley on the shoulder. "No more separations," he said. "We're going up that hill together."

"Ah'm sorry for what ah said. But I'm glad he went by himself."

He knew Rawley was just trying to help them both along. Kincaid refused to say anything more, but he nodded when told they'd head out in a V-formation ten to fifteen feet apart.

It was very quiet now as if the Germans were sleeping or watching their progress indifferently, and the silence was more unnerving than constant fire because it gave you time to think about your vulnerability. Miller could hear the crunch of his boots against the dried leaves and far-off the honking of a solitary goose. Was it on the wing or swimming on some pristine pond beyond the bloodshed? Back home he'd be look-ing for quail or rabbit, but there was no flutter of wings and no forest creatures raised their heads. No matter because he didn't want to shoot anything ever again. He knew this was an illusion and gripped the stock of the Springfield more tightly. How could he come this far and do what he had done only to surrender without a fight? It was too bad Hal wasn't here. He would have understood about the German. Miller had seen the look on his face when he'd told him he'd lifted his shoulder and that was why his shot had left the bear alive. *If you had only one chance to put anything out of its misery, you had to use it.* That was what he had written in the notebook. *But he knew the German wasn't the bear. He hadn't shot him in the back while he was running away or pulled the trigger when he was staring into his eyes.* The three sentences would begin a story one day. His knuckles were white on the stock. Yes, they would have to begin a story.

After two or three minutes of unchecked advance, it was clear the Germans had withdrawn from the forest, and a great cheer went up and down the Marine front line. For the first time Miller felt part of the huge company of men to which he officially belonged. It was crazy that everything they'd been through yesterday and today had been organized on a collective scale and was not just the haphazard experience of chaos. But he knew, despite such organization, his individual choice to leave the still-breathing sniper where he lay remained impulsive, and the deaths of Scott, Munson, and probably Davis resulted from personal and arbitrary encounters with violence. Headquarters would have a plan to take the hill, no doubt, whose success was based on the proper use of sheer numbers and weaponry, but it would take random, disconnected acts of courage and folly to win the day. Who was around to raise the flag depended more on good fortune than good tactics. If you didn't have the former you died in the Somme mud or the gas-clouds of Ypres by the tens of thousands no matter how certain your officers or slick the action of your guns.

The trees didn't thin out as they approached the eastern side of the forest, so there was plenty of cover as they came to the fringe and surveyed what was waiting for them. Where the trees ended the short grass began and stretched all the way to the base of the hill, which was surprisingly close, perhaps fifty or sixty yards away. The incline was quite steep and offered little cover except for irregular piles of rocks. The Germans had cut down the few stands of birch and poplar on the slope but had scattered the trunks and branches so these would offer little protection. Worse, Miller was afraid headquarters would wait until the next morning to attack when the sun would be in their eyes and would stay there for hours. The best time to go would be late afternoon when the Germans would be staring into the western light. He knew that firing downhill was difficult under any conditions. Because of the angle, the bullet's trajectory and line of sight didn't match up and you had to deal with a gravity drop of more than a foot at a hundred yards. He hoped there were some hunters making the decisions on the Marines' behalf.

They lay on their stomachs looking out and up between two close-set oaks. When the same sergeant went by behind them Miller asked how many would make the assault.

"We've got what's left of three of our companies and two of the Frenchies. They didn't get much resistance so they're near full strength. As for us, I can't be sure, but some sectors behind us were pretty rough.

If I had to guess I'd say we've still got six or seven hundred altogether. Plus you three, of course," he added with a laugh.

"And up there?"

"God knows," the sergeant said.

They could see the rim of the summit, but no sign of the Germans. Now the Marines were so close their heavy artillery couldn't angle down with any accuracy, so it would be mortars and small-arms fire they'd have to wade through. Almost directly in front of them at the foot of the slope was a low rock formation that Kincaid pointed to.

"I figure ten seconds from here to there. That's if they let us run."

"Those Minenwerfers will open up as soon as we move," Miller said, "and their best sharpshooters will pick off anyone still standing. If we do run, don't go in a straight line. I know it's tempting, but you should cut back and forth."

He wanted to tell them how easy it was to hit a deer that ran straight without altering its speed, but once the salvos began their impact would speak louder than any of his words. He didn't know if he could force his own legs to follow his hunter's advice, just like they hadn't when he and Scott had walked so unswervingly into the grain.

"It's funny," Rawley said.

"What's that?"

"How yuh kin come all this way an' still die."

Kincaid chewed on his bottom lip but said nothing.

Miller opened his mouth to reply, and for the rest of his life would wish he'd pushed out words that Rawley deserved to hear, their potential solace hidden forever because the whistles sounded, and then they were on their feet looking down the line at officers charging ahead through exploding columns of dirt and grass.

"Ten seconds, boys," Kincaid cried and began to run into the smoke.

There were so many men around him Miller couldn't zigzag without tripping over them, and it seemed they were all heading for the same pile of rocks. Suddenly there was a tremendous jolting of the air and he was tossed sideways into another body, landing face down on the ground, his Springfield thrown from his hands, and his pack slamming against the back of his skull. Far off he heard a voice calling to him: "Git up, Miller. Ah've got your rifle."

He pushed himself to his knees through a fog of pain and confusion. The thud of the mortars was very loud, and the ringing in his head wouldn't stop. Through the smoke he glimpsed a green refuge of trees. That's where he had to go, so he started to crawl on his knees until a hand grabbed his shoulder and the same voice yelled in his ear: "Yer goin' the wrong way, Miller, git up and run!" As he staggered to his feet a familiar figure whose name he couldn't recall pushed a weapon into his hands, spun him around, and pulled him forward. Who was he? Who was he? It would be rude to ask, but he didn't like his own stupidity. As they stumbled toward some rocks where another man was crouching, it suddenly came to him and he smiled at his companion and clapped him on his back. "Thanks, Hal," he said. "My ankle's okay."

The three of them stayed behind the rocks for a long time, enough for his mind to clear and recognitions to return. All along the foot of the hill men had taken shelter as best they could, digging into the edge of the slope and throwing up primitive earth-works or making small barricades with their packs. The mortars couldn't get them now, though the Mausers and Bergmanns could, and the sleet of bullets was relentless. Marines who safely protected their heads and torsos would get hit in the legs, and many had drawn themselves up into foetal positions, their Springfields resting on their home-made parapets, bayonets glistening in the morning sun. He couldn't remember getting here and asked Rawley how that was so.

"Ah guess you got hit by a shell-blast. Didn't know where you wuz."

"The fuckin' hero carried you in," Kincaid said, but there was approval in his voice rather than the usual scorn. "By the way, who's Hal? Your brother or somethin'? You kept talkin' to him like he was here. It was kind of spooky."

"He's just a friend," Miller replied. "He saved my life in a forest fire." He nodded at Rawley. "I guess that's two of you now. Thanks."

Rawley chuckled. "Hell, if I'd let you go you wudda been back in them trees soon enough."

"Yeah, people might have got the wrong idea," Kincaid added.

Miller flushed. "I ain't yellow if that's what you mean."

Kincaid stared at him without blinking. Finally he said: "No. That's one thing you're not."

He peeked over the top of a rock. It was about a thirty-degree rise that ran for a few hundred feet to the summit. There were some other rocks and a few fallen trees between them and the Germans but not much else. If they made it to the top it would be hand-hand fighting, close-range shots and bayonets. Then there'd be a flag. There needed to be a marker for all those mangled bodies that nobody was going to speak over any time soon. Sure, a chaplain would come along eventually, but until then they'd unfurl Old Glory. He didn't believe in all the pieties, the ones that painted the faces of the dead in red, white, and blue and promised salvation, the ones that echoed Sidney Carton's sentiments about sacrifice and reward in Dickens' novel when war was really all about an eye for an eye and always had been. If he ever wrote about the taking of this hill, he'd keep it simple and true. Crane was better than Dickens with those lines in *The Red Badge of Courage* that he'd never forgotten: "He now thought that he wished he was dead. He believed that he envied those men whose bodies lay strewn over the grass of the fields and on the fallen leaves of the forest."

Rawley took a crust of bread and piece of cheese from his pack. "Might as well have us some lunch," he said.

"I'd rather have a good stiff drink," Kincaid responded with a chuckle. "But I'd settle for a whiskey."

Miller took a chance. "You get up this hill with me, and I'll buy you more than one."

Kincaid's face didn't give an inch. Well, I tried, Miller said to himself. Then he heard him say: "Rawley Phillips, what's your real name?"

"Armistead," Rawley replied. "It's after a North Carolina gen'ral who died at Gettysburg."

Kincaid put out his hand, which Rawley grasped. "Jack," he said. "Jack Kincaid." He glanced across at Miller and held out his hand again without changing his expression. "It's after Jack Daniel's."

"Armistead Phillips," Miller whispered as the dark came down and they settled into their long wait. "Who would have guessed?"

"Ah've been around more than you think," Rawley said with a smile.

By mid-morning the sun had risen over the crest of the hill and shone down on the waiting Marines who had to shade their eyes to see anything beyond a glare. Miller cursed those in command. It wasn't enough to climb the steep slope against withering fire, they had to be blind as well. Stumbling across any cover would be a miracle, as would picking out any human targets. All they could depend upon was the force of numbers and maybe fire-power too as their own artillery opened up an hour before the attack was to begin. They could hear the eruptions above and didn't envy the Germans hunkered down under the bombardment. It was impossible to know if there had been any direct hits or the damage done. There should be a spotter plane, Miller thought, but there wasn't anything in the cobalt sky except small grey clouds drifting north. There could be concrete bunkers up there with slits for enfilade fire. If luck got them that far, even the Marines who made it to the summit were in trouble.

Hal

My throat's dry and I can't get the words out too readily. We're at the bottom of that hill I mentioned before, waiting for the bugler to sound the charge. A little too much like the Little Big Horn for my liking even if we've got more men than Custer had. The slope's steeper than most ridges in Michigan, and the Germans made sure there's no trees left on it. I wish there were trees. I wish I could walk through them, touching their trunks and smelling their leaves. I'd get up in one and sit on a high branch looking over the countryside. It would be peaceful because if there were trees there'd be no Germans and no bullets trying to cut me down. I almost killed a wounded German kid yesterday. He was in bad shape and I felt I couldn't leave him there to die. Rawley said it would be like murdering him, and that stopped me in the end.

He knew the German wasn't the bear. He hadn't shot him in the back while he was running away. *That's what I wrote afterwards. Maybe words will be enough one day to stop the bleeding. I don't know. As for this morning, Rawley and Kincaid will go with me. I don't see how any of us are going to get to the top. And, like the sergeant said, God knows what's waiting for us up there.*

Miller

P.S. If I don't come back, you'll get the notebook.

7.

The same runner crawled by.

"It's every man for himself once we charge," he told them.

"No kidding," Kincaid said.

Rawley pulled a tiny jar of jam from his pack. "Ah've been savin' this for when it's all over. But ah think we should have it now." He unscrewed the lid. "Each of us can dip a finger," he said, and passed the jar to Kincaid. Miller watched him lower the tip of his pinkie so slowly and delicately it was like he was setting a fly down on quiet water, and when he did the same and tasted the sweetness on his tongue he said: "Come visit me in Michigan, and I'll take you into thickets of berries you'll never want to leave."

With a swoop of his arm, Rawley tossed the jar over the rock like a grenade, but there was no explosion, just a soft clinking sound then a few seconds of silence broken by the whistle blasts. When the whistles sounded they threw on their packs, gripped their Springfields tightly, and stepped into the open.

Miller could see other men strung out along the slope, the more athletic leaders yards ahead, legs pumping like steam-engine pistons, bayonets pointed to the sky. More than one of them was ripped by a stream of bullets and flung back into his comrades who took his weight and bore him to the ground. Then as the men bunched together whole groups were cut down at once, falling in piles their successors hid behind until officers prodded them with batons or screams he couldn't hear in the din. He saw Kincaid ahead of him move toward a small cluster of rocks then disappear on its far side. He and Rawley, gasping for breath, managed to reach a pile of branches just below. The noise of the machine-guns and rifles was so loud and unrelenting he feared he would go deaf from the assault then told himself that wouldn't be such a bad thing after all. For a brief moment he thought of lying in silence in that trench with Hal while the roar of flames passed over them. But you couldn't bury yourself away from the war, could you? They'd dig you up and haul you in front of a firing squad.

Rawley put his mouth next to Miller's ear and shouted: "Ah think Kincaid's hurt. Ah saw his hand in the air, like he wuz tryin' to grab somethin' and hold on."

Miller peered through the branches as best he could. The rocks were ten or twelve yards away and not even waist-high. Why wasn't Kincaid on this side of them? Was there more cover they couldn't see, a log maybe or another rock? He crawled on his belly his body's length through the bottom of the branches and hollered as loudly as he could: "Kincaid, can you hear me? Hold up your rifle if you're okay."

It was as if the Germans not Kincaid heard him because a Bergmann zeroed in on their position and bullets pranged off the rocks and shredded the tops of the branches just a few inches from his helmet. How the hell were they supposed to win out against this? He was about to tell Rawley they should try to move sideways away from the centre of the advance when he saw him take off his pack and set himself as if about to start a race.

"He's hurt, ah know it. We've got to git him outa there."

Miller could see his fingers tense and the toes of his boots press into the soft earth, and before he could put out an arm to stop him he took off, leaping through the foliage and giving a cry that sounded like an Indian war-whoop but must have been a rebel yell. "No, Rawley," he called feebly, and heard the Bergmann snap again.

When Rawley fell, Miller felt a stab of pain in his chest. It was so searing he clenched his teeth and fists in protest and felt tears come to his eyes. They were both gone, and that left only him for no reason at all. He lay there with his head down for a long time while flames devoured him. When he finally looked up through the leaves he could see one of Rawley's boots sticking over the top of a rock at an odd angle, the rest of him hidden on the far side with Kincaid. His heart raced. By God, he'd made it! But he was either dead or badly wounded, the boot told him that. There was a lot of smoke drifting his way as if someone somewhere on the slope had lit a cooking fire. That was impossible! No, for once the officers were thinking straight and were creating a screen to hide the advance and give the Marines a fighting chance. He didn't care about the battle, though. He'd use the smoke to reach his friends and then he'd find a medic. How he'd do that he didn't know, but his war was over until he did. Maybe it was just over. He didn't want to fight anymore, not without those who'd died instead of him. He had to save Rawley and Kincaid so there was no more dying.

When the pall descended and he could barely see the tips of the branches, he stood up and ran toward the rocks. As he jumped over them he could see Rawley face-down lying on top of Kincaid whose open, glassy eyes stared at nothing, the top part of his skull laid open as if by an amateur surgeon, some brain matter smeared across his cheek. Rawley groaned as Miller knelt down and turned him over, the blood oozing from a throat wound that had punched through his Adam's apple and left him sucking air through its ragged remains.

"I'll get you back, Rawley," Miller said. "I'll get you back to Ocracoke."

Rawley couldn't speak, but he blinked in apparent recognition of the words and Miller felt his fingers grip his pant leg and give a little tug.

"I'll find a medic," he said, but Rawley would not let go. The smoke was thinning, and he knew he'd have to move soon. A minute or two at the most.

Then Rawley slowly held up his other hand and pressed his straightened index finger to his temple, smiling at Miller and giving a slight nod.

Miller slapped the hand away, but the finger came back, this time curling around an invisible trigger before extending itself again. The Rawley coughed and blood spilled from the wound.

"I can't, I can't! You called it murder. Not you, not you!"

He wouldn't leave him, then. He'd stay until he died or they both died together. But how long would that take, and how much would Rawley suffer while he lasted? He looked down at the southern boy whose chest still rose and fell, who'd survived hurricane winds and, like he'd said, come this far just to die. At that moment Miller loved him more than anyone he'd ever known, even more than he loved Hal. Would he shoot Hal if he were like this? Yes, he knew he would. Not back on the ridge in Michigan because the fire wasn't personal, but here because the Germans tried to steal everything from you, and you had to stop such robbery. He wasn't making sense. He shouldn't do anything when he wasn't making sense. There was so much noise he couldn't think, but his rifle barrel touched Rawley's chest as he leaned over him. Then there was a sudden searing pain in his right knee and a dull thud inside his head that silenced everything. The Springfield jerked in his hands as the last strands of smoke swirled away and he saw how close the summit was.

New York Times
April 1920

Junior Reporter Wins Pulitzer

A junior reporter for the St. Louis Post-Dispatch *has won the Pulitzer Prize for a series of short articles about his experience as a U.S. Marine at the battle of Belleau Wood in June, 1918. Miller Sark, just 20 years of age and recipient of the Navy Cross for bravery, produced, in the words of the prize committee, "a remarkable study of men at war in a direct, unassuming prose style that emphasizes courage under fire yet leaves his reader exhausted by the horror and waste of battle." In his pieces, Mr. Sark traces the path of his infantry squad, consisting of himself and five other men, as they struggle through Belleau Wood and ultimately take Hill 142 at great cost (all of his companions were killed in a three-day span). In particular, he tells of his encounter with a badly-wounded German sniper whom he shot out of a tree and then tended until he died. General John J. Pershing, who commanded all American Troops during the war, has called Sark's work "dramatic testimony to the achievements of our troops and to the experience of the individual soldier."*

Across the River

1.

Hal did spend two weeks in early September with his mother's aging cousins in their comfortable Brownstone in Brooklyn Heights, politely answering all their questions about the mid-West, fending off the attentions of a grand-niece whose bobbed hair was the rage, and sleeping late in the mornings so as to miss at least one meal around the overly solicitous table. The neighbourhood, on a steep slope above the East River, provided a panoramic view of the Manhattan skyline, and in the afternoons he looked for accommodation, turning down room after room until he found one perched by the bridge with its window facing the cabled towers he likened to wings soaring above the water. His Italian landlady, her accent still bearing traces of the old country, told him she had come to America the year the President was assassinated. At first he thought she was referring to McKinley, then realized she must have meant Garfield, and was astonished to learn she had been a girl of ten when she landed at the New Jersey docks to hear of a great war that had just ended. Three days later Lincoln was shot.

The widow Capalca (she had married her Luigi at sixteen) charged seven dollars a week for room and board, he wrote his mother, but it was worth every penny as her meals were hearty and delicious—soups, pastas, wonderful fresh bread and vegetables. That left him only twelve dollars a month from his allowance, but he was sure to find employment soon. This was the greatest city on earth, after all, filled with opportunity for those who would chronicle its attributes as Whitman had done. He might begin, he said, by writing a poem called "Crossing Brooklyn Bridge," which would be a worthy successor to the bard's celebrated ferry journey across the river. Once he had settled in and found a job, they would have to paint the town together, though of course she'd be aware that his paid employment and his writing would take up most of his time. He didn't tell her that Mrs. Capalca had a spare bedroom for guests of her boarders. The cousins' place, only several blocks away, would be close enough during the prolonged visit she'd want to have with him.

The truth was he didn't really fancy a full-time job except for the funds it would obviously bring in. He wanted to work alright, but on his long poem and other verse, not in some dreary office to which he'd have to travel with thousands of other slaves. The subway system was a marvel, whisking him from Central Park to the Woolworth Building, Greenwich Village to Times Square in mere minutes, but he didn't want his admiration of its speed and power to be dulled by timetable and repetition. Besides, he much preferred to walk the streets, absorbing the sights and sounds at his leisure and choosing his routes arbitrarily, ending up in areas where faces and voices were completely new and regular maps no guide at all.

He found the Metropolitan Museum of Art in a less haphazard manner and returned to it more than once, particularly drawn to an Etruscan burial chariot burnished with bronze plates that depicted Achilles and his goddess mother Thetis before he went off to Troy. Legend had it she'd dipped her son in the river Styx to make him immortal but left his heel exposed. He thought of his own mother immersing him in the dark waters of her possessiveness that would lead him inevitably to the docklands and a military uniform to strip off rather than don. He'd read an abridged version of the *Iliad* in school and knew Achilles loved a boy who wore his armour and was slain in a case of mistaken identity by Hector. When Achilles died their bones were mixed together and their ashes buried in the same urn. Homer called the boy his "beloved." He thought of his own battle up there on the ridge with Miller and the kiss he had given him when they were about to die. Wasn't Miller a more suitable Achilles, the seemingly invincible warrior off to fight in his own great war? If so, what was his mortal weakness and how would it be revealed? He hadn't yet heard from his friend, though his mother had promised to forward any mail.

When he could no longer avoid a serious search for employment it was difficult to stave off depression. He could be a messenger boy or lowly clerk in dozens of offices that dealt with business facts and figures as if they were of biblical significance. For submitting to such torture, he'd be paid ten or twelve dollars a week, almost six of which would go for subway and lunch costs. With his allowance leftovers he'd have around thirty a month for entertainment, clothing, and the cheap red wine that kept loneliness at bay most evenings. He was now going hatless and staving off the rain with an umbrella, but when the cold came he'd need a fedora and new coat. That would be a week's savings gone at one blow. Determined not to mention such difficulties in his letters home, he kept his news cheery and tried to summon up alternatives to his penurious lifestyle.

He was saved quite literally by an accident. Early one afternoon he'd set off for an interview in Manhattan that, if successfully passed, would have him copy-editing advertising sheets for a baby carriage company. As he was about to enter the Clark Street station, a small truck collided with a trolley, throwing its young driver into the street where he lay yelling in pain. Hal ran over, took off his jacket and slid it under injured man's head. An older passenger emerged from behind a dented front door as a crowd gathered.

"Jimmy, Jimmy, what'd ya turn right there for? Lookit the truck!"

Someone said they should get the kid to a hospital and started to lift him to his feet.

"Careful," Hal said, "his arm's broken."

The passenger sighed loudly. "Christ, that's all we need," he declared. Then he addressed Hal directly. "How'd ya know about his arm? There's no blood or nothin'."

"It's the way it's bent. See how the elbow is twisted around."

By this time a policeman had arrived and was asking questions. "You the owner," he asked Hal, nodding at the truck.

"Naw, that's me," the passenger said, as Hal noticed the sign on the truck's hand-painted panel for the first time. *Steve Costopoulos Carpentry Brooklyn Heights* in two rows of bright red letters.

The policeman took down the details and sent the trolley on its way.

"Let's get your truck to the curb," he said. "Come down to the station later and sign the report I've got to file."

When the injured Jimmy had been driven off to the hospital by a jitney driver, Hal, who had forgotten all about his appointment, helped push the battered vehicle off to the side of the road. There he dusted off his jacket and listened to the old man's lament.

"He'll be off work for weeks now. Who's gonna get up on the roof with me?"

Suddenly he saw his release from office prison. No subway, no slow death under a perambulator, and all the fresh air he could breathe. "I can climb," he said.

The accident happened on a Friday. Early the following Monday morning he showed up at the Costopoulos garage off Clark Street and not far from the cemetery. It hadn't been easy getting out of bed before sunrise, but he felt awfully lucky as he walked the six blocks to work amidst the Manhattan-bound crowd, knowing no trip on the Flatbush line was waiting. He was wearing corduroy pants and a fairly decent sweater under his one windbreaker that he hoped wouldn't get too dirty or, worse, torn. On the Saturday he'd paid two dollars for an old pair of work-boots and two more for a new pair of padded gloves in a store that sold everything from dishes to axe-handles. Surely Steve would provide him with whatever else he needed or at least point him to a cheap supply of hammers, screwdrivers, and other tools. Maybe he could borrow Jimmy's tools for awhile, but he didn't know how close carpenters felt to their equipment or if there was some superstitious ban on lending it. When he'd offered himself for the job he hadn't stopped to think about such details, and the old Greek had seemed so relieved to find a replacement that nothing much had been discussed except his wage of fifteen dollars a week as long as he could do what was asked of him until Jimmy came back, then they'd see.

The first few days they spent tied to one another on opposite sides of a steep-pitched roof laying shingles after Steve had schooled him in the basics he said a carpenter had to remember. Hal liked being up there and had no sensation of vertigo. The view was spectacular all around, but especially to the north and west where the sun glinted on the river, the bridge towers, and Manhattan. He could see boats heading out of the Navy Yard, and far off in the opposite direction was Liberty Island welcoming trans-Atlantic craft. Steve chatted to him from the other side of the ridgeline, asking him where he was from, why he'd come to New York, and what plans he had beyond being a carpenter's helper. Hal answered as best he could, appreciative of the friendly interest and glad to be able to talk to someone besides Mrs. Capalca whose conversations at dinner were centered on his getting married and having lots of healthy *bambinos*. There were two other boarders in her house, both of whom were elderly men who'd lived with her for years, and he didn't have much in common with their jingoistic views of the war, wondering how Miller would have handled their zealous acceptance of American death in the trenches. The one empty rental bedroom she hoped to have occupied at the end the month by a young New England man. She didn't know what he did, but he'd been highly recommended to her by a cousin in Boston.

He learned of Steve's voyage to the States in 1880 when the statue was half-complete and long before the Brooklyn Bridge and subway. The youthful immigrant had read dime novels about the wild west and thought about heading out to fight the Indians, but from what he could tell they were pretty much all gone by then and he wanted a steady job with a future. Mrs. Capalca would have approved of his immediately settling into the Greek community in Astoria and looking for a wife.

"I found my Maria in just one year," he said as they climbed down the ladder for a lunch break. When he crossed himself at the bottom Hal knew she was dead. "And she gave me two strong sons and a beautiful daughter." Before Hal could ask, he heard: "It was a fever that took her. Not even a grandmother, but God had other plans."

"I'm sorry," Hal said. "Where are your children now?"

Steve raised a closed hand and flicked his fingers open. "Scattered, just like that. Costas, he's on the ships. He's been everywhere, even back home. Christos owns a restaurant in Pittsburgh, and my daughter Irene is in Boston married to a big-shot banker. Christos and Irene got four kids each, gettin' too old for grandpa now. I see them once in a while, maybe for Christmas." He listed them all by name. "Jimmy, he's my grand-nephew from Maria's sister's girl."

Hal tried to keep track of everyone, but aside from the injured Jimmy, it was the unmarried sailor who stuck in his mind. Then he forced himself to concentrate and asked Steve what it had been like when he'd first arrived. There were no immigrants in his long poem because he hadn't met anyone like this unassuming Greek before. He learned about the crowded tenements and the gangs of unemployed men who roamed the streets looking for work and trouble, and about the neighbourhood divisions no different from today but more strictly enforced. "We stayed with our own, and it was family in Greek-town that kept us together. Ah, the parties we had and the dancin'!"

"Did you get along with the Italians?" Hal asked, thinking there might have been a Mediterranean alliance of sorts.

"Naw, not really. We respected one another but didn't cross the lines, except on the ferry and the bridge when it got built a few years later. We worked together on this side of the river and over in Manhattan, and that's how our English got better. I didn't speak no Italian or Portuguese and they didn't have any Greek, but I had to find some way to say 'Pass me a hammer and some nails' so everybody understood. Today's the same for the new ones. Pretty soon they speak like you and me."

Their exchange emphasized how insulated he'd been in Oak Park. After all, in two weeks in San Francisco he'd seen more people of different races than in his eighteen years in the mid-west. The Embarcadero had been a grab-bag territory of faces and voices where he could have ended up with a Chinese or Russian sailor as easily as he had with Nicky. The thought excited him now and not just sexually. He didn't care about a man's background only about his nature, and that surely meant he could write about all men and their experience equally. Steve and others like him would go into his poem, he'd make certain of that. He just had to listen to their stories and embrace what they offered of their lives.

His old-country hammer
Swings in time
To newly-formed words
Nailing American sounds
Proudly into place

Mrs. Capalca handed him the envelope containing the card one fall evening not long before Thanksgiving. He'd heard nothing else from Miller unless his mother hadn't forwarded his letters. No, she'd never do that because if Miller sent them to Oak Park she had no excuse. It was more likely that his friend had been wholly preoccupied with his training life. After all, his own New York existence took up most of his time. On week-nights he was usually too tired to do anything but read and make entries in his notebook. Besides, he had no address for the Marine base in New Jersey and didn't want to write anything that had a good chance of going astray. It didn't matter. Here was the news that Miller would be leaving on the 17th, the day after tomorrow. Typical, though. Just the name of the ship, but no pier number or time of departure. He wanted to find that pier and be there, even if it was just to wave his new fedora, but he couldn't afford the time off and knew that Steve needed him. Jimmy was back at work, but his arm was still giving him some pain so he couldn't lift heavy materials or hold himself comfortably on the ladder. As luck would have it, on the morning of the 17th there was shingling to be done on a house on Vine Street almost under the shadow of the bridge. He was up on the roof by 8 a.m. hoping that ships hadn't sailed at dawn. He'd told Steve about Miller, and the old man agreed to keep an eye out for the flotilla, though that was Hal's word not his and he wasn't sure if it was too grand a term. He spread the tar and hammered the asphalt pieces down for two hours when suddenly there was a shout.

"There they are!' Steve cried, and Hal looked up to see four grey ... what? Destroyers? Cruisers? He knew they were too small to be battleships like those giants he'd seen on the front page of the *Post*. There were flags and pennants flying and hordes of men lined up in straight rows on the decks, and the sounds of a brass band, though he couldn't see any musicians to tell if they were on board or blaring a send-off from the far shore. Somewhere in that assembly was Miller, and Hal ached to see his face and shake his hand one more time. If he sent the card surely he'd write letters from France. There'd be so much to talk about when he got back. Warning Steve to take up the rope slack, then standing up precariously, he waved the woollen cap he wore against the autumn chill, his arm going back and forth like a metronome until the craft disappeared around the western edge of Governor's Island. "So long, Miller," he whispered as he crouched over his hammer again. "For now," he added, and then, to his surprise, something his mother might have said tumbled from his lips. "God bless."

2.

On Saturdays he liked to spend his time in Greenwich Village. In the early afternoon he'd board the Flatbush line and disembark at Christopher Street where Frank Shay's bookstore was waiting. Famous writers had begun to autograph the narrow interior door that hung between the shop and the back office. There was Dreiser's hand, though the great man was living in Chicago where Hal would have had a much better chance of meeting him. Apparently Edward Arlington Robinson came down from his country refuge in Maine once in a while, and Vachel Lindsay had stopped by at least once when he wasn't off traveling across the country by foot. Standing in the aisle or sitting on a stool that also allowed access to higher shelves, Hal read as much as he could, struck by the bluntness of Robinson's famous "Richard Cory" and what one critic called on the cover of a Lindsay collection the "roaring, epic, rag-time tune" that was "The Congo." But, for him, the most prominent missing signature belonged to Edgar Lee Masters whose Spoon River epitaphs spoken by the dead themselves had their origins in central Illinois. Masters might have been focusing on local histories, but there was an appealing grandness in such lines as "Of what Abe Lincoln said/One time at Springfield."

He browsed for hours looking for the one book above all others he might purchase as a first monthly gift to himself. The funds his father had left him were bound to run out by the next summer and he'd have only fifteen dollars a week to live on, providing Steve wanted to keep him once Jimmy was at full strength. So he was very selective as he ran his fingers over dust-jackets and tried to settle on a choice. He'd brought a volume of *Leaves of Grass* with him from home, but thinking of Miller after he'd read "Vigil Strange I Kept on the Field one Night" and "Come Up From the Fields, Father" he bought *Drum-Taps* and found Whitman's war-hospital poems even more disturbing in their depictions of suffering and loss than the battlefield verse.

At night he walked the streets, taking in the traffic of people and vehicles, walking along Christopher and then 4th to Washington Square which seemed like the New York equivalent of the Embarcadero. There was no waterfront, of course, or market stall area, but there was that vast array of humanity that so attracted him and buzzed with a non-stop energy until the early hours. Beneath the memorial arch and around the fountain negroes and whites mingled freely, and he caught accents that summoned up Mrs. Capalca, Steve, and a host of other nations he could only guess at. He'd heard the Village had been an underground railroad site during the Civil war and called Little Africa for many years after that. Miller had told him that a number of characters in Crane's stories were based on negro tough's who ruled the district until Teddy Roosevelt became Police Commissioner and cracked down. While the night air filled with colours and voices rippled deliciously over his skin, he looked for packs of sailors roaming in their blue and white colours and loudly announcing their presence as they entered and exited clubs and bars.

More especially, he sought out the straggler who hung back from the gang as if slightly out of his depth or, completely the opposite, appeared confident in his solitary status. On Bleecker Street he discovered the Black Rabbit Club that hosted men and women who preferred the company of their own sex and welcomed the individual traveler seeking a companion. It was on the club steps where he first heard the word 'queer', the term hurled hatefully by someone who stayed outside the door but, as he soon learned, proudly adopted by those who entered without hesitation. He began to drink there every weekend and, as a result, had more than one tryst in the adjacent alley or later in a nearby flophouse. Once he woke at dawn in a strange bed with his head pounding from whiskey to find a naked woman beside him. Stirring, she opened her eyes and saw the shocked look on his face. He watched her pat her crotch lovingly and heard her laugh.

"Don't worry, honey, I prefer what's between *my* legs, not yours. You fucked a sailor, that's all, my roommate's brother. He had to get back to his ship, and you were in no shape to move."

He told himself that a whole neighbourhood of queers couldn't be wrong in its conduct, and the glow that intimacy with the male body gave him before the whiskey brought him down was worth every twinge of doubt or spasm of guilt. Other times, when in the climactic grip of a husky voyager, he would recall his dream of Miller's closed eyes as he drifted downstream from the naked Nicky and how, the next morning, when he was about to tell his friend who he really was, the fire had intervened.

There was also the Artists' Club on 13th Street that attracted a higher-class clientele. He didn't want to spend the night with any of the effete intellectuals, but he did enjoy their repartees over books and paintings. It was there he was introduced to Picasso and cubism, startled then mesmerized by an autochrome print of "Les Demoiselles d'Avignon" and another of Duchamp's "Nude Descending a Staircase." No one he knew of was writing in this way, breaking the rules so brazenly and flaunting innovative versions of figure and line. Miller had said Paris culture was more than the equal of New York's, and for the first time he had a basis for comparison. Small galleries caught his attention and recent work by American painters, but nothing, even when he went back further to Winslow Homer, Whistler, and Sergeant, could match the Europeans' vision of the immediate. He began to see his bear and Young Man in different shapes and guises and how these could change the perspectives in his still-developing long poem. Sundays he struggled with its content and experimented with its form, but he became more confident in his creative efforts once he met Garrett, the new boarder at Mrs. Capalca's.

It turned out Garrett wasn't from New England at all, but from Fredericksburg, Virginia through which flowed the Rappahannock River mentioned in Crane's novel. Though a huge Civil War battle had been fought there, he told Hal, it was not the one Henry Fleming had run from. A few years older, Garrett had a literature degree from Boston College and was determined to become a literary critic in New York.

"*Harper's,* the *Times,* the *Post,* I can cover them all. I had a good contact at the *Atlantic* when I was in Boston but they wanted someone with more experience, so here I am."

Hal had liked him from the moment of their first encounter on Mrs. Capalca's front porch. Garrett was tall and thin with blue eyes that contrasted with his dark head of hair combed straight back and rather long behind. He was wearing a suit and Hal was very conscious, when shaking his hand, of his own dusty work clothes permanently flecked with bits of tar and grease. His hand was dirty too, but Garrett didn't seem to mind.

"I've got the room at the end of the hall," he said enthusiastically, as if it were a gift granted by the royal lady of the house. "If I press my nose against the pane and turn my head I can see the bridge."

It was a Friday night so Hal was ready to relax. They went for a meal at a cheap Hungarian place on a dead-end street off Columbia Heights where they ordered schnitzel and Tokay. The wine had always been a little sweet for Hal, but Garrett urged him to savour the iron and lime from the Carpathian Mountains where the long Indian summer let the grapes ripen until the skins became transparent.

"I didn't know they had Indians over there," Hal said with a grin.

"Why certainly, my dear chap. Haven't you heard of those great warriors the Budapests and the Danubes? Say, you *have* heard of Sandor Petőfi, the great 19th-century revolutionary poet from Hungary, haven't you?"

Hal had to admit he hadn't and that in fact his reading in European literature was fairly restricted.

"Well, he wrote a poem in 1848 that called for class uprising and the freeing of political prisoners. The refrain was 'We vow/We vow, that we will be slaves/No longer.' Powerful stuff, and nothing like it here."

"What about Whitman? People called him 'the poet of democracy,' and he certainly had a lot to say about politics and slavery."

Garrett took a large gulp of wine. "I stand corrected, though I've always thought his concern for others was bound up with his personal search for identity. I don't mean this as a criticism, but 'Song of Myself' trumps anything else in *Leaves of Grass*, doesn't it?"

Hal liked the way he avoided declaration with a question and that he seemed eager to hear a response. They talked about Whitman for an hour or more, downing a second bottle of wine with some chocolate torte. He knew Garrett wasn't queer and had mentioned a childhood sweetheart back in Virginia so he hesitated to bring the poet's sexuality to the fore. But Whitman's man-love vision was part and parcel of what he wrote, an opened vein in the blood flow of his vocabulary and images. How could he deny the many powerful lines in the poem Garrett had said was above the others? "You settled your head athwart my hips and quickly turned over upon me,/And parted the shirt from my bosom-bones and plunged your tongue/To my bare-stript heart."

When he offered the quote Garrett exclaimed: "But that's what I mean. It's Walt's immersion in the self. The lover is any lover, but the reception of his love is unique. He's being personally exact when he says: 'Through me forbidden voices' and 'Is this then a touch? quivering me to a new identity.'"

Hal was impressed that someone knew the poem as well as he did, but wanted to argue these sexual expressions allowed for an expansive voicing of America that stretched, like his own intended epic, from sea to sea even though, as far as he knew, Whitman had not been west of the Adirondacks. When he tried to convey this to Garrett, his new friend laughed and provided a final quote for the evening that both conceded Hal's point and kept his own intact: "'This heart's geography map,'" he said, and they raised their glasses to travels everywhere, real and imagined.

The next day Hal shared his own creative plans and read some passages from different sections of his ambitious but still-ragged draft.

"I really like the consistency of concept in these passages," Garrett said. "It's the bear that gathers together the different strands of history. But you shouldn't be afraid of what you were emphasizing about Whitman. Get more personal. I don't think you can sexualize the bear, but maybe from time to time your furry seer can get his human fellow-traveller to grasp some of the intricacies of resisting the straight-and-narrow of American existence. And I mean now as well as then."

3.

The first letter came from Miller not long before Christmas, sent on by his mother who attached her own note reminding him of her plans for a holiday visit. He'd put her off at Thanksgiving, not yet ready for a maternal invasion, telling her they'd have more time in December as the big day fell on a Saturday and the following Monday would be the Boxing Day holiday. The truth was he didn't know if he'd be ready for her even by then. His new life was running along an uneven but necessary track taking him further and further from Oak Park manners and family loyalties. There was the question of what to do with her. Certainly the Village would be out of bounds, and after turkey dinner and stuffed conversation at the cousins that was where he'd want to go. The museums would be closed that weekend, though surely there'd be a concert somewhere they could attend. Garrett, of whom she'd approve, was leaving for Virginia before her arrival and wouldn't be back until early January, which was just as well because there was supposed to be a big bash at the Black Rabbit on New Year's Eve. He hoped his mother would be gone by then, but if not she'd just have to accept that he wouldn't be in Times Square with her.

Miller's news was a breath of fresh air given the stultifying effect of the Oak Park missive. His words and images, as usual, were simple and direct and Hal could see and smell the heads of grain bursting as the Marines ran through the field. He could tell Miller was in his element with a small squad to command. He could keep his eye on each one of them and move quickly and surely with only five of them in his wake. Hal knew the war was messy and that people died horribly, but the letter's only real reference to this was in its brief, penultimate paragraph, and even that was muted. Elsewhere, the Crane and Tolstoy references provided distance and the one-line description of the forest made it sound like a Michigan wood in summer. He was more concerned with the features of the day-to-day—the characteristics of his men, the brothel girls, and the carousing—but of course these were food for his notebook that in turn was a rehearsal for finished stories to come. Hal was interested in the *Stars and Stripes* and wondered if it would accept anything more serious than sad hound material. The Chekhov story about the lady and her dog, for example. Miller could write something like that.

Unfortunately, the censors had been at work. They allowed the grain field and forest to stand but clearly didn't want the geography associated with specific troop positions. The last line of the letter, which Hal was sure was a return address, had been blacked out.

Dear Miller

I know you've got a big reputation, but if I send this off to 'Corporal Miller Sark, Somewhere in France,' it might not arrive before the war's over. Tell your censor-boys to provide a General Delivery site, maybe c/o one of those brothels you frequent. In the meantime, I'm writing anyway and will put a stamp on the envelope when Marine Command sees fit to reveal your location.

New York is a tremendously exciting place to be. I have a rather dull weekday existence in Brooklyn where I rent a room (Brooklyn Heights, actually) and a carpentry job. My Greek boss is a good man, and we get on famously, but conversation, morning and afternoon, is of the hammer and nail type or the price of butter or reports of German submarines off our coast. Like the Prince of Denmark, I may be able to tell 'a hawk from a handsaw,' but also like him I tend to see things more 'in my mind's eye' than in the hard and fast measurements of a carpenter's rule or plum bob. The outdoor life keeps me awake until the weekend when I get over to Greenwich Village. Existence over there is full of music and booze ...

He was going to say 'and women', as he knew he should, but couldn't push the lie.

and what brothels thrive on at home and abroad,

There was a lantern-jawed young actor at the Black Rabbit who, dressed in garters and stockings, would take you upstairs for an hour's private entertainment.

but most of all there's talk talk talk about poems and stories being published in little journals and magazines and what's good and not good in American writing. Speaking of that, you'd like Garrett, my rooming-house mate. He's a true literary type and wouldn't survive long in the wilderness, but boy does he know his stuff! I read him lines and stanzas from my notebooks and he lets me know why some things work and others don't. I'm sure he'd like the way you put words on the page because he's so straightforward and direct in everything he says. While he only writes criticism himself, he's convinced me that's a craft in its own right, provided there's no rancour or self-centeredness to it. When you and I get our books out, we'll need him and those like him to let the world know.

One thing I'm trying to do is create a dialogue between my bear and a human figure who turns up from time to time to expand though never undermine the animal perspective. It's a 'we're in this together' kind of thing when it comes to America. I'm still wandering all over the country, but every day I get more confident I'll be able to pull it together. It may take me years, but one thing I've got is lots of time. We'll get to the top, you and I, or die trying.

Keep your head down, and try to figure a way to let me know your whereabouts as you conquer Europe.

Hal

The truth was he had pages and pages of passages that he couldn't con-
nect. The bear's vision of the country's expansion, tempered by the view
of the Young Man he met periodically along history's trail, was the
bedrock of the poem, but there was so much to deal with that insight
tended to be overwhelmed by physical details. He thought it over and
shared his concerns with Garrett, and they both decided it would be
better for him to back off from the big picture and concentrate on a
specific period or event until he'd finished with that and could move on
to another. He shouldn't worry about doing this in any sort of chrono-
logical order because it wasn't clear yet whether the final version would
unfold in ordered fashion. So he could begin, for example, with the
Revolution or the war against the Indians in 1876. He needed to accept,
as he'd told Miller, that it was going to take years to complete, maybe
even a decade, but, said Garrett, if he could succeed there'd be no other
poem like it in America.

> *The only good Indian*
> *Is a dead Indian*
> *Phil Sheridan*
> *Told the world*
> *And Custer rode*
> *With that in mind*
> *While the bear clan*
> *Watched and waited*

> *Years later*
> *Brave Teddy disagreed:*
> *'Nine out of ten*
> *Would be fine' he said*
> *And charged the White House*
> *Aptly named*

4.

When his mother stepped from the train in Grand Central Station he saw a middle-aged, fashionable lady from a by-gone age whose comportment nevertheless suggested an inner strength and sense of purpose that had survived her era. He knew that purpose involved him and was determined to resist its potency.

"You've spent too much time outdoors," she said, noting his wind-burned cheeks and chapped lips.

"Hello, mother," he replied, bending down to kiss her cheek, The taste of rouge stayed on his lips as he decided to push back a little. "No more than in the woods last summer. Besides, I like my job. I spend a lot of time behind a desk in the evenings and on weekends as it is. I don't want to do the same in an office from Monday to Friday."

"Mmm. Of course you shouldn't."

The ambiguity of this response unsettled him. Was she criticizing his writing now?

"Well, dear," she said, "we'll talk things over once I get settled. But first I want to see your rooms."

He was about to correct her use of the plural, but that wouldn't help matters. She wasn't going to approve anyway even if he'd had the run of Mrs. Capalca's whole top floor. Insisting they should travel to Brooklyn by subway because she wanted to immerse herself in the city right away, she gave in only when Hal persuaded her that her two heavy suitcases would be a real impediment to their progress.

"How can I see to you and to your bags at the same time? Besides, it's getting on to rush hour, and you probably won't find a seat."

"Alright, but you must promise that starting tomorrow we go underground or by trolley."

He reminded her that the next day was Tuesday and he had to work right up until Christmas Eve on the coming Friday night.

"Surely your Greek man will give you some time off under the circumstances?"

Steve's circumstances were that he couldn't afford to slacken off on any job, and he was being very generous by allowing Hal the entire afternoon to meet and deal with his mother. "Go, go," he had said. "How often does your family come to town?" Hal knew the Boxing Day holiday on the Monday would be a sacrifice as well.

"It can't be done, mother. But I'll have the evenings with you and then the entire weekend." He didn't mention the extra day, which he'd set aside for the reading and writing time he'd lose with her.

"And then you'll be back at work."

"Yes."

There was a flash of restrained anger in the pursing of her lips, but then it was his turn to subdue his emotions as she announced that least they'd have New Year's together.

"You're not going home until after that?" he said, trying to keep an even tone.

"Not until the third of the month." She gave a little laugh. "I'm looking forward to seeing the ball drop at midnight and fireworks in Times Square."

Hal thought of his plans for the Black Rabbit that night that would involve explosions his mother wouldn't dream of. As for balls, the lantern-jawed actor had done things with his that were from another time zone altogether.

He hailed a Checker cab that took them slowly down Park Avenue onto 4th and then Bowery leading eventually to the bridge entrance. She'd been to New York as a girl and later with Hal's father when they were first married, but the height of the buildings and the amount of traffic clearly overwhelmed her, and she kept commenting on the sheer size of everything as the twilight came on. By the time they got to the bridge Hal was wishing he'd hefted the bags onto the subway and saved the five-dollar cab fare, but his mother's exclamations at the beauty of the structure almost made the surface trip worthwhile.

"We walked across, your father and I, back in 1895 on our delayed honeymoon. I'll never forget the sense of freedom I felt with the wind blowing back my hair, which had come unpinned. I'd taken off my hat and didn't care who saw me in such a state. Your father, of course, stayed every inch the gentleman even though I could see out of the corner of my eye that he didn't mind my behaviour one bit."

Hal had his doubts about such a story, but her enthusiasm won him over. "Isn't the view grand when the bridge macadam is under your feet," he said. "You feel as if all the city is waiting for you as you approach, and that life can be anything you want it to be."

She wasn't ready for such an embrace. "Oh, we were heading in the direction of Brooklyn, dear, so I didn't have the view you're describing. Later we took a cab back to our hotel in Manhattan. I just meant there was nothing like it in Oak Park, that's all."

But he wouldn't let her retreat. "Did you know, mother, that Roebling, the man who designed the bridge, died from a foot-injury infection while surveys were still going on. Then his son, who had taken over, got a disease from going down inside the caissons, the big concrete structures that anchor the bridge under the water. His wife, the son's I mean, supervised the construction for the next ten years. Quite an accomplishment for a woman in those days! Think of the freedom she felt up there on the towers!"

She murmured something he couldn't quite catch about a woman's place, and the ghost of Emily Roebling slipped away to haunt a more open-minded voyager across her domain.

In an aside at the station he had given the cab driver the cousins' address. It was enough to deal with his mother's direct presence in his life again, and he wasn't ready for the inevitable criticisms her inspection of his residence would bring. Mrs. Capalca had invited her to dinner during her stay, and he cringed at the certainty of social collisions with that worthy woman whose unpretentious, down-to-earth character would arouse his mother's bourgeois defenses. Not to mention her jealousy of a home-cooked Italian repast that would threaten whatever culinary expertise she thought she possessed. No, it was better to endure the rest of the day with the cousins who would be very much her ally in any encounter with immigrant life. He'd eat their overdone roast beef and sickly caramelized pudding just as he'd done when he first met them and respond politely when they asked him about his work. Anything to keep the wolf from his own door for as long as possible.

But the wolf was on the prowl as she made known her disappointment at not seeing his rooms right away, insisting they walk over after she'd rested a bit and filled the cousins in on her news.

"You don't need to go to any trouble for me," she said as they sipped coffee after the predictable meal, though he had to admit the wine had been decent even if doled out in pygmy-sized glasses. "As long as there's a comfortable chair for me to sit in I'll be fine."

The combined problem and saving grace of his room was that there was only the bed and a cane-bottomed desk chair to sit on. That meant his mother wasn't likely to stay long, but it also meant her complaints and criticisms would be amplified.

As they walked the few blocks arm-in-arm under lowering late afternoon skies she plied him with questions about his plans for the future.

"Surely you don't want to be a carpenter all your life?" The interrogative was barely perceptible.

"I'm not a carpenter, mother. I'm a writer who helps a carpenter out and makes a sufficient wage for room and board."

"But you couldn't support your writing without your funds from home?" Again, barely a whisper of actual inquiry.

What did she mean by 'home'? The money his father had given him was in a bank account that his mother drew on every month to send him the needed forty dollars. There was still three hundred remaining. "No, I couldn't," he answered. "But that's not an issue right now, is it?"

"So what will you do when the fund runs out?" This time a real question with a hint of aggression not far below the still-unruffled surface.

"I don't know yet. There's seven or eight months before I have to find a second job." That was a clear signal he was happy with Steve.

Just then a truck cut off a taxi at the intersection right in front of them. There was loud bang and subsequent cursing and he saw his mother wince under the four-letter blitz.

"Let's go this way," he said, leading her down a side street that would eventually bring them around to his place.

"There's another thing," she declared after they'd walked a block in silence. "You need to find a decent place to live."

"You haven't even seen where I am yet."

She looked up at the building walls beside and above her, their windows staring back blankly at this Midwest intruder who was judging their size and shape as well as the streaks of pigeon dirt—'shit, actually,' he almost said aloud—that ran down the brickwork in thick streaks rain never washed away.

"I can imagine it," she replied.

Mrs. Capalca, in anticipation of her honoured guest, had washed her living room curtains and hung a poinsettia basket in the front hall.

> *The red leaves bled*
> *Into surrounding air*

he said to himself

> *As he breathed*
> *His last transfusion*

Not very good, but he was dying the death of a thousand cuts, after all.

"How beautiful," his mother said of the flowering plant. Then he saw her take in the pile of galoshes by the door, the worn carpet, and the uncovered light bulb that lit the staircase. She raised her chin and sniffed twice, and he realized the pungent smell of garlic was leaking from the kitchen in back.

"That's my landlady," he told her. "Probably making some of her delicious spaghetti sauce. She's invited you to dinner, you know."

"Let's see your room, dear." He knew the singular now defined this place forever.

When he had opened his door upstairs she stood at the threshold for a few moments surveying the damage. He'd tidied up that morning. His bedspread was evenly in place, the extra blanket folded at its foot, and the papers on his desk neatly arranged in a small stack beside his dictionary. He'd even dusted the tops of his books in their row on the strip of sheet metal over the radiator. As he looked over her shoulder he could see one suspension cable of the bridge curving like a mythic cord between heaven and the river. Concentrating on this image, he followed her in, her low-heeled Mary Janes quietly tapping the bare floor until they stopped just short of his unlaced work boots protruding noisily from under the bed. She bent over and prodded the mattress then looked around helplessly for refuge. Quickly he pulled the chair out from his desk and with a sweep of his arm offered her a seat, feeling awkward, in his muteness, like a servant in the presence of a monarch used to cushioned thrones.

The queen sat there for a long time clearly absorbing this outlying and impoverished portion of her realm. If this was a hovel, he thought, it had a view to rival that from any palace, but he knew she was more concerned with its paucity of comforts and failure—or was it ironically its success?—in meeting her expectations. Finally, as he was about to ask her if he could make her a cup of tea on his hotplate, she sighed heavily and issued her edict.

"I want you to come home, Hal."

He'd been expecting disapproval and even reproach but not such complete censure of his new existence. He wasn't following an easy path and felt deserving of some credit for that, not outright rejection of his journey. She must have noticed the papers and books. Didn't she care about his creative efforts? As long as he was writing, what did it matter where he lived? As long as he wasn't destitute why should his accommodations mean so much to her? He was happy in this room, watching over the bridge or having it watch over him, talking to Garrett about literature and life, and following his bear across the country not like a hunter or scavenger but as a boon companion whose record of their travels would one day be recognized. There was no need to ask her why; he knew why. She wanted him presentable and conforming to Oak Park sensibilities which could only come about through living with her and seeking proper employment, the kind that would temper his poetic desires and perhaps even eliminate them altogether. So he simply refused her as she had refused him.

"No, mother. I can't do that."

"Of course, you can. Give up this ..."—she waved a hand imperiously—"this distraction, and settle into a real life."

"You mean a caramelized life in blinders!"

"What are you talking about?" she cried. "I want only what is good for you!"

"Then leave me here without any more judgement," he said. "I'll be fine."

She opened her mouth to reply, then paused. He could tell by the rapid blinking of her eyes and her clenched fists she was overwrought and without any flexibility, but he was nonetheless shocked by her eventual, tight-lipped pronouncement. "I'll cut off your funding, Hal. You have no legal control of it until you're twenty-one. How do you think you'll get by for the next six months?"

"You'd do that?" Part of his mind was racing with alternatives to his dependence on her charity. How much of a raise could he ask Steve for? Could he get some training somewhere that would help find him a job to bring in another thirty or forty a month? Maybe he could work in a bookstore on weekends. He knew everything there was to know about books, didn't he? The other part contained only anger that she would threaten him this way, and that was the part that won. So he lashed out with the biggest weapon he had.

"I can't ever come home in the way you want."

"Why on earth not?"

"Because I'm queer, mother." He picked up a paperclip from his desk and pulled the ends away from one another, twisting the wire into new shapes. "Bent like that."

"I don't understand," she said, her fingers tense against the grainy surface of the desk.

He could have backed off and quickly explained that he was just different from most of Oak Park society and couldn't fit in anymore, as in 'I'm a queer sort, mother,' and 'I'd bend too many rules.' He could see how vulnerable she was to any unexpected attack, which revelation of his true sexual nature certainly would be, and if he simply held her and stroked her greying head (despite the henna) she would be fine and laugh off the fright he'd given her. But then she'd just return to the attack, and how long could his commonplace defences hold out? That included his writing, he realized, because how many young men had come to New York to find fame if not fortune in the publishing world, their dreams of words gaining notoriety on the public page fading with their youthful aspirations. It was true he had been here for only a few months, but he had nothing ready for the little magazines and journals, let alone *Harper's* or *The Atlantic*. He was hanging by a creative thread, living purely on faith that what he was trying to write was worthwhile and one day he'd achieve the recognition he sought. How could he expect to convince her he was an exception to the usual rule of failure?

Garrett believed in him, and Miller wherever he was trying to survive. Miller! Now there was someone who wouldn't retreat from who he was or return to Oak Park or even the Michigan cottage to live, even though he had a special relationship with his father. He'd seize whatever opportunities were given him to further his ambitions and treat them as fodder for his fiction. I have to let her go, he thought, or I'll end up giving in and never finish the poem or begin a new one. Down through the history he was trying to chronicle countless sons and daughters had left home and moved on, not abandoning the past but placing it in a perspective that included those figures they had yet to become. The ones they *had* to become if life was more than mere repetition.

None of this would convince her, however. If he succeeded on the New York and eventually the national stage she would be very proud, but she was incapable of facilitating such accomplishment and able only to hold him back. He didn't think he was being unfair. She was basically a good woman, and he didn't blame her for her lack of vision that prevented any awareness of this room as a crucible of thoughts, feelings, and words that might yield coherent, long-lasting results. She saw the thin bedspread, the scuffed boots and floor, and even the view of the bridge itself through her son's grimy pane as rude reminders of a world that threatened her sense of refinement and stability. She wanted to rescue him from such a plight whose surface she only glimpsed and in whose depths he swam. What had Conrad's character said in *Lord Jim*? 'In the destructive element immerse.' He could see the copy of that novel lying on the mantel above the fireplace at the Sark cottage. On the flyleaf Miller's father had written: 'For my son, who would never abandon ship.' I'm just staying aboard, he told himself, though he was about to stir the still-flat sea into a tempest.

She took a handkerchief from her sleeve and wiped some invisible dust from her fingers she had lifted from the desk. In that instant, even though he had not yet uttered the unspeakable, he felt himself erased as if she was anticipating in her action the need to remove all traces of reprehensible matter from her person. Those same fingers he could not help thinking must have stroked the most private areas of his father's body before he was conceived, and now that he too was about to reveal himself before her they could never be cleansed.

"I mean I like men, mother, not women."

She dropped the handkerchief and gave a little scream. He thought she would fall from the chair and reached out to support her, but she gathered herself, patted her chignon, and said: "Nonsense, Hal. You're upset. I shouldn't have put things as strongly as I did." She looked up at him with a claiming smile. "You'll still have your allowance back home, you know, and if you like you can find your own place, though it would be sad if your tower bedroom went to waste." Despite the soft tone, it was a kind of ruthlessness he had to match.

"Can I bring a sailor home on weekends?"

She blanched and clenched her jaw. In his final act on her behalf he bent and retrieved her handkerchief, handing it to her as carefully as a loaded weapon. When she spoke the sneer in her voice was undisguised.

"You're disgusting," she said, her last spoken words to him.

Everything after that was a blur. She was going down the stairs before he could react, and he heard Mrs. Capalca greet her in the front hall. It must have taken all her iron will to respond politely to this swarthy woman whose apron bore inescapable kitchen smells and stains that represented her son's betrayal as much as any aspect of this obviously corrupt city. He didn't catch her reply but heard the door open and close immediately after. She'd never find her way back to the cousins alone, he realized, and ran downstairs to find his landlady with a puzzled look on her face as if she had been slapped with a courteous hand.

"What did she say?" he asked.

"She told me garlic always gave her gas and she couldn't accept my invitation."

When he opened the door, Ruth Pierce was stepping into a cab, mid-west hem swirling above her exposed heels.

As darkness fell, he sat in the kitchen and explained to Mrs. Capalca in a subdued voice that since his mother didn't approve of his life in New York he didn't think they'd be spending Christmas Day together, or the previous evening for that matter. Having absorbed the remark about the garlic and the disturbing condition of her favourite tenant, his landlady had some emotional indigestion of her own, but she rallied to insist that he spend the special day with her extended family of children and grandchildren at the boarding house.

"You know Mario and Guido live in Jersey and have three kids each. Did I tell you Maria's husband, Tony, is a pharmacist, and Guido, who's married to Sophia, drives a platform truck in a lumber yard? No? Never mind. We'll have turkey with all the trimmings, and you'll be our guest of honour! The kids make a lot of noise, but Christmas is really for them, isn't it, thanks be to God," she said, crossing herself. "They'll have lots of questions for you, the kids, I mean."

He hadn't met them all at Thanksgiving because he'd stayed in the Village, but whatever his plans for New Year's, Hal didn't want to be alone for Christmas. He'd always yearned to spend the holiday at Miller's place, laughing and talking, rather than in the enforced quietude of his mother's parlour interrupted only by the occasional visit of friends who stayed for a sip of sherry and slice of gossip. After his father had left, they sat there year after year while the kitchen help hired for that one day only prepared the meal. So, since he was never a little boy with parents who took their Santa responsibilities to heart, Christmas was a boring time of year when he listened to his mother and her visitors, melancholy hovering over their predictable exchanges like a bird of prey. For them only the sherry and forced good cheer held off the bird's dark descent, but there was no liquor for him to stave off the beating of wings as artificial laughter caught in their throats. Mrs. Capalca's kitchen and dining-room wouldn't be like that, and there would be good Italian wine rather than sherry. He thanked her profusely and gave her a hug. Why couldn't she adopt him?

At work the next day Steve inquired about his mother, and rather than go into any detail Hal made light of the situation. "She's under the weather and I'm not the right medicine for her, I guess."

Steve chuckled. "I loved my old lady, may she rest in peace, but I was always glad she never left Greece."

He spent Christmas Eve quietly reading in his room, eating his way through a bag of mixed nuts, sipping some eggnog Mrs. Capalca had provided and that he'd spiked with rum. After he awakened on the Saturday morning, he shaved, had a bath, and put on his best outfit, which consisted of trousers that had not quite lost their crease, a clean white shirt and checkered tie. Over this he wore a wool cardigan his mother had given him precisely one year ago. Down in the kitchen he made himself a cup of coffee and calmly anticipated the unfolding of the day. There were no expectations to be met, but he was curious about how he would fit in, an unmarried mid-west boy who didn't speak any Italian. Not only that, though he might learn Italian at some point, he'd never marry. Of course, he wouldn't make any announcement on the subject that or give any indication as to why this was so. Better to focus on his foreign language deficiencies. He'd be able to talk to Guido about his job. That lumber from his yard probably made its way into Steve's supply of boards. As for the pharmacist, well, maybe he read poetry when he wasn't filling prescriptions. Or maybe their wives had secret leather notebooks like he did, and they could share the pleasures of entries and revisions.

As it was, Guido was the cultured one, avid about ragtime and Broadway productions. Had Hal been to the new Belasco Theatre with its Tiffany lighting and wood panels? Mary Pickford had been wonderful there last fall in *A Good Little Devil*. His Sophia was warm and outgoing and put Hal at ease with her questions about his carpentry and how he found her mother-in-law's place. She was very attractive with her long curling tresses and high cheekbones, and he could imagine falling in love with her had he been so inclined. Maria and the chubby Tony were more reserved, perhaps a little suspicious as to why a boarder had no place to go on such a day even if he was fairly new to the city. Didn't he have any family here or friends? they asked. No, he told them, his family was far away. Yes, he had a good friend who also lived at the boarding house but was away in Virginia. They'd be spending New Year's together, he said. Fortunately, Mrs. Capalca, who knew of his mother's proximity and the date of Garrett's return, was fussing with the gravy and vegetables and didn't offer any correction.

It was the kids who made it all worthwhile. They'd already opened their presents at home, but there were still gifts from grandma, and Hal watched all six of them hungrily tear at the wrapping to find their dolls and tin soldiers ready for play. The three girls and three boys ranged from three to eight years and were allowed a freedom of movement and expression that Hal could only envy in comparison to his own childhood. Perhaps it was having siblings and cousins that made a difference, but he knew it was the loving matriarch of the house who allowed them to be their eager, happy selves. When he looked above their heads there was no dark bird, just a clear blue sky of present and future days.

After supper, which lived up to Mrs. Capalca's promise—turkey and potatoes smothered in gravy, turnips and green beans, olives and avocados, fresh-baked rolls, an original Italian pudding filled with raisins and pine nuts, and a fine Neapolitan red that he sipped fastidiously, determined not to become in the slightest way tipsy—and after the dishes had been rinsed and neatly stacked for washing, Hal swearing to no avail that he would gladly do them all, everyone gathered in the front room decked with ribbons and boughs of evergreen. It was apparently the custom in the family that on this special eve the parents and grandmother would each or together tell a story about themselves to the children. Hal listened as Guido and Sophia had their audience in stitches with their tale of mama trying to drive the platform truck one Friday night when she met papa after work and the boss was gone.

"It was lucky she ran into the wire fence," Guido said straight-faced. "Otherwise, she would have ended up in the river!"

Sophia's version was just as funny only quite different. She described the fence running into her and how she bent it back into place after its accident.

He wasn't expecting much from the more reserved Maria and Tony, but they managed to turn their rather patriotic account of their first visit to the Statue of Liberty into a hilarious lesson about biting off exactly what you can chew. It seems Tony, somewhat overweight already and puffing badly, sat down halfway up the stairs to the torch and demanded a treat if he was going to continue the trek to the top. He refused to budge, and Maria had to march all the way to the bottom and back again with a cone full of melting chocolate ice-cream.

Then it was grandma's turn, and she held them all in thrall with her memory of a village harvest festival when she was a girl. Musicians came from miles around, and she was allowed to stay up past midnight while the adults sang and danced, and the sound of clinking glasses rivalled that of the fiddles and tambourines as libations were poured to the gods of heaven and earth.

When she had finished to great applause, all the faces turned expectedly to him. "Your turn! Your turn!" the children cried. Flustered and unsure what he could possibly say to entertain them, he tried to beg off, saying his life had been much less interesting than theirs, but they refused his pleas.

"Think of something special you've done," Mrs. Capalca said, and the children nodded.

Taking a deep breath, he told them how one summer morning he and his good friend Miller had crossed the border river to the Canadian side and looked back to see the fire. "We knew we had to get out quick, so we swam for our lives, packed up our stuff and tried to get over the ridge." Then he got separated from Miller, who hurt his ankle, but heard his whistle through the smoke. When the wind shifted, he said, they were in great danger, but he was always sure they would get out safely because Miller knew the woods so well. The rapt looks of attention on the children's faces and even those of their parents and grandmother got him past this second fib of the evening. Downplaying his own role in their survival, he described how they'd both dug a trench and covered one another with dirt before they felt the flames pass over them.

"Was it very hot?" one boy asked.

"Yes," Hal said. "I bet you could have fried an egg on my back!"

That broke the tension, and all the kids said it was the best story they'd ever heard. He looked down at their beatific faces and for just one moment thought, peacefully and without self-recrimination: 'If I weren't a queer poet I could be a father.'

"Where's your friend now?" Guido asked.

"In a bigger fire, I think." And he told them what Miller had said in his letter about the grain field and the hill.

"May God protect him," Mrs. Capalca said, crossing herself, and everyone followed suit.

5.

Hal got riotously drunk on New Year's Eve. He had heard nothing from his mother and refused to attend the cousins' house where he knew a tearful, accusatory scene would unfold. Perhaps she had left early for Oak Park or perhaps she was waiting, maternal cudgel in hand, for his appearance and repentance on her doorstep. He felt guilty for having pained her so but liberated from her domination. He was who he was, and she would just have to accept it. If not ... well, if not he would get on without her. The idea frightened him. She was the only close family he had, though she couldn't match the open and generous domesticity of the Capalcas and their offspring. Of course, he'd just been a guest in their holiday household without any responsibilities except those of an entertainer whose story pushed his audience briefly beyond their regular bounds.

Work saved him that week. He, Steve, and Jimmy had a deadline to meet with the installation of flooring on two levels of a renovated house. After the Boxing Day break, they toiled ten hours for four days straight to finish the job. He had no energy left for thought and, after supper and a hot bath to ease his aching muscles and knees, he tumbled into bed each night grateful for the oblivion. The big party at the Black Rabbit was set for 10 p.m. on Friday, and he wondered if he'd be fit and present given his condition. Steve seemed to recognize that concern because when they were about to part, wishing each other well for the next year's new beginning, he told Hal not to hit the bottle too hard.

"You might enjoy yourself, but in the morning your head will be added to all that other soreness. Believe me, it's not worth it."

The unintentional sexual suggestiveness made him smile, but he knew the old man cared about him and realized he'd taken Steve's holiday for granted not having asked with whom he'd spent Christmas. Had he seen his son or daughter with the grandkids or been alone? It was time to make some amends. He couldn't take Steve to the Village, but he could buy him a drink—and Jimmy too—what about right now?

"Yeah, I think we all deserve a cold one after this week, though given the occasion I might have a brandy instead."

Jimmy begged off because he was meeting some friends, so Hal and his boss drove a few blocks to a whitewashed restaurant-tavern called The Spartan where they both had a five-star Metaxa that covered Hal's taste buds in pepper and cinnamon and his nostrils with the scent of roses. Steve told him his daughter and the big-shot banker had come down from Boston with the grandkids, so he'd had a good time. A waiter brought them a plate of black olives and some bread. Sitting there, listening to the click of dominoes and the Greek phrases from nearby tables while the liquor warmed his blood, Hal relaxed as he hadn't done since his mother's arrival, grateful to be included in a space that made no demands. Steve was clearly at home here, calling out to other patrons and clapping his hands at something they'd say. After a second brandy he asked Hal if he wanted to stay and eat with him but understood when he politely declined, explaining he'd be eating a lot later and should save his appetite.

"Drinkin', yes. But the food very little, I think," Steve replied, wagging his finger in admonition. "Remember the sore head. But, go on, you're young, and that's what nights like these are for."

"Will you stay here until twelve?"

Steve scoffed. "Twelve! I'll be asleep long before then. I can't remember the last time I saw the New Year come in. That don't mean I won't enjoy myself though." And he raised his hand for another Metaxa.

As he walked the several blocks to his room, Hal thought for the first time about finding a space in America that would welcome him for more than an afternoon or evening, one quite separate from the demands of having to earn a living and the physical and mental price paid to them. Garrett had mentioned writers' grants that were available for short periods of support. You had to have a project you were working on and he certainly met that qualification, but to be seriously eligible he had to get some work published in recognized venues. Resolving to discuss the literary marketplace with his friend when he returned and to focus on some short lyric pieces he could send out, he turned his attention to the night at hand.

As it happened, he met some Village acquaintances who steered him to the Artists' Club just before ten o'clock, telling him the Black Rabbit party wouldn't really get started for another hour and was going to continue until dawn, so why not soak his mind for a short time before he drowned his body? He was sceptical of the reward but went along, deciding to have a coffee before he indulged in anything stronger, the after-taste of the brandy still lingering.

Someone in the crowd introduced himself and told him Margaret Anderson's *The Little Review* had just moved to the Village from Chicago and was looking for contributions. The journal was going to serialize a new novel by James Joyce. Had Hal read his *A Portrait of the Artist as a Young Man*? 'Simply splendid,' the man said rather pompously. When Hal said no, he hadn't, he was advised to begin with Joyce's short story collection, *Dubliners*, especially the last long tale, "The Dead." Despite the expense, he resolved to buy both books the next week, then, feeling entirely ignorant, asked the man what poets had appeared in *The Little Review*.

"Why everyone!" came the astonished reply. "Pound, Lowell, Doo-little—you know, the one married to Aldington—and lots of new ones. You should get in on it."

Hal discovered during a few more minutes of conversation that Garrett had spread the word he was working on a 'big' poem about America.

"If they'll serialize Joyce," the man said, "maybe they'll do you as well."

Buoyed by the prospect but well aware of his minor status as a writer, he downed his coffee and headed for the other half of his life.

Perhaps it was his guilt over his mother, perhaps his insecurity about his writing future, but after staying reasonably sober until the first stroke of 1918 he then made every attempt to obliterate the Hal who had always feared her disapproval and the one who wrote alone yet was desperate for the wide world's esteem. The club was overflowing with customers pressed together like sardines in a can, but instead of folded gills there were open hands everywhere. More than once he closed his legs against assault, more than once he opened them to the promise of gratification. He drank copiously until he couldn't taste what was in his glass and the scent of roses was replaced by the stench of breath too close to his own lips and demanding entrance. At some lost point he felt himself being half-carried downstairs and out a door. Then he was stumbling along an alley through puddles and waste while dirty words sang around him and laughter chopped at his head until he realized it was his own axe he was wielding and there was no way to put it down. He hacked and hacked in manic display so that breath could find its way in not just his mouth but his eyes and ears and finally that compliant part of his body that mothers and poems could never mention. Hours later on a mattress of splintered bottles, he stared brokenly at the morning sky and wept.

Flowers of glass
Beneath him lie
Colour like petals
The morning mud

Snapping a calyx
From nameless mast
To hold it high
Above his blood

In alley's bone
Six children cry
To hear his tale
And call him home

6.

Two letters from France arrived months apart. The first contained a baseball story written for *Stars and Stripes*, a note that said only "Keeping my hand in," and a scrawled signature. Hal read the piece with interest, noting Miller's usual attention to detail and how the hilarious sporting contest, if you read between the lines, emphasized that allies who could play together would probably win the war. The second letter told a darker tale as it was clear Miller and his men were on the very eve of battle and there were no punches to be pulled about danger and death. Hal could sense the reference to the 'beauty spot' in the whore was an insistence that survival was possible and prayed that his friend had made it across the grain field and into the relative safety of the trees he'd mentioned previously. From all the newspaper coverage of American triumph it must have been Belleau Wood he'd been talking about. The AEF post office had held on to the second letter until the battle was over because now there was a return address on the packet that read '9th Infantry, 5th Marines' and the name of a French town. Refusing to contemplate the worst, he wasted no time in writing back, discarding the first attempt that was still in its stamped envelope.

> *Dear Miller*
>
> *The powers that be blacked out your address in your first letter and I've only just received your second plus your baseball story. The latter is terrific, and I hope you're getting a chance to do more reporting, whether from ball games or ...*

he almost said 'whorehouses' but caught himself

> *the front line. I especially like your description of the French shortstop picking up a grounder and stopping to take a puff on his cigarette before he throws the ball to first. The Yankees could use him this year. I didn't get anything from you about an Ojibway girl, but maybe it'll turn up. I guess, such times aside,*

*it's pretty rough over there, and my life here in Brooklyn is a
cinch in comparison. My weekday reveille is 6 a.m. when I rise,
eat a quick breakfast, and head off to whatever place I'm helping
build or repair. My boss Steve, a Greek-American, is a good man
with a heart of gold. He and his nephew and I are quite the
carpentry crew, and when you get back I'll show you a few of the
sites we've hammered and sawed. The outdoor life, as you know,
is much better than working inside all day, and most of the time
I have splendid views of the East River and the Brooklyn Bridge
from upper floors and roof tops. I live in a boarding house run by
an Italian widow who feeds me and includes me in her family
gatherings, which is a good thing since I appear to have broken
off with my mother who expected other directions for my life*

he wasn't going to say what his own particular direction was, not now
at least

and stormed back to Oak Park after an aborted Christmas visit.
 Garrett's already steered me to The Little Review *where he
works, which has just moved to New York. I'm going to submit
some shorter pieces (I include one here) and maybe even part of
the bear poem. It—the bear—is still spread all over the map and
I wish you were here to advise me on how to say more with less.
I've recently learned* The Dial *in Chicago (publishers of Yeats
and Anderson, among others) is starting up an annual award of
$2000 for published writers, so you and I had better get busy.
Wouldn't it be great to have that kind of dough to live on for a
year! From what the newspapers say, your great victory at
Belleau Wood brought the Germans to their knees and the
war could be over soon. When that happens be sure to tell me
when you'll be hitting the streets of Manhattan.*

 Hal

*P.S. What's the French girl's name? If you're going to get married
over there I'll have to come to Paris.*

Sporting his degree from Boston College, Garrett had marched into the Village offices of *The Little Review* soon after his return from Fredericksburg and convinced Margaret Anderson to hire him as an assistant editor. He brought previous issues home and Hal was able to read stories and poems by those writers the man at the Black Rabbit party had referred to. He also found a copy of *Dubliners* at Frank Shay's bookstore and read "The Dead," which stunned him with its devastating portrait of human frailty beneath mortality's weight. The final lyrical scene in which Gabriel Conroy imagined the snow falling on the living and the dead all over Ireland was so powerfully evoked he couldn't imagine finer writing anywhere. These pieces reminded him how far he had to go, but Garrett was eager to help and when Hal showed him his poem beginning "Flowers of glass," he declared it was good enough to appear in the magazine.

"What's the title?"

He thought it over. Titles had never seemed important. "It might be part of a sequence. I don't know yet." Then, remembering the nightmare site that had released the words, he said: "Let's call it 'Passageways.'"

Margaret Anderson agreed with Garrett's judgement, and Hal sent a quick note off to Miller with a copy of the poem. "I'm getting busy, so delve into your notebook."

In the Mirror

1.

He'd had two days in New York with Hal before boarding the troop train back to St. Louis where he'd been discharged. His knee was healing slowly, but he still used a cane to get around. The doctors said bits of shrapnel would be working their way out for years to come. There was other stuff inside him as well. After the medics had found him, he was taken back to the hospital in the town, half-conscious and unable to recall his wounding. Apparently, he told them the others were all dead, but he couldn't remember their names or give any details. There was a snake crawling somewhere, but it was crazy to think so, and he felt awfully bad as the one survivor. He did recall fragments of an exchange about shooting someone, but whoever he was talking with had no face or a face he didn't recognize, and after a while he stopped trying to figure it out. The morphine kept him groggy, but eventually they cut back the dosage and his mind cleared a little. Some officers came by and told him he'd been recommended for a medal.

"What for?" he asked.

"Even with that knee, you somehow kept going," they said. "You were the first on the summit. You shot three Germans before you passed out from blood loss."

"They should all get a medal," he said.

For a moment they thought he meant the enemy and didn't understand.

"My men," he told them. "The ones who died."

The older colonel in charge chided him. "You get decorated for killing not dying, Corporal." His juniors, discomfited by such bluntness, looked away.

"Fuck you," Miller said, but they had turned to other business in the ward.

Hal seemed in great shape when they met, though very much the civilian. His physical labour was obviously doing him good and he was making some inroads into the New York publishing world. In the hospital Miller had read "Passageways" and thought it strong if a bit obscure. Thank God he wasn't a poet and could write things down as they were, not filtered through endless sensibility that suggested without ever confirming. That was harsh judgement to be sure, and he believed Hal was destined for great things, but he wanted a bigger audience and the only way to get that was by stripping away embellishments and talking straight to the reader.

They'd discussed their future plans over a few beers in a Brooklyn tavern and then at a nearby restaurant where they went through three bottles of wine with their meal, his knee aching despite the vintage anaesthetic. Miller was aghast at the price of each bottle of red.

"I could drink for a week in France on what it's cost us tonight."

"What it's cost me. You're the returning hero and deserve to be fêted."

Miller shook his head. "A hero sets out to do things. Like write a great book, for example. Up on that hill I didn't set out to do anything at all." After his obscenity that the Colonel didn't hear, he'd kept quiet about his citation for bravery, and this was the first time he'd tried to convey how he saw the actions for which he'd been rewarded. If honesty wasn't about blowing your own horn, it also wasn't about keeping everything to yourself, especially with your best friend, but he wanted to put it on the page, which would demand a different kind of truth. On the ship bits and pieces had started to come back to him from that final day, though there was no overall clarity yet.

He took the medal from his uniform chest pocket and held it out, a bronze cross beneath blue and white ribbon. "That's what five men look like in the end. You keep it for me, Hal. I can't carry them around with me like this."

Hal protested, of course, but was finally convinced Miller would otherwise throw it away. "I'll find a case for it. You can have it back whenever you want."

There was a decent chance of a job at a St. Louis newspaper, he said. "I'll show them the *Stars and Stripes* story and some pieces about the fighting I worked on aboard ship. Of course, I can always cover the fire beat given our experience up on that ridgeline. Well, I'll do anything to get started. I've got to make a living so I can buy time to do the stories I have in mind. Anyway, tell me about your work. I liked that poem you sent me, the one about the alleyway. Has it been published?"

"It's coming out in *The Little Review*. The issue after the next. I'm writing more short poems. That's the way to get known."

"What about the bear?"

Hal told him of Garrett's advice to finish individual sections of the epic one by one. "Even so, it's going to take me years. There's so much I want to say in it. Now there's the war, for example."

"What do you know about the war?" He'd snapped it out but was a little angry.

Hal flushed. "Not like you, obviously, but what do I know about the Civil War or the Indian conflicts? I wasn't there, was I? Come on, Miller, the imagination's worth something."

"You should write about what you know, Hal. You were on the ridgeline. That was first-hand experience. That was your war."

Now it was Hal's turn for anger, and the force of it surprised him. "That's just stupid, Miller. If writers restricted themselves to first-hand experience we'd have isolated historical commentaries that weren't connected. Look at Crane, for Christ's sake! He made up Henry Fleming and his war from things he'd read and imagined."

He knew this was right, but what he remembered of the grain before and after the onslaught had taught him you had to have been there to really nail it. Crane had written a great book, but Miller Sark was going to write a greater one because he'd draw on more than the imagination. He'd make a partnership with words and promise never to betray them through phoney ornamentations or visions. Meanwhile, miles away in his own territory of expression, Hal was waiting for his reply. They wouldn't see each other again for months, probably longer, whatever promises they made. There was no need to lob any shells behind his defences.

"I'm sorry, Hal. I know you're on the right track. Different ways of doing the same thing, that's all." He put out his hand. "C'mon, old pal, shake on it."

Hal smiled. "'I see us matched with fair/bright rivals, and I see/ those lesser rivals flee.' Hilda Doolittle with just one word changed." Then he added in a strangely pompous voice: "She married Aldington."

Over another glass of wine he told Hal about Amélie and her fiancé, Georges. "I think he was her pimp," he said with more bitterness than he thought was left in him from the affair. "After that first day in the field I forgot all about her." That wasn't the case, of course, since he'd talked about her in the letter he wrote in his head that Hal never got to read, the one in which he must have described the snake and how Munson had been at the tail and got killed. That was after Scott and Davis, wasn't it? His promise to drag her along with his men and make them into an unbreakable chain of words had jumped out at him at sea. Wasn't in the letter that he'd told Hal he'd have a 'love-'em-and-leave-'em' attitude towards women from then on? Well, he'd find more than one woman in St. Louis that was for sure.

"What about you? You must be stepping out after all this time in the big city?"

Hal took a big gulp of wine. "There's a good crowd in the Village," he said. "I'll show you some places there tomorrow. But, no, I haven't got anybody right now."

Miller pondered this and concluded his friend needed to take the bull by the horns—or, more to the point, the cow by the udder. He was shy, that's all, and focused too much on his work. There was a time and place for everything. In the Marines they called it a furlough when they went to the brothel.

To give Hal some breathing room, he asked about his mother. "What made her drop you like a hot potato? It always seemed to me she liked to hold on even when her palm was burning."

Hal didn't answer him directly, but he put it down to those years of dependence on her, ones that couldn't allow any insult.

"Wrong shape of spud, I guess," Hal said, and maybe his laughter went on too long. "Seriously, though, she wanted me to settle down, get married, and give her grandkids. I told her I wasn't ready."

The next afternoon they went to a post-Impressionist show at the Metropolitan.

"It's all gone, now," Miller said as they stood before van Gogh's *Wheat Field with Reaper.*

"What is?"

"The old France. The one where the light blessed everything."

"Remember when you threw me in the lake so things wouldn't sneak up on me? Well, they snuck up on me over there."

"You swam through them alright didn't you?"

He wanted to say some part of him had drowned even as he'd kept his head above water. But if he admitted that out loud he'd lose sight of the other swimmers altogether. "Yeah, I did," he lied.

His trip home to see his father was relaxing except for that one brief exchange. Henry Sark knew better than to quiz him about his experience at the front but was solicitous about his wound. Because of his knee they couldn't hike anywhere to fish and had to be satisfied with throwing their lines in from the dock or canoe. Miller told him of his newspaper plans, and the old man approved. He wasn't an old man really, just a weathered woodsman who'd lost a step or two since he'd initiated his son in the ways of the wild. It was good to have a week with him in and around the cottage where so much of his boyhood had unfolded. How he wished he had the strength to take the train north and tramp up to the border river. There'd be new vegetation growing on the ridge and the fish would be jumping. But, of course, Hal wouldn't be there, so it wouldn't be the same.

2.

His boarding house in the Little Bohemia district of St. Louis was bigger than the one Hal had described in Brooklyn Heights. A dozen or so young men gathered each night around the dining table to share the tureens of soup and stew produced by the elderly owner with the unpronounceable last name.

"Call me Magda," she told him with no trace of an accent. "Everyone else does." She had been born in a country village outside Warsaw, married young, and came to the States when she was barely out of her teens. Her husband Mike had worked in the stockyards for years and now retired spent most of his time in the local tavern playing cards. They had four children and many grandchildren who turned up at the house from time to time but kept mainly to the kitchen. Despite her otherwise flawless English, she called him "Meeller," praised him unreservedly for serving his country, and always gave him the largest helpings at the table.

His room was in the southwest corner of the third floor with a view over the rooftops towards the downtown. Along with his bed, chest of drawers, and a small table he used as a desk there was a comfortable armchair in which he could sit and read. That's what he did in the evenings after supper when he'd spent the day exploring the city, mostly riding the trolley because of his knee, which was slowly improving but pained him if he stayed on his feet too long. Sometimes he'd wake at night and feel it locked into a position he knew he'd have to change or he wouldn't be able to walk easily in the morning. So he'd cup it between his hands and gingerly turn it one way or the other until the pressure eased and he could sleep again. From trolley windows he saw the Anheuser-Busch brewery on South Broadway, the stockyards and rows of packing houses, and the vast parkland that had been the site of the 1904 World's Fair. There was an openness to the city's layout he liked, which was expanded by the meeting of the two great rivers, one carrying the residue of six states in the culmination of its twenty-five-hundred mile flow and the other only halfway on its storied journey to the sea.

After two weeks of such R & R he made an appointment and went down to the editorial offices of the *Post-Dispatch* carrying his *Stars and Stripes* story in a folder along with the pieces on the fighting he'd mentioned to Hal. He thought about wearing his uniform, which he was entitled to do, but didn't want that to be a factor in any hiring decision. They'd find out soon enough from his subject-matter that he was a veteran, but it was the writing itself that would have to win them.

He sat on a wooden bench in a hallway watching people rush back and forth with sheaves of papers in their hands, some occasionally stopping to take a pencil from behind an ear and mark copy against a wall or a willing colleague's back. The turmoil didn't bother him. All he'd need was a desk and a typewriter, though his two-finger method was rather slow. As he'd told Hal, he was willing to work in any section so long as he got to write stories. If they didn't think he was good enough he'd try some place else. There were the *Globe-Democrat* and several prominent weeklies, and if that didn't pan out he could always apply to be a local correspondent for a paper out of New York or Chicago. But it was the *Post-Dispatch* with the Pulitzer legend behind it that he really wanted to be part of.

"Miller Sark?"

The man was a few years older than him, tall and thin with a receding hairline and the beginnings of a moustache. When Miller stood to shake his hand, he introduced himself as Dan Fitzgibbon. "The receptionist has passed you on to me," he said, "so I guess this is your lucky day."

"Why's that?"

"Well, I presume you want work as a reporter. The usual judges of your ability would be very wary of competition, but me, I'm a cartoonist so unless you can draw and have a certain level of wit in you there's no need for worry."

Miller was puzzled and annoyed. What would a cartoonist know about the quality of his writing? Were they trying to discourage applicants? If so, they should just say straight out that there weren't any openings. He was about to turn and leave when Fitzgibbon said: "I was at the Art Institute of Chicago. We had to provide succinct and credible descriptions of paintings and photographs as part of our training. So, to paraphrase the Mad Hatter, 'I can tell a raven from a writing desk.'"

Encouraged by the literary reference and the man's background in art, he followed him into a cramped office with an oversized cartoon on one wall of a youth in pince-nez creeping away from a Massachusetts recruiting station in the Civil War. He looked like a coward until you read the caption: 'I'd rather be in the Lincoln Brigade.'

"That soldier-to-be is the original Pulitzer, Joey the German, long before he bought this paper and a few others. Right off the boat from Hungary and only seventeen he served in the Lincoln cavalry for the last eight months of the war. The cartoon got me this job. I guess his son admired the likeness. Anyway, you didn't come here to talk about me or Mr. Pulitzer Sr. What have you got to show me?"

Miller handed over the folder and watched as Fitzgibbon read the baseball story, chuckling as he did so and muttering a few French words in accompaniment. "It's very funny," he said, "but very poignant as well. The last inning for so many of them, wasn't it?"

"Yes, we never got to play another game. There wouldn't have been enough of us after Belleau Wood." He hadn't meant to say anything about where he'd been unless asked directly and was angry at drawing attention to himself in such fashion. But the cartoonist had moved on to the remaining pieces and appeared not to have heard. He took his time, which Miller appreciated, although each of the vignettes about the fighting was no more than a brief paragraph or two in length. He had laboured for hours on them, carving and shaping the actuality and mood from the intense experience he had endured. After a long time, Fitzgibbon put the folder down on his desk. "I've never read anything quite like it," he said. "You take me there and leave me there. It's dangerous stuff."

At first he was pleased, but in the ensuing silence became concerned that he'd overwhelmed his reader who wouldn't be able to make an objective judgement about his work. "I haven't finished them yet," he said defensively to buy them both time. Fitzgibbon didn't reply, but from his air of concentration appeared to be thinking things over, and this was confirmed when he finally declared: "I see what has to be done here."

Before he could respond, Fitzgibbon made him an outright offer of twenty-five dollars a week as a junior reporter, probably in the sports pages because there was an opening there and he obviously knew baseball. But he would only be hired if he agreed to keep working on the vignettes and would allow the paper to publish them as a series beginning as soon as possible. "I'm prepared to recommend this, at least. But the big boys usually take my advice. What do you say?"

He was assigned to cover the Browns and Cardinals who were sharing Sportsman's Park that year, which meant he could see American and National league games from one press box. Both teams were mediocre overall, but each had an outstanding player who made every plate appearance worth watching. Gorgeous George Sisler, or Gentleman George as some called him, was the Brown's first baseman and a born batter who looked capable of breaking Cobb's single season hit record and could steal bases as well. But the true boy wonder was the younger Rogers Hornsby, the Cardinal's shortstop who hit for average and had real power from the right side, though the park favoured left-handed swingers.

There was a game almost every day, and as his knee improved he began to walk partway to the park, arriving as the players took batting practice, talking with a few of them, and making his way upstairs to the narrow press room behind and above home plate. There a half-dozen reporters, including those covering the visiting team, sat before cups of coffee, boxes of doughnuts, and typewriters, banging out stories as they unfolded, each trying to outdo his colleagues and rivals with purple descriptions of brush-back pitches, collisions on the base-paths, and the soaring arcs of occasional home runs into the bleachers. He was much less effusive and got compliments from the players who appreciated his acknowledgement of their daily grind.

> Just as the grain in the bat's white ash can determine the flight of a ball, so the grain of a man's character can determine the path of his career. Sometimes a professional team is not successful but the individuals on it are because they do not flinch from fastballs or worry about broken bones as they slide into second or defy gravity in pursuit of flies or grounders. These are men who leave a mark on the basement walls if not the upper floors of a season's structure, and their efforts deserve our recognition and applause.

Fitzgibbon badgered him about the war sketches, and he began to work carefully on the eighteen drafts he had one by one. Almost everything that had been missing or blurred came back clearly to him—the surprisingly quick fall of Scott, the disappearance of Davis, crawling through the field with the three others and Munson's death, then the encounter with the German sniper in the woods. Only the action on the hill remained hidden. He could now remember himself, Kincaid, and Rawley at the bottom but not anything that happened after that. Of course, he'd been told of his reaching the summit after the shrapnel had torn into his knee and what he'd done to the three Germans in a bunker there, but he couldn't write about an official report that gave reasons for his medal so he had to find another way to deal with his apparent heroism. What he did do first of all was cut everything extraneous away from his basic description of fear, indecision, and fierce bonding with his five companions. There was some dialogue, but most of it took place inside his head as he wondered which way to lead them and where the best cover was. He tried to bring out in a few brief images the essence of each man—Scott's physical presence and dependability; Davis's grounding in his northwest outdoor origins; Munson's slightness belied by his dogged determination; Kincaid's absolute refusal to compromise; and soft-spoken Rawley as the decent centre of their increasingly restricted universe.

He began in the camp and town when they were still untested, briefly alluding to the ways they found to relieve their tensions. Although he never used the word "whore," he didn't disguise the soldier's need for female company and, drawing on his best memories of Amélie, indicated to his readers that if he had not been fired by passion in the nights before the battle he would have faced the enemy with far less belief in his cause. It was a great chance he took as with one swift image he suggested patriotism was braced by carnal touch:

Her body finally covered me like a flag.

"It won't fly," Fitzgibbon told him when Miller read him the passage concluding with these words. "I might as well draw the literal depiction of what you're saying. How far do you think I'd get with that no matter how true it might be? Maybe if you were writing fiction, but you're not. Decorated war heroes don't talk like that in what our subscribers like to think is real life."

That night he tried to push Amélie into the distance and find another way of joining his intimate pursuit to the great cause. But the longer the flag as sexual icon stayed with him the more he realized it was the right emblem for the wrong place. Fitzgibbon had told him where it belonged, so he XXX-d it out on the typewriter and wrote it by hand on a clean notebook page, the first or last line of a story yet to come.

He didn't glorify their deaths because he said glory was irrelevant when a man's life was wasted, but he did make their loss personal by describing his shock when the seemingly invincible Scott fell and how Munson touched the slug on his hand before he died. Davis, he wrote, simply disappeared after his mock salute, which seemed impossible when all he wanted to do was take Miller up one of his fast-water Oregon rivers and show him Mount Rainier's snowy peak high above. As for Kincaid and Rawley, he'd been told the pile of rocks where they'd died was almost half-way up the hill and only after that did the reports say he was alone. What he did at the summit, he wrote, any one of them would have done, and he took no credit for his blind achievement. He had been lucky, that was all, and a man needed luck in war when all the things he had relied on had been destroyed. Fitzgibbon agreed that since the war was over those still in command wouldn't blame him for being a hero who hadn't acted primarily as a result of his training and pride of country, but one who emphasized instead his supposedly courageous actions were the result of loyalty to his men. What offset such a vexed issue, Fitzgibbon said reassuringly, was the central story of the German sniper.

It was the longest piece but still no more than a few hundred words. Miller indicated how, despite the three of them having been pinned down in the beech and oak, their semi-circle approach with him in the middle had succeeded in bringing the man down from his limbed perch. He was badly wounded and entreated Miller through hand gestures to end his misery, but Kincaid and Rawley had dissuaded him, and all three of them, still under fire, tended his wounds until he died. That was what you did sometimes, he wrote, believing it as if it had happened. You tried to save your enemy because he was you in a mirror world, and if you shattered the glass with a shot something in you would die as well.

It was a fine sentiment whose integrity was sustained by the forceful description of those fateful moments, but of course, whatever his powers of persuasion, it wasn't true. Why didn't he write about the bear and how it ran through his thoughts as he watched the dying man or about Kincaid and Rawley's very different reasons for letting him live? Well, few would understand his lingering alone with the German then walking away, and Hal especially would not condone this. But you didn't shoot a man in cold blood the way you shot an animal no matter the circumstances. Oh really? Wasn't that their action in bringing him down from the tree? No, they'd been defending themselves then, but afterwards when the German lay defenceless before them there was no more heat of the chase just calculations about suffering versus survival and, of course, murder versus mercy. Rawley had come down on one side, but had he called it right? Burning with uncertainty and ambition, Miller saw how he could complicate such plain oppositions with further fictions though it might take a novel not a journalistic vignette to achieve any resolution. For the first time writing truthfully wasn't necessarily the same as writing what was true.

> *The German looked at me as if I had betrayed him, but I was loyal to something other than his desire to die. It seemed as if in that forest glade life of any kind was at a premium, and we were determined to preserve it.*

It would do for now.

"The three of you deserved medals for that," Fitzgibbon declared.

After filing a report each evening when a home game was over, he usually went out for a beer with his fellow scribes or listened to ragtime and band music at an outdoor site near his boarding house, surprising himself by preferring free-spirited New Orleans rhythms to Sousa's formal marching melodies. In the mornings he'd work on the vignettes for a couple of hours before heading to the park once again. Though neither the Browns or Cardinals finished above .500, something interesting always occurred there, like reliever Rasty Wright getting three outs on three pitches in the bottom of the ninth or Hornsby telling him "I can't remember anything that happened before I had a baseball in my hand" and then being handed a message that his brother had been shot and killed in a Texas saloon.

The real news of the season was the Black Sox scandal in the World Series. Miller had covered the games, taking the train to Cincinnati three hundred miles away and wiring his reports in time for the early edition. Before the best-of-nine competition started there were ru-mours of a fix, but it was hard to believe enough members of a profes-sional team could be bought, especially the stars of south-side Chicago who had been world champions two years before. Left fielder Joe Jack-son had hit .351 after taking a year off because of the war, second base-man Eddie Collins had a .400 on-base percentage, and pitcher Eddie's Cicotte's record was a stellar 29-7. But all the players rubbed shoulders every day with gamblers and gangsters in the crime-ridden city, and once things got underway it was difficult to ignore unforced errors and plain lousy efforts. Lefty Williams lost three games in a row by throw-ing fastballs Miller could have wacked over the fence, and Cicotte lost two, including game four in which he made two crucial fielding mis-takes that had the home fans booing. When it was all over, Hugh Ful-lerton of the *Chicago Herald & Examiner* wrote openly that the Series had been "thrown" and said that in his opinion it should never be played again. Still somewhat sceptical, Miller pointed out in his sum-mary that the Sox had one less error than the Reds and only five fewer hits in eight games, but he was eventually reduced to defending Jackson who, despite a .375 average and setting a Series record for hits, would be banned for life along with seven others. There was something about the South Carolina country boy that reminded him of Rawley.

In the final vignette, the one about his hill-top accomplishment, he took a different approach, putting himself into the third-person and creating a dream-like state for his protagonist who left his dead companions below as he crawled up the hill with his perforated knee-cap, shot three German machine-gunners at point-blank range with his .30.06, then woke up in a field hospital surrounded by a group of congratulatory officers.

When he opened his eyes he didn't know where he was. There was a dull feeling in his head as if he were hung-over. Someone in the grinning circle said he was a hero. It had to be a mistake, he thought. The last thing he remembered was coming out of the forest and seeing the steepness of the hill.

In November, a year after the armistice, Fitzgibbon told him. "We're going to start running them next week. I've been feeding them to the editorial board all along, and they think they're worth a Pulitzer nomination. We'll wait for the public response, naturally."

He was very happy when the first one appeared on the front page beneath a brief introduction by Fitzgibbon, though he didn't like the title they'd given the series, "Belleau Wood Warriors." The reason for their choice, of course, was that any large-print tribute to apparent heroism would sell papers. At first it was only his restrained prose that attracted attention because he was describing behind-the-line perspectives, but after a few days it became evident to readers his subdued outlook and vocabulary reflected a cynical attitude towards the violence while underscoring the basic decency of those he commanded. The debate began in letters to the editor as to whether someone in charge, if only of a squad of five, should detach himself from a sense of duty and patriotism the way he had done. More than one correspondent accused him of downplaying the sacrifice his men had given in death, even of betraying it. But others lauded him for telling the truth as he saw it on the battlefield and refusing to 'go over the top' in his writing the way troops had been ordered at Ypres and the Somme, if not at Belleau Wood because there had been no deep trenches there. By far, his refusal to shoot the German sniper drew the greatest reaction. Readers were fascinated by his self-control under duress and by the shared humanity of Rawley and Kincaid whose origins he had revealed to the extent that he knew them.

His basically fictional passage about the summit had furthered his ambitions to attempt a novel, one in which he would reveal the journey of a character from training camp to medalled achievement, his view of the war growing less jingoistic and assured as he plodded with several others toward his last battle. He wouldn't pull *any* punches when he wrote this, so bodies in love and slaughter would be covered by the same flag.

In the spring he won the Pulitzer in the Feature Writing category for his "distinguished work giving prime consideration to high literary quality and originality," and between this and national syndication he was suddenly famous. The paper offered him a $15.00 a week increase and his own byline in the editorial section. New York publishers contacted him asking if he had any book plans. The telegram from Hal was special.

I ALWAYS KNEW YOU HAD IT IN YOU STOP
DON'T LET ANYTHING DISTRACT YOU FROM
WHAT YOU CAN DO NOW STOP

But a month later a personal letter arrived from Ocracoke Island, pleasing and troubling him at the same time.

Dear Mr. Sark,

I am grateful for your portrait of my son Armistead. He was a good boy and did not deserve to die the way he did. I am living here permanently now with my sister, and if you ever visit the Outer Banks you would be most welcome in our home.

Yours truly,

Anna Mae Phillips

Her sentiments were very special, but had he betrayed Rawley by not remembering his end, and could he ever look this woman in the eye if that were so? "Geez, Miller, it's jus' lak we was watchin' the game rat nayow." Wasn't that the response to his work that mattered most? Anyway, the $2000 prize money wasn't going to take him south but over to Paris for a year where he'd become a real writer.

3.

Given his new-found fame, the paper agreed to grant him a twelve-month leave provided he stay on for two months until they could find a replacement for the baseball beat. He was also not to accept a job with any other newspaper until he had returned and given the *Post-Dispatch* two more years. Things changed when he met Sally Morgan.

On a rare day when the Browns and Cardinals were both out of town, the city editor called him in and asked if he'd like to interview a barnstorming aviator out at Fairground Park. It would be something different and, besides, he might get a free ride.

"What's his name?"

"Sally" was the laconic reply.

When he got to the field she was in the air and he fell into a conversation with a young mechanic about her biplane. It was a Curtiss JN-4 that had been used as a training aircraft early in the war, $5000 new, but the kid heard she'd picked it up for several hundred. Miller watched it spin, dive, and go through what he was told were barrel rolls and loop-the-loops high above. In the cloudless sky it looked and sounded like a mad insect without direction to its flight. But occasionally, drifting on the currents between sharp manoeuvres, it became more gracefully hawk-like, and he envied her perspective and passage through the blue depths.

"She's just practising," the kid said. "Come see her when it's for real."

After half an hour or so she landed not far from the terminal and he walked out to meet her, introducing himself as she undid her harness. He hadn't really thought about what he was expecting, not a dowager in long skirts certainly, but not a long-legged pilot either, roughly his age, in jodhpurs and a leather jacket, who climbed down and shook his hand with something of a man's grip.

"The paper said they'd be sending somebody out. You want to talk or fly first?" Almost his height, she stood with her fingers resting lightly on her hips and her eyes intently on him, a contrast of manner or purpose that suggested either answer would do.

"Let's go up," he said. "But you'll need a rest first, won't you?"

She pointed to the rear seat. "There's a pair of goggles in there. Don't forget to buckle your shoulder harness."

From below the insect's frantic activity had been contained by his constant field of vision, but as they lifted away from the earth and he saw so much space beneath him he recognized the true dimensions of its activity. At first, he was mesmerized by the remarkable view as the city fell away in seconds to the east where the two great rivers silently embraced and rolled south as one. The green and brown grasslands looked very flat as the sun glinted off the tops of silos and barns, though to the south-west he could see the heights of the Ozark Plateau stretching down into Arkansas and wondered how long it would take to get there. When he shouted to her, asking how fast they were going, his words were torn from his lips and scattered like bits of paper in the wind. That violence sent off an alarm in his head, so he wasn't caught completely by surprise when they suddenly went into a steep climb. Now he couldn't see the earth, only the back of her head and the wing struts vibrating like harp-strings as the frame of the instrument threatened to crack, and he held on to the sides of the cockpit hoping she'd done all her extreme practice for the day. But evidently the interview that would follow down below was meant to begin on her terms with the reporter's heart in his mouth, *if* they landed safely, making it difficult for him to maintain any professional composure. At some invisible point of their ascent the engine's roar simply stopped and, powerless, they began to drop silently out of the sky, spinning downward at an alarming speed towards the now featureless ground rising up to meet them, the promised impact just seconds away. It was all in the moment with no time to be afraid even though, eyes open wide behind his goggles, he was very aware it was death rushing noiselessly over the wings. Then the engine coughed a couple of times and caught, and she pulled the doomed craft from its collision course so close to the roof of a building he could almost reach out and touch a lightning rod bolted to the shingled curve of the ridgeline.

After a few minutes at low level that allowed some part of his equilibrium to return, she eased into a gentle glide and they touched down with a slight bump not far from the main hangar where the mechanic was waiting.

"Though you'd lost her for a second," the kid said after he placed the chocks behind the wheels.

"Another cough and I'd have been worried," she replied. "What about you?" she asked, turning to Miller. "Did you lose faith?"

Under that forceful gaze he realized she wasn't mocking him but posing a question she'd asked herself many times before. *Her* faith lay in the machinery, which she knew, however god-like its powers, wasn't flawless. How often did she lay awake at night calculating the odds that kept her from the lightning-rod's sharp spear? Was she holding on to belief or letting it go completely day after day when she coaxed the engine back to life for an audience that secretly prayed it wouldn't catch? How could he answer her?

"Not all of me," he said finally, unsure of what he could preserve from the need behind her question.

They had lunch in a greasy spoon that fed the airport workers lukewarm soup and overdone hamburgers along with coffee that hadn't been ground from any bean he recognized.

She laughed as he washed the meat down with a large swallow of the oil-coloured liquid. "I try to get into town for better fare when I can. That is, when there is a town. Most places are so small, it's the airfield and a general store. Mind you, I've had some great farmhouse meals after a successful show. Missouri home-cooking isn't bad at all. Or Iowa or Kansas or ... well, you know what I mean."

He'd taken out his pad and pencil, though he hoped they would be able to relax together without the constraints of a formal exchange. Her looks and her physical courage dazzled him, and he knew he would write her down in his notebook afterwards. Whatever her expertise, they could easily have died together, their bodies broken by impact and consumed by fire with nobody but the mechanic as witness. He didn't like being party to such vulnerability and all it implied about the loss of what it was he had still to do with his life. But their shared survival seemed to bind them together in way reminiscent of his attachment to Rawley and the others as long as they had stayed alive against the odds.

"Where are you from?" he asked, leaving his pencil on the table to signal it wasn't a reporter's question.

"Originally? Johnstown, Pennsylvania. That was home base when I was in school. My dad was an oil well trouble-shooter. He traveled around putting out fires by capping the wells—Oklahoma, Texas, California. He got to know the business, and now he owns quite a few wells in those places and a refinery outside of Philadelphia."

Miller blinked. She was a millionaire's daughter, so what was she doing making fifty bucks a dangerous show and living out of a leather grip when she could be married to one of her father's henchmen and taking it easy in a high society kind of way?

She must have sensed his puzzlement because she laughed again and said: "The life of Reilley doesn't interest me."

"The what?"

She sang in a high light voice, "'Faith and my name is Kelly, Michael Kelly/but I'm living the life of Reilley just the same.' Irish blarney from the Morgan vault, but it just about says it right."

"In other words, you're having a good enough time flying a plane."

"Yes, but don't bring it up with my father. He's a bit sensitive about having a grown daughter who refused a coming-out party."

He steered things around, not without cooperation, to her barnstorming exploits. How did she get started? Where did she learn her tricks? His pencil was still on the table between them.

"I knew the first day I saw a plane overhead before we got into the war that I wanted to fly. I badgered Daddy until he let me take flying lessons as soon as I turned sixteen. He thought it would pass, but when I got my licence and he saw how serious I was he bought me the Curtiss. If I could have gone to France with it, I would have. But it was a boys' club in the sky over there just like everything else."

Not angry but not resigned either, he thought.

"Anyway, I swore I'd make my own name even if it wasn't in dogfights. I found an instructor who took me through all the moves until I could do them in my sleep, and here I am talking to you. By the way, what you went through in that stall was just the beginning. Stick around and I'll show you some real seat-of-the-pants action." She looked at him steadily. "Since you're not writing any of this down, I take it we're off the record. In that case, tell me about yourself."

He recounted a little of his Oak Park and Michigan wilderness background, mentioning Hal as the one constant companion who put up with his desire and obsession in forest and stream. Then he spoke generally about Belleau Wood, saying only that he'd been a corporal in the Marines who'd fought with some good men.

"I can see in your eyes there's more to it than that, but I won't press you."

He sensed the demands of living on the edge produced her own kind of warfare. She wasn't dodging flak and other planes like Albert Ball and von Richthofen, but she was an ace in her own right who obviously understood what it meant to expect death daily.

"Do you have a base? Somewhere you stay so I can see you again with your feet on the ground?"

Her smile was open and inviting. "I've always liked St. Louis," she said.

When they'd been lovers for awhile and the idea of leaving her wasn't a pleasant one, he went to the editorial board and told them he wanted to postpone his departure, offering to cover the upcoming ball season and see how things stood in the fall, assuring them the earliest he'd head for Europe would be after the New Year's holiday. Still eager to gain publicity and sales from promotion of his Pulitzer status the board agreed and stuck by the raise originally offered.

Before that, they'd shared a lot about themselves, and although she'd never heard of the big prize she was mightily impressed, for a millionaire's daughter, when he mentioned how much it was worth.

"What'll you do with it? Buy a house and settle down?"

He knew she was probing and warning him at the same time. No domestic ties for Sally Morgan, at least not the usual kind.

"Well, I was planning to go to Europe—Paris, actually—and spend a year writing."

"That's exciting," she said. "Daddy took me there before the war. The Eiffel Tower was wonderful, the highest I'd ever been and would be until I went up for my first lesson. I wonder how much the city has changed?" Before he could answer, she asked: "What do you mean by 'writing'? Are you going to work for a French newspaper or the *Paris Herald*?" Whatever his interest might be in her, she clearly assumed he'd stick to his plans.

When he told her he wanted to write fiction, she was astonished. "You mean like *Little Women*?"

He smiled and nodded.

"I loved that book when I was a kid!" she exclaimed. "It was as if Jo March knew me, long before I'd thought about flying, because she told her sister Laurie: 'I've got the keys to my castle in the air, but whether I can unlock the door remains to be seen.' My mother always said I was like Jo, who would have worn pants if they'd made them for girls back then."

While she continued to barnstorm through the Midwest, she rented a small apartment near the river, a two-room affair with a small kitchen and bathroom down the hall, so they could spend the night together when she was in town. Now she was lying naked on her bed where they did all their love-making because of Magda's strict house rules. Her limber form and tousled hair always aroused him, and he doubted the virginal Louisa May Alcott would approve, but for the moment Sally's question about his writing was more important than sex.

He almost hadn't finished the copy of Alcott's book that was part of his older sister's small collection at the cottage, but he had so enjoyed Jo's tomboy independence and, above all, her writing of plays and stories, that he kept going to the end. "I want to write a novel—more than one—but the first will be about the war. Before that, though, I'll warm up with some short stories."

"You got a medal for bravery, didn't you?"

"How do you know that?"

"Oh, I asked around. I like to know who I take up in my plane." She gave a little gyration to her hips and, along with his discomfort about the medal, the contentious image of the flag came back to him.

"Did they tell you I couldn't remember my bravery?"

"The first time I came out of a spin, about two hundred feet above the ground, I didn't know how I got there. It doesn't matter. You do what you can do. Is that what you want to write about, not remembering?"

"That'll be part of it, yes, but mainly I want to tell a story about how men, sometimes very different men, learn to get along under fire. What it is that makes them tick when they're always an inch from death."

"Reporters tell me I'm always an inch from death, but I don't think about it. Maybe if there were others with me, a wing-walker, for example, I'd be more aware. I guess my problem is I don't want any company up there."

"And down here?" he asked. "I was going to leave in another month or so, but I can wait."

"Wait for what?" She leaned into him and Miss Alcott's approval was no longer an issue.

The truth was, despite his pleasure in her company and the consequent arrangement he'd made with the paper, he was anxious about surrendering his prospective Paris freedom. As long as he had to cover the ball games every day and see Sally whenever she was in town, which was usually once a week or sometimes every second weekend for a couple of nights, there'd be little time for sustained creative effort on a longer work. He'd never met anyone like her—no woman certainly—but while their mutual attraction was evident, their unpredictable meeting schedule meant neither of them felt tied down. Despite the struggle between his relationship with words and the powerful instinctive force of their intimacy, he gave no deliberate thought to a long-term association.

Dear Hal

The Pulitzer award came with enough money to put me up in Paris for a year. I was all set to go when I met Sally. She's a barnstorming pilot who likes to compare herself to Jo in Little Women. *But there's much more to her than that. The guts it takes to fly a plane like she does is a rare thing. I've been up with her, and it takes great effort to keep your balance when it feels like the wings are going to rip off as you tumble toward the ground, then you realize it will hardly*

matter if they do because the inevitable impact will destroy
them and you immediately. Without pulling any punches, let
me say she's great in the sack as well, maybe because she
relaxes as hard as she works. Anyway, I put my trip off and
will be staying with the Post-Dispatch *for the next few*
months at least. I feel good because I'm with her—though the
shows she does keep her out of town a lot. On the other hand,
I'm not writing what I want to write. You and I both turn
twenty-one in a couple of months, and especially after the war
I always have to wonder how much time is left. Whatever
happens, I am going to finish some stories about Michigan
this summer and send them out. I liked that poem about
Faust's temptation you sent me and submitted to The Dial.
He was an interesting guy. I wonder which of us could really
refuse Mephistopheles and his offers? Let me know if there's
any new publications on the horizon.

    Miller

One thing Sally had told him he found especially attractive in the short-term. Her family owned a house and property on the Isle of Pines in the Caribbean. A great-uncle on her mother's side had cut lumber there after the Civil War and left a ramshackle place that had been passed down to the present generation of Morgans, none of whom seemed interested in visiting or sprucing up the building. The island, which had been discovered by Columbus's second expedition in 1494, lay about fifty miles off the south coast of Cuba and two hundred miles by sea from Havana. Accounts of its landscapes had apparently influenced descriptions in *Peter Pan* and *Treasure Island*. Unlike his slow completion of *Little Women*, he had devoured Stevenson's novel as a boy and was intrigued by the idea of a trip south where'd he heard there was plenty of good fishing as well.

To his surprise she became quite excited when he mentioned the possibility of a fall trip after the World Series was over. They could use a bit of his Pulitzer money, he said. A month down there, as long as the house was habitable, wouldn't cost them much at all. What he didn't say was that he could get some writing done or that if things worked out they could eventually make arrangements for Paris together.

"I absolutely begged my parents to take me there," she told him, "but they always said it would be too hot when I had my summer holidays. It'll be nice and cool in late October. Maybe we could rent a plane in Havana and fly in like Peter. I'll ask Daddy if there's an airstrip?" Then she whooped with laughter. "If I'm Peter that'd make you Wendy Darling," she cried.

"That's not funny."

"Maybe not, but I'll tell you what is," she said, catching her breath before breaking into laughter again. "We'd have to get hitched. My mother would never allow us to use the property otherwise. And Daddy won't buck her on that." Her eyes were sparkling vividly like she was daring him even to consider this.

He didn't know what to say it was so completely unexpected.

"I know," she cried. "It would be crazy. We still hardly know one another. Who tries a completely new trick with the plane without easing into it?"

The only woman he'd ever thought of marrying was Amélie, but he'd been head over heels with her. Did he love Sally? He greatly enjoyed their conversations and love-making, and deeply admired her physical courage, but was that the basis for a marriage? And how would 'settling down' interfere with his writing? It was one thing to go to Paris with her unattached. She wouldn't stop flying. He'd pictured her barnstorming through various French skies while he held down a fort by the Seine, his typewriter clacking while her struts hummed in the distance. If they couldn't make a go of it, they'd just part without any messy legal complications or demands. It would be a kind of wing-and-a-prayer agreement between them for which no licence was required.

Apparently she shared his sense of the situation. "Tell you what," she said. "Let's see how things go this summer. I want to fly. You want to write. Maybe we can work something out, maybe not. But let's not let that spoil what we've got right now. One way or another we'll get to the island."

After they had made love that night and he was drifting off, he thought of the trench Hal had dug on the ridgeline. It could have been their grave but ended up as their salvation. He lay beside her in the dark and wondered if marriage could last as long as friendship.

4.

The Browns and Cardinals struggled that summer, though Sisler and Hornsby were having great years. He went out to the park every day, chatted with the boys in the press box, did his compulsory interviews, and tried to write some memorable prose about line drives and inside curves. But his heart wasn't really in it. If he wasn't going to get to Paris any time soon, he wanted to head south with Sally, put a fishing line in the Caribbean and write some stories that would transcend every-day reporting. Meanwhile, Sally confined her shows to Missouri and to Illinois towns across the river within a hundred-mile range and was able to fly home two or three nights a week. He spent so much time at her apartment that Magda began to suspect he had a serious sweetheart. Wagging her finger at him in disapproval, she scolded him for too much dreaming about romance and not making this girl an honest woman. When she discovered he was courting a flier, Sally became 'the one with her head in the clouds.'

"How can she have babies at such a height?" she moaned. "No, before that, how can you marry her up there?"

They didn't talk any more about marriage, but he found he was growing used to the idea of a more permanent tie between them. After all, they each had their own lives to lead, and there was no reason to suspect that would change just because they became an official couple in the eyes of his landlady and the rest of the world. Maybe it was the best sort of relationship for him—a bright and lovely companion he enjoyed spending time with who didn't crowd his writing hours and protected her independence as fiercely he did his own, an autonomy that for both of them, if in quite different ways, was a matter of life and death. He knew her flying took her to the edge of mortality where he had walked as the mortar shells fell and the machine-gun fire raked the grain, but he also knew that part of him died every time he couldn't put the right words on the page. He'd come back from this death-by-creativity more than once and suspected such return would continue only at great expense to himself and whomever he was with. That was why the on-and-off-again time with Sally was a good thing. When she stared at the earth hurtling toward her at eighty miles an hour she had her own price to pay and resurrection to endure. Hell, he thought, we're both crazy to do what we do.

On the 4th of July weekend, the Browns were in Philadelphia playing the Athletics. He and Sally took the overnight train so he could cover the game and meet her parents.

"I thought we were supposed to be legitimate before they allowed us to do anything," he said as they boarded the sleeping car.

"My mother will assume we had separate berths. It's easier for her that way."

"And your father?"

"Oh, he'll assume we didn't, but just won't say anything about it. It's easier for *him* that way."

He was more than a little nervous about gaining their good opinion, which annoyed him because, aside from permission to use the Isle of Pines property, he didn't want anything from them. He might not be a millionaire, but he had sufficient funds to support himself, as did Sally, and he wasn't going to play the role of some vassal on bended knee seeking the lord's and lady's consent to court and presumably marry their daughter.

"I told you," she said as they hailed a cab outside the Broad Street station. "This is just so they know who you are if we decide to sign on the dotted line. If not, there's no harm done. I'll bring up the island in passing so we can find out if the house is liveable, that's all. By the way, I mentioned your medal."

When he opened his mouth to protest, she held up her hand. "They're both great patriots and were already on your side because you volunteered. The rest just helps things along."

To his great surprise he liked them both, and their good opinion, as she'd suggested, was already in place. Sally may have pointed out his military decoration, but John Morgan had done his homework and knew the prestige of a Pulitzer Prize.

"I found your pieces about the war very honest and moving," he said as they sipped some chilled white wine on the patio of a mansion that would have swallowed Magda's boarding house whole. A coloured man in white livery had brought the bottle in an ice bucket and glasses on a silver tray. They weren't the descriptive words Miller expected from an oil magnate, and when he simply nodded his thanks, Morgan seemed to understand his reticence and moved the conversation to the post-war state of Europe. When he learned Miller was thinking of going to Paris he spoke knowingly about the Louvre, where he had passed many hours as a young man and then again when, as husband and father, he'd travelled to France with his wife and Sally.

"We've only a few who come close to the European masters," he said. "Whistler, Homer, Sergeant."

"Perhaps so, sir, but our writers are every bit their equal. Whitman, Crane, Jack London."

"London? Isn't he all tooth and claw, man against the wilderness type of thing?"

"There's that to his work, no doubt. But if you're interested in art's place in the modern world, read his great novel *Martin Eden*." He regretted the words as soon as they were out of his mouth. London's working-class protagonist loved a wealthy girl and struggled against huge odds to become a successful writer. If John Morgan did read the book would he think Miller was lecturing him and pleading his own case? Of course, Martin Eden killed himself in the end out of despair that art cannot overcome the shallowness of the material world, and Miller didn't accept that despair for one moment.

Fortunately, Mrs. Morgan—"Edith," she told him, smiling in a friendly manner—stepped in and steered them to safer ground. "Sally tells us you write about St. Louis baseball. Did you know that many years ago in Akron, Ohio I taught history and geography to George Sisler? He was quite a handsome lad back then and a little gentleman, so both his nicknames today are entirely appropriate."

She, Miller, and Sally talked animatedly about 'America's pastime'. Both Philadelphia teams were in last place and appeared to be mired there, but the Indians from her hometown were in first thanks to the batting and fielding of Tris Speaker. Her knowledge of the game was impressive, and he asked if she'd like to attend the Browns-Athletics game the next day. Turning to her husband he added: "Of course, you're welcome too, sir. I'd venture to say Sisler is an artist at what he does."

"Oh, my wife has already convinced me of that. Yes, we'll all go." The coloured man suddenly appeared with a new bottle and fresh ice.

During the game the Morgans engaged him in a wide-ranging conversation about President Wilson's policies, the upcoming vote on in Congress on Prohibition, and Mack Sennett comedies, but when Sally went off to the concourse to buy some sandwiches, they turned to her flying and expressed their great concern for her safety.

"But I think she's an artist, too," Edith said. "And women artists are a rarity. We can't discourage them."

John Morgan agreed but also wondered what his talented, headstrong daughter would do when her flying days were over. Miller thought he was about to say she should get married and settle down before too long, but then Sally returned and everyone smiled. It was clear her parents weren't going to try to direct her future. In the bottom of the ninth, Joe Duggan, the Athletics' best batter, smacked a game-winning ball over the right-field fence and the happy crowd celebrated noisily.

"If they're so open-minded about so much," he said that night as they headed for their separate bedrooms across the hall from one another, "why would they object to a Caribbean holiday without a wedding?"

"Mother's a baseball fan," she said. "She believes in statistics. And the statistics say young people in love get married. As for Daddy, I honestly don't think he cares that much, but he's the star player only in his boardroom. At home, she's the manager and if she says take a pitch, he takes a pitch."

"Are we in love?" he asked with a smile.

"You were always a sucker for the fastball," she replied as she opened her door and drew him in.

5.

When they returned to St. Louis she told him it made sense to move in with her. That way they could get an idea of what it would be like to be married without any vows attached. He felt reasonably comfortable with such an arrangement since it would allow them to decide their future together while proceeding on a day-by-day basis. After all, whatever his aspirations, he never sat down in front of the typewriter with a finished design in his head just the faith that words would come if there was a story he wanted to tell. He and Sally weren't blank pages, either of them, but already deep into their shared narrative that now included other characters like her parents. If he remained at the boarding house it would be a signal he wanted to stay at a distance from the unpredictable unfolding of feelings that close range would encourage, and that would make him something of a coward in his own eyes as well as hers. So he gave Magda a week's notice and borrowed a wheelbarrow to carry his books and clothes, along with the typewriter and a small desk he'd purchased, over to Sally's place in two trips. Having learned there were no wedding plans in the offing, his landlady admonished him once again, and made him solemnly promise he would not elope but have a proper ceremony to which she would be invited.

"You want to tell your children you didn't run away," she told him, and despite her hectoring tone he knew she had his best interests at heart.

One thing Sally had learned at the breakfast table the day they left Philadelphia was that the Isle of Pines house was intact and weatherproof. It was looked after by a local caretaker on a few acres of land overlooking the river that ran down to the sea through the capital Nueva Gerona.

"It would be nice, I suppose, to make a visit," her mother said. "But what would one do there?"

"You could always join the American revolution against Cuba," her father replied. "Since the timber trade died, there's just a few planters left. From what I've heard they're a blinkered lot who spend most of their energy protesting the government treaty that gave the island to Havana. That was over fifteen years ago and they're still denying its legality." He looked pointedly at his wife. "If your uncle was alive he'd be leading the charge."

"That was my great-uncle Ralph," she told Miller. "He was with Roosevelt at San Juan Hill and thought the Cubans should be more grateful once the Spanish were vanquished."

Her mother brought out an album and he looked at faded photos of white men in high collars and tailored suits standing proprietarily near giant piles of logs while shorter, darker men in white blouses and shabby pants stared at the camera as if it were their last chance at recognition. Behind them in one picture a valley sloped down to the sea where a two-masted schooner waited patiently for its cargo.

"I understand much of it has grown up again, the timber I mean. But since 1904 Cuba hasn't wanted anything exported, so there it sits."

Back in St. Louis they talked about the trip.

"Let's go in December and stay through the holidays," she said.

"Alright," he answered, imagining a room with a view of the hills and water, its only furniture a pine table and chair. "I'll work every day," he told her.

"I know you will," she said, "but I'll have to find a plane down there."

"What about the Curtiss?"

"Daddy says there's no airstrip, and it doesn't have pontoons."

Her apartment—*their* apartment—was peaceful in the evenings when she was away. He missed her, of course, but it was good to settle down at his desk and write despite his tiredness from the day. He began one story with the line he'd sent to Hal about the Ojibway girl, in which his young Michigan protagonist convinced himself initially he could marry into the tribe and become a hunter-fisherman like her father and brothers. Then one day he was in town with his parents and saw her approaching along the wooden sidewalk. Without thinking he took his mother's arm and turned her into a shop doorway, saying there was something of interest he wanted to show her. Inside, he felt rather than saw the girl pass by and knew her head was down in deference to his father who stood waiting by the entrance. When his mother asked him what he had in mind, he laughed and said he couldn't remember anymore. That's what the title was, 'Something of Interest,' and he closed it with a brief encounter between the two lovers by the lakeshore where they held hands and silently pondered their separate fates. He typed up a second copy and sent it off to *The Dial* in New York. Wouldn't it be great if he and Hal could have their first publications accepted in the same year!

He'd written about the war in his newspaper vignettes and wanted to save anything more on the subject for his novel, so he focused on the things he knew best outside of his time in France. In the tale of two friends caught in a forest fire while fishing near the Canadian border he described their very different personalities bound by their love for the outdoors, one boy slightly older who always took the lead and the other something of a dreamer who, though nearly as skilled in the woods, was happy to follow. When the fire hit, he wrote, the leader was in his element, and took them into the middle of a stream with hollow reeds to help them breathe underwater. With burning branches and limbs falling all around they managed to survive, despite the dreamer's submerged panic. He read over this betrayal of Hal several times, then wrote another account, this time giving the dreamer credit for digging a trench where they could outlast the flames. The leader had broken his ankle so he couldn't perform to the best of his abilities, but it was he who suggested the trench in the first place. The final line left things up in the air by not identifying the speaker: "'I couldn't have done it without you,' one of them said." But this was still the more honest version, and he knew it. He put both versions in a drawer.

As the season wound down, it became clear the Brooklyn Robins were probably going to meet Mrs. Morgan's Indians in the Series, though Cleveland ended up winning the American League by only two games over the White Sox. George Sisler was having wonderful year, leading the American League in batting and second in home runs. But the extraordinary performance that had everyone talking was by the

Yankees' Babe Ruth who was on a tear to hit fifty homers. It didn't seem possible that one man could hit thirty more balls over the fence than any other. Ruth had a massive barrel chest but skinny legs, and as Miller watched him he realized it was all in the timing of his swing and the strength of his wrists. The bat came around in a short, swift stroke that cracked the ball like a rifle shot and launched it so quickly over the outfielders' heads they didn't have time to move.

For several weeks they'd been talking about the island as if their trip there were a foregone conclusion. "What do you think?" Sally asked him with that same intense gleam in her eye he recalled from their first meeting. "Should we invite them to Cleveland for a game and make a wedding out of it?"

It was time to bite the bullet or whatever you did when you got hitched. He still didn't know if he loved her, but he liked being with her far too much to say no. Most of all, he wanted to get away from the daily grind and put all his efforts into the stories. Who knew but he'd make a start on the novel, though he did want to wait for Paris to begin. To complete a collection of stories before they left for Europe was his true goal, and he'd need the island to do that.

Land and Sea

1.

By 1924 he had what he jokingly referred to among his friends and acquaintances as a near-flung national reputation. What this meant was his poetry was read by a small group of connoisseurs in New York, Chicago, San Francisco, and perhaps one or two other large centers in the literary landscape. Besides in *The Little Review* his shorter lyrics had appeared on more than one occasion in *The Dial* run by Marianne Moore, *Poetry* (with its redundant subtitle *a Magazine of Verse*) edited by Harriet Munroe and Ezra Pound, the newer *Modern Review*, and *The Fugitive*. Publishers had come after him for a book, but he had been slow to work things into a collection, partly because he wanted his completed grand endeavour, which he was now publicly calling *An American Odyssey*, to appear first, and partly because he was nervous he would give too much away about himself all at once. But he could no longer resist the pressure for a finished manuscript from Garrett and others. The long poem was still unorganized and largely disconnected, probably still years away from completion, and it was foolish to believe in any distinction for readers and critics between revelations found in scattered lyrics and those gathered together in one volume. Those who had no first-hand knowledge of his Village adventures would undoubtedly put some pieces of his personal puzzle together no matter their format. When one publisher learned that Garrett had offered to edit the fifty poems he'd gathered with Hal's permission, he promised a two-hundred-dollar advance and an alluring cover that would not be forgotten.

"What does he mean by that?"

"Something that sells. Look, bring the book out and you'll definitely get one of those *Dial* prizes. Then you can leave all this dross behind and go off and write to your heart's content."

That's what he wanted. In the last year, Miller, who had already won his first Pulitzer and then published a collection of stories about Michigan, had been given the big prize again for his first novel. The *Times* had trumpeted it as "a searing portrait of men at war," written in his usual brilliant, understated way, and Hal agreed, though it was obvious how much his friend was haunted by what he'd gone through in France. His fame pervaded the country from New York bookstores and libraries to those in small towns from coast to coast and even crossed the ocean into British accent and French translation. On the strength of the award stipend and the monstrous sales of his book, he was now living comfortably in Paris and working on new fiction. The poet's version of Miller's success might not be as lucrative, but it was time to take advantage of whatever benefits were available. He and Miller had assured each other about their inevitable triumph when they met in New York after the highly-publicized launch of the short story volume.

"Three years is a long time, but a bear doesn't change his spots," Miller said, laughing, after they'd shaken hands and vigorously clapped one another on the back. Hal had wanted to hug him, but it wasn't the time or place. The room was filled with literary types, publishing bigwigs, and social climbers. The sophisticated crowd included critics from the *Times* and *World*, plus Dorothy Parker from *Vanity Fair*, men and women he'd soon need to review his own work, so there was a need for restraint by the famous and lesser-known alike. They hadn't been able to get more than a couple of minutes to themselves in the clamour, Hal noting his friend's deeply-tanned features and confident manner as well-wishers greeted him in passing before insistent palms were cupping his elbows and drawing him away. They hurriedly agreed to meet for lunch the next day at Lindy's on 7th Avenue before the launch continued in Boston and Philadelphia. He was basking in the glow of their renewed contact when he heard a woman's voice beside him. "You must be the famous Hal Pierce," the voice said assuredly, and he turned toward its owner.

She was almost as tall as him but lighter in frame. Despite her slim beauty he felt the strength of her grip as she took his hand for a moment and said: "I'm Sally, Miller's ... um, pilot."

He laughed. "No, you're really Jo March, the barn-stormer."

She laughed in return. "Miller's told me all about you as well."

There was no insinuation he could read, but two could play the game.

"I guess that makes us even," he said.

"I guess so," she replied, letting the contest go almost too quickly for him to feel comfortable. She looked across the room at her husband. "He's in his element," she said with affection.

"You might set out to be famous, but it's not without good reason if you make it."

"He showed me some of your work. I don't pretend to understand most of it, but some of your lines are ... well, like a plane perfectly-balanced between heaven and earth."

It was an image he'd never been offered before, one whose visual precision came out of her own deep experience, not of words but of a life on the edge both readers and non-readers could admire.

They wandered about together, sipping their wine and remarking on the appearance of various guests. Garrett came over to them and was introduced.

"You're the one Hal lives with," she said when she heard his name.

"A mere squire, I'm afraid, following the knight-errant."

"Why do you?" she asked. "Follow him, I mean." Again Hal could detect no innuendo, but he was on his guard nonetheless.

Garrett wasn't about to be caught by beauty or strength. "Well, because he's irresistible." Someone patted him on the sleeve and pointed across the room. "Excuse me," he said, "duty calls. Very nice to have met you."

"Likewise," Sally said and turned back to Hal.

"He loves you, you know."

"Garrett?"

She smiled. "Oh, probably in his way. But I mean Miller."

"I know he does. And I love him."

"Yes, you do. That's just it, isn't it?"

"What do you mean?" Though he knew what was coming.

"You're queer, aren't you?" she said softly and with no trace of malice.

It was as if the room went totally silent except for the cacophony of words ringing in his ears. No one outside the Village had ever spoken this directly to him before, though he'd often imagined it happening in accusatory fashion even if he'd never imagined how he'd reply. It was just as well she didn't seem to be accusing him of anything, just remarking on a fact, because there was nowhere to hide.

He took a deep breath. "I didn't think it was that obvious in mixed company."

"It isn't. Let's just say I can read the wind."

"So can Miller, but he doesn't know," he said, which was confirmation as much as assertion.

"He doesn't *want* to know, and he won't unless you decide to tell him." She pressed his arm. "How long have *you* known?" she asked.

He walked her arm-in-arm along the Embarcadero and told her briefly about Nicky. For some reason he trusted her with this without knowing why.

"How was it when you shared a tent together?"

"I wanted to tell him the last time up near the Canadian border, but we were too busy trying to save our lives to think about anything else. I'm sure he's told you about the fire." He wouldn't mention the kiss. That was between him and Miller alone.

She leaned over and brushed his cheek with her lips. "You've always been good for him, Hal, whoever you are."

He loved her too in that moment. 'Whoever' not 'whatever.'

The next day he and Miller talked over beer and smoked meat sandwiches, so much to catch up on in so short a time. Hal was nervous at first, looking for any signs that Sally might have betrayed his trust of the night before, but Miller was his old voluble self, talking about the New York elite who couldn't understand a boy from Michigan but who would sit up and pay the right kind of attention when he handed in his war novel.

"I had to write those stories first," he said, "otherwise I would have been denying where I came from as a writer. Where *we* came from, Hal. You know I would have dedicated the book to you but for my father."

"It's okay, you wrote that story about the fire, didn't you." He liked the ambiguity of its ending, which blended them together.

"Yeah, what did you think of it?"

"It made me feel as if I was there, even if I was. I guess that's the best way I can put it." Miller had superbly filtered event and feeling through memory to re-invent the past. What had actually happened didn't matter as much as what could have. Somewhere in limbo Hal Pierce's own version of escape was waiting.

"What about you? How's the big poem coming along? Jesus, I'll be glad when I don't have to ask you that anymore!"

"I know, I know. It's been on the back burner while I've been putting together a collection of shorter verse. Garrett's editing it for me, and I think it should be out in the next six months or so."

"Just like me then. Our second books will be the big ones."

"Oh, I think mine's going to take a lot longer than yours, from what you say."

"You need to find a place to write away from all this big city shit. Your own Isle of Pines."

Miller had written him about the island and how relatively easy it was to produce prose there, let alone poetry, amidst all the sun and sea. "If I get one of those *Dial* prizes, I will."

"Are you still on the outs with your mother?" It came suddenly, but he wasn't surprised. After all, Miller was the only one left who knew her.

"Yes, she's never forgiven me for not wanting to go back to Oak Park and become an office manager of one kind or another."

"Think it's always going to be that way?"

"Nothing will change," he said, apparently of her but meaning his own invariable nature. It was time for a more flexible exchange. "Sally's a great girl. You're a lucky guy."

Miller smiled broadly. "I am! When her hand is on the throttle up there she's like an artist painting the sky. She's a painter, I'm a writer, so we're not competitors." He laughed. "That's grounds for a very good time in all sorts of ways."

"I hear you told her all about me."

"Naw, just that we've been together since birth and fished most of the streams in northern Michigan. She asked if you've got a girl, by the way. Do you?"

He wondered when she had asked. "No, but I know some great dames." He hoped the general slang would cover the specific absence.

"You need to take one home to mother. Maybe then she'll leave you alone to write."

"She's already done that."

They did hug one another when they parted, a quick manly embrace, Hal surmised, that their subsequent firm hand clasp put in proper perspective for any casual observers.

"Take care of yourself, brother," Miller said.

2.

He titled his volume *Passageways* because included were ten inter-related poems dealing with aspects of his journey after those imagined flowers of glass from that anguished morning in the alley. In these particularly, his intense images were dependent on symbolic implication rather than literal interpretation, so for most readers the puzzle of Hal Pierce would remain a work-in-progress. In the forty other pieces he focused more on the external world but with similar undertones that opened up everything from trout fishing to boarding-house life into territories of larger association.

Sung through pools	*Her kitchen rag*
In blooded scales	*Waved like a flag*
Of rising melody	*In colours of her mind*
The humming hook	*Lingoed with smells*
With feathered lie	*She left behind …*
Swims silver in the air	

The critical reception was mixed. Allen Tate, whose opinion mattered, called the poems "transcendental" and said the collection was filled with "fresh creative language." Others were less effusive but praised his ambitious pursuit of the mythic in the everyday. Unfortunately, there were those with some influence who found his style "pretentious" and "over-blown" and advised he should return to prosody's starting line where simpler forms were waiting. The result was, despite Tate's glowing review, not even a mention when potential Pulitzer nominees were discussed in the papers. While he couldn't really argue with Edward Arlington Robinson winning the prize for his collected poems, he was disappointed that it always seemed to be the old school that rose to the top. Nonetheless, as Garrett had predicted, he did receive a *Dial* Award and the prestige and $2000 that went with it. This meant he could have a year or so to kick his *Odyssey* into shape. The question was, where did he want to live while doing so? Staying in New York was not an option. He needed a fresh start.

When Steve had suffered a heart attack two years before and had to give up his business, Hal found a job at Frank Shay's bookstore on Christopher Street, and worked his way up from lowly clerk to assistant manager of acquisitions. He missed the outdoor work and the comfort zone of Brooklyn Heights because not only was he inside for eight hours a day, but he'd also moved with Garrett to an apartment on the edge of the Village. Mrs. Capalca had been tremendously upset when he left and made him promise he'd come for Sunday dinners once in awhile at least. Her grandkids were growing but still viewed him as the world's greatest story-teller, and as he hugged her on the last day, he knew he was leaving a family situation so much warmer and more tolerant than any he had known in Oak Park. For his part, Steve had told him that when the trolley had hit his truck it had been one of the luckiest days of his life.

"You helped me last longer than I woulda, up there," he said, pointing to the rooftops outside his kitchen window. He had lost weight after the attack and there was a rasp to his voice that emphasized his failing strength. "What'll ya do with yourself, Hal?"

"Well, I won't work for any other carpenter, that's for sure." He laughed. "I guess it's time, as they say, for this young man to go west, as far as Manhattan anyway."

The bookstore was stimulating because Shay entrusted him with purchase decisions about new and contemporary writers, and his status in this regard was amplified by the publication of his own verse and readings he gave at various venues, including one at the prestigious New York Public Library. His social world expanded on the strength of his growing status as a poet, and he was soon rubbing shoulders with those who funded the city arts scene to a considerable extent, business-men and lawyers who sat on the boards of the Metropolitan Museum and the city's nationally-renowned symphony orchestra. Literature wasn't very lucrative, but it had a celebrated European lineage they couldn't ignore, and he felt it was his job to keep them informed of what was going on in their own country. They knew about Shakespeare, Dickens, and Conrad, but what about Frost, Anderson, and Miller Sark?

In the meantime, he was having difficulty keeping his late-night Village excesses separate from the sedateness of early evening cocktail parties and dinners. His writing couldn't relieve his sexual longings and his ongoing immersion in Black Rabbit activities. To his surprise, Garrett broached the subject even as he suggested they share a place together.

"I'm just trying to look out for you."

Amused at his friend's naivety, he brazenly announced: "You don't know how far you'll have to look."

The shock was instant and harsh. "Yes, I do, Hal. Do you think you have any secrets left?"

"Secrets?"

"I suspected when I first met you. All those weekends you disap-peared and never offered an explanation that it was a young woman—or women in general for that matter—whose arms you couldn't leave. Then, word gets around. Whether you like it or not, you have a reputa-tion in the Village. It might not have reached back to Brooklyn Heights yet or upper echelons on the other side of the river, but it's alive and well for many, make no mistake. Besides, there was that episode with your mother. When I came back from Virginia, she'd been banished from your life or you from hers. That wouldn't have happened simply over your employment or staying in New York as you tried to tell me."

He saw the swirling hem of the only woman he had ever loved disappearing into the taxi and felt the crushing weight of her subsequent silence. He would never forgive her or himself for what had broken their bond. But that was different from being exposed to the public eye. He shuddered at the thought. Any desire for personal recognition was bound up with his creativity not his libido, and he didn't want to jeopardize his attainments as a writer. Those in charge, from Frank Shay to the Metropolitan elite might tolerate his preference for male company but not any open carnality, and for that matter neither would most of those who made decisions about book publication and funding. He'd been stupid not to see this and lucky his wilful blindness hadn't cost him yet. Just the other night he been traipsing drunkenly through Washington Square with yet another sailor—a beautiful boy with a cupid's mouth—singing uproariously the lyrics to one dirty limerick after another. It wasn't even that late. Anyone respectable might still have been around. He soberly considered Garrett's roommate offer as a ticket to his propriety.

"Won't people just think you and I are … well …?"

"Queer? No, for one thing I have my own repute as a lover of female company. For another, enough of those we care about will understand my motive is to keep you toned down. No one is suggesting you change who you are, Hal, just that you, ironically, become even more Greek."

"Meaning?"

"Meaning Solon of Athens: 'everything in moderation.'"

So they'd moved into a second-floor flat on Sullivan Street about ten minutes' walk from the Square in one direction and the bookstore in another. His life did change in that he spent more social time with Garrett and hence with young women as well as straight men who might have been titillated by Black Rabbit escapades but disturbed by any invitation to join in. Of course, he'd still go off to the club or find pick-ups in the streets, but he was quieter in his prowling and with any captures he made, and nearly always stayed in control of situations to make sure he turned the key to his own lock early on Saturday or Sunday mornings and fell alone into his own bed. His schedule became more flexible, and the time he set aside for writing was a more fluid, less formal period that he didn't feel he was snatching from unrelated demands of the day. The result was completion of the lyric manuscript, some limited but vital critical acclaim, and the year's freedom he could now purchase with the *Dial* money.

"I want to go some place warm where I can be outside when I'm not working." He was sitting one September night at a table in the Artists' Club with an assorted group of writers and their hangers-on. Everyone was jealous of his success but wanted to be part of its future as well. Friendly suggestions were offered about California, the Carolinas, and the south-west. He thought about San Francisco, but the daily fog was cold and there'd be too much temptation from the Embarcadero. Then a boy on the edge of the crowd mentioned Key West at the tip of Florida.

"It's beautiful," he said. "You can swim all year round and rent a place for very little. No one bothers you, but a good crowd comes through on their yachts in the winter. By 'good' I don't mean 'a lot,' just that they've got manners and know how to host a party. And if you want to slum it, there's always the merchant marine bars."

He'd meant what he'd said about being outside. Since he'd stopped working with Steve his previously ruddy complexion had declined to a pallid hue, and because he carried nothing heavier than the occasional box of books no more than a few feet, his muscle tone was shot. Miller would have scoffed at his condition. He wrote from Paris that he was running every day and had been on several fishing trips to the *Massif Central* where the gorges were steep and demanding.

"What about fishing?" he asked.

"I never did any myself," the boy said. "But I saw plenty of rods." Everybody laughed, including Hal, then another man spoke up. "I've seen photos of record-size fish down there. You can't miss."

Garrett made some enquiries and thought it a good bet. "You can get an entire house for fifty dollars a month, which means plenty of room for visitors like me and … transient guests. Plus it's only ninety miles from Cuba, so you could easily get over to Havana for a break."

He knew Miller had loved his time on the Isle of Pines, where he'd completed his short story collection, because his letters had been full of the Caribbean lifestyle and tales of flying with Sally. He probably wouldn't spend a lot of time on the water, but if he could throw a line in every morning from the shore and catch his breakfast or lunch that would be fine. The idea of swimming in January was just fine too.

Frank Shay promised to hold his job, and Garrett would find a room-mate for the year, maybe even, he hinted, a young and pretty one to help cook and clean.

"You'll never take me back," Hal said.

"I'll take you back on one condition, Homer. You finish that god-damn poem!"

In early October he boarded the Atlantic Coastline train that would take him south to Jacksonville. From there he'd travel on the Florida East Coast railway to Miami and then on the Overseas track that connected the Keys all the way to his destination.

"See you at New Year's," Garrett said.

3.

Dear Miller

What a place! As you probably know, Key West is an island joined to other islands and the mainland by ferry and by a railway line built over the water. I've been here a month now and am still getting used to all the vibrant sights and colours. There's flora and fauna of every description raging from over-sized cactus to date palms, mangos, and the ubiquitous mangroves. The perfume of jasmine and other flowering plants is everywhere, and the sky is filled with birds—from tiny wrens to giant turkey buzzards and thousands of peregrine falcons that have headed south for the coming winter. There are also amazing numbers of migrating butterflies, the same kind we'd see back in Michigan. Every morning I rise early and fish for red snapper and barracuda

*in the old submarine pens at the navy yard, and every morning
I catch something for breakfast. The 'cuda are certainly an
acquired taste, and, after hitting them firmly but carefully
over the head, I usually give them to an old fellow who runs a
stall in the center of town, but the friendlier snapper, fried in
oil, are delicious. I've got a small house on a side street for
forty dollars a month—yes, an entire house with guest room!
You'll have to drop by. Just turn west out of Rue Montmartre.
I'll be the one with the tan and big smile on his face.*

    *Anyway, after breakfast I sit down at my desk overlooking
a garden covered in poinsettia plants and work on my
"Odyssey." I've become a perfectionist in my old age and keep
looking for the diamond in the coal-bin, but I can see the
individual sections falling into place even if there's still a lot of
work to be done on specific lines and images. By the time I
return to New York next spring I should have some parts of it
ready to send out. After a lunch of oysters (so cheap!) and
greens with a little chilled plonk I take a short siesta then
walk over to Mallory Square by the waterfront, buy a day-old
copy of The Times, and sit for an hour or two perusing
concert reviews and letters to the editor. Later I have a swim
back at the pens. I've made a few acquaintances and generally
meet them following a light supper at home, saving my funds
for the local speakeasies. The bootleggers bring in rum from
Havana and whiskey from Nassau (you're so lucky to be
living in a civilized country when it comes to booze). I try not
to overdo it since I have my morning regimen, but there are
occasional sprees when I wake up under a palm tree with
sand in my teeth and a head that won't quit. You know how it
is. I've never been happier, not since our backwoods days.
Send me Paris news and some indication of what you're
working on. If you top the last one ... well, you've already got
the literary world by the tail so I don't know what's left.*

    Hal

What he'd said in his letter was by and large the case. His powers of concentration seemed to have increased according to the degree of his financial independence. When he didn't have to worry about whether he had the means to be a full-time poet he was able to organize himself and his work along consistent lines of purpose and production. As exposed as it was to hurricane fury and the hunger of Gulf Stream currents, the tiny coral outpost, officially declared the southernmost point in the U.S., gave him a solid base from which to consider the rest of the country, past and present. The bear wandered more securely through history because, for the first time in his life, the Young Man who sometimes accompanied the observant creature was content with whom he was and what he was doing. The best illustration of this was that he finished the original opening section in which, from a hill where *boarding-house windows one day would shine*, the bear watched a ship under full sail enter the river *that waited patiently to herald its captain's name*. He saw the shallop rowed ashore and the *trinket meeting* between Indians and crew, the former never guessing this was *the beginning of their end/the place where souls and beads were traded*. The bear then followed the ship on its one-hundred-and-fifty-mile voyage up the river to the site where *Alba burned for fifty years/in the fireplace of the Mohawk nation/rising from ashes / Hudson had no match to understand*. Eventually the English Hudson, hired by the Dutch East Indies Company to find a northwest passage, resumed his main commercial course and headed north to *mutinied abandonment in ice and snow/as wind carved ghosts beneath the pole*. If America was born out of duplicity and death and continued to be haunted by their presence in its advancement, he would have to work hard to show its glory.

Of course, he hadn't been entirely truthful with Miller. Although he had cut down on his drinking and felt better for it, his late-night lust for sailors had not abated. The submarine base had closed down after the war along with the training field for naval aviators, but Key West remained an important port for merchant ships carrying loads from Kingston, Vera Cruz, Havana, and the rest of the Caribbean to Miami and destinations on the east coast. The docks area provided easy pickings and the usual brief adventures without responsibility that he

south to offload everything from lumber and machinery to bourbon and medical supplies. On the return trip north the delivery would include rum, sugar, and coffee, before citrus fruits were put aboard.

"I've been here for over a month and haven't seen you!"

"Sometimes we don't get shore leave, depending on the work we have to do." He was standing in faded dungarees in Hal's living-room, the only sailor allowed in.

Hal couldn't believe it had been seven years since their one-night stand in San Francisco, those few hours of sexual release that had changed him utterly. For all the weathering Nicky must have withstood under the tropic sun and then as gale-force winds hurtled Pacific spray over the railings, his face was remarkably unlined. His hair was cut short, and the tan on his arms and neck indicated exactly where his t-shirt sleeves and collar began. His muscled torso was testimony to un-ceasing manual labour and left Hal feeling soft and lazy about his own work, but under the heat of the unforgotten green gaze he remembered leaving his mother in the train compartment to swim beneath the pole-star "in keener/currents of the sea" and how he had almost dedicated the poem to his first lover. Where was that original stanza of the poem now? In a box back at the apartment with Garrett. But he'd brought it with him on the printed page as well.

They'd had one drink in the bar with his crew then Hal led him back to the house.

"What are you doing here anyway?"

"It's a long story. I'll tell you later."

Nicky didn't protest, just whistled when Hal pushed open the gar-den gate and took out his key. "Whatever you are doing, it's paying off."

"It's only forty a month for the whole place."

"You could fit our entire living quarters on your ground floor. That's for thirty men!"

"Let me show you around."

"There's only one room I want to see," Nicky said, taking his hand.

They fell onto the bed locked together in a kiss so fierce and full of promise there was no embrace from all his dockland and Village adven-tures that could compare. Their mouths and hands were everywhere, making impossible claims on willing territories of breath and touch, sweat glazing their lips and fingertips, and those salty rivers of blood rising then overflowing until there was only one body left they could call their own.

For the first time in his life Hal felt loyalty to a sexual partner, leaving behind dingy rooms, alleyways, and more recent sandy wastes with this stranger who had initiated him so long ago and now confirmed him in his desires. But he didn't want him to remain a stranger. Why couldn't they live here together whenever Nicky was in port and then back in New York when his *Dial* money ran out? If a poet could work in a bookstore, maybe a sailor could become a stevedore without much problem and come home every night after his shift. Foolish romance or not, based on one glorious encounter in seven years, they would talk about it in the morning, sitting over a coffee in *their* kitchen, he assured himself as he drifted off. Somewhere in his dreams a warm wind dried his skin.

At sunrise he was up to grind the beans and fill the percolator with water before stepping under the patio shower, hesitating for a moment before washing away the residue of a fleeting tryst so filled with promise. Pulling on his shorts and shirt he stepped back into the house where Nicky was by the window with its view of the harbour, barefoot in his dungarees, the long curve of his back dappled by the shadows of the room. Given that shore leave wasn't always granted, Hal began to doubt the smoothness of his future plans.

"Maybe you could do something else," he said tentatively.

"What do you mean?"

"I mean ..." But Nicky had picked up his only copy of *Passageways* and was riffling through it.

"What's this?" he asked. "Is that your name on it?"

This is what happens to the poet who works in the bookstore, he thought, when someone he cares for deeply regards the bookstore as his whole world. He hadn't thought about trying to tell Nicky he was a writer, that he was here, in fact, because he was a *good* writer with a New York reputation that maybe stretched to sections of Charleston and Baltimore if not yet Kingston and Havana. Where should he begin?

Nicky flipped through the pages again then stopped to read a poem. "What's a calyx?" he asked. There was vulnerability in his voice not ignorance, but the distance between them was suddenly enormous.

"It's the part of a flower that protects the bud," he said.

"Why doesn't it say that?"

There were different kinds of clarity that needed to be addressed.

"There's one in there that's special." He took the book from his sailor's hands and found the poem he'd finished years later. "After you left me in the Embarcadero, I wrote the first verse so you wouldn't entirely disappear." He read it aloud now, his voice trembling a little as he admitted his love.

The pole-star left a mark
In your green eyes
A fiery fleck
To burn the brine
Without crime or shame
We swam in keener
Currents of the sea

As algae glowed
Like tiny points of light
So far so near
We could not tell the source
But held our course
Until the tumbled dawn
Caressed us lying here

Only in legend
Were we too young
To swim beyond
Where dreams are born
And now this page is torn
Our hearts must drown
To finally set us free

Nicky took the volume from him and turned each separate page. Hal knew what he was looking for.

"It's the only one without a title. Why's that?"

"I scratched it out a long time ago." He went to his desk and picked up a pen. "I'll write it in now," he said.

That was how his regular life began. Nicky would work extra shifts in Kingston or Vera Cruz so he could take certain shore leave when his ship docked in Key West. At least once a month he would have several days with Hal when they would make love, sleep, have their meals, and wander the beach like any normal couple. Later he would think they got away with it because it was so infrequent a liaison that no one paid any attention outside of their small circle of acquaintances. But at the time he felt it was because they strolled along the blessed edge of the continent beyond straight and narrow judgements in an eternal summer, as he liked to put it to himself, of no discontent. The loyalty that he felt on that first morning stayed complete, and there were no more bleary-eyed awakenings under the date-palms after escapades he could barely recall. He missed Nicky when he was away but kept to the original schedule he had described to Miller, rising early to fish at the pens, working through the morning, then spending a relaxing afternoon with the *Times* before a return to the old naval yard to dive from the concrete walls into the clean, clear channels where the subs once were moored. Every time he surfaced the bright new world was waiting for him in which approval and accomplishment were never in doubt and the impact on his writing only beneficial.

> *Hear us call to you Walt Whitman*
> *Down the long lanes of our country*
> *Cry out our need for you*
> *In a garden still wet with dew*

Despite such optimism, he could only make poetry, like Whitman, from striding beyond the lanes into the often twisted, potential of America with its 600,000 lost to the North and South and slavery's *sinful torpor of pillared porch and darkling death.* Even these iniquities had their heroes who *refused to wear the chains/or suffer auction on history's callous block.* Thus, the abolitionists led by Douglass rising, after his escape from the cotton fields, to nomination for Vice-President, running with the suffragist Victoria Woodhull for the Equal Rights Party; the deluded John Brown who wanted action rather than talk and whose soul *marched on in battle-hymn formation*; the doomed President, of course,

> *Whose words were writ in dirt*
> *Of Manassas and Cold Harbour*
> *Earth turned by limbs and organs*
> *Of young men from Georgia and Vermont*
> *Who wanted first to laugh before they died*
> *His own blood flowing into theirs*
> *As they lay down in futile glory*
> *And he in glory all his own*

He backtracked to Melville's *mythic white whale muse that sang men to their doom/with the last story-teller floating on a worded coffin*; to the great raging ride of the Comanche in 1840 from mid-Texas to the sea where they sacked the coastal town of Linville, survivors huddling in boats on the bay *full of prayer that scalped all sense of feathered fury*; to the last buffalo *lost in that final canyon or stand of western plain/where repeating rifles levered their message of doom/and Bowie's blade skinned all nature's dignity for gain.* The bear felt the harpoon and knife edge cutting deep and *wept for all extinction.*

It was just as well Garrett wrote him before Christmas to say Manhattan had waylaid him so the New Year's trip was off because he wanted to keep writing and not have to talk about what he was attempting on the page. The happy surprise was that his friend was engaged to a New York girl he'd met at a gallery opening. Her family was well-connected enough to pass the social test with his parents but not wealthy enough to threaten their sense that money came from established class rather than the other way round. They were to be married in the spring, and if Hal couldn't be at the cathedral perhaps they could spend a delayed, springtime honeymoon in the Keys. As for the apartment, should he let it go at the time of the wedding or sublet it for the months Hal would still be away? Keep it, by hook or by crook, Hal wrote back, along with his congratulations. Without mentioning Nicky, he assured Garrett he'd be able to come up with the rent money.

As luck had it, Nicky's schedule would allow them to spend New Year's together, although on Christmas Day one of them would be somewhere between Jamaica and Cuba while the other decorated a houseplant with a few bulbs and tinsel. During the rest of the year his mother rarely came to mind. She had no idea where he was or, unless someone he couldn't imagine had told her, anything of his success as a poet. What *she* could certainly imagine had come true. Her worst fears when he had revealed himself to her would be realized if she ever saw him walking hand-in-hand with his lover, undisguised and unashamed. It was better she was gone, but even so Christmas brought memories of pre-Embarcadero boyhood when, whatever the stultifications, he had felt reasonably secure and, besides, always had Miller to get away with. The holiday also reminded him of that magical time with Mrs. Capalca's family and especially her grandchildren. He might not be Ishmael's equal as a storyteller, but those kids would never forget the forest fire adventure. He'd send them a postcard care of her address and write her a letter too.

Dear Mrs. C.

How I miss those carefree days of home-cooking and grandkids' visits when I didn't know how lucky I was. If you ever feel like leaving Brooklyn for a holiday, you're more than welcome here. I have my own house with guest room and set quite a decent table if you like salads and fresh fish. Garrett was going to visit me at New Year's but wrote to say he's become engaged to a New York girl. I'm sure you'll receive an invitation for that happy day not far down the road, and I hope to see you then. As for me, I don't think I'll ever get

married (you see, I can hear your well-intentioned question)
because to have and to hold that special someone would prove
very difficult. Please give my best to all your family.

with love,

Hal

He didn't think she was one to read between the lines, her heart too
much in the right place of Sunday gatherings and *bambinos*.

As it turned out, he didn't have to spend a lonely evening on the
25th because there was a turkey dinner provided for all the sailors and
their friends at the Elk's Lodge in town. He almost didn't go because of
the organization's openly racist membership policies, but then he
thought to work such prejudice into his poem along with KKK extrem-
ism so he decided to view the enemy up close. The young men's company was very enjoyable, and he was pleased he had no quivers of temptation, but his most memorable moment came in an exchange with an
elderly man who referred to himself as an "Esteemed Leading Knight"
of the Order. He told Hal the Elks, when they were forming, had almost
called themselves the Buffalo.

"Thank God we didn't associate ourselves with a dead species," he
proclaimed.

"Too bad the negroes won't cooperate," Hal said, and walked away.

5.

When Nicky returned four days after Christmas they impulsively decided
to take an overnight freighter to Havana and spend New Year's there.
Nicky could catch his ship from the island to Vera Cruz on the 2nd. Hal
was excited to see the city Miller had told him about in letters from the
Isle of Pines, and Nicky was eager to show him some of the haunts he

knew from years of stopovers. They stayed in a hotel near the *Plaza Vieja*, which in the old days had been the site of executions and bullfights. The surrounding area showed off the baroque architecture of the cathedral and other buildings, including many private apartments, that were marvellous to look at but inescapably the products of colonial wealth based on class inequality and slavery. He knew there had been Spanish plantations on the island, and Miller had written that workers were still toiling in cane and tobacco fields as they had in previous centuries, only now for American-owned companies.

They spent the last afternoon of the year walking the avenue beside the seawall then took a skiff across the mouth of the bay to see the sunset from the limestone ridge where Morro Castle had guarded the harbour entrance since the late 16th century. There were no heights like this on Key West, but the spectacle of sea and coastline reminded him of the view from Telegraph Hill. Maybe there was mixed blood in his lineage because the Keys, like San Francisco, had been settled by Spaniards too.

"I could always ask my mother," he said aloud.

"Ask her what?"

"Oh, if everything's as pure as it's made out to be."

"Don't ever think so," Nicky replied.

When an itinerant photographer offered to take their picture for a few pesos, they stood with their arms draped over one another's shoulders and smiled into the sun. The man said he would deliver the *imagen* to them the next day and asked if they wanted a frame, two pesos extra.

"No," Nicky said. "Don't fence us in."

"*Qué?*" the man asked.

"We're hard to translate," Hal said, and they both laughed at the insinuation.

That night in the Plaza there was a carnival of fireworks and processions, and they sat at a table on the cobblestones sipping the best rum Hal had ever tasted, watching the bright explosions and trailing plumes of smoke. He told Nicky he wished they had time to visit San Juan Hill, but it was too far away at the south-east end of the island.

"What's so important?" Nicky asked, and at first Hal thought he was kidding.

"That's where Roosevelt won the Spanish-American War in 1899 and set himself up for the Presidency."

"He was a hero, I know that. I was asking why you wanted to go there."

"I want to write about it." He hesitated. When he'd showed Nicky the poem in *Passages* and penned in its dedicatory title, his "companion, lover, friend" had smiled, kissed him, and then closed the volume. As far as Hal could tell, he had never opened it again. Nicky certainly wasn't illiterate because he'd read Miller's novel and thought it "really honest." However, when he'd discovered Hal had been friends since boyhood with the famous author, he seemed jealous, saying he'd have to confront Miller and warn him off, but Hal couldn't tell how much was an act and how much actual resentment.

"Don't worry, Miller's as straight as an arrow. But even if he wasn't, despite your stevedore muscles, I doubt you could discourage him. We went through some tight times together."

"Sounds like you're in love with him."

"Jesus, Nicky, he's like a brother! We were born on the same day and we almost died on the same day. I'm not *in* love with him, but I do love him, that's for sure. Listen, let me tell you a story."

So he described the fishing trip and the fire, emphasizing that he wouldn't have known to dig the trench if the injured Miller hadn't told him. "I've never forgotten lying there with my mouth cupped in my hands taking shallow breaths while the flames licked at my back. By then I was too scared to think about dying." He didn't mention the goodbye kiss or his dream about Miller and Nicky the night before.

Now in the Havana plaza Nicky brought up Miller again. "It says on the back of his novel he won a medal in the war and some kind of big prize for writing about it."

"The Pulitzer. I'd like to win that one day."

"How did he win the medal?"

Hal told him about Miller's charge up the hill after all his men had been lost and that he killed three German machine-gunners at the top.

"His own San Juan," Nicky said, and Hal heard the irony. "Do you think he wants to be President?"

He laughed a little too loudly. "Not Miller. He just wants to be the best writer in the world. You can't get elected to that position. You just have to do it."

"What about you?"

"I just want to finish what I started a long time ago. It's a long poem about ..."

"I'll bet it's about heroes." This time there was no irony at all.

Nicky left Havana the next morning, and they held on to one another for a long time on the wharf. Hal knew something had shifted slightly between them during the conversation about Miller back in Key West, and even more so over the issue of heroes the day before. Maybe if he'd told him about the kiss on the ridgeline there'd always be the possibility of that physical confrontation Nicky imagined and a lover's victory, but it was their writing that joined him and Miller in Nicky's eyes, and there was no way for a stevedore to deal with that. It meant, of course, he was jealous of the one thing Hal could not surrender to him, which had everything and nothing to do with Miller. He didn't want to win the Pulitzer because Miller had, but because it would verify his own work, take it off his desk and into the world where ambition would be sated and his almost decade-long voyage be ended. He didn't know what he would do if that ever happened, didn't know if there would be anything left to consume him creatively. Maybe he could just settle down then with Nicky and write the occasional lyric about red snappers or the smooth taste of Cuban rum. Keats had stopped at twenty-five, his own age now. But, of course, disease had claimed the Englishman not an end to inspiration.

He wandered through the back streets of the old city past newspaper stands and bookstalls, running his fingertips over the spines of leather-bound volumes in Spanish he would never read. Then on a wooden shelf beneath a shop window he saw the title *Simple Verses* by José Martí. He had picked it up when the shop owner appeared in his doorway, obviously recognizing him for the *gringo* he was, and hailing him in more than passable English.

"Our greatest poet, *señor*. The Apostle of Our Revolution."

Hal could hear the capital letters ringing off the man's tongue and knew Martí had been granted national designation.

"Here," the man said, taking the book gently from his hands, "let me show you his most famous work." He turned the pages for a few moments then handed it back.

The poem repeated its title in the opening line then wrapped what the writer could give himself and others in petals of metaphor.

I have a white rose to tend
In July as in January
I give it to the true friend
Who offers his frank hand to me.

As for the cruel one whose blows
Break the heart by which I live,
Thistle nor thorn do I give
For him, too, I have a white rose.

Not a flower of glass, but, like "six children," living, breathing possibility. There were tears in his eyes as the shopkeeper spoke to him again.

"Do you know he dwelled in your country for fifteen years? For his health at first and then because he was leading the revolution and could not return here."

"Where in the States?"

"Why New York, *señor*. And in *Cayo Hueso* where he and his compatriots formed the Revolutionary Party."

"That's Key West!"

"*Si, señor. Cayo Hueso.*"

"How much for the book?"

"I can see how much you care for him. *Es nada.*" When Hal began to protest, he held up his hand. "Your country gave Marti a great deal, *señor*. It is easy to return the favour."

When he got back to Key West he read all the poems and wrote to Garrett, extolling Marti's verse and asking if there was a biography of him available. After a couple of weeks, Garrett replied saying he'd been unable to find anything, but on Hal's recommendation he'd read *Simple Verses* and a compelling essay translated as "Our America" in which the poet called for an end to cultural and governmental colonialism in Latin America, declaring dramatically: "Our own Greece is preferable to the Greece that is not ours."

He began to think about expanding his *Odyssey* to include this remarkable figure who was only forty-two when he was cut down in battle after returning to Cuba from exile. Then he realized Martí and his struggle, let alone his poetry, deserved a literary paean of their own. Other Caribbean figures, no doubt, had fought against the Spanish, British, and Dutch on other islands and perhaps even written about their efforts. There'd be plenty of time for such research once he'd finished his first long poem.

Dear Miller

I'm sending you this copy of a poem by the Cuban revolutionary José Martí. Perhaps you heard about him in your travels to Havana. Did you know he lived in New York for fifteen years and spent time in Key West? I've learned a little about his role in Cuban independence and his vision for a united South America. How I envy those writers whose lives are entirely grounded in what goes on around them, violently and beautifully, from the time of their birth until they die from their loyalty to its unfolding. You are something like that kind of writer. The war gave you the basis for those initial pieces of journalism, then your novel. And in between you brought the wilderness you've known into stories that will last as long as the rivers and pines. I, as you once told me, am busy making up words out of places I have never been and people I can never know. Some might say it's a lesser art, but it's still worth the effort. You didn't say very much about Passageways when I sent it to you, but I like to think there's a Martí poem or two in there. I guess you're waiting for the big one. One day, brother, one day.

Hal

6.

On the freighter home, despite his relatively positive frame of mind, he had been disturbed by Nicky's ongoing mistrust of Miller and his implied mockery of his friend's physical courage. If there had to be a reckoning sooner or later, he didn't see what more he could say to alleviate his lover's suspicions. Miller was a force in their relationship, but surely not a threatening one. His presence lay in the occasional letter and in his international notoriety, but it wasn't as if Hal had ever slept with him or paraded him like a tempting rival who could upset the status quo at any time. Nicky knew that, so what was going on? The more he thought about it, the more he was convinced it wasn't sexual jealousy but envy of Miller's creative prowess and, by association, his own artistic efforts. How to reconcile the body and the mind? It frightened him that maybe you couldn't. When he and Nicky were joined in the flesh poetry might be the powerful after-thought, but the gift of tongues was immediate and wordless. When he did write, it was page not body he was inscribing, and the result transcended corporeal exchange. He certainly wasn't superior to Nicky, but he did feel different, and he wondered if such difference meant the inevitable incompatibility he'd hinted at to Mrs. Capalca. On the other hand, while he sensed an extraordinary creative affinity with Miller, the sexual disparity between them was enormous, so what did that portend for *their* future?

Unable to sleep in the tiny airless cabin, he flicked on the light and tried to read some Martí, but he was too restless to concentrate. Pulling on a sweater over his pyjamas, he went up on deck and walked along silently with his hand on the railing. The stars were legion above him, and his own insignificance weighed heavily as he gazed up at them and out at the black encompassing sea. What was the point of it all? Trying to love someone and leaving traces of your earthly passing in so many words didn't amount to very much in relation to stellar distances or even ocean depths. Since he couldn't fly into the heavens, he looked down at the water and its startling promise of union with something larger than personal disquiet. Or was it just oblivion he was aching for, an end to thoughts of poetry's irrelevance along with the inconsequence of orgasmic bonds? The cuffs of his pyjama trousers were flapping pathetically in the wind as his fingers curled around the railing and he stared into the darkness below. Later his aching calf muscles told him how long they had anticipated the leap before a memory of Martí miraculously broke the plane of despair and released his tension. The poet's lines had included him for the moment, but he wasn't sure how long he could be worthy of such association.

> *May they not bury me in darkness*
> *To die like a traitor*
> *I am a good man and as a good man*
> *I will die facing the sun.*

As he shivered beneath his thin blanket and drifted off into sleep, he swore to himself there would be no solitary, veiled betrayal of his character or his craft. Whenever and wherever the exit he would not hide from heat or light.

Warned by the full-time residents of how hot the Keys became even before high summer, he decided to return to New York at the end of May. Not that the city would be much better in July and August, but he and Nicky could spend as much time as possible at Brighton Beach or out on the Far Rockaway peninsula where the swimming was excellent. After Cuba Nicky didn't bring up Miller again nor did Hal mention him or any of his own work. The mutual silence was golden, and they relaxed into a relationship in which loyalty was comfortably taken for granted and sexual pleasure a balm for days and nights apart. Hal knew that their future together wasn't assured given their differences, but neither was there any guarantee he'd ever be able to answer that question about reconciliation of body and mind, so he was willing to take the chance. The sharing of a Village apartment would succeed only if the Key West situation could be moved north and he could do his work uninterrupted most days of the month. Nicky would have to accept his bookshelves filled with volumes of verse and fiction, but he'd make sure all his writing papers were put away when the ship was in dock. After all, he'd have Garrett to talk to about his work and those at the Artists' Club for further support.

For the first time since he was a boy he considered his parents' failure to get along. His mother's domineering personality meant his father had to have something to fall back on, but apparently whatever it had been wasn't enough. Well, that was never going to be the case with him. Your partner didn't have to be domineering, but if you loved him hard enough there had to be relief at hand. Nicky, after all, had the sea-life for weeks on end, and his own immersion in his writing was a voyage across immense distances of vision and expression. New York was to be their shared port-of-call and should be the richer for it. Meanwhile, he wrote about wagon-trains bound for California pressing their mark into prairie vastness, miner and settler aspirations clashing with indigenous desire.

> *Ponies circle dreams of gold*
> *Ruts are tracks before the plough*
> *Hooves hard shod and manes undone*
> *Both sides yearn to live unbowed*

The winter sea was warm enough for swimming, but it wasn't until early April that he and Nicky began to spend as much time in the water as they could. They learned to snorkel in the sub pens, pinching their nostrils when they dove and blowing out the pressure on their ears. This way they could descend a few metres down and happily anticipate the depths offshore. Of course, there was no coral in the pens so plant growth was at a minimum, but it was great fun to get up close to the barracuda that hovered within reach like house-pets in the gentle currents before exploding away to remind amateur observers they were anything but tame. When they felt confident enough they rented a skiff and began to explore the inner reef, Nicky exacting a promise that Hal would never go out alone. In his absence it was frustrating to stick close to shore when the spectacular display of coral, marine life, and waving fronds were waiting just a hundred yards away, but he recognized the dangers of any solitary activity out there, especially as local fishermen warned him of hammerheads where the reef fell away into blue-black expanse.

The first time they anchored the skiff and went down the sights were overwhelming. Small striped fish darted ahead of them and followed in their wake as if they were all part of a parade, while larger groupers drifted lazily in the currents to a different drummer. Pink coral forms thrust upward like small cacti or blossomed into firm flowery shapes they almost reached out to pluck. Each of them would touch the other's arm and point excitedly at some new and wondrous sculpture or finned performance, straining to hold their breath just a little longer and trying to time the breathless distance to the surface. When they did come up and tossed off their masks, arms supporting them on the gunwale as the sun's heat beaded the salt on their shoulders, the air seemed charged with exhilaration and bliss and they half-creatures of the sea who could stay this way forever.

"Why would anyone ever leave this place?" Nicky asked as he rowed back one day, the boat's prow slipping smoothly through the chop that usually appeared around noon along with a south-east wind.

"So they could find it all again for the first time," Hal said. To swim the reef was like immersing yourself in words, he thought. In each case eternity was your medium, but it was finding eternity anew each day that kept it holy.

"Sometimes I wish I could paint. All the underwater photos I've seen are in black and white, but a painter could do it justice, couldn't he?"

Hal imagined Picasso's "Les Poissons d'Avignon," stifling his laugh because he didn't want to hurt Nicky's feelings, and naming a few realist artists whose results, he would have to agree, would be stunning. Then his mind went back to writing and what a struggle it would be with words to present the reef in all its glory. Eliot, to be sure, had "lingered in the chambers of the sea" and seen the "sea-girls wreathed in seaweed red and brown," but that poem was so damned depressing, people getting bald and old and never taking chances. There had to be a more positive portrait that reflected the absolute quality of the light down there and the energy you brought back from an unspoiled realm.

"If you descend not stairs
But fathomed paths without a rail
Hurry up please it's time to feel
The universe ripple as you dare"

"What?" Nicky asked.

"Nothing. Just thinking aloud."

One morning towards the end of the month there was a sheen on the water as they rowed out, and when Hal looked below he couldn't see the sandy bottom as clearly as usual or the beginnings of the coral. When they anchored in a new spot and dove down everything was pristine and precise in outline, but the reef here seemed magnified in shape and size with huge rectangular boulders strewn about or strangely aligned to create twisting alleys of stone. He felt uneasy as if a hammerhead could be lurking behind one of the giant rocks, but they were well away from the drop-off the fisherman had described and he thought it too shallow here for such large predators. When they came up for air Nicky was eager to explore a tunnel through the rocks that schools of tiny fish had entered but he hadn't seen come out.

"There might be a cave of some kind in there with thousands of them swimming around."

"There might be barracuda in there eating them, which is why they're not reappearing."

"C'mon, Hal, we have to have a look at least."

The entrance was too narrow for them to swim side by side and, following behind Nicky, he found himself enclosed by rugged slabs of stone angling together overhead to permit only a thin strip of light to penetrate from above. He didn't like the claustrophobic sensation or the way the rock rubbed against his legs and shoulders as the tunnel tapered downward. There was no sign of a cave and they'd have to exit very soon or else pull themselves backward, which wouldn't be a simple task. After a few more moments he punched Nicky's heel with his fist signalling his need to retreat. Grasping at the walls he struggled to reverse his forward momentum, his own heels and elbows banging against the rock, bubbles escaping now from his mouth as he desperately tried to hold his breath, forgetting about Nicky and everything else except the need to escape before he drowned. At last his torso came free and he propelled himself upward, but in his panic his mouth opened to let the sea pour in and he saved himself only by swallowing the surge until he could hold no more and began to die. It was his head sharply striking the bottom of the skiff that yanked him from surrender and allowed him to choke his way back into the world.

He clung to the gunwale, his chest heaving and throat burning with brine, lost to any rational perception of what had happened until his heart finally slowed and he realized Nicky was not beside him. He gazed out over the flat, indifferent surface of the water and saw nothing but emptiness. Christ! How long had he been holding on? He had to go back down. Spitting in his mask and rinsing it to remove the condensation he donned it again and flipped over into a dive. He thought he'd be right above the tunnel, but the reef topography was deceptive now and he panicked again as he frantically sought the entrance, stroking and kicking back and forth uselessly until he had to surface sucking in oxygen and awareness that too much time was passing. Below once more he tried to map his way with marker rocks and not repeat his route, but there was nothing at all except fronds and rigid flowers until he glimpsed the pale hand in the current, fingers spread and waving slightly like a crenellated fan.

Nicky had tried to squeeze through the end of the passage, but his shoulders were too broad and held him in place without mercy. He must have fought, but in his staring green eyes there was no evidence of strife just bewilderment that space and time had closed in so quickly. Hal went up for more air, looking back for signposts, and when he returned swam into the entrance and down to grasp Nicky's heels and pull him loose. He did not come readily, but when Hal finally held him in his arms a school of miniature fish emerged from the tunnel and danced around them in panoplies of praise.

Happy All Alone

1.

Watching Sally do a barrel-roll over Le Bourget Airport, he remembered the first time she'd done that with him in the rear cockpit back in St. Louis. Once you knew what was going on, it was scarier in ways to see her perform the stunt from ground-level because you could see how small the plane was in the blue depths. They'd been here a year now, and everything was working out. On the strength of her reputation, which had preceded her across the Atlantic—"Woman Flier Greatest Daredevil!"—she was able to purchase a Blériot-SPAD biplane on the cheap. Though it always seemed to have maintenance problems, she liked the way it handled, and when she took thrill-seekers up the side-by-side seating gave her a chance to call out in advance of any sudden moves. There was a trick, she said, to yelling between your teeth and not opening your mouth too wide.

"No wonder your voice is hoarse," Miller said. "Every move you do is sudden."

They had a flat on the Rue Dante on the Left Bank not far from the Seine. He liked to walk over to a riverside *café* in the early morning for a coffee and *beignet* where he would watch the boats and read the *Herald-Tribune* with its three-day-old box scores and reports of the President's wit. When Dorothy Parker told Coolidge she'd bet against a man who'd said it was impossible to get him to say more than two words at a time, 'Silent Cal' had replied: "You lose." Well, win or lose, he'd never felt more relaxed than he did in Paris. The French didn't rush about anything, and his return to the flat around ten a.m. to write for a few hours was in time with the regular unfolding of a Gallic day.

In the late afternoon he would stop in at *Shakespeare and Company* and chat with Sylvia Beach who was a dyke, but that didn't matter because she sure had a wonderful collection of books for sale and he could meet other writers there. The expatriate American community flourished in the city, and everyone seemed to be writing a new novel. Well, at least he had two fictions under his belt, the last of which had brought him quite a lot of money not to mention a measure of notoriety that meant he was always being asked for advice about plots and characters or what he was working on. He liked being famous, but he didn't want to sell out to fame and measured his responses carefully. His enemies, mainly back home, saw him in the pretentious role of a senior literary statesman who wasn't much past his mid-twenties, and mocked him accordingly, but he didn't care.

Sally barnstormed all around the country, sometimes absent for a week or two at a time. He missed her when she was away but always worked better when the flat was empty and he could stick strictly to his own schedule. When she was home she was always restless and they'd have to *do* something like stroll in the Luxembourg Gardens or go out to the track at Longchamp and bet on the thoroughbreds or, at night, take in the splashy costumes of the dancers at the *Folies Bergère*. It was always a bit exhausting, but he supposed when she wasn't flying she had to stay in motion so he didn't complain. Besides, he still enjoyed the way she moved in bed, her lithe body taking off eagerly into sex and never landing until, as she was fond of saying, her runways had been cleared. For her part she appeared happy with their life, assuring him they shared the best of all possible worlds in which their combination of love and self-sufficiency kept them together through thick and thin.

"What's the thin?" he asked.

"That's when I've had a lousy series of shows because the weather closed in for a week, and I come home in a funk and you're too busy to hold my hand."

"And the thick?"

"When I get to hold something else."

He enjoyed this banter but felt, after all this time together, they often hid behind it, afraid to step out in the open and admit any uncertainties about their relationship. He'd once sworn never to let a woman rob him of his words the way Amélie had, and he wondered if the controlled repartee between them was designed on his part to prevent such theft. But even if that was the case, she had to have her own motives based in her counterpart to his writing—her flying and the way she disappeared into it. Just as he was invisible when he was writing, so was she when she took off into what made her tick. Just as he couldn't share or explain the space from which his characters emerged, she couldn't emotionally or intellectually divvy up the sky where she spread her wings. They were two of a kind, two artists who could only meet half-way, and if that meant restricted vocabulary between them was the price for basic contentment, so be it.

She hadn't ever said much about their brief New York meeting, but he was sure Sally approved of Hal, and how could any man resist her nerve and ability, not to mention her good looks? He never mentioned any women, though Miller was sure he didn't abstain. There'd been no word for quite a while, and he was a little worried. It wasn't like his friend to keep his news to himself. The last letter he had from him was full of enthusiasm for the Cuban poet Martí whom he had been intending to read since his first trip to the Isle of Pines. He had finally found a copy of *Simple Verses* on Sylvia's shelves and had to admit the man could deliver the goods. He was a genuine hero and had died a good death fighting against Spain. Hal's own book of poems had been moderately successful, but he must still be working on his magnum opus and that unending task might be the reason for his silence. Nonetheless, what he'd written about Key West suggested a fine outdoors life just like they'd had when they were young, and surely that couldn't have done anything but inspire. Wouldn't it have been great to swim the reef and fish together at the sub pens? Hal was probably back in New York by now. Maybe when they resumed their correspondence he'd invite him to Paris or they'd get down to Florida and make up for lost time, though he didn't know when he and Sally would ever go home.

2.

After the wedding in Cleveland had gone as planned, they'd taken a train to Miami and boarded a ship for Havana. Just six months after T.R.'s charge up San Juan Hill and the expulsion of the Spanish, the U.S. had allowed the island's independence, but until very recently had reserved the right to intervene militarily in Cuban affairs. That policy included the Isle of Pines, and the American colony there when he and Sally had arrived had been far too jingoistic for his taste, so he kept his distance.

Nueva Gerona was a small town not far from the coast and clinging to the banks of a river that ran quietly down to the sea. The house was a mile or so outside of town, close enough to walk in for groceries and a cold *cerveza* but far enough out to give him peace and quiet for his work. There was no airstrip, so Sally was frustrated until she took a ship to Cienfuegos on Cuba's south shore and found an Aeromarine 39 at the U.S. army base there. It was badly in need of repair, and she manoeuvred the price to an acceptable level before making several trips across the thirty-mile strait to work on the 100-horsepower engine and replace the tattered wing canvas. The main reason they decided they could afford it was that it was a pontoon craft, which meant she could land and tie it up in the sanctuary of the river's lower reaches. He didn't like her flying over the open sea, because there was no search and rescue available, but knew it did no good to try and dissuade her. She talked of barnstorming in Cuba because it would give her a focus and bring in some money, and eventually she was able to arrange some shows in and around Havana.

When he watched her take off from the river-mouth she simply vanished into the clouds or became a tiny speck that disappeared over the horizon, and he wouldn't know if she'd made it across the strait and then the forests and hills into the city where crosswinds off the water made for a tricky landing. Back in St. Louis she'd brought home a battered copy of *Little Women* from a county fair stall and pointed out a passage he wouldn't soon forget. 'You are the gull, Jo, strong and wild, fond of the storm in the wind, flying far out to sea and happy all alone.' There was nothing to do but return to the house and sit at the desk in front of the north-facing window, looking up from his typewriter after a few days had passed to scan the sky for her return flight. It was useless to worry because she usually flew too low for a 'chute, and if she went down there wouldn't be much hope unless she survived the crash and a fishing boat was passing by. So he concentrated on his work, which was a little like flying by the seat of his pants. He had a compass and vague sense of his destination, but the weather of words was always unpredictable, and there was no such thing as a parachute for a writer.

He stayed away from the war in his stories. Having dealt with it in reportorial fashion in the newspaper vignettes for which he'd won the Pulitzer, in the future he wanted to transform rather than straightforwardly present the experiences he'd had in France. That transformation would be the basis of the novel he planned to write about the conflict, but first he wanted to say something about growing up in Michigan. His old notebook was very useful because he could read over the jottings he'd made years before about such things as a high school football game, the sunlight glinting off speckled scales as a fish leapt in a rapids pool, and the crooked lope of a wounded deer before the final shot. These were beginnings of coming of age tales, ones in which a youth on the verge of manhood glimpsed something more than the surface of life he had taken for granted—a star quarterback saw the leg bone of a teammate protruding through his skin after a vicious tackle and decided to give up the game though no one, least of all his stern father, understood; a young fisherman entered into a contest with a friend to see how many trout they could catch in a day, and was ashamed to look at the rows of pallid corpses in the grass even though he had won; a hunter revelled in his first kill, then, as he was about to skin his prize, heard the bear moan softly before expiring and wondered what it would be like to turn the gun on himself. The irony for each of the main characters lay in the further, complex interaction with the world that had prompted the dark inner visions in the first place. Thus the quarterback thought of studying to become a doctor but could only do so if he accepted a sports scholarship; the fisherman tried to explain his shame to his younger brother but promised to take him to the same pool in the spring; and when the hunter wrote a faithful account of the incident in the woods for his school yearbook his teacher derided him for his cowardice.

He decided to revise and combine the two versions of the forest fire into a single long story in which the narrative moved back and forth between the two friends, each of them with a point of view that seemed above board and even admirable as they remembered danger closing in. The older boy, who was the leader, recalled leading them to safety in the river *because that was what he had been trained all his life to do,* while the younger one, who had always been a prisoner of his dreams, *saw unfettered survival for them both as he dug the trench.* He placed the original last line of the second version, *'What would I have done without you?'* as the ending of the entire piece still without identifying the speaker. The reader would either have to choose between the escapes or accept the duality of truth under pressure.

First love was glimpsed in a house on the edge of a lumber town where a college boy was working for the summer. He went to the Indian whores with the men who worked in the saw-mill because he feared their derision if he stayed behind, but they found out somehow it was his first time. When he'd had two whiskeys for fortification, many pairs of hands clapped him on the back and indecent words of advice rang in his ears as he stumbled upstairs. There he followed the trail of cheap perfume to a room with a bare bulb suspended above a thin blanket and straw mattress, a jug of water, and a Bible left by the Gideons. While he laboured over the girl and she worked beneath him, her face was turned away as if to meet his gaze would alter the economy of their impersonal agreement. He heard the men laughing distantly below and the soughing of wind in the trees outside the window. All he could see was lines of shadow like bars across her cheek and strands of her hair bathed in sweat. All he could do was wonder at the dullness of his feeling and her indifference until, at the sudden climactic release he'd been assured downstairs would be his alone, she turned her head and he glimpsed the muted pleasure in her eyes.

Miller knew that readers might think this story mirrored too closely "Something of Interest" that had appeared in the *Dial* two years before. But for him the contrast was obvious between his first protagonist's betrayal of the *dark pearl* who never sold herself and the college boy's bond with the Ojibway girl who took his money in the end. He decided to include them both in the collection.

Then he surprised himself by writing about a newspaper reporter who met a beautiful female flier and learned more about the nature of courage than he ever did in the wilderness as a boy. Of course there was practical accomplishment in finding shelter in a storm and starting a fire with wet kindling and logs, and a certain strength of body and mind necessary to hike through the woods alone while you kept your imagination in check. You never knew what lurked in the denser stands of trees or whether your hand would be steady if you had to shoot to save your life. But to put your trust in pistons and cylinders as well as bits of wire and canvas a thousand feet in the air involved skill and achievement of heroic proportions. The reporter tried to reconcile such a fact with his strong sexual attraction to the pilot, going up with her time and again in an attempt to discover the link between bravery and the emotion that had claimed him. The climax came as they attempted to fly over Lake Michigan together in the winter and got caught in a blizzard. When she took the plane down almost to water level to escape the high-altitude winds and he was sure they were going to die, her loveliness faded into the commonplace movements of her hands on the stick and the cold deliberation with which she manipulated their fate. He learned that on the sheer edge of existence there was little room for feeling and that heroes felt least of all. They finally made it to the other side of the lake, but when he told her of his discovery she scoffed at his innocence.

'Every part of me was humming up there,' she said, 'but it was the plane fucking me, not you.'

Since the censors would inevitably prevail, he went with innuendo instead.

'Every part of me was humming up there, but the plane was doing it, not you.'

In the ensuing weeks he finished five more stories to make an even dozen for the volume, dedicating it to his father and titling it Something of Interest as a draw to readers but also because The Dial's acceptance of that story had put him on his way as a writer of fiction. A large New York house brought the book out eight months later and the critics all admired his prose, one calling it "as clean and original as the rivers and streams he writes about" and another saying he was the best young stylist in the country. But most of them were troubled by the "disturbing, at times sordid, quality of his subject matter." Why were all his characters so depressed and depressing? Why did he focus so much on carnality and death? The public, on the other hand weren't deterred and the book quickly went into a second printing. He was, as he wrote to Hal, in the company of many best-selling artists who were appreciated everywhere in the country except the Upper East Side of New York.

In the afternoons when he'd written enough, he explored the island, passing through extensive stands of pine that reminded him of Michigan, and hiking to the crumbling limestone cliffs on the west coast that were nearly a hundred feet high. He and Sally went to the mineral springs to bathe in their warm waters and swam off the black sand beach that was evidence of volcanic eruption centuries ago. On the way to these places there were unfenced citrus groves and vegetable gardens near modest haciendas with red-tiled roofs, whitewashed walls, and tiny wrought-iron balconies above their main entrances. On his journeys alone he waved to the occupants, usually of Indian or Spanish descent who, if he was close enough, would beckon him into the courtyard for a cup of water, unfazed by his failure to understand their welcoming chatter. The Americans, whose places were not so modest, weren't much interested in an itinerant countryman who wasn't a property owner and had too much free time on his hands. They'd talk if he stopped and addressed them, which wasn't often because all they seemed to do was complain about Cuban aggression against the lumbering interests they would never surrender.

At the port he made friends with several fishermen who took him out into deep waters where tarpon, marlin, and even the occasional swordfish would take a trailing hand-line.

"Did you ever try to fight a big fish on a hand-line?" he asked Sally. "Those guys can do it, but their palms and fingers are so calloused they can't feel a thing. Look!" He held up his own palms so she could see the scorched red strip cutting across each one. "That's from a hundred-pounder, and I couldn't haul him in. Next time we come down here I need to get myself some proper gear."

She was pleased by his apparently spontaneous suggestion of return, but the truth was he could see she wasn't yet convinced Paris was for her, and if they weren't going to get overseas soon, he needed this kind of place to write the first draft of his novel. He could deal with subsequent revisions anywhere at all as long as he had a quiet working-space, even if newspaper responsibilities would eat up a large part of his day. He'd helped her buy the plane out of his Pulitzer funds, but that meant he'd certainly have to go back to work for the *Post-Dispatch* for awhile. With his editorial by-line he could write about anything at all from Rogers Hornsby to the new American novel that was all the rage about a self-made millionaire's dream of buying back lost love. Sally could get regular barnstorming work in the States, which would increase their income, so he figured they could be back on the island next winter before Christmas. Maybe his book of stories would bring in some royalties. Well, even if it didn't, he was sure the novel would. They'd get to Paris by '24 one way or another.

On his final free day he went out fishing with a grizzled Cuban named Manuel who had fought in the 1895 uprising against the Spaniards. On a whim Miller asked him if there were any Cubans who had written about the war.

"Si, *senor* Miller, there was José Martí. He was a great leader of our revolution. Without him we would still be licking Spanish boots."

He held the wheel casually with one hand, but Miller could see the cords of muscle in his forearm that held the boat on course. Then to his astonishment, in a voice worn with war and weather, the old man recited lines of poetry that could only have been Martí's.

Cultivo una rosa blanca
En juilo como en enero,
Para el amigo sincere
Que me das su mano franca

Y para el cruel que me arranca
El Corazon con que vivo,
Cardo ni ortiga cultivo,
Cultivo una rosa blanca

"It is a pity I cannot say it in English," he said. "It is very beautiful."

"A friend of mine would like it very much," Miller replied. "He writes poems almost as good." His faith in Hal's work was strong, but he knew not to insult his host.

"If that is so, *señor*, I would like to meet him." He paused. "There is something else."

"Yes?"

"I saw him die."

"You saw who die?"

"Martí, *señor*."

Miller blinked in surprise. "How did it happen?"

"We were on the Cauto River and the Spanish were hidden in the trees. Martí always wore black and with his white horse they could see him without trouble. A courier rode by and, for a reason we did not know why, Martí told him, '*a la cargal*,' which meant to charge them. They shot him down, and after that we nearly lost the war until your country helped us."

They were out in the Caribbean current now, and while he baited a hand line with a small appledore and dropped it into the blue chop, he thought once again about waiting to charge up the hill with Rawley and Kincaid before everything went blank and how he woke up in the hospital to hear the story of his bravery under fire. He had lived and Martí had died. That was the only difference between them, that and the fact the Cuban was a writer who had left his mark on an entire country. When he got back to the States he'd have to find the poems Martí surely wrote about the war. Hal would know, and maybe even had copies in that bookstore he worked in. Sometimes you got your best writing done before you died in the war, but sometimes you survived so you could do your best work afterwards. He didn't care for black clothing, and they didn't ride white horses into battle anymore, but he could cultivate his own flower of expression that somebody could quote one day. No, not a flower, but a tree, a giant white pine by a border river that was impervious to fire and young death.

3.

"Let's fly back," Sally said the week before.

"Are you crazy? It's way too far."

"No, I've thought about it. From here to Havana. Havana to Key West. Then hopping up through the south to St. Louis. It'll take a week, not much longer than going by boat and train. Besides, I'm used to the plane now, and you know the pontoons can eventually come off and wheels be put on."

"The Curtiss will be jealous," he said. "Besides what about our luggage?"

"We just send it on home. It can't cost that much."

"I'm keeping my manuscript."

"Okay," she said, "but no typewriter. It's too heavy."

He wished he'd made a copy he could put in his suitcase with instructions to Hal or Fitzgibbon so if they went down maybe it could still be published. But it was too late for that, so he crammed the pages into his knapsack that would sit at his feet along with enough socks and underwear to last him on the journey. When they checked with the shipping office they were told if their big bags went to New Orleans then straight north they would be waiting for them when they arrived in St. Louis.

On a bright January morning just after dawn they took off from the river-mouth and headed for Cuba. Normally, they would have spent a couple of days in Havana, but with few personal items at hand they had to keep going. There was a build-up of thunderheads to the west, but luckily the skies stayed clear all the way to Key West where in the early evening Sally set the plane down in the calm water just outside the old submarine pens. He liked the site of the town and the American company of merchant sailors they found in the restaurant and bar on Flagler Avenue, named after the guy who had built the railway from the mainland through the keys. But he could tell this was a tourist town and it would never be peaceful enough for him to work in. Their island was preferable by far, and in Paris one day the distractions wouldn't be gaudy shirts and loud Nebraskan businessmen and their wives, but great art galleries and alien accents he could ignore when necessary.

Sally hadn't mentioned winter when she planned their flight, and as they got farther north the clouds began to close in. They spent an extra day in Mobile because of wind-driven rain and another in Memphis for the same reason. By the time they were flying over Missouri there was snow on the ground and Miller shivered despite an old lined jacket he'd purchased at a surplus store in Poplar Bluff to take him the last hundred miles.

"What if there's ice on the river?"

"Then we'll just ski in on the pontoons." When she saw the look on his face, she laughed. "Haven't you heard of a wing and a prayer?"

His father died that spring, and he took the train to Oak Park alone, having convinced Sally there was no need for her to go along as, apart from some aging cousins, he was the only family left so the ceremony would be brief and without fanfare. He regretted never having taken her home while his father was still living, although they'd talked about the possibility of a visit in the coming summer. But right after their wedding they'd been focused on getting to the island, and once they'd arrived it was memories of Michigan that prevailed rather than a desire to see the place again.

The one letter he'd written to Henry was all about how the sea looked on calm mornings or when the wind was up and the white caps seemed to come all the way from Venezuela. He'd described the true wilderness lying offshore in the currents and deeper streams, the island itself like the little northern towns of Wolverine or Indian River in the midst of unmapped, surrounding country. He'd told his father too about the great flocks of water-birds that nested on the limestone cliffs— storm petrels, gannets, and cormorants that rose and fell on tides of air and when they landed rode the waves like perfect ships—and the smaller land-based aviators—bluebirds and sparrows, meadowlarks and finches that you would see back home. The last thing he'd written was a two-sentence paean to the cottage as he remembered it and his father's place there: "At dawn on fishing days you'd prod my shoulder and wake me to the smell of coffee brewing. I'd rise from my pallet on the porch and see the lake waiting patiently forever."

The house in Oak Park had been sold soon after Miller left for the war, and the cottage was where Henry Sark had lived alone for many years and where he had died sitting at the oak table in the main room with the fly-tying vice and bits of feather and thread in front of him. When Miller got there the local undertaker had laid him out in a pine box whose ends rested on two chairs. Henry had no suit, but he did own a white shirt and patterned tie that were complemented somehow by his checked woodsman's jacket with its oil-stained cuffs and one missing button. Neighbours came by to pay their respects and shake the son's hand solemnly, saying they remembered him as a boy and how proud his father had always been of him. He didn't think they knew he was a writer until one of them said how much she admired his stories about the war that she'd read in the newspaper.

"You all tried so hard to be brave," she told him, and he smiled politely and thanked her, thinking how courage had come naturally to Rawley and that Kincaid would have scoffed at any conscious display of valour.

He owned the cottage now but didn't know when he'd return. The only thing he took with him to St. Louis was the old lever-action Henry had given him for his sixteenth birthday. "It's a man's gun," he'd said of the Winchester. "You need to go after bigger game now."

His father would have been pleased with the dedication to the book of stories, and Miller regretted not having told him he'd done this as he'd wanted it to be a surprise. With the exception of the one based on Sally's flying prowess, all the tales had come out of his Michigan boyhood in one way or another, especially how he had been taught to depend on his senses and instincts for survival. He wished he could put the body in a canoe and set in on fire before pushing it out into the lake or maybe build a platform and let paternal flesh return to dust through the beaks of birds and the power of the elements. But he did neither, of course, simply stood by the side of the grave in the local cemetery and listened to the well-intentioned words of the Lutheran minister who handled all the Protestant funerals, including those of the Indians who'd been to church more than once, their first time counting only as a visit. Miller had told the man his father hadn't been religious but had loved the natural world as if it were Heaven itself, and he was grateful for the suitable choice of words from *Ecclesiastes* about the earth abiding forever.

Dear Hal

My old man died last week and I'm home at the cottage dealing with things. He would have been happy at the way he went with pieces of feather on his fingers and a new fly in the vice. Fifty-five isn't a long enough life, of course, but it still seems a long way off for you and me. There's so much lying around here from years ago—rods and reels, a few guns (including my Winchester, which I'm taking with me), and rows and rows of books on the shelves. He taught me to fish and shoot, but he also gave me Tolstoy and Crane and encouraged me to love words as freely as he did. I don't think you go anywhere when you die, and that giving up the ghost, as they say, is letting go of what you are haunted by when you're alive, in my father's case by the water and woods that went everywhere with him so the ghost was a spirit really that lived within and around him from beginning to end. I think you understand this because you spent so much time with us back then, and whatever we did together when we hiked and camped was all wrapped up in what he instructed us to do. When I told you to dig that trench, you shaped it in your own way, but it was all an inheritance that came down through him. Maybe we'll have kids one day and pass things on ourselves. I've finished my book of stories and will make sure you get a copy when it comes out in the fall. Sally and I will go back to Isle of Pines sometime after that and I'll work on the novel about the war. We still plan to get to Paris, but before that you and I have to meet up. It's been too long.

Miller

Fitzgibbon had welcomed him back to the *Post-Dispatch* newsroom and suggested almost immediately that they work on a series of commentaries and cartoons together.

"You supply the subject-matter, and I'll take care of the rest, everything from baseball to the White House."

He thought it over and began with a piece on Hornsby's celebrated fight with Cardinal owner-manager Branch Rickey in the clubhouse after Rickey had given a batter the 'take' sign with Hornsby prepared to run home from third. You didn't leave a star player stranded like that, Miller wrote, but Hornsby was wrong to get in a fight with Rickey off the field. He should have strolled home, been tagged out, and then punched the pompous ass in full view of the fans. Owners shouldn't be in the dugout. They had too much power as it was. He wasn't covering the sports beat anymore so he could get away with this partisan advice, but Rickey was incensed by the column and even more so by Fitzgibbon's accompanying visual that showed a hawk with a "Rajah" crest on its cap swinging a bat to sock a tiny uniformed cardinal over the Sportsman's Park fence. "Take That!" the caption read beneath.

More serious confrontation between opponents became the theme of the series as Miller wrote about railroad shop workers across the country battling with the oligarchs of business and government; the massacre of sugar plantation labourers in Hawaii over wages and working conditions; and the federal government's continuing support of Prohibition, which he saw as upheld by special interests ranging from the Women's Christian Temperance Union to a new kind of owner-manager, the gangster who profited from the speakeasy trade. Fitzgibbon altered a popular poster of Uncle Sam pointing his finger and announcing 'I Want You To Stay Sober' by giving the flag-draped icon a drunken leer and arming him with a sub-machine gun. Many readers were outraged, and the paper was forced to issue an apology, though secretly the editors were delighted by the publicity garnered by the series they refused to shut down. After all this was the work of a Pulitzer Prize winner and nationally-syndicated cartoonist and no other paper in the country could boast of such a team. What all this publicity and accompanying sales did through the summer and fall was give Miller the leverage in bargaining for another leave, this one to be several months in duration, with a promise to give the *Post-Dispatch* an excerpt from his novel before publication.

"I should put you in a cartoon," Fitzgibbon told him. "You're sitting on a tropical isle that's shaped like a typewriter, festooned in Panama hat and sandals. Maybe there's a highball in your hand, say a Lime Rickey for those in the know. The caption reads: 'Twenty-Six Keys To Success.'"

"That's not me," he said gruffly, but was pleased by the implicit suggestion it was his writing that counted.

Despite all his talk about the war novel, he really didn't have any outline in his head or definite sense of how he would write it. The newspaper vignettes about Rawley and the others had taken care of actual experience, and he didn't want to go over the same ground twice. But it wasn't all actual, was it? He'd changed what happened with the German sniper in the woods and hadn't focused at all on what it might be like to kill your enemy in cold blood. As well, there was the question of heroism when the hero couldn't remember anything he did to get the medal. War was like that anyway. You put your thoughts on hold except the ones that would help you survive from one moment to the next, and once you pulled a trigger or threw a grenade you moved on to the next movement of your finger or arm, provided they were still intact and the figure opposing you on the other side of the line hadn't been that little bit quicker.

He wanted to get back to the Caribbean and start writing. It didn't do to think about things too much. That was what Hal had done with his bear poem that might stay a great work-in-waiting because it couldn't escape the idea of what it was or could be. The few hours they'd had together in New York had been great, and some of the poems in *Passageways* were wonderful, but like his own stories they should only be preparations for the best that was yet to come. *Sure* to come if you just put your mind to it. He worried about his friend because there always seemed to be a measure of restraint about him as if that boy who had been so free in the wilderness wasn't free any longer, trapped by the failed relationship with his mother and the fact that poetry would always be a hand-to-mouth production incapable of providing the real independence he needed to complete his great work. As well, the problem was he had no stability in his life, the kind a woman like Sally brought to a relationship. That guy Garrett seemed affected to him, maybe even a bit swishy. When he mentioned this to her, she laughed.

"I don't think Garrett's going to bother him."

"Why not?"

"Hal gets around more than you think."

A casual attribution that he hoped was right. Rawley had said the same thing of himself at the bottom of the hill, hadn't he, a contented smile on his face that danger couldn't wipe away. He wished they could have met, these two, the haunting Carolina ghost who had saved him from the mortars and the living wilderness brother who had kept him from the flames.

4.

At the beginning of the novel, his protagonist, Matty Compton, was visiting an unnamed island in the Gulf of Mexico while a massive hurricane was brewing offshore. When the wind and waves hit he thought he would die alone, but a fishing smack rescued him from the rocky outcrop where he was stranded, and he and the crew rode out the tempest at sea-anchor in a semi-sheltered bay. When the weather calmed, they put in at a demolished village where there was no respite from the sight and stench of death. To provide distance between himself and the disaster, he enlisted in the AEF that was preparing to go overseas. He carried with him a cynicism about any individual effort to overcome large forces of catastrophe and didn't consider how the war would reflect the extremities of the storm.

Once he encountered the carnage of the front lines Matty built a wall to protect his emotions, at first cutting himself off from camaraderie and the tiny moments of human warmth that refused to be quelled by machine-gun fire and heavy shelling.

*He looked into the eyes of his men and saw their useless
efforts to preserve their humanity with jokes and bluster, the
occasional hand on a shoulder, or a kind word. Why couldn't
they see such things didn't matter anymore and they were all
simply waiting for extinction? He had lain in the long grass
while the German artillery found its range and blasted entire
companies to pieces. He had seen officers wave squads of
young boys into the woods where snipers picked them off one
by one and their bodies were left to rot because it was too
dangerous to retrieve them. He had heard those same officers
speak of the dead as if they were mere numbers whose
subtraction from the world deserved no more attention than
the ordnance lost in battle. He didn't expect to survive the war,
but he knew that pain and suffering would have a long life
and there was nothing he could do to make any difference ...*

*The efforts of those around him to maintain their self-respect
and encourage others to do the same, even if in rude and
awkward fashion, slowly won him over. He began to depend
on their personal quirks and signatures of behaviour as he did
on the familiar smell of coffee from the mess-tent in the
mornings and of tinned meat that had an imaginary gourmet
taste all its own.*

Most of the narrative action concerned the separation of him and his
squad from the main body of troops and following muddy tracks while
the German lines closed in around them. As they walked through the
afternoon and into the evening before eventually finding a resting-spot
in a grove of trees, each of the five men told a story about himself revealing something of his background and character and his personal
reasons for volunteering. When it came his turn Matty faltered, not wanting to bring the horrors of the storm into the awfulness of their present
plight, but pressured to follow their paths of disclosure he described
finding the body of a young girl lying in the village street as if she were
asleep, a rag doll clutched to her breast and a strand of muddied hair

across her eyes. "I brushed away the strand," he told them, "and saw her eyes were open. They looked right through me but included me at the same time. I can't explain that." As he spoke and saw them hanging on his every word, he realized he didn't want to let her go and that the only way he could keep her would be to write her down. The same was true of his connection with these men in front of him, and when he had finished talking and took first watch he made entries in his notebook about the tales they had told. His pencil was worn to a stub by the time he was relieved, but before he slept he wrote the name and address of his closest friend back home on the inside cover. His friend, whom he hadn't seen since long before the storm, wasn't a writer either, but that didn't matter. It was enough to pass the stories on.

Sally had told him she didn't want to stay on the island for more than a month. A barnstorming circus was being set up out of San Diego and she wanted to join. It would require a lot more traveling, but, as she said, she traveled every day in her portable office. It also meant he'd be alone from mid-January until he completed the manuscript, and although he was used to her absences, he had a few qualms about what he'd do without her over such a prolonged period.

"You know, once a week or so when my writing day's done I like to relax with you."

"You'll drink too much," she said. "But you should get out on the boat with Manuel and make sure you do a lot of hiking."

He carried her knapsack down to the river's edge where she kissed him fervently.

"See you at Easter."

"Remember," he told her. "More than kisses, letters mingle souls."

Her cheeks blossomed with colour. "That may be the most beautiful thing you've ever said to me. I'm as lucky as you the words are always there."

When the pontoons had cleared the water he shouted out: "Donne, not Sark." But she was already focused on the sea. Hell, he was never a poet, but as long as the truth showed up eventually, it could take its time.

The date she set gave him a goal, and he was determined to write a thousand words a day with Sundays off for such good behaviour. He wrote in the mornings, which meant after lunch he could fish or find some other kind of relief from the typewriter. To keep himself in shape he began to run to and from different parts of the island. From the house to the village square was a mile, mostly downhill, so he'd walk there at a leisurely pace, check the post office for mail and a week-old copy of the *Post-Dispatch*, then turn and push himself up to speed along the incline until he was breathing hard as he neared the front gate. On other days, he'd run the southwest track toward the limestone cliffs, going a little farther each time, helped by gulps of water from a stream that would be nearly dry in the summer months but now rushed down from the high ground in cold clear channels. Usually he went out with Manuel on Saturday afternoons revelling in the use of his new rod and reel that meant he no longer had to drag the line by hand. He liked to have a drink or two on the boat and burn the midnight oil with several more at the *cantina*. Since he didn't write on Sunday mornings he could rise late and make himself a big pot of coffee to clear away any excess fumes. There were a few times he couldn't remember walking home, but that didn't happen often. He wanted to stick to his schedule and be able to tell Sally he was almost done the first draft when she returned.

What happened to Matty was what happened to all men in war. He watched men die who, one moment before, had been alive like him, hurled into oblivion because they didn't move quickly enough, or it didn't matter whether they moved at all since skilful Germans could pack the mortar blasts together and destroy anything above ground within a certain radius.

> *Your only chance was to find an obstacle like a mound of dirt or old tree stump and keep your head down because usually there was no warning except the tumbling whoosh of the Minenwerfers just before they exploded. Three of the squad died in the same blast though they all heard the shell coming. He saw one crumpled face-down in the mud with his legs cut off above the knees, bright splintered bones protruding from*

bloody thighs, and another with a gaping chest wound in
which his exposed heart still beat, its red pulse obscenely
ticking off the last seconds. The third man had simply
vanished. It didn't matter they had spoken about their
boyhoods the night before, laughing over mistakes they had
made and announcing confidently there would be no
repetition. It didn't matter they had listened to their
comrades, absorbing the shapes of syllables and images
conjured from shared American experience, telling themselves
this was what it meant to be alive and they would not let the
meaning go. When the heart's rhythms finally ceased, Matty
swore he'd find a way to convey to the wider world what
they'd said to each other, such grace before such devastation.
He touched the notebook in his jacket pocket where their
words were breathing still.

Miller had Matty and the two others press on, uncertain of the German positions or where their own lines lay. They spoke little now except to indicate their fatigue and need to rest. Each of them carried his rifle and a nearly-empty canteen of water, their packs with a change of socks, a blanket, and bit of food. Matty had a collapsible spade slung on his belt he'd never have time to use unless the Germans stopped firing mortars and marched at them from a long way off so they could dig in. In his mind he wrote letters home, telling his parents he was having a fine time and his younger brother he'd better remember to feed the rabbits in the back-yard hutch or else he wouldn't get the enemy helmet he'd been promised. He also wrote to a girl he'd never talked to who had always walked through the school hallways as if she owned them, though her dark beauty softened her imperious manner. Strangely, he told her the truth about the war, or at least in a way he did, describing what it was like to hug the earth as if she were a lover while jealous suitors of bullets and shells tried to tear you from her arms and leave you without hope. And she wrote back to him in his head, saying she would lie down with him and never let him go and talked about all the things they would do together when he got home

until one of the men, Billy Catania from Brooklyn, said he
was too tired and was going to lie down in that barn over
there, maybe there'd be some straw and, if they were lucky, a
home-cooked meal the farmer's wife had left behind. Carter, a
tough ex-stevedore from Chicago, scoffed at his optimism.
They made their way to the shelter, although it wasn't much
of one because the wind blew through the slats and there was
only sky where the roof had been and the straw that Billy
yearned for was damp and uninviting. They piled some
rotting boards against a wall to block any view from outside
and built a small fire to heat their cans of stew. Their chewing
and swallowing sounds were accompanied by occasional
groans of satisfaction that something warm was going into
their bellies, however lousy the taste.

"How long do you think we can keep going like this?"
Billy asked.

Carter let out a loud exhalation of breath. "What's
wrong?" he said. "It's just a Sunday stroll, ain't it?"

Billy wondered what would happen if they tried to
surrender.

"How're you going to do that?" Matty asked. "You need
somebody to surrender to."

"Next time the mortars come in we just walk in the
direction they've come from waving our handkerchiefs."

"And they welcome us with flowers and chocolate."

"Naw, but they do stop trying to kill us."

"You can do that if you want," Carter announced. "I
didn't watch our guys die just so I could give up." He looked at
Matty. "Where do you stand, Corporal?"

Matty didn't know how he felt. It was fine to be brave,
but not so much if it got you killed. On the other hand, he'd
heard bad things about being a prisoner-of-war.

"I guess I'm neutral," he said. "Right now, anyway."

"Sooner or later you'll have to choose," Carter told him.

As he slept fitfully Matty dreamed about a whore he'd

visited more than once when their outfit first arrived in France and they'd been billeted in a small town. She was quite a bit older than him but not so much so that he didn't fall for her shapely curves and long tresses. The pupils of her eyes were like black suns, their heat keeping his cold imaginings of front-line dangers at a distance when he lay with her, and although she didn't speak much English and his French was limited to oui, non, *and* un verre du vin, *their bodies spoke the same language plainly enough. Maybe he should just keep walking until he found her again. Yes, that was a good idea. Just find the place where he could stop walking and become a permanent citizen instead of a transient foreigner with a stripe on his shoulder. Could you marry a whore? Why not? If men could destroy one another so ruthlessly what did it matter who you married? The world was crazy when it tried to make you pick and choose according to its skewed versions of morality. Her name was Mathilde, and maybe he loved her. When he awoke Billy told him he'd been talking about a woman in his sleep. "You're lucky," he said. "All I got was my old boss yelling at me for being late to work."*

Miller knew what he was doing. The three men were lost in a fictional version of Belleau Wood, heading inevitably toward a reckoning that would provide deliverance or damnation for his protagonist or some strange combination of the two that would hold indeterminate forever his own memory of faces and events. It wasn't so simple as his manipulating plot and character to release himself with words on the page like Matty wanted to do because there was a hill waiting for him in the real world that would write itself if he ever got there. He still couldn't recall what had happened after he, Rawley, and Kincaid left the woods and started to climb. Those who had given him the decoration had assured him of the outcome, but what had gone on before he charged uphill alone and wreaked some kind of vengeance on the Germans at the top was still a mystery. Wasn't the novel his way of finding out? Why else create the would-be writer, the down-to-earth Billy, and the unrelenting figure of Carter with their intersecting fates? Well, there was nothing for it but to keep going with the actual and imagined right to the end. If he said it all as clearly and honestly as he could it might be a story to outlast any real-life discovery.

Standing on the tarmac at Le Bourget as Sally circled her plane for landing he thought back to her arrival that Easter and how the whole island was blooming with flowers as the pontoons touched down off the river mouth. He had conquered the first draft as promised and was proud of his accomplishment. But the liberation he'd sought from the past remained incomplete just as Matty realized his well-intentioned prose would fail to redeem the trauma on the hill they tried to ascend. Miller had to make up his conclusion from whole cloth because he was resolved not to leave Billy and Carter in the silence in which Rawley and Kincaid stayed wrapped, despite battering himself against the locked door of their final moments together. It was Matty's heroism that was left hanging not the deaths of his two men cut down by the Germans before they had climbed very far. He took cover behind their bodies, and when he left them it was because he could not stay there under the withering Maxim fire and survive. As he crawled to the summit in the last few lines of the manuscript, his feelings of inadequacy and guilt were so strong it was doubtful he'd have the presence of mind to pull a trigger.

Dear Hal

> *I finished the novel yesterday or at least the first draft. It was a struggle not just because I was reliving parts of the war but because I couldn't easily reconcile memory with what I was trying to say. And there were some places where memory wouldn't accompany me but wouldn't completely abandon me either, so I didn't always know what to do. Something happened on that hill in France before I got to the summit and supposedly did all those brave things that got me the decoration, and I'll never know what it was because if my*

writing can't make it visible I don't know what can. But I think I've written the big one anyway, and that's what finally matters because it's out in the open and I can't hide. The critics who weren't there will lob their own conscientious objector shells into it, but there's plenty of readers who stayed home who'll recognize themselves in the characters I've portrayed. I've got a long way to go with revisions, but everything essential will stay the same. I'm dedicating it to the men who died instead of me and for me. Their names are on their gravestones, of course, but even so I like to think words on a page last longer than stone.

Sally's here now and we'll be on the island for another couple of weeks. Everything's in flower and the colours are spectacular. We'll head for St. Louis at the end of the month and I'll work at the newspaper while editing the manuscript. If everything goes well, I expect to submit it in the winter with publication maybe next year at this time. After that I'm determined to head for Paris with or without another Pulitzer. I shouldn't put a hex on the book, I know, but I'm feeling pretty good about its chances.

It's your turn now. Get out of New York and find yourself a warm place to hunker down in and finish the greatest poem in American literature even if not everyone sees it that way. Never forget, just like those civilian readers who'll follow what I've said about men in war, there'll be those who can track a bear through all those vagrant histories you provide.

Miller

P.S. I almost forget to tell you I've titled the book What This Has Cost, words of General Lewis Armistead who died at Gettysburg.

5.

In his dream he was in the boat with Manuel, farther out than he had ever been before. It was very hot and there was not a whisper of wind on the sea. The birds that usually trailed in the wake were gone except for one man-o'-war that hovered over them with its bright red pouch distended. He'd set his rod in the metal holder Manuel had bolted to the stern gunwale and the line was stretched out a hundred yards behind weighted by the heavy hooks and sinkers. Many hours passed as they drifted in the current, and his eyes were smarting from the constant glare despite the glasses he wore and the peak of his cap that protected his forehead. He wished he had brought a book with him or his typewriter so he could work as he waited. Then, where the end of the line should have been, he saw a dark shadow ripple briefly across the surface of the water and called to Manuel.

"*Qué es?*" he asked.

The old man studied the calm until the shadow appeared again. He drew in his breath sharply. "*Madre de Dios,*" he said. "You must reel in."

"But why?" Miller asked. "We can catch whatever it is."

"No, we cannot. This is *El Recuerdo.*"

"What is that?"

"The fish of memory, *señor.* The one who keeps what we have chosen to forget."

"I'm a writer," Miller said. "I remember it all." He picked up the rod and set the butt against his stomach, waiting patiently for the strike. When it came suddenly, he let the line run then jerked back to set the hook. The weight of the fish was enormous, and after bringing in the initial slack he couldn't turn the crank handle a single inch.

"Let him run," Manuel told him. "If you will not cut the line it is your only hope."

"I will let him run because he will grow tired," he replied, releasing the drag, but instead of surging away as expected the fish sounded, sinking into the depths and nearly stripping the reel in just a few seconds of descent. He knew the creature was real not a myth, and the ocean here was far too deep for it to reach the bottom and rest. Besides, the length of line would not permit this, so he was surprised when the line went slack again and he had to bring it taut. It meant the fish was strangely suspended in the mid-air of the current as if biding its time before its next move.

After several minutes his arms began to tire and he wondered if he would lose this waiting game. Manuel removed his cap and glasses to pour water from a drinking bottle over his head. "Cut the line," he said. "He is giving you a chance."

"No," Miller answered. "To hell with his mercy."

At that moment he felt the line go loose. "He's coming up," he yelled. "Get ready."

But Manuel would not pick up the gaff as he frantically wound the crank until the rod tip curled into the water and he knew his catch was just below the surface. Kneeling down to bend over the transom he reached out for the dark amorphous shape that was shockingly small for all its strength and weight.

"This is crazy," he yelled as his fingers brushed cloth instead of scales.

"No, *señor*, it is the truth."

The shadowy form spun free several times before he grasped it and pulled it close. As it turned slowly between his hands, he saw it was the body of a man in a forest green uniform, the buttons on the tunic displaying the Marine Corps eagle. He could see through the buttons to the other side and the words 'Waterbury Button Co. Conn.' magnified in the clear water.

"You're not a fish," he said, as Rawley's face floated toward him, bubbles escaping his friend's open mouth as if he were drowning or trying to speak, the hook cruelly embedded in his tongue. Miller recoiled before reaching in frantically to free the barb, weeping at his ineptitude as his hand twisted and turned to no avail. Then Manuel's hand was on his shoulder.

"Let him go now. You have seen the past, and that is enough."

His head was throbbing and there was a terrific pain in one of his knees. He wanted to hold Rawley in his arms and tell him he was sorry, but all he could say was: "Why did you come back?" There was no answer and, finally, nodding wearily at his failure, he took Manuel's offered knife to slice the line where it joined the leader.

"You were wrong," he said, turning to the old man. "I haven't forgotten anything about him."

"*Señor*, if that were so, *El Recuerdo* would never have caught you."

He would not return to Belleau Wood and visit the nearby cemetery even though it was only sixty miles from Paris. Instead he preferred to sit by the fountain in the Rue Charlemagne behind the St. Louis-St. Paul church. In the marble structure a small bronze boy holding a sea-shell above his head stood on basin supported by a school of fish. Sometimes Miller was the boy and other times it was Rawley they carried on their backs. Either way the war hadn't happened yet.

Ambos Mundos

1.

When Nicky drowned Hal retreated to New York, broken and guilt-ridden. If only he'd kept going forward, instead of madly trying to escape the coral tunnel, he might have pushed Nicky through the opening or pulled him free by the legs. But, given his panic, he'd almost run out of air during his retreat and the extra seconds submerged could have been fatal. Then there was his muddled behaviour once he'd surfaced. An instant fresh breath and dive might have given a chance of rescue instead of his clinging to the boat for far too long while Nicky was desperately reaching for salvation. Either way he'd been useless and there was no self-forgiveness.

He stayed in his cabin for the entire voyage, feigning illness and persuading the steward to bring him his meals on a tray. Most of the time, he slept or fought to keep from collapsing altogether. Garrett met the ship at the Wall Street pier and took him back to the apartment. His new roommate was at work, but, given the situation, had volunteered to stay with some friends for a few days until Hal was back on his feet and some permanent accommodation could be found.

"I'd like to ask him to leave, but I can't," Garrett said. "His lease runs until the end of the month."

Hal didn't really care one way or the other. He just wanted to be alone with his grief. "I'll manage," he said, though he had no idea what he was talking about when he declared this. Hunched on the couch with his hands between his knees, he wept while Garrett made tea then took a bottle of whiskey and two glasses from the cupboard and poured each of them a healthy shot.

The telegram from Key West had been terse but Garrett knew he wouldn't have cut short his stay without powerful motivation. "FRIEND DROWNED STOP LEAVING FOR HOME STOP ARRIVE SS ORIZABA 12TH." Hal tried to find a way with words to explain his pain, but language became a tangle of emotions and thoughts that crashed into a brick wall at the end of a dark and terrible cul-de-sac. It seemed stupid and futile to say he loved Nicky, but that was what he ended up saying over and over again, and when Garrett, at a loss, could only nod sympathetically, he rambled on about having found happiness for the first time in his life. At some point it occurred to him that if he had ever been able to imagine such culpability and sorrow, he would have put them down on paper, but now he didn't care if he ever wrote anything again. The bear, critically wounded, moved slowly across a distorted landscape and disappeared.

He poured himself another whiskey. "Weren't you supposed to get married?"

"Yes, the wedding's in six weeks, in fact. The invitations, yours included, are on the desk. But that's not a priority under the circumstances."

"Of course it is. Tell me about her. Does she have green eyes?"

"No, blue. And long, light-brown hair. She doesn't like the bob."

"Good, I don't like the bob either." They both laughed weakly.

"And she's rich?"

"Her family's very well-off."

"So you can quit work and become a man of leisure." He was on his third whiskey now. It must be that because the burning in his throat had softened. "She doesn't have green eyes," he said.

"No."

"They buried him at sea, Garrett, wrapped in a Merchant Marine flag. I stood there and watched him vanish. 'We have lingered in the chambers of sea ...' Is that what he's doing? Goddamn poetry!" he shouted. "Doesn't make a fucking bit of difference."

"Tell me about him, Hal."

As it turned out the roommate could stay with his friends until it was time to renew the lease, and he offered to share the apartment with Hal after that. It seemed like the best arrangement until Garrett, worried about his torpor and the great silences that blanketed such inactivity, suggested he move in with him and Anne for a couple of months after the wedding. He'd have his own room and they'd both be out during the day—she worked in the gallery where Garrett had met her—so he wouldn't be overwhelmed in any way. Hal had met Anne, and liked her, but knew he had no business interfering in their new life together. He thought about going back to Mrs. Capalca's except there'd be so much explaining to do and the old woman's kindliness would have been too much to handle. No, he didn't want to live with anyone ever again. His grant money would run out soon and he'd have to find a job, just enough of an income to get him a room with a hotplate so he didn't have to sit around a crowded table and tell people who he was and where he'd been.

Frank Shay had found another acquisitions manager who decided he didn't need an assistant, but Frank was fond enough of Hal to hire him as a sales clerk for fifteen a week, a position that kept him in touch with the world at large so he didn't fade completely into despair. The wage was barely enough to live on when he paid almost half of it for his room on the edge of the meatpacking district a few blocks north of the Village. He went into the bookstore six days a week, cooked meals for himself, drank a cheap bottle of wine every evening, and stayed away from the old crowd at the Black Rabbit and Artists' Club. The fact was he couldn't afford any kind of night life, and if Garrett hadn't quietly supplemented his salary he wouldn't have been able to afford the bottle.

Dear Miller

I left Key West rather abruptly because a friend of mine drowned there and it was just too painful to stick around. His name was Nicky and he was in the Merchant Marine. We went diving on the inner reef and he got caught in a coral tunnel. People told me I couldn't have saved him, and I guess that's true, but I didn't want to stare out at the water every day and think about it, so here I am in New York again working at Shay's bookstore and doing no writing at all. How's Paris? What are you writing these days?

Say hello to Sally for me. I wish I could go up in her plane and do some wing-walking. Sure it's dangerous, but I don't feel I've got much to lose anymore.

Hal

Garrett and Anne were married in mid-June at her parents' sprawling Long Island property. There were over two hundred very well-off guests, plus Garrett's colleagues at *The Little Review* and in the publishing world, including Margaret Anderson.

"Hello, Hal," she said as he stood at the edge of the garden with an empty champagne glass in his hand watching the ebb and flow of the crowd across the lawn and wondering how to make his escape. He'd come all the way out here in a car full of strangers, and it would be difficult to head back to Manhattan alone. Margaret was to be valued and admired not only for her literary judgement and generosity but also because she lived openly with Jane Heap, her co-founder at the *Review*, and they'd survived the absurd obscenity charges when they'd been fined and forced to discontinue their serialization of Joyce's *Ulysses*. She was a large woman with a winning smile, and if anyone was going to interrupt his self-imposed wedding exile he'd rather it was her.

"Garrett told me what happened in Florida. I'm sorry for his passing. Nicky, wasn't it?"

Tears welled up in his eyes to hear the name spoken so compassionately and because he knew she understood his love not just rationally but intuitively as well.

"Yes," he said. "Thank you."

She put a hand on his shoulder. "We're all worried about you, Hal, those of us who know your talent and that you still have so much to write. Your loss was tragic, no one understands that better than me, but it shouldn't silence you. The war did that to too many writers."

"Writing seems so pointless, Margaret," he replied. "It changes nothing but gives the illusion that it does."

"Perhaps so, but what about Miller?"

"What about him?"

She withdrew her hand so slowly he almost didn't notice. "That novel of his came out of pain so large I don't know how he fought it onto the page. He pretends otherwise, but the prose doesn't lie. And aren't we all the beneficiaries of that fight? You were born a writer Hal, like him, and to deny it at the time of your greatest trauma is to deny the very essence of who you are."

"Maybe that's what I want to do."

"No, really I think you want to write but you're afraid. Not that the words won't measure up but that they will. And if they do, you'll have to measure Nicky against them. Every artist finally has to insist that what he writes or paints or composes is ultimately how he marks the world and the trace he leaves behind."

Hal thought of Mrs. Capalca's six grandchildren and her trace in them. For the first time, he wondered if Miller and Sally wanted a child and whether that would change his friend's single-minded intensity to be the best. It seemed Margaret with Jane had adopted the two sons of her sick sister while they were living in Paris but had given them up when they returned to the States. They were now being raised by, of all people, Gertrude Stein and Alice B. Toklas. He wanted to ask Margaret if the *Review* made up for the children's absence, but what did he know about the comparison?

"I want you to send me something from your long poem," she told him. "Even twenty lines will do. But I have a proviso. Make them twenty new lines." The crowd's twisting and turning was almost upon them. "I'm saving the space," she said as she moved away.

Grateful to Margaret for her support, he sent her a note to say she had stirred him that afternoon. He'd write and publish those twenty lines, he knew. But if he ever returned to Key West he'd seal a copy in a watertight box and place it in the tunnel for a different kind of posterity.

2.

Over the next year he kept mainly to himself, seeing Garrett and Anne once a week for dinner and avoiding other company, though he could chat with Frank Shay and various bookstore colleagues when the occasion demanded or even wax enthusiastic with a prospective customer about new fiction or poetry. His celibacy, as he stayed away from his old haunts, surprised him, but he wanted nothing to do with fleshly pursuits. It wasn't a matter of loyalty to Nicky, but a fear he would break into pieces beneath another man's demands, his limbs betraying the fragmentation of his thoughts and feelings.

On weekends he walked endlessly, from the Village to the Lower East Side where he could look across at Brooklyn Heights and recall his roofline work with Steve, or north to Central Park and Harlem where the 'New Negro' was writing and composing a storm of literature and jazz. He'd read Jean Toomer's *Cane* with its experimental rendition of race struggles in America and listened on Garrett's wind-up Victrola to Ma Rainey and Bessie Smith wail the blues that made him wish he could change the colour of his skin and merge with a larger woe. Of course, he'd only fail as a negro who took nothing for granted just as he he'd failed as a white man who assumed everything would unfold as it should—poetry, sex, friendship, love, they'd all been contorted by his pride and refusal to see their fragility as his body and mind shaped them, insistent on their permanent place in his life. Even when he stood up to what needed to be opposed, as with his mother, he'd been too superior in his resistance. He could hear Bessie singing "After You've Gone," which seemed a paean to so much he'd lost. Ironically, it was an encounter with a street musician on Lenox Avenue that altered his steady slide into oblivion.

He couldn't afford the better clubs and kept his day-time drinking to a minimum, preferring to go home after his walks and drown his sorrows with the wine in his room. Occasionally he'd head down to a working-man's tavern on a nearby corner and treat himself to something a little stronger than cheap plonk, but it was more expensive, as well, so he didn't indulge often. If he was feeling especially low when he began his weekly treks, he'd carry a bottle in a paper bag and sip from it as he stood watching the ship traffic on the river or listening to trumpet or sax players trying to emulate the rapidly aging King Oliver or the young virtuoso Sidney Bechet.

One Saturday afternoon he stopped outside a grocery store just above 115th Street where a crowd had gathered around a clarinetist who was dancing while he played and drawing enthusiastic applause as his feet left the ground with the high notes. Hal stayed off to the side by a plate-glass window, behind which fruits and vegetables were lined up in rows, and he could see his reflection back-lit by a crate of oranges. The musician seemed tireless as his fingers on the keys never faltered and the shuffling of his shoes provided a constant accompaniment like brushes on a cymbal. He didn't move on from one tune or improvisation to another but pulled connections out of the air so the symphony of his sound never let up. Hal sipped his wine and tapped his foot, feeling if not genuinely happy at least free from his cares for a bit. After fifteen or twenty minutes the performance didn't really end but slid into an interval that would be filled by someone else stepping up to play. Meanwhile, the crowd threw coins into a leather instrument case, and a few individuals shook the man's hand or clapped him on the back effusively before moving on. As people scattered, Hal approached the musician who was counting the change carefully and even testing one or two of the coins with his teeth.

He glanced up at the white stranger. "Never can be too careful. All the brothers and sisters is well-intentioned, but they ain't all rich."

Hal laughed. "I don't think you do it for the money."

"Don't kid yourself. I'm makin' a livin' jus' like ever'one else."

"You should be inside one of the clubs. You're good enough."

"Think so? Well, I tried that. They want too much."

"You mean a percentage of your take."

"I mean a percentage of *me*."

"But don't you want to be recorded and maybe become famous?" Hal admired his independence but was puzzled by his nonchalance about success.

"You don't get it, do you? Out here I am who I am, not someone's idea of what I should be, not even my own idea. The music, man, that's where it's at."

Hal handed him the bag. "Have a swig on me," he said. He had no illusions of any extended conversation, and the wine was one way to close things gently.

On the walk back he stopped in the Park and lay down under a white pine whose shape and scent reminded him of the hikes with Miller where the needled forest floor absorbed their footfalls and there was no distant traffic noise to remind them of civilization. He'd left the dregs of the bottle with the musician but not the crucial nature of their exchange. Hal Pierce had once been inside the clubs of poetry where others certainly felt they had a good idea of who he was and where he was going. Whatever word-play disguises he'd thrown up in the way of their complete certainty, that younger and more innocent writer was definitely concerned with personal accomplishment and public success. Nicky's death had exploded the worth of such things, but if aspects of the negro's undoubtedly difficult life had blown up his plans and dreams with more than equal force, the man was still playing and dancing. Why? Because he believed in the music and, although he hadn't said it exactly, the quality of his performance clearly indicated the music believed in him. He breathed himself and what he had learned from others into the mouth of the clarinet, and what came out through the bell was charged in its transformation. Now I'm on the outside, Hal thought, in the streets, where the club-goers can't touch me, but I'm not playing anything at all. He wriggled his toes. Hell, I'm not dancing either. He took off his shoes and stood up. If anyone had been watching they would have seen a smiling young man in shaggy pants and sweater moving to invisible rhythms over the grass.

At first things went very slowly, but over the next many months he made his way on, deeper into the long poem where structure melded with themes in a more seamless fashion than ever before, and images cohered as if they were notes on a scale that could be followed or left behind with comparable precision and impression. As he wrote he organized, and as he organized he pushed himself further into lyric adventures in which his delineation of American experience rang true because he gave up any self-consciousness about what he was doing and how it would be received. He wrote because, like the fated nation with all its triumphs and disasters, he was a man inevitable as an artist who would live then die within these connections of past and present that would finally be his epitaph.

Into its swirling pages came Steve and Mrs. Capalca and their first views of Liberty Island that permeated family vision; the *frontier's final stand* on the paths of the Embarcadero and the shoreline of Key West that admitted forbidden love (though readers like his mother would have read it a mere promiscuity); all he could say about the best and the worst of negro life in the story of a *brilliant, blowing* street musician who could not escape the confines of a slavery that kept *ankle-chains and lynch-mobs unbroken/in emancipation's ether*; the contents of bookstore shelves telling stories of courage and cowardice, moral heights and dissipated depths, as piecemeal digging for gold of one kind or another was vanquished by industrial excavation.

But, above all, hope for the future.

At ocean's end the statue havens
All bells of ships with battered hulls
Tough ancient ones in anchored need
Stone fingers hauling down their sails

Lost halyard grace is riveting
To throngs that forge the modern
In trusting scraps of children's eyes ...

Back and forth he went between lament and celebration until one day he wrote both Miller and Margaret Anderson to say, for better or worse, he had completed his *Odyssey* and was ready to begin the shorter voyage of revision. She answered there was even more space reserved in the *Review* when he was ready. In his reply Miller quoted Homer from Books Two and Four of the ancient epic. "It's either *What he greatly thought, he nobly dared* or just *The windy satisfaction of the tongue.*" Then he added: "Actually, I prefer Sark: *About bloody time!*"

3.

In the summer of 1926 Miller worked steadily on a novel about expatriates in Paris after the war. In real life the male *émigrés* were cynical about their survival, and the women had learned not to depend on them because of this. Everyone drank a great deal and took chances in their relationships that they wouldn't have done back home. There was a lot of money floating around in the hands of a few and it made for considerable largesse but even more tension as the rich and not-so-rich collided in bars and clubs over politics, art, and home-town accents. The best of the people Miller met actually knew something about France's occupation of the Ruhr in order to claim reparations from Germany, or about Dada and the Bauhaus. They also didn't care much where you were from as long as you didn't cheat them or run on at the mouth. These were the ones who formed the main characters in his novel, but the trouble was all their knowledge and open-mindedness didn't put the war to bed. They carried their role in the conflict around with them in elegant valises or scruffy knapsacks, taking it out every so often when they were alone and empty or if some English fool made a bar-room crack about Americans coming late to the conflict.

His protagonist, David Winters, had seen action along the Marne and walked with a slight limp because of shrapnel in his knee. He was a drummer in a jazz trio that played the clubs in Montparnasse, and his main problem was he was in love with a whore who was already married to her pimp. What Miller wanted to portray was the night-life, in bed or on the stage, as never enough to sustain the musician in the early morning hours when he couldn't sleep and roamed his flat with a whiskey in his hand, reliving several violent incidents at once but especially one in which he was afraid he'd been a coward. He'd been wounded and his knee permanently damaged while preparing to lead a charge, and he couldn't recall if he sent men over the top when he couldn't go himself or whether the order had been given the instant before he was hit. He wasn't sure, and never would be. All witnesses to his potential shame were dead. The only way he coped, aside from the booze and despite his infirmity, was to climb in the Alps along the French-Swiss border. Avoiding falling rocks or clinging to a ledge no wider then a thumbnail, he forgot about the war and put all his energy and focus into the moment in which he was living and then the next moment after that. Mostly he climbed alone, but one day he met a female French guide who offered to take him up the east face of Mount Blanc. Miller wasn't sure what was going to happen next, but he knew the fictional woman had Sally's guts and proficiency.

Her reputation and demand as a flier were unparalleled in France as far as he could tell. She had to turn down countless offers for shows in major centers, yet often agreed to perform at small rural venues with grass runways and crowds of fifty or less.

"You know what?" she told him. "They're the ones who'll remember the show for the rest of their lives from the cough of the stalled engine to my scarf streaming in the wind. The privileged crew in Paris or Lyon are always betting on my not making it—and I mean literally betting— and when I do they yawn and sip their absinthe, or whatever concoction their money buys, and they couldn't tell you the colour of my plane."

Sometimes he went with her to the wealthy gatherings, like the one down at Harry Crosby's estate near Ermenonville. The likeable nephew of J.P. Morgan held court with his wife Caresse, watching with the others as Sally looped across the blue expanse before buzzing them so closely he could see the red polish on her fingernails as she passed.

"Don't you ever want to fuck her up there?" Harry asked him without the least intention of insult.

"There's not enough room," he replied nonchalantly. "And besides, when she's flying no man can compete."

"A bit suicidal, don't you think? For you as well."

"I never thought of it that way."

"So, how did the betting go today?" she asked. They were lying in bed in a hangar-shaped room whose silk curtains looked like banners for a tournament.

"I don't know about the rest, but I put my money on the pilot."

"Do you always win?"

"Now you're sounding like Harry."

Dear Hal

*It's tough about your friend. There is no good way to die,
but no one deserves to go like that. I know what you mean
about staring at the water. I've never been back to Belleau
Wood because I don't want to look at the field or the forest or
the hill. There are some things you pay for at the time and
you shouldn't have to keep putting money in the register.
Sally's fine. I don't think she's ever taken up a wing-walker,
but I'll mention your name if you don't get yourself out of
your funk. I'm sure your friend would want you to keep your
feet on the ground. Why don't you think about applying for a
Guggenheim and coming over here for a few months? If you
don't get one I'll provide the funds. Last week I went fishing
for bream in a backwater of the Seine outside of town. They
don't put up much of a fight but in wine sauce they make you
forget about how easy it was to catch them. I still remember
how the trout tasted when we ate them from the frying pan
and how a bubbling can of stew was true haute-cuisine.*

Miller

He had Winters and Marie, the guide, make the ascent of Mount Blanc
on a July day when the temperature on the heights was blistering in the
sun and dipped down close to freezing in the shade. It wasn't just the
steepness of the pitches that concerned them but the sheer size of the
mountain as well. Winters knew the British team trying to conquer
gigantic Everest had met with tragedy. Mallory, probably the best
climber of his generation, had died, and he couldn't imagine tackling a
peak almost twice the height of the one he was on now. When he mentioned this to Marie, she laughed.

"It's all about doing what you can't do" was the best way he could
translate her response.

Miller didn't want her to die, but he didn't see how he could avoid
it, if not here then somewhere else in the novel. The main thing would

be the impact on Winters who was, in his way, clinging to a thread not a rope he could depend on to hold his pain.

He'd meant what he'd said to Hal about giving him the money to cross the Atlantic. Hal hadn't been in the army, but it seemed he was always fighting his own little war, first with his mother, then with just making a living while trying to be a poet, and now with this drowning for which he was clearly blaming himself. These battles had prevented him for so long from finishing that damn poem about America that might vault him to prominence and certainly give his damaged ego the shot it needed. Maybe, if he came to France and left his memories behind, he could start something new and push on unimpeded by whatever anger or guilt he was carrying. Paris was a big enough place to absorb Hal Pierce, and the combination of Gallic insouciance, erotic night-life, and intellectual passions could exhilarate and change him. The trouble was unless you got away from that cloying New York self-centeredness you couldn't see your art for what it was worth and set yourself creative tasks limited by beginnings, middles, and ends.

Miller was somewhat surprised Hal hadn't advanced with things in Key West and that the recent writing spur had to come from the death of his friend. In contrast, he'd written steadily on the Isle of Pines and was working just as effectively here in Paris. Of course, he was lucky enough to have a steady life with Sally and to be able to support himself, and her when she let him, through his writing. Well, you had to be good to be lucky because there were lots of people his age struggling to get published while countless critics had confirmed the quality of his stories and novel, and people like Harry with his Black Sun Press were begging him for anything at all. It didn't do to let it go to your head, though. Every time he sat down at the typewriter he was vulnerable because he wondered where he was going. It was ironic that Hal's imagination was so dependent on the external world, a place where he hadn't fared well, but out of which he conjured his content if not his form. Miller had once asked Joyce, an expert on such matters, about the difference between writing poetry and fiction. The pinch-faced Irishman had told him rather enigmatically that poetry was always a revolt against actuality.

"And fiction?"

"Cold polished stones sinking through a quagmire, my dear Sark. Nothing more, nothing less."

4.

He wasn't there when she crashed on a summer's day. He was supposed to be because she'd invited him to the dirt field outside of Rouen to see a new manoeuvre she'd invented, a quick two-and-a-half roll she'd come out of upside down before arcing into a screaming dive over the spectators and twisting at the final second to right herself. The way she'd described it, the stunt was a piece of cake.

"Just have to be sure about the wind," she said wryly. "It needs to be on my side."

He'd meant to attend as he often done elsewhere, but he had Winters and Marie on a treacherous rock face and he didn't want to let go.

"Just let them hang there," she suggested when he explained without revealing too much.

"I can't, they're depending on me."

She made the one-hour flight from Le Bourget in the morning. The summer sky was cloudless, and he was glad of that because clouds spoiled the view for the audience and could disorient even a skilled pilot when she came out of them. He worked for a few hours as the climbers inched their way upward and over the top of the precipice where they lay on a ledge and Winters told Marie a story about an old man in the Dolomites who'd climbed a wall so smooth and high that young men refused to consider an ascent. From below they saw him sitting at the top until night came down and he wasn't visible anymore. At first light he was gone. There was no body at the bottom of the wall and above it was a precipitous two thousand feet of snow and ice impossible to ascend to the summit. No one could say what the old man was looking for at such a height, he told her.

"What do you think?" Marie asked him.

Just then the telephone rang in the downstairs hall and then the concierge was calling to him. He almost shouted that she should take a message because he didn't yet know what Winters' reply would be. When he took the receiver the voice on the other end of the line spoke rapidly, but he understood *percuté* and *morte* well enough. At the top of the stairs his hero was still waiting for his line, but Miller didn't know him at all.

Apparently, the show had begun under shadow. The field mechanic had suffered a minor heart attack just before Sally was due to take off. By the time the ambulance had arrived and he was driven to the local hospital, the weather had changed somewhat. A cold front was blowing in from the Atlantic and there was a slight mist in the air. The officials indicated she should wait for it to clear, but Sally insisted this was only a brief disturbance in an otherwise perfect day and rolled along the runway to the cheers of the crowd. Once at height, as the mist did indeed dissipate, she did a series of loops and spins to warm-up before launching into the multiple roll, coming out of it parallel to the ground and held in only by her harness. Then she began her long curving dive that would right her and have the plane bottom out just fifty feet above the grandstand. Her speedometer would register 80 mph, but she would be going much faster. There was nothing to obscure her sight yet inexplicably she misjudged the radius of her half-circle and never made it through the arc. The Bleriot smashed into the hard Normandy earth with surprisingly little noise the police told him later. Yes, he thought, there was the heavy engine, but most of the plane was made from a wing and a prayer.

Dear Hal

Sally died three days ago. She was performing at the Rouen airfield when something went wrong and she never came out of a dive. I took the train there and saw the wreck, though they had taken what was left of her body to the hospital morgue. The engine went right through the cockpit so she never had a chance. She told me if she ever went down I should

take her ashes home and scatter them in the sea between
Cuba and the Isle of Pines. I guess I'll do that eventually. I
guess I'll do a lot of things eventually, but right now I just
want to drink whiskey and be alone. I was working well on a
new novel. No one who isn't a writer can understand what
that means. And no one who isn't a writer can understand
how it hurts to know writing's not enough when death comes
along. I was happy with her. Hell, I loved her, Hal, and now
she's gone forever. There aren't enough books in the world to
make up for that. I telegraphed her parents and they've
agreed we'll have a ceremony in Philadelphia when I get
there, maybe next month. It must be terrible for them, she
was such a great girl. We all want to die with our boots on.
That's what she did, but it doesn't help.

Miller

It was a simple September service at a Presbyterian church. Two of Sally's school friends spoke about her good nature and joked gently about how she always had her head in the clouds even before she learned to fly. Mrs. Morgan was too broken to say anything, but her father described her fierce enthusiasm for what he called her "craft" and said that the agony of losing her was eased a tiny bit because she died doing what she was born to do. Everyone was waiting for Miller to address the congregation, especially the press. He'd refused any interviews and they were eager to glean anything of his condition and ask about his future plans. Standing to face them all, he glimpsed Hal near the back of the nave.

"The fact that I am a writer means nothing at all right now. How can any man provide words equal to the loss of a loved one? Some have tried. The prophet Isaiah said: 'But they who wait for the Lord shall renew their strength; they shall mount up with wings like eagles.' For Sally, flying was a passion akin to faith, and before she died she soared like an eagle beyond all earthly confines. Stephen Crane, whose own life was cut short, told us: 'You cannot choose your battlefield. God does that for you. But you can plant a standard where a standard never flew.'

When Sally flew her courage and laughter in the face of death were a flag for us all."

Miller paused. He had laboured on what he was about to say for many hours, struggling as he wept and swallowed shot after shot of whiskey to carve a concise memorial into a prop against his pain. "There is no lonelier man in death," he said as the scribes scribbled, "except the suicide, than that man who has lived many years with a good wife and then outlives her. If two people love each other there can be no happy end to it."

When the reception back at the Morgan house was over, he and Hal walked in the garden or, more properly, the small park at the back of the property. Although so much of his focus was turned inward, he saw the wear and tear in his friend's face and imagined his own attrition reflected there.

"How did we get so old, pal?" he asked. "We're not even thirty."

"It comes from holding on with both hands, I think. Neither of us has done anything lightly."

"Is the poem really finished?"

"Yes, except for a few revisions here and there. Margaret Anderson wants to serialize it in the *Dial*. I've applied for a Guggenheim like you suggested. I should hear any day now."

"That's all good. Listen, I'm going down to the island for as long as it takes to sort myself out. I'll be there for at least a few months. Why don't you meet me in Havana when you're ready? I can show you the city and then we can take a bus over the mountains and catch a boat across the channel. Like I said before, if you don't get the G-grant I'll foot the bill. It will be good just to relax and talk, maybe do a little fishing too. Come to think of it, we should get back to Michigan sometime and get up into the woods again."

"You'll never leave her behind anywhere, Miller."

"I don't want to leave her behind."

He suddenly remembered David Winters and the woman waiting for his answer on the alpine ledge. If he'd been the one to die, Sally would have gone on flying.

Six weeks later Hal heard from the secretary of the Guggenheim Board and learned he had won the prestigious grant. The Board's letter offered congratulations and asked for a detailed list of proposed expenses, reminding him that $2000 was the maximum allowed an individual artist. It also quoted from the Selection Committee's decision: "Mr. Pierce's poem is a paean to the beating heart of America and the blood that flows in all our veins no matter our origins or outcomes. He takes many chances in individual sections of the work, but the consistently bold sweep of his narrative and lyric annotations of history reward the overall gamble."

He was elated by the stamp of approval and immediately wrote Miller to plan his trip south. The reply wasn't long in coming.

Dear Hal

That's the best news I've had since the Cardinals won the World Series. That was only a few days ago, but still. You deserve the prize for endurance alone. Bring the manuscript with you so I can determine if the writing warrants the same praise. Seriously, I want you to read it to me from start to finish. People need to read novels in their heads, but poetry needs to be declaimed, and you can do that from the rooftops of Havana or even the ramparts of the Morro if you like. Just send me the date when your boat docks and I'll make reservations at the Hotel Inglaterra. It's a grand old place with floor to ceiling windows in the rooms, and in a park right across the street is a statue of your hero Martí. We can talk and carouse for a few days then we'll head to the island.

Miller

P.S. I'm okay. I have dreams of Sally that make me weep, but I hope they never end. If I ever finish my Paris novel, I'm going to try to write one about flying.

5.

Before he left New York Hal had lunch with Margaret Anderson who had read the poem from beginning to end and planned to publish it in four parts over the next year. She'd arranged for it then to be published in book form by Harry Crosby who promised European as well as American distribution.

"You'll never look back, Hal. It's a magnificent national epic, and I expect it to win a Pulitzer when Harry brings it out. My main question is what are you going to do now?"

"Relax with Miller. Tweak the poem. See how the island stirs me. And afterwards go to Mexico. Well, I told the Guggenheim people that was my plan. When it's over I don't think I want to come back to New York just to have to scrape out a living as I've been doing. I can't stay a bookstore clerk all my life."

"This poem is going to make you famous, Hal. I'm sure there'll be some prospective employers amongst your readership. Make sure you leave me a copy before you go. You don't want to lose it on a boat or a bus." She took a sip of her tea and wiped her lips with her napkin. "There's something else, though."

"Which is?"

"You need to settle down. Oh, I know your roaring days appear to be done and you've been celibate for quite a while, but you need to find a partner, Hal. You need to have a life off the page and see if you can be happy."

"I was happy, Margaret. But I lost him."

"I know, dear boy, I know, but that's no reason to be a monk for the rest of your existence. Who can tell, maybe you'll meet someone down there in the sun."

"Well I can't carry on about the possibility to Miller."

"No, I don't imagine you can."

Once again he made the rounds and said goodbye to those who had supported him, especially since his return from Key West. Allen Tate told him to forget the fifty dollars he'd loaned him in the spring, and Frank Shay shook his hand and told him to keep an eye out for cheap

English-language first editions that often turned up in flea markets south of the border. One afternoon he went up to Harlem and found the clarinetist on the same corner. This time he had a full bottle to hand him, and when the man gave him a puzzled look in return Hal said: "You won't remember me but I just wanted to tell you I'm staying outside and dancing to the music."

"Only place to be, brother. Only thing to hear."

"Do you know Bessie Smith's 'After You've Gone'?"

"Sure do." He began to play the slow and easy introduction, and Hal shuffled his feet in time.

The boat south hugged the coastline, putting in at more ports than usual, but there was still plenty of opportunity to sit on a deck chair and watch the white-capped swells rolling in all directions into a vastness he could barely comprehend. There was a history out there but an invisible one that lay far beneath the spindrift and made surface concerns so paltry in comparison. Tomorrow there would be no evidence he had ever been in this particular spot except in the ship's log and that was simply the imposition of longitude and latitude on the unfathomable, the desperate measuring of what could not be contained. For all intents and purposes, the bottom of the sea was as distant as the most far-flung stars, and in between the depths and heights men and women carried on as if terra firma were not an illusion. How long had he and Nicky known one another? A few months, no more. Yet that relationship was the gauge of every encounter he'd yet have on this third planet from the sun. He hadn't told Margaret Anderson he didn't want to find another partner, hadn't said he couldn't chance the loss of anyone else. That was his problem. He couldn't really talk to anyone about who he was and what he'd been through, yet here he was headed toward the one man left to love whose embrace would not allow for open arms.

He knew Miller needed to talk about Sally. That was only normal and expected, and he would listen willingly though he didn't pretend to understand women, especially those with physical courage to match that of Miller Sark. So why couldn't he talk about what Miller couldn't understand, a sailor-stevedore with the beauty to win Hal's heart? Sally, Nicky, what in God's name was the distinction? Miller was going to write a novel about flying. Why couldn't a poem reveal a world in which little boys wore their mother's and sister's clothes and went off in staggeringly different directions? Just another kind of flight, after all. If he wrote what he knew he should, it would tear the covers off the comfortable literary beds America slept in. But Whitman had already tried that, hadn't he? He stared out at the indifferent sea and wondered if he fell in clutching such a poem whether it would be a life-buoy or deadly weight to drag him down.

The ship passed by Key West late at night heading straight for Havana. The lights of Flagler Street were flickering in the distance. When he came down the gangway the next morning a bearded burly figure he almost didn't recognize was waiting for him.

6.

Miller spent most of his time alone brooding and gaining weight. Except for an occasional afternoon with Manuel on the boat he didn't seek any company and passed many hours sitting at a south window staring down over the town to the sea. When he felt like exercise he'd walk to the limestone cliffs, hardly pausing there to note the great gatherings of birds before he turned around and headed back. He'd told Hal about his affecting dreams of Sally and how he hoped they'd never end, but he didn't mention the recurring nightmare that left him bathed in sweat and gasping for breath when he came out of it morning after morning. In this dream he wandered through the flattened field of grain and past the blackened stumps of trees broken by shelling to a green hollow in the forest where the five were always waiting. Scott, Munson, and Davis were sitting on a fallen log, but Kincaid and Rawley stood off to one side beneath the heavy, spreading branches of an oak. He took his place in front of them, tin helmet in hand, as if before a court of judgement, each time their verdict pending though after his first vision of them he knew the preliminary words by heart.

"We died in the field," Scott said.

"Yes, I saw you fall," he answered, then nodded at Munson. "You were the tail of the snake. It was my fault you were unprotected." He noticed the slug on the back of Munson's hand inching its way forward without seeming to move at all.

"No, Munson replied, "someone had to bring up the rear." Then he smiled. "I always liked your stories, Miller, especially the one about the fire."

"I didn't know I'd told you that one."

"I tried to call to you when I was hit," Davis said. "It was a stomach wound and I was awfully thirsty."

Miller thought about the glacier-fed streams that Davis had drunk from when he was a boy. "I'm sorry," he said and put out his hand though he knew the distance between life and death was too great for either of them to shake.

"We don't blame you," Scott told him. "You tried to take us through, but there were too many bullets and mortars."

He looked over at Kincaid and Rawley. "But you blame me, don't you?" he said quietly.

"Tell us what happened," Kincaid said.

"We crawled through the woods together and that German sniper was in a tree."

"But he was still alive after we brought him down, wasn't he?"

"Yes."

"Why did you let us think he'd died before you had a chance to shoot him?"

"I was afraid."

"Then or when you wrote the story?"

"Both times."

"So he died and we moved on to the bottom of the hill. What happened then?"

"I don't remember."

"Ah remember," Rawley said, and the strange combination of joy and sadness in his face made Miller want to reach out and comfort him.

"Me and Kincaid got ahead of you and headed for a pile of rocks. Both of us got hit. Kincaid was dead, but ah waited for you because ah knew you wouldn't leave me there to die alone the way you left the German."

"What happened?" Miller cried. "Tell me!"

"Yuh'll have to tell yourself," Rawley said softly. "Yuh need to find a way."

He always woke up after Rawley spoke, his heart pounding as his mind writhed in contortions he couldn't stifle or appease. So he'd get up and pace through the house until the thin band of light on the eastern horizon brought him some respite and he made coffee so strong the bitter taste stayed on his tongue even when the sun was high in the sky.

Maybe he'd try to tell Hal about things when he got here. Hal was the only one who'd understand why he couldn't pull the trigger on the dying sniper. "You had to shoot the bear," he'd say, "but this was different." Then he'd take Hal to the bottom of the hill and introduce him to Kincaid and Rawley, and the four of them would talk about what to do next. Hal would go with them when they went up, and he'd find out what happened before the shrapnel shredded his knee and somehow he crawled on to the top. If Hal was there like he'd been on the ridgeline so long ago they'd get out of it together. Then maybe the nightmare would stop, and he'd be able to write about it at last.

He'd tried to work on his Paris book, getting David Winters back to the city after his climb on Mount Blanc. Everyone seemed so jaded and fed up with life, except as it could entertain them. They wore him down, and he didn't want to give them the privilege of being on the page anymore. He almost put the manuscript away, but found it was soothing to write about the music Winters played so intensely and how it reverberated down the narrow streets and alleys to bring at least some of their citizens out of cynicism's shadow. He began to see a new direction for the novel in which the pulsing combination of drums, piano, and saxophone, as well as other forms of music in the clubs and along the avenues, would bring the world-weary generation back to affirmations of life. But these were imagined sounds, and he had to find his own healing rhythms before he could complete the fictional score.

When Hal wrote to say he'd won the Guggenheim and would get to Havana if Miller would set a date, he was relieved the visit would get him away from his daily and nightly routines. They'd spend a few days in the city and catch up on so much of what distance and time had prevented them from sharing. He'd been serious when he'd suggested they return to Michigan and fish the rivers there again. What he hadn't said was how much he wanted to go back to that border river and finish the trip they'd never been properly able to complete. Everything would have grown over as if the fire had never occurred, and he'd bet that in the ten years that had passed those trout had only gotten bigger and the wilderness had never lost its piney innocence. They might never be boys again, but goddamn it they could sure have a good time trying!

Once he confirmed his plans with Hal by sending a telegram to say he'd meet him at the dock on the last day of November, he thought his anxieties would cool and the Marine tribunal would rest for awhile. If anything, however, the questions of Kincaid and Rawley became more insistent each night as if he were resolutely refusing to cooperate in the search for the truth his memories of them must contain.

"We're convenient ghosts," Kincaid told him, expanding the familiar dialogue.

"What do you mean?"

"I mean we haunt you only as much as you let us. You need Rawley and me but only to a point."

"What's that point?" he asked.

"The one where you stop typing us in your head and let us be ourselves."

"But I haven't written about you for a long time."

"In your head you're writing this dream," Rawley said.

He had a flashing glimpse of something passing between them, a violence and a beauty he could not comprehend but wanted desperately to clasp. Suddenly the forest scene disappeared, and he saw Kincaid moving on the hill toward a small cluster of rocks before he disappeared on their far side. When he didn't answer their call Rawley, whooping like an Indian, ran to help him. Miller felt a knife in his chest when his friend fell and he saw his boot sticking over the edge of a rock at an odd angle. He was about to go to him, but the smoke got so thick he couldn't see to move.

He thought Hal looked thin and run-down, so after they'd dropped his suitcase at the hotel he took him to a place in the old city that served mounds of prawn *paella* and pitchers of cold Cuban beer. They lingered through the afternoon at a patio table, trading stories about the smaller details of their lives and staying away from larger concerns. Then Hal got around to speaking of Margaret Anderson's generosity with his poem and how Harry Crosby's Black Sun Press was bringing out *An American Odyssey* the next winter after Margaret had serialized it.

"If she and Harry have given it their blessing, you must have hit a home run," Miller said.

"I just hope all those literate fans haven't left the park waiting for me to finish the game." Hal had never been to the new Yankee Stadium or to Ebbets Field in Brooklyn where the Dodgers played, but he was happy enough about his completed work to joke around with any kind of metaphor.

"I want you to read as much as you can before it gets dark. Then we'll go out and celebrate. Meanwhile, let's get some inspiration from Mister Martí."

They walked back past the Capitol Building and the *Gran Téatro* to the *Parque Central* opposite the hotel where the island's 'Apostle' chiselled from white marble had a few pigeons as acolytes. He looked as if he were about to speak, though the Cuban people not the birds were his intended audience.

"You know they replaced the original statue here of Isabel II after the Republic was formed. It seemed they didn't want to be kissing her hem anymore."

"The only American poet who can compare is Whitman," Hal said.

"I think Martí was more of a man."

"More of a man?"

"Yeah, he was on the front lines while Walt was playing Florence Nightingale back in Washington hospitals."

"That's not fair! Somebody had to comfort the wounded. Better it was a poet than a minister offering false hope or some Washington bureaucrat hawking his wares. And in case you want the real stamp of approval, Martí wrote an essay on him and translated some of his poems."

Miller laughed. "I haven't got any quarrel with the poems. 'O Captain! My Captain! Rise up and hear the bells/Rise up—for you the flag is flung—for you the bugle trills.' Listen anyone who writes like that is okay by me." Miller laughed and slapped him on the shoulder. "Hell, you're okay by me."

Hal flinched as much from the unintended slight as the weight of Miller's hand. How did front-line assessments of manhood Miller had written about compare to Whitman's judgement that "your very flesh shall be a great poem," which certain sections of his own work dealt with without disguise?

They spent much of the late afternoon and early evening slowly walking the *Malecón* or sitting on benches in front of the breakwater, watching the lines of surf roll in from the north. Hal had returned to their room at the *Inglaterra* and taken his manuscript from the suitcase, leaving it wrapped in a checked shirt as protection against the wind. Miller insisted he start at the beginning and work his way through.

"We've got three days here after all. I'll bet old Walt could have declaimed for that long," he said as if trying to make amends.

The reading went slowly because Miller couldn't help interrupting him to ask about the origins of certain images and symbols or where he'd found the historical information embedded in so many lines. He liked the opening-of-the-West passages, especially the allusion to Byron as *the Comanche rode down/like wolves on Linville's sheep* and the *stark hungered love* of the Donner family caught in a high Sierra pass and doomed to cannibalism for survival. He also approved the homage to the immigrant waves that *washed up on Liberty's redemptive shores/became the honest future blood to cleanse the war-dead veins/ and forge another nation under God.* When he told the story of the Harlem musician whose *dance gave boot to slavery/his song sound restitution for a racist thrum* Miller whistled in admiration.

"You're saying it all. There's no novel that could do it this way. I'd have to write one about the Negro and another about the Indians. There wouldn't be enough time."

And one about the Embarcadero and another about Key West, Hal mused, but we haven't got there yet.

At twilight they stopped in a waterfront bar for a beer, though each of them had a glass of rum as well. Hal was feeling good and a bit remorseful about doing so because he knew Miller was suffering.

"Enough poetry for now. I want to know how you're doing."

Miller stroked his beard and put his hand up for another slug of Varadero. "She's always with me, if that's what you mean."

"I don't know how you do it. Go on without her."

"No, I don't guess you do since you've never been married."

He'd meant it as simple fact, and when Hal flushed Miller took it as embarrassment rather than anger. "Sorry, it's just when you commit that way the loss is all the greater."

Hal knew he should let it go. But Nicky never left him alone either. "I don't think any piece of paper defines love." No matter how many times he repeated it in his mind, that poem in *Passageways* didn't really help.

Miller blinked. Why was Hal pushing the issue? "Yeah, I guess you could live with a woman long enough so you wouldn't need to sign on any dotted lines. But you haven't done that, have you?" He was a little angry now. Despite the lingering presence of Sally, he wasn't doing well at all, but he was afraid to reveal this, afraid, despite his previous determination, to take Hal to the hill.

"No, I haven't, but can I read you something else?"

"Why not?" He needed to think things through, that's all, and find a way to get to Kincaid and Rawley that Hal would understand. Maybe he could try to do that later on if they both stayed sober enough. At first, he barely heard the eloquent voice as it traversed the plains and Rockies to arrive in San Francisco and at the waterfront there, but images of sailors' dives and a perceptible hunger that approached the Donners' need began to reel him in from his distance. *Caress of lips and fingers softly caught/turned hard as night rose all around/and darkness proved their first desire.* Hal wasn't pulling any punches, was he? He shook his head. Too much booze. Too many dreams crashing into one another. He opened his mouth, but Hal had put down the manuscript and was saying something else.

"There's a section like that on Key West as well. Only this time I say his name."

"How's that?" Miller wasn't sure he'd heard him correctly.

Relieved, Hal gave him what he seemed to be asking for. "Nicky," he said, and trembled at the revelation after all these years.

Miller squinted although his back was to the harsh street-lights. "That was the guy who drowned."

"Yes, my lover." He wouldn't stop now. Expecting eruption and accusation he was surprised by Miller's apparent calm.

"How long?" What was it Whitman had said? 'Be curious, not judgemental.' Well, who was he to judge? "How long have you ..."

"Been queer, is that what you want to say? Ever since ..." If he took this now to their innocent times memories would be rewritten and there would be no possibility of return, but he couldn't just *partly* show himself for who he really was. He had to shed all his protective layers and stand naked and unashamed before the one he had loved the longest. So he leapt over the Embarcadero.

"Since that time on the ridge."

"The fire?"

"Yes, you were unconscious and I held on to you thinking we were going to die. I said goodbye in my mind, but it wasn't enough. So I kissed you. Then you woke up for a moment and told me to dig."

Miller's stared at him fixedly, but Hal could see something in his eyes, a dark fleck of pain like a charred stump of recognition that remained after a burned-out forest became green again. "Miller," he said.

The smoke had cleared now, and Miller could see Rawley's foot bent over the rock once more. He tried to concentrate. It was okay, Hal had kissed him on the forehead like a brother saying goodbye. What did he care about the other stuff? They were both still writers even if poetry had to pound experience with hammer-blows of hyperbole rather than understating or even choosing to leave things out that mattered as much as what was on the page. Never mind, they'd always have that border river before the fire. What did one fucking kiss matter anyway?

Hal couldn't stop. He owed it to Nicky and the poem. He owed it to all those sailors in New York who'd kept him alive even in the blackest of alleys amidst those flowers of glass. And he owed it to Miller because they had both saved one another on the ridgeline and brought each other out of the woods to the brink of whatever they would make of their lives. There was no going back to before the fire, but surely there was a going forward based on the authenticity of stories that Miller always insisted mattered more than facts.

"It wasn't chaste," he said. "Maybe I couldn't admit it then, but I kissed you on the lips not just because I loved you but because right then I wanted to love you too."

For the first time Miller watched himself crossing the open ground to the rock pile and jumping behind the protective wall to find Rawley lying on Kincaid whose head had been laid open by a shell, bits of brain matter stuck to his cheeks. He turned Rawley over and saw the blood oozing from his throat. He was trying to say something to the dying man, and suddenly it was as if Hal's last words had become his own.

Recoiling from the apparition as if slammed by a bullet, he jumped to his feet and swiped the beer bottles from the table. "Shut-up, shut-up you faggot!" He swung as hard as he could and hit Hal on the side of the jaw, hearing the cheekbone crack beneath his fist. As Hal fell to the ground, Miller heard a voice in his mind tell him to dig. But he knew there was no saving either of them from the flames that roared over their intimacy. He threw some peso bills on the table. "What this has cost," the same voice said.

7.

As he watched Miller stride away from the bar, his rigid posture an angry wall of rejection, Hal lay on the cobblestones in shock for several minutes. The waiter brought him a wet towel and asked if he wanted the police. No, he replied, it wasn't necessary. They were supposed to take a bus across the mountains to the port of Majana where Manuel would be waiting for them with his boat, but that wasn't going to happen.

"You are not staying, senõr?" The Inglaterra's night clerk looked at Hal's swelling jaw. "Someone beat you up perhaps?"

"Is there an overnight boat to the States?"

The man handed him a schedule and he saw there was just time to catch a midnight departure to New York on the familiar *Orizaba*. There was no sign Miller had returned to the room before him. He thought of leaving a note, but everything had already been said.

Most of the night was spent in his cabin with an ice pack pressed to his cheek. The ship's doctor had given him some aspirin, saying his jaw was badly bruised but not broken and the swelling would go down in a day or two. The blow's damage would subside, but he was devastated by Miller's violence and hateful outburst. Even though he was such a man's man, Hal had never expected a clenched fist from him or a furious end to their relationship. Of course, he'd always been uncertain how Miller would respond to any unmasking and recognized how much he'd tried to protect himself from such a moment. Why, for example, hadn't he come clean years ago, especially when he was pressed about the absence of women in his life? He almost had, of course, when they'd swum across to Canada, but the fire had intervened, though the dream he'd had the night before of Miller's wilful blindness in the face of his and Nicky's nakedness in the river should have been a warning rather than a basis for confession. As well, so sudden and final had been the subsequent break with his mother it could hardly be explained away by his wanting to stay in New York against her wishes, but Miller had interpreted the rift as an inevitable split between generations, especially since writing was involved, and he hadn't attempted to correct him. Sally, on the other hand, had seen him for who he was almost from the moment they met. Why had Miller ignored the signs? Why did he never say, even jokingly: "You're not queer are you?" Despite what Hal had proclaimed in the bar a few hours before, his love for him, even when he'd kissed him on the ridge, ultimately transcended any bodily need, and he could have answered with a laugh: "Yes, but not for you." Garrett had figured him out but knew he'd never cross any lines when they lived together. His sexuality was never an issue with Frank Shay or even Steve because, like Garrett, they were secure in themselves. Why wasn't Miller Sark?

He searched in vain for indications in their shared past that suggested any unease between them, but if it was there it all seemed to come from his side—the dream, the hesitation in revealing himself even in letters that would have cushioned the surprise, the aggressive way he'd spoken out the previous night. He'd been the same way with his mother, driving in the knife when persuasion might have saved the day. The only possible excuse back then was that his Village life had been full of excess and remorse, but later he'd found Nicky and settled down, and his memory of Nicky should have been his guide with Miller. He didn't have to say anything about the kiss or, once he had, suggest he'd wanted it to lead to more. What consistently dark side of his nature, hiding in an alley, had prompted his antagonism that rather than his carnal choices had unleashed Miller's hostility? Had his secret defect always been in the form not the content of his life? Perhaps, but something else had been bothering Miller, he was sure, a furtiveness of his own. That dark fleck of pain in his eyes might mirror Sally's death and his own evasion but didn't tell the entire story, what had been deliberately left between the lines. His entire head was aching now, so he went out to find the doctor and get some more aspirin. For some reason he picked up the manuscript from his open suitcase.

A sliver of light fired the line of clouds that hid the rising sun. He walked slowly towards the stern, one hand on the railing and the other clutching the images with which he'd tried to invoke his vision. It was too bad he hadn't yet made a copy for Margaret. But even if he had how long would it last for readers on their different voyages? The Gulf was choppy and there was a greasy sheen on the crest of the small waves as if the ship was leaking oil or slick dew had fallen during the night. Barely visible to the north, maybe five miles off, the solidity of the last Key dropped away to a brilliant underwater reef. He'd been happy the moment before he and Nicky had entered the rocky tunnel just as he had been the instant before Miller spotted the flames on the tops of the pines. He'd tried, Walt was his witness, but if he couldn't marry word and flesh he would have to let go of them both. Opening his hand he scattered the pages over the water as the sun's rays broke through the clouds to melt the waves' patina. He clung to the top railing for a few moments as if looking toward Cuba for reprieve, then leapt into the wake. The inscribed sea broke over him like a cry.

Miller retreated to the island within hours after the debacle in Havana, telling Manuel on the crossing only that his friend had to leave. He shouldn't have used his fist or mouth so cruelly, but his altercation with Hal had threatened him in ways he didn't understand. All night he sat at his desk and tried to write about it by hand, but the words didn't make sense. Just before dawn, he gathered up the letters Hal had sent him through the years, placing them in a small metal box. On the path to the limestone cliffs he could smell the sweetness of the jasmine and tang of the pines. From the edge of the precipice he threw the box into the sea, wondering idly if Hornsby's arm was still as strong as ever. Back at the house he sat at his desk and poured himself a whiskey. They were lost to each other, and he'd never see the bear again.

Despite the opportunity through the years he'd never examined Hal's situation closely. Maybe if they'd lived in the same city and had seen one another regularly this altercation would have occurred long ago, but nothing as fierce and uncompromising to destroy their friend-ship. What was it to him that Hal preferred men? Why had he been so disturbed by his description of the kiss? He downed the whiskey and glanced out the window at the northern sky where Sally's plane would always appear on the horizon after a show in Cuba. She wasn't coming home anymore. He wished he could talk to her about all this, but those days of possibility were gone. Hal gets around more than you think, she'd said, and he hadn't really listened.

He drank some more and stared at his typewriter. There were only a few chapters to go in his Paris novel, but that didn't help his dark mood. His mind drifted back to Michigan and the boyhood trek. He could see himself and Hal hooting and hollering as their feet dangled from the open box-car door heading north to their grand adventure. He watched as they swam to the Canadian shore and how he reached down to help Hal from the water just before he saw the fire. They'd almost died there in the shallow trench. They'd almost died on the hill when the mortar claimed him before the Mausers could. But Rawley and Kincaid *had* died while he and Hal survived. He'd told them about Hal, hadn't he? It was all mixed-up because here they were both beneath him, one with his broken jaw and the other with blood on his throat asking him to ... asking what? He couldn't talk through that pitiless wound. Then suddenly Rawley's finger was pointing at his own temple and curling around an invisible trigger, requesting what the German sniper was denied.

"No!" Miller yelled, but the vision persisted, and he saw its sequence and entirety for the first time. The barrel of his rifle grazed the wounded man's chest as he leaned down to kiss him on the forehead, but instead their lips touched and Rawley smiled and nodded. The Springfield jerked in his hands, the shrapnel ripped into his knee, and memory exploded into silence.

A wind had come up and there were whitecaps on the distant sea. Miller stared at the spume flaring in the morning light. Even if Rawley had only a few minutes remaining, he had kissed him goodbye and taken his life rather than hold him close to the end. Surely he had done so to stop his suffering, and mercy had condoned their brief intimacy as much as it sanctioned his pulling of the trigger. Yes, that would be a good story. But *El Recuerdo*, the nightmare dialogue with his squad, and the elusions in his fiction all embodied his doubts about the final choice he had made, doubts that had erupted with Hal's revelations about death and desire. As for the most recent story he had tried to write down, he saw now his brutal slur and blow were fatal shots to Hal's heart, fusing the separate pairs on hill and ridgeline remorselessly into one.

A more famous poet than Hal had been wrong. You *could* embrace in a grave. He'd done it twice, but now he was alone. Pressing his palms against the knotted grain of his desk, he glanced at the confusing array of words on the page and knew what he had to do. In a cupboard behind him the old Winchester stood waiting.

Notes

The title of this novel is taken from a line in Hart Crane's poem "Legend," which appeared in his *White Buildings* in 1926.

The geography of Michigan's Upper Peninsula has been somewhat altered to accommodate Miller's and Hal's borderline fishing trip in the opening chapter.

pages 203, 206, 221: the Spanish quotation from the poetry of José Martí is taken from his *Versos Sencillos* [*Simple Verses*] published in 1891. An English-language version of this book (Trans. Fountain) was published by McFarland and Company (Jefferson, North Carolina) in 2005.

p. 256: the line from Joyce beginning "Cold polished stones ..." can be found in his short story *Giacomo Joyce*, written in 1914 and published in book form by Faber and Faber in 1968.

p. 256: the reference to the old man on Mount Blanc was inspired by Hemingway's epigraph to his short story "The Snows of Kiliman-jaro" in which he describes the body of a leopard found high on the African mountain: "No one has explained what the leopard was seeking at that altitude." Ernest Hemingway, *The Fifth Column and the First Forty-Nine Stories* (New York: Scribner's, 1939).

p. 259: "There is no lonelier man in death ..." can be found in Chapter 11 of Hemingway's *Death in the Afternoon* (New York: Scribner's, 1932).

p. 268: "O Captain! My Captain!" by Walt Whitman, *Collected Poems* (London: Penguin, 1986). "...and your very flesh shall be a great poem" is from his Preface to *Leaves of Grass* (1855). Hart Crane's creative attachment to Whitman is best revealed in the "Cape Hatteras" section of his epic poem *The Bridge*.

Acknowledgements

My thanks for over fifty years of creative conversations with Philip Hamilton, Peter Goddard, and Marlene Markle. We've grown older together, and the words still matter.

For several decades there have been rewarding exchanges with Ken Sherman, Larry Gaudet, Victor Li, and Chris Arthur.

Newer friends John Justice, Albert Busch, Shao-Pin Luo, and Jim Raffan have kept the conversations going.

My family has always been there for me: Eric, Chris, Jennifer, and Alyson, but most of all Marjorie without whom I certainly would not have written what I have over the past three-and-a-half decades.

Thank you, as well, to Guernica publisher Michael Mirolla and the book's designer David Moratto who guided this work to fruition.

About the Author

J.A. Wainwright was born in Toronto in 1946. He attended the University of Toronto and graduated with an Honours degree in English and History in 1969. *Moving Outward*, his first book of poems, was published in 1970, and he was awarded a short-term Canada Council Grant that enabled him to live in Spain and Greece for an extended period. He received his M.A. (1973) and his PhD (1978) in English from Dalhousie University. For the next thirty years he taught in the English Department there, specializing in Canadian literature, creative writing, and the lyrics of Bob Dylan. Between 1976 and 2018 he published four more books of poetry, five novels, and two critical biographies. Along with Dylan, those writers who have had the most influence on his work are Patrick White and Lawrence Durrell. He lives with his partner, Marjorie Stone, in Halifax where he is McCulloch Emeritus Professor in English at Dalhousie.

Books by J.A. Wainwright

Poetry

Moving Outward
The Requiem Journals
After the War
Flight of the Falcon: Scott's Journey to the South Pole 1910=1912
Landscape and Desire: Poems Selected and New

Fiction

A Deathful Ridge: a Novel of Everest
A Far Time
The Confluence
The Last Artist
The Grace of Our Affections

Non-Fiction

World Enough and Time: Charles Bruce, a Literary Biography
Blazing Figures: a Life of Robert Markle

Editor

Notes for a Native Land: a New Encounter with Canada
A Very Large Soul: Selected Letters from Margaret Laurence to
    Canadian Writers
Every Grain of Sand: Canadian Perspectives on Ecology and
    Environment